POWERS
AND
PRINCIPALITIES

VOLUME 1

J.E MUZZIO

SWEETSPIRE LITERATURE
— MANAGEMENT —

CONTENTS

Acknowledgement

I would like to acknowledge every peep and plum town in Florida, (the towns where if you peep around the corner, you're plum out of town). My respect and fondness goes out to every one of the vigorous cowboys, and precious, bless your heart ladies that inhabit those towns. To my grandmother's guava bush, I have mourned your passing, dear shrub I thank you for the Sunday afternoons that you kept me safely hidden under your branches whilst the high-spirited boys played croquet. I pay homage to your protection.

Dedication: To: My father, my hero, who always said that I am able to do whatever I wish, even dance on the stars. **To:** My mother Pearl, a gem of great value, and a beautiful yankee lady, who taught me that if you want to dance you have to pay the fiddler. **And To:** The high-spirited boys that I love.

Author's Note: It has been brought to my attention, a time or two, mostly through gritted teeth, that I never say I'm sorry; that may be true, maybe not. Once I was asked how my stories are inspired. I answered "imagination." I sadly own that bare bones answer and for that I am truly sorry. Imagination is the inspiration of Fiction. Fiction is a line that begins with A and ends with infinity. The line is created by what we know and what we have known. What we know is built upon what we hear and what we have heard. The average person hears and speaks more than 860,000,000 words in a lifetime. Even if you agree, disagree, believe the words or dismiss the words as completely unbelievable, the words are wedged somewhere between A and infinity.

It's been said that I have lived a storied life. I'm not sure if that's accurate but ultimately it is what it is, or was. Being a Tampa native, I have been exposed to the comings and goings of the distinct cultures and subcultures of Tampanian society. The studies of Christian, Judaic and Kabbalistic mysticism have bolstered my understanding of the interactions of spiritualism over various faiths and beliefs.

I now live quietly content, in the shadow of The Big Guava. I drink wine from a coffee mug, put the understanding of my experiences into the essence of my writing, and mind the welfare of my children. This author hopes you will enjoy the fiction and always embrace the words.

JMuzzio

I feel compelled to write this story, but each time I sit to put words to paper my mind is consumed with thoughts of earthworms and coconut heads. I am certain that if this story is not unlocked from the nether regions of my mind, surely the earthworms and coconut heads will be.

December 31,1899

Georgia - The Empire State as the otherworld holds forth.

"Please, gentleladies and certain gentlemen, don't cry why me and gnash your teeth when evil calls. No, there ought not to be although there shall be, the renting of clothing and the sitting in ashes when evil leaves you as an empty crust. I say there ought not for this account, your very soul knew the evil was upon you but regrettably the soul follows the heart. Oh? Says you? Evil will never have its way with me, for I will never look into its repulsive face, nor will I accept as truth its malicious lies. Ah, but alas, the sad truth being this innocent naivety is what the evil pursues. It will not come into view with a disgusting appearance, spewing clear vicious lies. The evil purpose will be unseen, the conversations will be sweet and dripping as thick honey; evils countenance will remain concealed.

Now, beware fine ladies and good gentlemen, when evil kisses your lips and the last living breath is sucked from your very soul, you will be left gasping into the face of iniquity. Furthermore, know that when evil comes a courting, it will not present itself as a repulsive troll, rather he will come to the fore as a prince."

November 9, 2015

Tampa, Florida—The Cigar City where the sun rises over Davis Islands. Three islands created of sand dredged from the bottom of the polluted Tampa Bay. The sand was then situated upon submerged foundations of garbage, discarded building materials, and more than one rotting corpse. Davis Islands—the final resting place for victims of gangland slayings, a testimony to Tampa's claim to infamy. Nonetheless, it has some of the most beautiful sunrises in the country.

As dawn burns through the morning fog, a young nun finds herself sitting on a cool, damp cement bench facing a spectacular sunrise. Life is escaping her body from a deep cut along the palm of her hand and across her wrist. Her blood is falling in large droplets and hiding in the folds of her heavy black clothing. The woman's mind races as she surveys her surroundings. She turns toward the Tampa skyline. The morning sun reflects from mirrored twenty, thirty, and forty-story buildings.

"If I wrap my hand tightly, the bleeding will stop," she mumbles. She twists her hand into the dark fabric, and the bleeding slows. She lays her head on the back of the bench.

"I am… alive." *Her eyes close in a quiet surrender to pain and fitful dreams that take her to another place and time.*

⁓

Jacob set his jaw and looked only toward the monastery looming ahead. Dark clouds were building; a storm was brewing. He picked up his pace. They would have to hurry.

"Please, Father, *listen* to me! I can help. I want to go with you. I am old enough, Father. I am sixteen years old, almost seventeen. I can help you. Please do not make me go there! I am strong and clever. I am the cleverest girl in my class, and I am smarter than any boy." The words flying from Miriam's lips were falling on her father's seemingly deaf ears. "Please, Father, let me go with you!"

Jacob drew a deep breath, glanced askew at his daughter, and strengthened his resolve. He took Miriam's hand to hasten their journey. Miriam pulled her hand from her father's grip, stepped back, and planted her feet firmly in the hardened sand of the dusty road.

"No! I will not go. I will not live there I cannot be like them, I will not!" Miriam's resolve matched her father's. Jacob turned to face his daughter. Now she could see the tears pouring down his cheeks. She could feel his heart breaking.

As she searched his eyes, they exchanged each other's sorrow. Falling to his knees and taking his precious child in his arms, Jacob gathered every ounce of strength in his being to speak the words that he knew he must now speak.

"Miriam Ruth Davidson, give me your promise. Give me your oath this day before God. Swear to me that you will do what you must. Obey the sisters and learn their ways. Live as one of them. Swear to me, Miriam. Swear that you will seek to understand the existence that will be granted to you."

viii

"I promise, Father." Miriam's tears fell as she gave her oath to her father in the presence of God. Now, she is bound by her promise. "But tell me why I cannot go with you."

"You read my journal."

"I am sorry, Father."

"The days of sorrow shall renew themselves." Jacob cried as he held his precious child.

～

"The days of sorrow shall renew themselves," the nun whispers.

The southern sun climbs high into the Florida sky, growing fiercer with each leg of its journey. The cool, misty morning changes into the relentless pounding taskmaster of the afternoon. From dawn through midday, the woman sits like an alabaster statue of a saintly nun from long ago. The cool damp cement bench beneath her has turned to a steaming stone oven.

Police officers, Vicky Knight and Mike De Augustino, respond to a call to investigate the strange specter that appeared at dawn, and now hours later, still sits bewildered and frightened. Vicky and Mike have been partners for six years. After a particularly nasty divorce, Vicky gave up on love and moved to the Tampa Bay area. Vicky has sworn to uphold the law and that no man will ever hurt her again, she has been true to her word. Vicky is a real Georgia peach, a Southern belle with a 9mm pistol. Mike is a Tampa native, as were his parents before him and their parents before them. He grew up in Ybor City, the historic Latin district of Tampa. Mike's father was a Tampa vice detective. Mike will soon take the detective's exam; he plans to continue his father's investigation into the Vicente crime syndicate.

The police officers start across the Boulevard to the Bayshore promenade. Mike assesses the woman as they approach. Her face is framed in white linen. Her head is covered by a black wool veil that falls past her shoulders and all but vanishes into the black of her heavy garb. She appears to be the vestige of a bygone conviction; her hazel eyes are still and lifeless. Her lips are dry and parched, and her fair skin is flushed, burned, and bruised.

"Whew," Mike whistles through his teeth. "Would you look at all of the regalia she has on? And who knows, she could have a weapon hidden under all that." Mike is cautious as he sizes up the woman.

"What sort of weapon does a nun usually carry, Michael?"

"Depends on what order they're from." Mike grins. He loves it that Vicky calls him Michael.

"Did I ever tell you about the time my friend Rolando and I dropped a cherry bomb firecracker down the toilet at the Sacred Heart School? Boy, did we suffer for that, but not as much as when we rolled the fire extinguishers down the staircase. We taped 'em open first." Mike chuckles as they walk. Vicky whispers, "Have you ever seen a nun who looks like that? She looks ancient."

Having been raised in the Freewill Baptist persuasion in southern Georgia, Vicky has little knowledge of nuns or anything else Catholic. For that matter, free will has been a fleeting fantasy to Vicky. It seems to her that the words "free will" and "Baptist" when strung together create the colossus of oxymoron.

"No, I've never seen one like that, not even when I was a kid at the Sacred Heart School. I've seen nuns like that in old pictures, sure, but not for real."

"You think she's real or what?"

"Or what."

"You're a smartass, Michael. So, since you're so smart, you go on and take this one."

"What? No, she's a female. You should take it."

"She's a nun. You know more about nuns than I do. I'll take the next one."

"Okay, I'll hold you to that." Mike smiles. He approaches the woman, and begins questioning her, "Can we help you? Can you hear me, ma'am?" Mike's concern grows with each unanswered question.

"It looks like she's been out here for a while, Michael. Maybe she's from the monastery over in Kumquat."

"The Holy Trinity? She might be," Mike says, keeping his attention on the woman.

The Holy Trinity Monastery was built by Klaus Duetzman. He then donated it to the Catholic Church in a desperate attempt to atone for his wretched life and in the direst hope that he would not spend eternity in purgatory——or worse. Klaus Duetzman has long since passed to his direst hope and probably worse, leaving his son Richard as patriarch of the Duetzman family. Richard, Red to his friends is now living his own wretched life amidst Tampa's high society. It has been said of the

Duetzman's that they have more money than God, not because they have so much money but because they have so little God. The Catholic Church teaches that the love of money is the root of all evil, yet the Duetzman family tree suckles unrepressed from that evil root and bears the fruit of that consequence.

To the gathering crowd of curious onlookers, Mike appears to genuflect in solemn respect to a holy icon as he drops to one knee and continues to question the young woman. "Can you tell me your name? Do you know where you are?" From somewhere far away, she can hear the sound of a voice, a man's voice, bringing her back to this strange place. "Do you know where you are?" the voice is asking. The woman wills her eyes to focus on the man kneeling before her. Fear and panic grip her as she realizes she is being questioned by a police officer. Her only hope to survive is to run and hide. The young woman struggles to her feet. She knows she must escape. She must find her father and the others. Then, she will be safe. But she finds no escape, only darkness, as she collapses into Mike's arms.

"Roll EMS!" Mike shouts. There are two sounds foremost in the woman's ears: the distant sound of a siren and the call of a raven. As the EMTs lift the stretcher with the woman into the waiting ambulance, she turns toward the sound of the raven's call.

～

"Sandalphon…" *she whispers as she returns to velvet darkness and dreams of sorrow.*

"I love you, Miriam." Jacob held his daughter for the last time. Taking a small black leather book from his coat, he placed it in her hands; a blank journal bound with ties so pages could be added.

The book was inscribed: *Hidden things belong to the Lord our God but revealed things belong to us and to our children, forever. Deuteronomy.*

THE DREAM

"Father, father!" Miriam quietly sobbed.

"Shh, do not cry, my darling." Mother Mary Gertrude knelt beside the crying child. She held Miriam, gently rocking the young girl as she tried to comfort her.

"What is to become of me?" Miriam looked into the kind and gentle eyes of the mother superior.

"Take heart, my child. God is watching. We will be strong together, ja?"

"Ja." Miriam cried.

Mother Mary Gertrude remembered the words she had spoken to her friend, Jacob:

"With my life, I will guard your child."

Jacob Davidson walked toward his home. Only a short while ago he had walked this dusty road with his daughter. Miriam is Jacob's dearly loved only child. "Strong and clever." Jacob smiled as he remembered her words. Miriam *was* strong and clever. She was truly her mother's daughter. Sara Rosa, Miriam's mother, was the only woman Jacob ever loved. He was certain they had been created in the heavens as one person, split apart to be born into this life, and then drawn back together as man and wife to be one again. Miriam was the miraculous result of that reunion.

As Jacob walked, he watched the dark clouds that had formed on the horizon. He felt the electricity in the air as thunder rolled from cloud to cloud. Miriam had been ushered into this world on a night much like this. That night, the lightning split the sky. The flashes of light that followed, one after another, transformed the minute of her birth into a surreal string of moments in time. Then there she was, Jacob's hope: Miriam; glorious, screaming feminine principal.

Jacob followed the dusty road along the bank of the Danube. Just ahead, he could see his home, a small stone cottage on the grassy slope of the dark river. His thoughts were on the day before. He had sat on that grassy slope that day, laughing and talking with Miriam as she picked at the clay that seemed to grow out of the riverbank.

"Heidi has not been in school for three days, Father," Miriam had said as her hands worked independently of any conscious thought, forming and reforming the piece of wet earth she held. *"I have gone by her house every day, but there is no one there. I think they have gone on a holiday. We are best friends and I do not know why she did not tell me she was going on a holiday; she tells me everything. One day in class she told me that their cow pushed over the rabbi's outbuilding; and he was in it! We laughed until we cried. The teacher asked what we were laughing at, so I told her Heidi told me a funny joke. Then the teacher made Heidi come to the front of the class and tell the joke. So, she did, and she told the whole class about the cow, the Rabbi, and the outbuilding. Then everyone was laughing except the teacher."* Miriam grinned and then shrugged.

"Do you ever breathe, my child?" Jacob gently teased. Miriam looked down at the clay form in her hands for several moments before looking up at her father.

"Why were you talking to the mayor two evenings ago?" Miriam held her father's eyes with her own.

"This is very good, Miriam. You search my eyes for the truth. You will always find the truth in the eyes for they are the windows of the soul." Jacob knew that he must now tell his daughter the truth for she had read his soul.

"Miriam, you know Wilhelm has been my friend since childhood, and his older sister, Emma, was like a second mother to me and to your Uncle Aaron. Wilhelm came to warn me that there are people coming here to question us. He said that Aaron and I should leave town quickly."

"Where shall we go, Father?"

"I am sorry, Miriam, but you must stay. Aaron and I will go." Jacob turned away. He could not allow his daughter to read the fear in his eyes.

"What… what do you mean I must stay? I cannot go with you? What am I to do? I cannot wait here alone until you and Uncle Aaron return!"

"Wilhelm's sister, Emma, is the mother superior at the monastery. Wilhelm and I have made arrangements with her for you to stay there until it is safe."

"Father, I should come with you and Uncle Aaron. I can help you. I have been studying for almost a year now."

"No, Miriam, you cannot come."

"Father, please!" Miriam dropped the clay form from her hand into the wet sand of the riverbank, slumped to the grassy slope, and sobbed. Jacob knelt beside her and tried to make her understand why it was necessary for her to stay at the monastery. However, as Jacob spoke, Miriam sobbed all the more.

"My decision is final, Miriam. We leave for the monastery on the morrow." The discussion ended. Jacob picked up the form that Miriam had dropped and studied it. She had transformed the piece of earth into the image of a large bird. "It is a raven. "He exclaimed.

"Yes, it is. Does it look like Sandalphon?" Miriam sniffled.

"Yes, he does look like my childhood pet. He looks as if he could fly away at any moment."

"But you said Sandalphon never flew away from you even though he was not caged." Miriam wiped her tears.

"No, he did not fly away. He trusted me, just as you must trust me now, Miriam."

"But, Father, why did Sandalphon trust you so?"

"I think he knew he would have died on the ground if I had not chanced upon him when he fell from his nest."

Miriam moved closer to her father and laid her head against his arm. "Tell me again about Sandalphon, Father."

"Sandalphon was my only playmate before your Uncle Aaron was born. He followed me everywhere. He even played tag with me."

"How, Father? Tell me how he played."

"No matter where I happened to be, Sandalphon always found me. Upon finding me, he would fly down. I would try to catch him in the air as he swooped toward me, and then at the very last second, he would avoid my grasp. He would play that game of tag for hours. He never seemed to tire of it."

"Now father, tell me about Sandalphon, the spirit and, Metatron, his brother."

"I am getting to that child. Be patient." Jacob smiled.

"Sandalphon is the spirit who stands on the first rung of Jacob's ladder. It is said that he is so tall that his head is in the heavens and his feet are on the ground, Metatron is Sandalphon's twin brother. He has the special job of watching the crystal children."

"Yes Father, Mother told me all about Metatron. I think he was her favorite." Jacob smiled down at his daughter and continued his story.

"Sandalphon is the guardian spirit of all humans. I will call this one Sandalphon also." Jacob studied his daughter's creation. Her mother's talent truly is in her hands.

～

"Jacob, Jacob. Is it done?" Aaron met his brother at the edge of their small village.

"Yes, it is done." The sound of his brother's voice drew Jacob out of his .memories.

Aaron looked at the dusky sky. "Come, we must hurry, the sun is setting."

"We will meet here tomorrow morning before the sun rises, and then we will join the others," Jacob spoke quietly to his brother.

"Yes brother, we meet here before sunrise. Is Auvil prepared to travel with us?"

"Yes, Aron, he is."

"Until the morrow then. Good Sabbath." Aaron hurried to his home before the sun set.

"Good Sabbath, Aaron."

Jacob entered his house and sat at his small table. He lit one candle, prayed to the God of the Universe, and held his glass to heaven in a toast to life. Then Jacob dropped his head and wept bitterly.

Before the appointed meeting hour, Jacob arose from his sleep, awakened by the approaching storm. The candle that Jacob had lit still burned. In the dim light, he fumbled through his bureau drawer. He took a small box from the drawer; tears filled his eyes as he opened it. He then took a small silver vial and Sara Rosa's wedding ring from the box and held it in his large, strong hands. He placed the ring, a symbol of their love, on the bureau next to the clay raven. As lightning flashed and electricity filled the air, Jacob read from his journal.

～

There was little chance that Jacob, Aaron, and Auvil would be seen as they pushed through the deep undergrowth of the Black Forest. It would take the men three days on foot to reach their destination of Freiberg, a port town on the Rhine River, almost seventy-five kilometers away. The men knew they must keep to the dense forest and not chance being seen in the open fields or on the highway.

As they walked, Jacob said, "I dreamed of Sara Rosa last night." Aaron had heard these words from his brother many times before. He knew that every dream, every thought, and every remembrance of Jacob's beloved Sara was sacred.

"Yes, Jacob?" Aaron looked into his brother's dark eyes.

"But this dream was much different than any dream I have ever had of her," Jacob said.

"Tell me how so, brother?"

"She spoke in this dream. She has never spoken to me in a dream before."

"Tell me the dream."

"I dreamed that I went to my bed to sleep. As I slept in my dream, I had a dream. Do you understand that?"

"Yes, you had a dream within a dream. Tell me the rest, Jacob."

"In this dream, I woke. I turned in my bed toward the wall. Upon turning, I saw that the wall was no longer there. I could see a horse and wagon approaching my house. I arose from my bed. Then, at once I was standing outside. As I stood in the path, the horse and wagon came to a stop in front of me. You, Aaron, were the driver. I saw that Sara was sitting in the wagon. I walked to the back of the wagon, so I could see more closely what she was doing. She was embroidering a scarf. As she made each stitch, I could see the pattern becoming ever more intricate. When she finished, the embroidered scarf had become a lace collar. I said, 'Sara, that is so beautiful. What do you call that pattern?' Life,' she answered. 'Life? Why?' I questioned. 'This collar is highly sought after and brings a great price for its intricate design and delicate stitch. But often the design and intricacies become bothersome, so the collar is wrapped in tissue paper and placed in a bureau drawer, awaiting a never appointed time to wear such an elaborate collar,' she explained. Although I was afraid of her answer, I asked, 'Who have you made this collar for?' 'Miriam,' she whispered as she offered the collar to me."

"I tell you, Aaron, my heart stood still as I put my hand out to receive the collar. When I took the collar, it ripped in half. I stood horrified. I saw the beautiful piece of torn lace fall from my hand to the ground. I watched as the half in Sara's hand fell between her fingers as it turned to dust. When I looked to the ground, the piece I had dropped was clean and new and had become a whole collar again. I looked up and Sara was gone. Then, I awoke. Can you tell me the meaning of this dream?" Aaron watched Auvil lumbering through the thick underbrush.

"Do you think he is able to talk?" Aaron asked as the Herculean figure of a man plowed through the thickets oblivious to the brambles and branches.

"Auvil? I don't know, he never has. It seems he has no need to talk. But what about the dream?"

"Let me think about it."

Three days later, Jacob, Aaron, and Auvil met five others at the river dock. Hiding in the predawn shadows, they watched as Captain Peter van Dague, a Dutch trader, and his first mate, Morris Taylor, load cargo onto the barge moored to the landing.

"No, not that one!" Captain van Dague stopped his shipmate as he picked up a crate lying off to the side and began to load it into the barge. "That one's our ace in the hole," the captain whispered to his first mate with a smile and a nod. They exchanged knowing glances and continued loading the cargo boxes that lined the dock.

"Good morning," Lieutenant Heinz Reichmann of the dock patrol addressed Captain van Dague in a genial manner.

"Good morning if you can call it that. With all this cargo and the fog slowing us, it's been a hell of a morning, a hell of a morning indeed," the captain grumbled good-naturedly. "I see you have your new right-hand man with you."

The young officer smiled, delighted to be recognized as an important addition to the dock patrol.

"What have you got here? This one has no dock stamp on it." Lieutenant Reichmann gestured to the ace-in-the-hole crate—the crate that van Dague had put aside specifically for this purpose. "Open the crate," Reichmann ordered.

"Ja, let's have a look." van Dague broke open the crate, revealing a case of Green Fairy, an opium-based absinth.

"Green Fairy, where did you get that? I have not seen any of this for almost twenty years!" Reichmann exclaimed.

"A Frenchman came across a whole cellar full of the stuff, I was lucky to acquire it from him. Ja, damn lucky," van Dague said.

"Still, you have no dock stamps. Tell me, did you say the Frenchman has more of this?" Reichmann asked.

"A whole cellar full, I think I said. Certainly enough for everyone here," van Dague repeated as Reichmann studied the case of rare liquor and weighed his options.

"Listen, my friend," Reichmann began. "If you give me three bottles of this, we will both go away happy and then perhaps you will remember me the next time you have a case of this."

"Three bottles, hmm? You drive a hard bargain, a hard bargain for certain, but well, worth it for the price I will get for the rest." Captain van Dague handed the three bottles to Reichmann and the young officer.

"Enjoy," van Dague called out as the soldiers hurried to their post, anxious to sample their contraband.

"I have only heard of this liquor," the young officer confessed upon reaching the post.

"Then this will really be a treat for you." Reichmann laughed, as he pried the cork out of the bottle with his pocketknife.

Two hours later, Reichmann and the young officer were unable to make even one more toast to the Fatherland as they slumped to the floor of their post in a drunken opium stupor.

As the dawn broke, Captain Peter van Dague and his first mate, Morris Taylor, were under way with their hold full of cargo, contraband liquor, and eight men hiding in crates.

～

"THE QUEEN IS A WHORE." A drunken American shouted.

Peter van Dague did not know if this statement was true, nor did he care. He gulped down the whiskey he had been nursing; but Morris Taylor, the brooding hulk of an Englishman who he had been drinking with all night took offence to the toast that was raised in the crowded pub by the American pilot. The bar brawl that ensued banded their friendship forever.

"That was a bloody good fight," The Englishman sputtered through loosened teeth and a bloodied lip. "Ja, sure and good whiskey too; sign on with me, Morris. I could use a good first mate, one with more brawn than brains." Peter van Dague laughed.

"Aye, aye Campth." Morris saluted van Dague and smiled a crooked smile through his swollen lip.

～

"Where are we taking them?" Morris asked van Dague as they stood on deck, watching the dark waters of the Rhine sacrificing itself to the bow of their ship.

"They are trying to get to England. They have come on foot from a town about seventy-five kilometers away. I've made arrangements for a Dutch vessel to pick them up in Rotterdam and take them to Port Carmarthen, England."

"I guess everyone is running somewhere." Morris kept his eyes on the water." van Dague took a long drag on his cigarette, flicked the butt into the water, and watched as the current carried it away.

"I'm going below. It's safe to let them out of the crates now."

AUVIL

"MAN OVERBOARD! MAN OVERBOARD!" Morris yelled. He ran to the alarm and sounded the shrill whistle. van Dague, Jacob, and a few of the other shipmates raced to the ship's rail where Morris stood.

"Morris, ready the dinghy now!" van Dague ordered.

"Aye, Captain." Morris raced to the dinghy and checked the cinch to the hoist. van Dague lowered the dinghy into the water. Morris rowed toward the floating man. He grabbed the man's arms and pulled him into the small boat. Morris then rowed back to the ship. The dinghy was hoisted back up onto the ship. Morris and van Dague pulled the man from the dinghy onto the ship's deck; Jacob, for the first time, saw the man's face.

"Aaron!" Jacob pushed through the men and dropped to his knees beside his brother. "Aaron, Aaron!" Jacob cried.

Seth, the physician traveling with Jacob, attended to Aaron.

Aaron spewed water and with several more hacking coughs, he spewed a bit more.

"That's a nasty bump he's got there. But I'd say he's lucky, damn lucky. Most don't bob back up after a fall into this muddy brine. Sure damn lucky, I'd say."

van Dague turned to Jacob and walked him out of Aaron's earshot. "Keep him below, warm and dry. This could go bad real fast. I've seen it before. Ja, real bad, real fast."

"My head..." Aaron looked to his brother.

"Morris, help take him below."

"Aye, Captain."

"Aaron, what were you doing? What happened?" Jacob asked as he and Morris guided Aaron into a dry corner of the cargo hold.

"My scarf. It blew overboard and got stuck on the ship. I thought I could reach it, but I fell over the rail and hit my head. I guess my scarf is lost."

"No, Aaron, I have it. Morris fished it off the side of the ship with a pole." Jacob finished dressing his brother in dry clothes and wrapped the scarf around him.

"A pole. That easy, hmm?" Aaron smiled sheepishly, closed his eyes, and gave himself over to exhaustion.

"Auvil, stay here and watch Aaron. I must speak to Seth again."

"Will he be all right?" Jacob asked Seth.

"I am afraid his skull is fractured, Jacob. There's nothing I can do. Keep him dry and warm. It is in God's hands now."

"Thank you, Seth."

"I will come back to check on him again later." Seth returned to the quiet conference of the other men. Jacob returned to Aaron.

Aaron opened his eyes and looked at his brother sitting next to him like a sentry. Jacob leaned forward and adjusted Aaron's scarf.

"When you gave this scarf to me so you would have an excuse to buy another from that Gypsy woman, I was worried. I never told you, but I went to the market to find her. You did not know this. I went to tell her that she is not one of us and to resist your advances. I knew it would be of no avail to tell you. You would not have listened to my advice, Jacob. You have always thought with your heart."

"But Aaron, you loved Sara."

"I did. That day, when I went to the market, I was expecting to find a thief. Instead, I met a beautiful, young woman who looked into my eyes. She looked in my eyes..." Aaron's eyes closed.

Jacob spoke to Auvil, who sat stoically at Aaron's feet. "When he was a baby, I watched him as he slept. I thought I would for all time be his big brother. I vowed to always watch over him. I kept my vow; even as he grew, I looked after him. However, at some point, that changed, and he became the one who was watching over me. I knew Aaron was concerned when I met Sara Rosa, but he remained silent about his concern. He accepted Sara Rosa for my sake at first, but he grew to love her. I, on the other hand, fell in love with her the minute I looked into her eyes. She was truly my split-apart."

"The dream, I know what it means." Aaron looked into Jacob's eyes and beyond.

"Quiet now. Tell me later."

"No, now. I must tell you now."

"Aaron, please."

"No. I must tell you now. I am not afraid of what is to come. Life, Jacob, the collar—it is about life. It is your life, Miriam's life, and Sara's life all woven together and then torn apart. Your life is out of your hands. Miriam's life has been made new, and Sara's life is gone…dust.

Jacob, I tried to save her. We heard the glass breaking. We ran, she tripped but scrambled to her feet. Her tiny silver box amulet fell to the ground. She did not notice. I picked it up and tucked it into my vest pocket. I tried to run to her, there were too many of them, too many… I tried to save her. I tried. Please forgive me, Jacob. Forgive me."

"I forgive you, Aaron. I forgive you," Jacob whispered as Aaron closed his eyes to sleep in the bosom of Abraham.

"*Seth*!" Jacob called across the crowded cargo hold. Seth hurried to Jacob's side. He searched Aaron's neck for a pulse.

"I am sorry." Seth covered Aaron's body.

Jacob sat in front of Auvil, rocking forward and back as if he were petitioning at the Temple Mount Wall.

"Is there even one small crevice for my prayers, Auvil? No, I think not." Lifting his eyes toward heaven, unable to contain his grief, he cried. "My God, I have mightily loved you. Since the day of my understanding, I have served you. I have followed your precepts, and I strive to keep your commandments. Now, I have lost my family, my home, and my country. Even so, my God, I remain your faithful servant. Although it appears that I serve an unjust God, I will continue in my understanding, knowing that you will vindicate yourself and my faithfulness."

Seth sat next to Jacob and quietly listened while Jacob openly mourned Aaron's death. Jacob would be allowed a year of mourning according to tradition, but now they needed to talk. They needed to plan; they needed to talk to van Dague. There would be time for mourning later.

"I am sorry, Jacob. Aaron was a good man and a true friend. This is a terrible loss. He will be missed." Seth was truly saddened.

"All he wanted was my forgiveness. He wanted my forgiveness for something he had no control over. The night Sara died; Aaron was with her." Seth listened as Jacob's story brought back the horror of the night of the broken glass.

"Every week, for years, Sara baked an extra loaf of bread for an old woman who lived less than a kilometer from our home. Usually, she finished baking early, but she had not seemed herself that day. It was getting late, but she promised she would hurry. She said she had something important to tell me when she got home. I suggested to her that she would be much quicker if Miriam stayed with me. I was anxious to hear what delicious foolishness she had contrived. Then, I made her promise she would hurry along and ask Aaron to walk with her. They made the journey to the woman's house. They left the bread with the woman, and just before the sunset, they began their walk home. Then, suddenly, motorcycles raced through the town. They came from every street and alley, the riders smashing every window and door as they rode through the town. Aaron and Sara heard the glass breaking. Everywhere they turned, there were fires from the oil lamps that had fallen, and broken glass that had been smashed from windows littered the streets. Some of the men saw Aaron and Sara run into an alley and followed them. They overtook Aaron, beat him, and left him for dead. Sara, they found hiding only a short distance from where they had left Aaron. When it was quiet, I went to the streets searching for Sara and Aaron. I was hoping against hope that they had been at the old woman's house when the nightmare began. I found Aaron in the alley, unconscious and badly injured. Sara, I found dead. I fell to my knees in a sea of broken glass. As I held her lifeless body, I screamed these words of the psalmist to the heavens…VINDICATE ME, OH GOD, AND PLEAD MY CAUSE AGAINST AN UNGODLY NATION. WHY DO YOU CAST ME OFF? WHY DO I GO ON MOURNING BECAUSE OF THE OPPRESSION OF THE ENEMY?"

"Jacob, I am sorry, but we must talk with van Dague," Seth interrupted. "Soon, we will be in Rotterdam, and plans must be made."

"I understand. The lives of many are at stake." They all knew the importance of reaching England soon.

In the privacy of the captain's cramped quarters, Seth and Jacob sat with van Dague. The captain poured the men a glass-full of Irish whiskey. Jacob spoke first, van Dague downed his drink before Jacob started his sentence.

"How long before we reach Rotterdam, van Dague?" Jacob asked.

"Tomorrow, early afternoon. Ja, afternoon is the earliest I can get there. I have to keep to my regular schedule, so as not to arouse suspicion.

Regular schedule, ja, puts us there tomorrow afternoon early." van Dague poured himself another glass of whiskey. Seth and Jacob declined. "Suit yourselves." He set the bottle down and continued, "I have two sets of false mariner's papers. When we reach port, your men will leave the ship, two at a time, with the false papers. Morris will escort them to the waiting ship. Morris will then return with the false papers and continue accompanying your men until they are all safely aboard the ship, and then you will be on your way to merry old England."

"What about Aaron?" Jacob asked.

"Don't worry, I'll take care of him as if he were one of my deck hands. I will say he died en route and has no family that I know of. Ja, none I know of. No one will question this. It happens often. Ja, often." Jacob trusted van Dague because he trusted his friend, the mayor. Wilhelm Herder had not only warned Jacob and the rest of the men of trouble but had also arranged for their escape. Auvil and Jacob would be the last two men to leave the ship. Seth and Ethan would leave first. The others would follow as van Dague had said.

Jacob returned to the ship's hold. He searched through Aaron's wet clothing for his vest. Safely tucked away in the pocket of Aaron's vest, Jacob found Sara Rosa's silver box; an amulet, a family heirloom that was supposed to be given to Miriam. Jacob tucked it away.

~

It was five o'clock, and van Dague was getting nervous. Morris had left the ship more than an hour ago. He should have been back. Jacob and Auvil, the only two men left on board, should have already been on their way to the waiting ship. This trip had been a royal pain in the ass. First, the logistics of hiding the men in the restricted space of his cargo hold was a daunting task, and eight men were more than he had ever moved at one time. Then, the accident and a body to dispose of and now Rotterdam was crawling with seaport police. Ja, a royal pain in the ass. The police had been doubled since the last time van Dague had been in port, and they were apparently searching for something. Something was wrong. Still, all in all, he would do the same thing over again. van Dague would do it over again because he could not abide the maniacal ranting of a madman. He would not salute, nor would he pledge allegiance to this evil little man.

"Heil Hitler, my ass," van Dague swore. From the vantage point on the bridge of his ship, van Dague watched the port police as they boarded and searched each vessel in the Rotterdam port. Now, it was his turn, van Dague met the soldiers at the gangplank.

"We have orders to search this vessel. Stand aside," the arrogant captain barked his orders to van Dague. The four soldiers stood on the deck of van Dague's ship.

"Help yourself." van Dague knew that Jacob and Auvil would not be easily found. They had hidden themselves behind the ship's false wall, the wall that he and Morris had built for an occasion such as this.

"You two guard the deck while we search the cargo hold," the captain ordered. van Dague led the officer and one soldier into the belly of the ship. The men stood in the hold surrounded by crates.

"What is all of this?" the officer said as he looked around.

"Moving crates. Some are empty. Some are full. That is what I do, move belongings. A lot of people are moving these days. Ja, a lot of people moving. The neighborhood has gone all to hell if you ask me." He smirked at the men standing beside him. van Dague knew that this was a dangerous game. He also knew that he must not show even the slightest hint of fear. The officer studied van Dague for an extended moment.

"Who is this?" the officer asked, pointing to Aaron's body.

"That's a stupid bastard who's dead." van Dague sat on an empty crate and lit a cigarette.

"What happened?"

"The stupid bastard fell overboard," van Dague exhaled. A heavy cloud of smoke hung in the air over his head.

"Why is he still lying here? You have been in port for more than five hours according to our records."

"He got himself killed on my time, and he will get himself buried on my time. I am a busy man, and he is not going anywhere. I have no time to waste. Ja, he is not going anywhere." van Dague extinguished the burning cigarette in the palm of his hand and dropped the butt into his shirt pocket, never breaking eye contact with the young officer. After the crates and boxes were thoroughly searched and inspected, the officer and the soldier turned to make their ascent back to the deck. Then, as if on some secret cue, they turned back to van Dague.

"There is one more thing."

"What is that?"

"Take his pants down."

"What?" van Dague was caught off guard by this request.

"I must see if he's cut, in the manner of a Jew.

The officer stood very close to van Dague. The other soldier stood more than a meter behind. Van Dague bent over Aaron's body and reached for the waistband of Aaron's trousers; van Dague struggled with the catch on Aaron's pants. The impatient officer leaned closer. When the officer had been manipulated into position, van Dague brought his elbow up sharply into the officer's solar plexus. The officer lost his breath and rocked backward for a moment, enough time for van Dague to pull the officer's pistol from its holster, but not enough time to shoot. The officer tried to regain control of the weapon.

The soldier standing behind drew his pistol but could find no opportunity for a clear shot at van Dague. He followed the wrestling match like a deadly referee. Jacob watched with his hand on the release bar that opened the wall. Auvil watched Jacob. The soldier stepped backward, tripping over a stack of boxes.

At that moment, Jacob pushed open the wall and rushed toward the soldier. Auvil advanced as the soldier turned and took aim at Jacob. In a matter of seconds, Auvil lifted the soldier over his head as if the man was weightless. The soldier's pistol fell to the floor just before his broken body fell from Auvil's hands. Jacob recovered the soldier's pistol. The port hatch opened. The two soldiers who had stood guard on deck hurried down the ladder to investigate the noises coming from the cargo hold. Shots rang out, and the soldiers fell victims of their comrade's pistol in Jacob's hand. The officer and van Dague continued their struggle for the weapon. Another shot rang out, van Dague and the officer stood frozen in a deadly embrace. The officer smiled into van Dague's eyes. The smug look of victory turned to confusion and then disbelief. Blood trickled from the officer's mouth as he fell to join his troop in the ranks of death. Morris withdrew his dagger from deep within the officer's back.

"Sorry I'm late, Captain." Morris stepped over the dead officer.

"This is a bad one." van Dague leaned against a cargo box clutching his bloodied chest. The officer's bullet had found its mark.

"No, Captain. We have too much to do yet." Morris caught his captain as he fell.

"Make it so, Morris." Van Dague gave his last command.

Morris gently laid his captain's body next to Aaron. Then he stuck the dead officer's pistol into his pants.

"Jacob, the two lanterns in the corner and the box of flares, get them up top." Morris opened the tool locker and selected a very large pipe wrench. Two pipes ran transverse overhead of the cargo hold. One pipe was the ship's fueling line, and the other, the gas line to the galley stove. While Jacob and Auvil stood on deck, Morris worked the fitting of the fuel line loose, spilling hundreds of gallons of fuel into the cargo hold. Then he opened the gas line and raced up the ladder. Considering what had just transpired below, it was amazingly quiet in the port. If anyone had heard the gunshots, they did not know where they had come from. The men had little time to act, and Morris obviously had a plan. Morris bounded through the cargo hatch and closed it behind himself.

"Give me the flares." Morris tore open the box, shoved it next to the cargo hatch, and laid one flare over the side of the box. "Jacob, give one lantern to me and take the other to the gangplank." Morris opened the well of the lantern and poured a trail of kerosene from the box of flares next to the cargo hatch to the lantern at the gangplank.

"Now, we walk off the ship like we're going to tea!"

Morris lit the lantern at the gangplank and followed Jacob and Auvil. From the dock, Morris turned, drew the dead officer's pistol from his pants, and shot the burning lantern. The fire from the broken lantern followed the line of kerosene to the flares. The fireworks that ensued sent an invitation to every soldier in port to board the ship. As the fireworks displayed, soldiers swarmed the vessel. Curious to investigate the cargo hold, a soldier opened the hatch. As thundering explosions, bellows of smoke and walls of fire filled the sky behind them, Jacob, Auvil, and Morris walked toward the safety of the waiting ship.

"What the bloody hell are they so anxious to find?" Morris wondered aloud.

"They are interested in what we have done," Jacob offered a vague answer. Morris was not satisfied.

"What is it that you have done that has enraged them so?" Morris demanded an explanation. "It is not so much what we have done as how we have done it that interests them."

Morris stopped walking and faced Jacob. "You better come forth with an explanation pretty damn quick."

"It would be better if I show you. Auvil, come this way." Jacob directed his companions into an alley just ahead. As they stood between the giant cargo boxes in the deserted alley, Jacob took the dead soldier's pistol from his coat. He turned the firearm in Morris's direction. Before Jacob could be stopped, he rang three shots into Auvil, who stood behind Morris.

"Have you gone mad?" Morris turned, braced to see Auvil lying in a heap on the alley floor. "What the bloody hell? He's standing... There's no blood. That is impossible! He has three bullets point blank in his middle!"

"We should hurry to the ship. I will explain later." Jacob started out of the alley. Morris grabbed Jacob by the arm and swung him around.

"I want bloody answers!" Auvil stepped between the two men, breaking Morris's hold.

"It's all right, Auvil." Jacob intervened before Auvil could act.

"I want an answer *now!*" Morris demanded.

"He is a golem. I made him. Can we go now?"

"No, we can't go now, and what the hell is a golem?"

"Morris, any minute, the police will come looking for us. I will explain once we are safely aboard the ship."

Morris sat on a crate in the alley and lit a cigarette. He inhaled deeply. Then studied his burning cigarette.

"I had thought of quitting. Nasty habit, but it's been a tough day. The ship is only a few hundred meters away. However, you can't board without me." Morris took another long drag on his cigarette. "So, until I have an explanation that's to my liking, I'm not going anywhere. I think I'll quit tomorrow, maybe tomorrow."

Jacob decided he had better talk, and talk fast.

"A golem is a soulless being created for protection. The others and I are Kabbalists, Jewish mystics. We have the knowledge to create these beings. We are traveling to England to join with the Alchemists. We will work with them against the Fuehrer and the German war agenda. The psychic to the Fuehrer has warned him that we will be a formidable deterrence to his ambition to cross the channel. They want to stop us from reaching England, and they want our knowledge in order to create an army of golems." Morris set his gaze on Jacob and Auvil. The cigarette he drew heavily on burned almost to his fingertips. Morris crushed the cigarette beneath his foot.

"We better hurry."

IN THE COUNCIL OF MANY

"JACOB! Welcome! Please sit at our table we have much to discuss." Alden ushered Jacob to his seat and the other men took their seats around the large oval table in the middle of a dimly lit room that was once a root cellar. It was not a large cellar, and it remained damp and dark, lit only by a few modest lanterns. The cellar tucked under a barn in the English countryside was hidden away from prying eyes and was now readied into a makeshift laboratory. The walls were crowded with shelves, each one teeming with the apothecaries' glass beakers and corked bottles. The array of bottles addressed every size, color, and form conceivable. The bottles, crucibles, and retort were readied on the shelves all the while screaming to the Alchemists, "Choose me; I am the secret to the elixir of which you search." However, the Alchemists pay no-heed to the willful cries. They just silently and persistently seek as is their foundation.

"I am relieved to finally see your face, Jacob. I heard there was trouble in Rotterdam."

"Yes, my friend, we lost Aaron and van Dague."

"I am sorry. They will be missed. It is a great loss. And you, Jacob, how are you faring?"

"Thank you for your kind words, Alden. Losing Aaron has been devastating, but I do not yet have time to mourn. Even though I suffer now, there are many in need of my help. As a result for the benefit of the living, I must put off my sorrow. There will be much time in the future for my grief."

"What of Morris?" Alden asked.

"Morris traveled with us, and he vows to continue the work he and van Dague started."

"And our friend, Wilhelm? I trust that you left him well, fat, and sassy." Alden's cheeks pinched his eyes closed when he grinned.

"He remains well and continues to take advantage of his aristocratic ancestry to keep himself safe from accusations of treason."

The conversation came to a lull as Alden hung his head and Jacob breathed a deep, mournful sigh. The Alchemists and the Kabbalists were keenly aware that the world and even the heavens have been beset with horrors that were only to just begin.

"Jacob, do not worry. I am certain that Wilhelm and Morris will be arranging transportation for a time yet. Now, tell me Jacob, I must hear of the golem. How is he holding up? Has there been any deterioration? Does he continue to obey?" Alden was anxious to get to the heart of the alliance that the Alchemists and the Kabbalists had entered into.

"Auvil is holding up very well; although it has been more than a year since we created him, I have not seen any deterioration. Furthermore, he never fails to follow my commands, and he seems to have a sense about my needs. I am curious if he will have a sense about you also since it was the combination of your elixir and my knowledge of golems that completed him."

"He is amazing, Jacob. No one would think he is anything other than a mere man. Amazing." Alden shook his head in wonderment.

"Yes, he is amazing, Alden. I think he is perfect for the work we will be doing; he is very much a human being and equally as much a spiritual being. It is your living essence that we have added to our traditional creation of a golem that has allowed us to create this being."

"This is an exciting time for us in alchemy," Alden said. "For centuries, we have sought to form a truly human and equally spiritual being. Unfortunately, all we could create are the Homunculi."

"Where are the Homunculi now?" Jacob is curious about the tiny creatures that the Alchemists had created.

"The Homunculi were weak and terribly difficult to sustain. They have all deteriorated, just as well I say. Those fellows are useless, disobedient and quite ill-tempered." Alden looked to his colleagues for confirmation. The Alchemists laughed as they agreed among themselves.

"We will begin our labors in the morning, Jacob. However, before we begin, we will go to the village market. There, I will introduce you to our trusted vendor. Then we will return to the cellar to set in motion our effort. I am anxious to start, but first we must all get a night's rest. Come, I will show you our quarters." Jacob, Alden, and the unlikely troupe of Kabbalists and Alchemists filed out into the dark night of the

English countryside. The Kabbalists were welcomed into a quite large and well-kept barn that sat above the cellar.

"These are our quarters, as you see they are spacious and afford enough room for all of us." He bent down and picked up a handful of clean dry straw. "And there is all the straw you can sleep on and more." Alden smiled as he allowed the straw to slowly fall from his fingers. In Jacob's mind's eye, he saw an image of Miriam as a young child playing with her puzzle sticks, trying and retrying to pick up the sticks, one stick at a time, without disturbing the next—a frustrating improbability.

"Thank you, Alden. I am very grateful, as are my men. We are also very tired from our journey." Jacob closed his eyes for a moment, not in exhaustion but to dismiss the vision of Miriam.

"Yes, yes, of course, Jacob. You and your men will find a storage room full of horse blankets. Feel free to use what you need."

"Thank you, Alden."

"Don't thank me. Thank the aristocrat's horses. Their master, Lord Smithe, has put them out of their palace and allowed us in to stay in their stead." Alden laughed a hearty laugh. Only a short time later, the barn fell silent, save for the sounds of men in fitful sleep. As the men slept, Jacob quietly spoke.

"Auvil, listen to me now and remember. Beginning on the morrow, you will have two masters, Alden and me. You must follow Alden's every command. Obey him and protect him just as you protect me. I must sleep now, Auvil." Jacob closed his eyes, and Auvil watched.

The rooster's song clamored in the men's ears. The cock's intention to welcome the dawn also served to warn any nefarious rival to be aware that he is the undisputed lord of the yard, and in due course, his boast brought the sleeping men reluctantly to their feet.

"Good morning," Alden greeted Jacob. "There is bread and cheese in the cellar for our breakfast. Afterwards, we shall go to the market in the village. The journey through the countryside to the small village was pleasant and afforded Jacob and Alden much time to discuss the daunting task that they would soon embark upon.

"I believe that Auvil will work well with you Alden. I ordered him last night to obey you, although I believe he would have anyway."

"Good Jacob, I am certain that we will all work well together."

"Yes, Alden, I believe so. We will be a commanding force against Hitler's agenda to cross the channel."

"Jacob, my friend, merely the fact that Hitler is so determined to learn the secret of Auvil's creation and to destroy us and any other like us attest to the strength of our opposition to him. That is our village just ahead," Alden said. "The first vendor we will visit is a trusted friend, but beware, there are whispers of Nazi sympathizers here, so we must be careful. I will introduce you as my cousin. It is best if only you and I come to the market. There is no sense in drawing undo attention to ourselves."

"Yes, Alden, I understand."

Alden smiled and headed into the market. Jacob followed Alden to the vendor's table where Alden greeted a particularly hairy and generously wide man with a grin and a bear hug. Alden wrestled away and introduced Jacob.

"Henry, old friend, this is my cousin, Jacob, the one that I told you about." Alden spoke in an uncharacteristically loud voice for the benefit of any curious eavesdroppers.

"Jacob, good to meet you. Alden speaks of you often." Henry shook Jacob's hand, and in doing so, he pulled him close and whispered "Alden has told me that you and your men have arrived with only the clothes on your backs. May I send clean clothes to the barn for you and your men? Are you and the others of a similar stature?"

"Thank you, Henry. It is good to be here. I trust we will all become powerful friends." Jacob followed suit and spoke gregariously, and then he whispered, "Yes, we are very close in size. A change of clothes will be appreciated." Henry looks around to make sure no one was paying attention to the newcomers. However, he still kept his voice low.

"Good. I will have my eldest daughter, Lydia, bring the clothes to the barn. I will also send a pot of hot mutton stew with her. There will be enough food for all of you."

"Ah, yes, a hot meal. We will all be looking forward to that. How much do I owe you for these carrots and eggs I have here?" Alden held a small wooden box filled to overflowing with a generous bunch of carrots and a half dozen large duck eggs.

"You owe nothing for the work that you and your men are doing. I am the one who owes you a debt that can never be repaid, as do all of your countrymen, yet they will never know. Take what you and your men need. I am honored to help the cause such as I can." Alden picked up a few more eggs and thanked his friend. He showed Jacob through the rest of the market and into the tiny village.

"The villagers are, for the most part, farmers and sheep herders. A millhouse, a creamery, a cobbler, and a pub make up the total exchange of the village. However, the pub gets the lion's share of the villagers' money." Alden laughed. Their final stop was the creamery for a liter of goat's milk, after which they started back toward the countryside. Just as they reached the edge of the village, Jacob turned and looked back.

"What is it, Jacob?"

"Nothing, nothing," Jacob answered, but it *was* something. "I thought my brother called to me." Jacob was certain that he had heard his brother call his name from the village. He would not travel to the village again without Auvil.

"Come let's hurry on to the barn. The men will be wondering about us if we do not make haste." Alden quickened his pace.

Finally, Jacob and Alden reached the barn. As they stood at the barn door, Jacob stopped. "Do you hear that, Alden?"

"Yes, I hear the sound of our men talking."

"But my men, they are laughing as they talk. It has been a long time since we have had any mirth. Hitler has made certain of it, it's good to hear their laughter again."

"They have hope now Jacob, so they make merry."

"Yes, here we have hope. There is no hope from where we came. In our ravaged country, the children are taught to inform on their parents, and citizens are rewarded for turning their neighbors over to government officials for perceived crimes. Entire families have been sent to the camps or have gone into hiding. Truly, Alden, our home has been transformed into a place of horror."

"Yes, and now we shall work together to end that horror, my friend." Alden gave Jacob a strong pat on the back and then slid the barn door open.

"Have we missed the meeting of the minds?" Alden laughed as he addressed the men.

"Not yet. We are just trading tales," Seth explained the great deal of levity that he and the men were taking pleasure in.

"We brought food and a promise of a change of clothes." Jacob's men cheered at the good news.

"Jacob, I would like to familiarize you with our laboratory. We will take this food down to the cellar and then I will show you around."

"Very good, but first I must tell my friends what I have learned today."

"Of course." Alden sat in the straw while Jacob told the others about the village market and the trusted friend, Henry. He warned of the Nazi sympathizers and the need to keep to themselves and not venture into town. Jacob would only return to the village with Alden and Auvil. The men agreed, then returned to their discussions.

In the cellar, Alden familiarized Jacob with the retort since refinement, the most important process, would be Jacob's first lesson. Alden picked up each bottle and explained the decoction or concoction that filled it. The mixtures were by large extracts of plants and animal parts. The most precious potions held the basic essence of minerals that had been captured in the distillation process. Now bottled and corked, the potions quite simply sit on the shelves in a state of flux, waiting for their moment to transmute or to merely cure a cough. Alden turned to face his colleague. Jacob could see the worry in his eyes.

"Jacob, I am concerned. You claim that you heard your dead brother call to you when we were leaving the village. I must ask. Do you think you are up to the work that lies before us? Perhaps you need a little more time to grieve. Certainly, Seth could step in for you. There's no shame in that."

"I appreciate your concern Alden, but truly, I am bearing up as I have said and honestly believe my priority is and must be with the living. I will grieve my brother when this is done," Jacob replied.

"But what about the voice you heard?"

"I believe it was a warning. My brother is still looking after me… but do not worry about it interfering with our work. I will merely take Auvil with me whenever we return to the village, and I suggest that you also take him when you venture out."

"So, you believe the ones that have passed to the spirit world can travel here. Is that so Jacob?"

"I do. I also believe that we can travel in the spirit, but I have not discovered how."

"What makes you think such thing?"

"Because of the story of our ancestor, Jacob, and the ladder he saw coming from the heavens and the spirits traveling to Earth from the spirit realm upon that ladder."

"Jacob that story speaks only of *angels* traveling on the ladder. Tell me why you think it relates to the physical being."

"The story tells of Jacob *wrestling* with an angel. Do you find that strange?"

"I have never thought of it as strange or otherwise."

"Please continue, Jacob."

"According to what I have been taught, a spirit, unlike an angel or a ghost, is not nor has it ever been corporal. It is totally spirit."

"Yes, I believe that also."

"However, Jacob was a man, a man created flesh *and* spirit by the Creator," Jacob continued. "I think when Jacob took hold of the spirit to wrestle him; he must have been in the ladder. Moreover, when he was in the ladder, he became more spirit than flesh. He, in other words, transmuted. Therefore, Jacob was able to take hold of the angel and wrestle with him to demand a blessing. The angel finally blessed him, but the damage Jacob sustained from the fight caused Jacob to walk with a limp from that night on. You see, Alden, that is the proof. The angel damaged Jacob because he was still flesh even though he was in the spirit. However, although Jacobs' flesh was weak, his spirit was strong, so he endured to the end. That is why he received his blessing. He endured to the end."

"That is incredible, Jacob. So, you are saying that you think it is possible to enter this ladder as flesh!"

"Yes, that is what I think. I also think that there are many of these ladders. I think they are doors to the spirit world."

"I am inclined to agree with you, Jacob."

"I do not imagine that you could disagree. It is a perfectly logical conclusion that I have drawn from the facts as I understand them."

Jacob sat on a hard-wooden bench, pulled off his boot, and groaned.

"Are you hurt?"

"I am fine, but I fear that my boots are quite worn." Jacob continued, "Perhaps, you have a sheet of old newsprint that I can have to build up the sole of my boot and protect my foot from the hole there within?"

"Certainly, I have a discarded piece of paper here, quite handy just perfect for your need. I am curious. Can you tell me what your first question to yourself was? The question that brought you to the amazing hypothesis that you have laid out?"

Jacob finished stuffing his boot with the folded newsprint and jammed his foot into the worn shoe. "To tell you, I must start at the beginning."

"All the better." Alden pulled a stool in front of the bench where Jacob sat and listened to his story.

"When I was a child," Jacob began, "my mother always brought me along to the spring in the field behind our home where she washed the clothes. Each week, she would wash, and I would run and play in the field. It was great fun. Then one day, I happened to catch my smallest toe on a stick. I sat on the ground and bemoaned my aching toe. My toe was no bigger than a field bean, but it had become the source of what I considered an unbearable pain. I studied my tiny toe. Then I covered it with my finger. Now, I could see only four toes. I thought this is how my foot would look if I had knocked the toe completely off. Then I realized that if I *had* actually knocked my toe off, I would still be me, Jacob Nathaniel Davidson. I then covered all of my toes, and I determined I was still Jacob Davidson. Amazed, I folded my leg under my haunch and sat on it. Still even without my entire leg, I found that I was still me. Realizing at that moment that I am not any part of my body; I became intent on knowing what exactly I am. I ran to my mother and asked, 'What am I, Mother?' She answered, 'You are my precious boy, Jacob.' Of course, I knew that and was slightly disappointed by her answer. It was then that I knew I must discover what I truly am. As a result, I have since searched for my actuality."

"Have you discovered it?"

"Only in part, Alden. Only in part. However, all will be revealed, I am certain."

"We will go to my uncle in the village. He is the cobbler. He will fix your boot. However, now, we must boil some carrots and duck eggs. Our men are undoubtedly hungry for their evening meal." The laboratory would now become the hungry men's dining room. They rehash the events of the day and then retire to clean dry straw and the warm horse blankets that await them.

SANDALPHON

November 9, 2015

The emergency room's nurse's station stands like an island in the sea of calamities. Orderlies and aids race gurneys down the halls and along corridors like Roman gladiators with the helpless patients strapped to their speeding chariots. Chest pain sufferers stumble blue-faced through the hospital doors. Wailing rises from treatment areas. Gang members and their rivals sit only a few feet from each other, separated only by curtain walls. They lament brothers that have fallen victim of a drive-by shooting, a knife wound, or some other act of violent aggression that was wielded in retribution for another act of real or imagined aggression.

Mike sidesteps a gurney as it speeds past.

"How 'bout Greek when we get outta here?" Mike whispers to Vicky.

"Papa Louie's? Sure, sounds good," Vicky agrees. They approach the nurse's station just as the desk phone rings.

"Tampa General Hospital, emergency room, nurse's station. No, this is Tampa General Hospital, not Tampa Community Hospital. Yes, you're welcome." The nurse returns the telephone to its receiver.

"Can I help you, officer?" Smiling, the nurse appraises Mike while ignoring Vicky. Vicky rolls her eyes and pretends to study her notepad. Mike, who considers himself a sensitive, caring, twenty-first-century deadly good-looking Italian man, smiles back.

"Can we see Sister Jane Doe?" he asks.

"Let me check her status. Wait here." Glancing back over her shoulder, the nurse smiles at Mike as she enters the curtained room.

"I don't know what you've got Mike, but you should bottle it. You'd make a fortune." Vicky looks up from her notepad just as the nurse walks back over.

"The doctor is in with her now. She hasn't regained consciousness yet," the nurse says.

"Can we speak with the doctor?" Mike asks.

"Just a minute. I'll check." A moment later, the nurse returns and leads Mike and Vicky into the treatment room.

Monitors beep, buzz, and chime a symphony as life-giving fluids drip intravenously. The resident doctor and the chief of staff stand over the unconscious woman.

"Hi, Mike. Are you on this one?" Doctor David Knowles greets his friend and cycling buddy.

"Yeah, me and Vicky. I'd like to finish up and get out of here as soon as I can. What can you tell us, David?" Vicky walks over to try to get a closer look at the woman.

"Not much, I'm afraid. It appears to be an attempted suicide. She has no identification. However, she does have a tattoo on the inside of her forearm. Not something you'd expect a young girl to have. No hearts, flowers, or butterflies—just two letters and a string of numbers. The only word she has spoken is 'Sandalphon'."

"Well, David, we'll keep in touch. I bet the little *boutana* has half the *cojones* in Tampa under her little nun outfit," Mike swears under his breath as he and Vicky turn to leave.

"And it looks like she's been tortured," Knowles adds.

"What?" Mike spins back around to face the doctor.

"By the marks on her wrists and ankles, it appears that she has been bound, very tightly. Someone wasn't playing. She has marks on her shoulders and neck that look to be cigarette burns, and it seems that she's been choked. We have a pretty good idea, but we won't know for sure about everything that has happened to her until she wakes up and we're able to talk to her."

"When she wakes up, give me a call. Will you, David? I want to talk to her as soon as she's able. Vicky, can you get a good picture of her face?"

"Sure thing. Vicky's phone flashed into the unconscious woman's face. Okay, I think I got a pretty good one. I'll get it printed out when we get back to the station."

"Good, we'll ask around about her." Mike turns back to David Knowles and takes a card from his shirt pocket. "Call me at this number, David. Tortured… *Mierda*," Mike mumbles as he and Vicky leave the room. Growing up in Tampa, Mike learned to swear fluently in three languages, four if you count English. Mike and Vicky leave the doctors with their sleeping enigma. As they walk past the nurse's station, the flirtatious nurse looks up from her charts, long enough to bid Mike farewell and flash one more dazzling smile. Mike takes another calling card from his shirt pocket.

"Will you call me the minute she wakes up?" Mike places the card in the nurse's hand, hesitating a moment as his fingertips brush hers.

"Oh, I surely will."

"Thanks. I really appreciate that." Mike winks at the nurse and then hurries to catch up to Vicky, who is waiting by the exit.

"Geez, you were laying it on kind of thick back there. Just try to keep your mind on the case, Michael," Vicky scolds.

"Never hurts to be nice." Mike gallantly holds the door for Vicky, she rolls her eyes as she walks through.

Doctor Knowles returns to the woman's bedside. The chief of staff, Doctor Sam, as he is affectionately known by the hospital staff, stands at the head of the bed, quietly assessing the unconscious young woman.

"Sandalphon... I know that word, Sandalphon. Hmm. It'll come to me," Doctor Sam says as he searches his memory.

"I'm sure it will. I don't know what we'll do when you retire. You've got just about everything stored up there." David points to Sam's noggin.

"Not everything, David, but I've seen my share of life, and I think I have a few good years left before I retire." Sam smiles.

"Well, what do you make of this tattoo?" The young resident lifts the woman's arm to study the tattoo one more time.

Doctor Sam looks away. "I've seen tattoos like that, but she's too young."

"It's been a long day. Transfer her to the ICU, David. I'll have her blood work sent to my office, and I'll call the monastery before I go home. We'll talk tomorrow."

"Good night, Sam."

"Good night, David." Doctor Sam walks directly to the nurses' station. "I want to know the minute that woman wakes up. I'll be in my office for a while. Call me if you need me."

"Yes, Doctor." The nurse's curiosity piques. Doctor Sam walks to his office and hangs his coat on the hall tree next to his carved mahogany desk. His office is comfortably elegant. The doctor's diploma from Oxford School of Medicine, *Magna Cum Laude,* is the only one of his many accolades that holds a place on his office wall alongside his vast collection of original watercolor art.

"Sandalphon." He shakes his head, repeating the familiar word as he sits at his desk. Still shaking his head, he rolls the cuff of his crisp, white shirt to his elbow. Stretching his arm across his desk, he studies his own tattoo—two letters and a string of numbers.

In 1945, the Allies liberated the Nazi death camps. The hardened battle-worn soldiers had come from bloody battlefields where their friends and comrades had suffered and died. These soldiers, with tears in their eyes, were the first to look upon a nation's inhumanity. Samuel David Rubinstein was eight years old when a soldier carried him, starving, and near death from such a camp. Doctor Sam buzzes his receptionist.

"Will you get me the number for the Holy Trinity Monastery? Yes, it's in Kumquat, and please ring it through?"

Kumquat, is a sleepy little township that sits a few miles past the edge of the Tampa city limits, just east of downtown Tampa. The town took its name from the small citrus fruit which grows in abundance there. The townspeople are standoffish, quite backward, and mostly disagreeable.

Doctor Sam was lost in the memories on his arm when the telephone rang.

"Hello, Doctor Rubinstein here."

"Hello, Doctor. I'm the prioress of the Holy Trinity Monastery. Your receptionist said you have a question for me?" Doctor Sam chooses his words as the caller identifies herself. Doctor Sam will not violate his patient's confidentiality, but the young woman's identity must somehow be discovered.

"Yes, Sister, we have a young woman who is unconscious in our ICU. She has no identification, but we think she is possibly one of your sisters. She was found sitting on a park bench here in Tampa. When she was brought into the hospital, she was wearing an outdated habit."

"A habit? You mean a full habit?"

"Yes, Sister, she was wearing a full habit."

"My word, that *is* unusual. We haven't been in full habit since Vatican II changed everything in the sixties. Can you tell me anything else about her?"

"The only word she has spoken is 'Sandalphon'. Does that word mean anything to you, Sister? Can you tell me if there are any sisters unaccounted for or missing from the monastery?"

"None of the sisters who live here are missing, Doctor, and Sandalphon doesn't mean anything to me, although we do have some visitors coming from Europe for our seventy-fifth anniversary celebration. They're due here tomorrow. She may be one of them. Many of the European sisters do still wear the full habit. I'll ask if they are missing anyone from their group in the morning when they arrive."

"Thank you for your time, Sister. Please call if you have any information."

"Of course. Good bye, Doctor."

"Good bye."

Doctor Sam's eyes fall on his tattoo once again.

"*Sandalphon… yes!*" Doctor Sam remembers. He chooses a book from the library table behind his desk. "Sandalphon, Sandalphon, Sandalphon…" he repeats as he turns the yellowed pages of the ancient book. "There you are! Sandalphon, the spirit on the first rung of Jacob's ladder," he reads out loud. "The guardian of all humans. All right, Sandalphon, you're in charge now. I'm going home!" Doctor Sam speaks to the air as he returns his father's Kabbalah to the table.

❧

Zoe beams every time Mike and Vicky come into Papa Louie's. As they take their usual table, Zoe teases the officers.

"Mike, Veekie, so good to see you. Have you two married yet?" She has been trying to push them in the direction of matrimony for years.

"No, maybe next time you ask." Mike laughs nervously. Unflustered, Vicky studies the menu. Zoe smiles.

"Not yet, eh? Such a shame, you two been coming here together for so many years and you, Mike, since you were so young." Zoe puts her hand out even with her shoulder to signify how tall Mike was then.

"Zoe, you're making me feel old now."

"We are only as old as our little finger, Mike." Zoe crooks her little finger and laughs. No one knows Zoe's age, what is known about Zoe is that for the twenty-five years Papa Louie's has been in business, she remains beautiful, gracious, and ever young.

Mike looks up from his Souvlaki sandwich just as the Duetzman family files in. The rapacious daughters and sons of Richard Duetzman and their ill-mannered children. Three generations of Tampa's society.

Children, grandchildren, nieces, and nephews are all followed by none other than the patriarch himself, Richard Duetzman.

"I'm glad I'm almost finished. I'm about to lose my appetite." Mike glares at the family.

"Just eat, Michael. Ignore him."

"I can't. You know he's gonna come over when he spots me. What a hypocrite." Mike fumes as he finished his sandwich.

"Mike! How ya doin'?" Red Duetzman spots Mike and limps over to the table.

"Let me take care of your check. This one's on me for all the good you boys in blue do. Oh, and girls. Excuse me miss." Red nods condescendingly to Vicky as he takes the bill from the table.

"That's not necessary." Mike snatches the bill from Duetzman's hand.

"How's your brother?"

"Fine."

Mike's radio crackles. "10-91d Bayshore and Bay to Bay." Mike and Vicky hurry to the register.

"I wonder why he limps." Vicky watches as Red makes his way back to his table.

"I heard he got thrown off the roof of a barn by an angry farm hand when he was a kid. It happened in Georgia at a tobacco farm that his family owned. They say the worker's son fell from the hay loft and Red's father wouldn't allow the doctor onto the farm to treat the kid. Supposedly, the kid died, and soon after, one of the workers threw Red off the roof. The worker was never seen or heard from again, and Red has limped ever since then. I don't know…that's just the story I heard." Mike shrugs.

"Well, my grandmother always said that the fruit doesn't fall far from the tree." Vicky shook her head.

"Yeah, I guess she was right. They're all bad apples, that's for sure, except Victor. Don't know what happened there, but he's really a good guy."

"Why did Red ask about your brother?" Vicky asks as they drove toward the station.

"Nick dated one of his daughters, nothing serious, but it worried the old man. One day, the old guy came to him with his checkbook and asked him what he'd take to disappear from her life. Nick told him to shove his money and dropped his daughter soon after that. Turns out, he should have dropped her sooner. She gave him herpes. You know the gift that keeps on giving." Mike is quiet for a moment.

"And I don't like Red's pal, Joe Vicente. My dad was working on a case against Vicente when he was killed. I was in high school at football practice when my father was shot. Red's son, Victor, was on the team. We were pretty good friends back then. Victor drove like a wild man, right up to the door of the emergency room. He got me to the hospital in time to say goodbye to my father. I will always be grateful to him for that." Vicky quietly listened as Michael once again shared his heart-rending story.

"Does Victor still live around here?" she asked.

"I haven't heard from him in years. I think he left the Tampa area. He's the only good one in the whole family. I figure he doesn't want to be associated with them."

"Do you want to go by the Bayshore and check out that mess they found? We've got some time before our shift ends." Mike turns the cruiser and heads toward Bayshore Boulevard, the longest most beautiful stretch of unbroken promenade in the world, according to the Tampa chamber of commerce.

"I know Wallace and Daniels got it, but we can check it out anyway. Bet you the next pizza it's a Santeria sacrifice." Mike wagered.

"Okay, you're on."

❧

"It's a dog."

"No way. It's a goat."

Officers Wallace and Daniels argue as they stand in a secluded niche of the Bayshore sidewalk. The bloody carnage of an animal sacrifice lay mutilated at their feet. Unfortunately, ritual sacrifices often litter the longest, most beautiful stretch of unbroken promenade in the world.

"Whatcha got, Wallace?" Mike interrupts.

"It's a goat."

"It's a dog," Daniels insists.

"Well, whatever it is, I just won a pizza."

AMICA MIA

Tap...tap...tap... Tap, tap, tap.

Standing in the doorway of Jane Doe's hospital room, Mike watches as an aged nun examines the habit that hangs beside the young woman's bed. The old sister slips her hand into the deep pocket of the habit and withdraws several pieces of broken blackboard chalk. She digs deeper into the pocket and finds an ornate silver rosary worked with amethyst beads.

Tap, tap, tap.

"Oh, mio Dio. Sai tu, Amica mia."

The nun crosses herself. "What happened to you?" she whispers as she stands looking into the face of the unconscious young woman. The aged nun turns and hurries from the woman's room. Mike steps aside to allow her to leave the room. As he watches the nun makes her way down the hospital corridor.

"Yeah, we all wonder what happened to your friend," Mike mutters.

Tap, tap, tap, tap, tap.

Mike's training and his gut tell him that there is something more to this case. There is something more than merely a beaten and tortured woman in a nun outfit—likely another prostitute dressed up for some john's odd amusement, and now the beaten and tortured woman is lying unconscious after an attempted suicide. Mike's gut is never wrong. There is more, but how much more could there be?

Tap, tap, tap, tap.

"Hey Mike, here for an update?" Doctor Knowles says as he and Doctor Sam enter the patient's room.

"Yeah. How is she today?"

Tap, tap, tap. Tap, tap, tap.

"Her vitals are good. She could wake up soon." Doctor Knowles makes notes on the patient's chart as he speaks.

"Why hasn't she come around?" Mike asks.

"It's not uncommon for a trauma patient to shut down and remain unresponsive."

"How long usually?"

"It's a measure of stress. It could be a long period, or it could be a short period."

Tap, tap, tap, tap.

"There was an old woman in here when I got here, a nun. Did she say she knows who this Jane Doe is?" Mike continues.

"She's visiting the Holy Trinity Monastery from somewhere in Europe. She said that she doesn't know who the girl is, but the sister did ask if she could come back tonight and give her Holy Communion if she is awake." Doctor Knowles looks up from the chart.

Tap, tap.

"She said she doesn't know her, but she wants to come back to give her communion that's odd." Mike analyzes this bit of new information. Mike's gut is whispering, *"I told you so."*

"Yeah, that's what she said. We just spoke to her in the hall as she was leaving." Doctor Knowles returns to studying his patient's chart.

Tap tap.

"What's that tapping sound?" Doctor Knowles closes the young woman's chart and looks from side to side. He checks and rechecks each monitor.

Tap, tap, tap, tap, tap.

"That noise is going to drive me crazy. I'll call maintenance. Maybe they can find where it's coming from." David Knowles' eyes dart around the room, searching for the cause of the tapping. Doctor Sam stands quietly beside the woman's bed. He turns toward the window and opens the mini blinds.

Tap, tap, tap, tap.

"Look. It's a raven. He's tapping on the window." The three men peer through the glass at a large raven.

"It might be her bird. I've heard that ravens can be tamed and that they can even be taught to talk." Mike leans closer to the window.

"Pretty bird, Pret-tee burrd," Mike coos through the glass.

"Pretty bird?" Doctor Knowles cannot contain his laughter. The sight of the police officer making 'smoochie' noises at the bird on the other side of the window glass is more than the sleep-deprived resident can seriously process.

Mike clears his throat and straightens up. "I'll come back later."

"David, you should get some sleep," Doctor Sam walks back toward his office.

Doctor Knowles finishes his report and continues his rounds.

Tap, tap, tap.

"I see you, Sandalphon. Is this a trick? English, they were speaking American English. Are they waiting for me to wake up, so they can begin their interrogation? I will keep my eyes closed and ears open until I devise a means of escape," the young woman speaks fondly to the only thing familiar to her in this strange and frightening place.

～

Vicky sits in a corner of the emergency room waiting area. A woman sits next to her, hesitantly answering Vicky's questions. Mike leans against the wall and listens as Vicky talks to one of her unfortunate ladies of the night.

"I don't want no trouble," Joniqua whispers.

"It looks to me like you've already got you some trouble." Vicky looks into the woman's bruised face and blackened eyes. "Joniqua, this isn't the first time I've seen you like this. Was it a john?"

"*No.* I told you I'm off the street. I've been off for months, and I'm not goin' back either." Joniqua was pretty once, but now she is tired, and she looks it. Years of working the streets of Tampa has taken its toll. Joniqua could pass for a good forty-five; she has just turned twenty-seven.

"Looks like you were mixin' it up with Vicente's boys, Joniqua." Standing over Joniqua, Mike takes the picture of Jane Doe from his shirt pocket. "Do you recognize this woman? Is she one of Vicente's girls?" Mike thrusts the picture in Joniqua's face.

"Mike, back off." Vicky gave Mike a stern look. Mike backed off. He knew he was in trouble with Vicky.

"I ain't never seen her before, like I said. I don't work for him anymore. I told you. I don't want no trouble. I have nothing more to say." Joniqua turns her face to the window and stares at the cold, dark Tampa Bay.

Vicky walks away in silent anger. She knows Joniqua was going to talk before Mike interrupted her. Mike follows Vicky to the hospital's courtyard. He is sure that there's more ire to come from his normally mild-tempered partner. Vicky is certain that Vicente had something to do with Joniqua's sudden outbreak of bumps and bruises. And certainly might have something to do with Jane Doe's. She has seen other women who had quit Vicente break out with the same symptoms. Vicky has worked for years to gain the trust of the street women. However, without a statement from one of the women, she is getting nowhere fast.

"Don't ever do that again. Joniqua was talking before that Vicente crack. Those women trust me, and they're a link to Vicente, our only link right now. Remember that Mike, before you let the chip on your shoulder get in the way of our job."

"I'm sorry. You're right," Mike apologizes as they buckle into the cruiser, and Mike starts the engine.

"You know you have to let go of some of this Vicente stuff if you want to pick up your father's investigation. You have to distance yourself or forget the whole thing. Hear?"

"That's kind of hard to do, Vicky. He had my father murdered, sure as hell." Mike defends himself even though he knows Vicky is right.

"Speaking of murder, the chief asked me to go over to Kumquat after my shift. Looks like some lady got herself murdered in her house last night."

"Don't try to change the subject, Mike. Maybe Vicente did have your dad killed. Maybe he didn't. Maybe you're just too close to this case to take it on. You better think about it, Mike."

Joseph Vicente headquarters the southeast crime syndicate from his home on the exclusive Davis Islands. He chose Davis Islands because of the canals that lead into the Gulf of Mexico, allowing easy access to the Tampa seaport's illegal drug trade. Vicente also relies on the Davis Islands' private airport to always ensure his fast getaway. Mike hopes to soon take the detective's exam and reopen the investigation of Joseph Vicente, the investigation which cost his father's life. "10-55. Channel Side Drive," the radio squawks. A body has been discovered on Channel Side.

"10-49. ETA, three minutes," Vicky answers.

There is already a crowd gathering on Channel Side when Mike and Vicky arrived at the scene.

"We'll probably be here the rest of the day. If you cordon off the area, I'll talk to the guy over there. I'm betting he found the body," Mike says.

"Gang stuff, I'm guessing." Vicky walks to the back of the cruiser and opens the trunk.

"I hope we can get this done quick so I can get back to the hospital. I want to question that old nun who visited Jane Doe this afternoon."

"I thought you said she didn't know Jane Doe." Vicky grabs a roll of crime scene tape.

"No, I said she *claims* she doesn't know her. Therein lies the difference, my good woman."

"So, you think she's lying? What makes you think that?"

"I overheard her talking to herself in the woman's hospital room. She called the Jane Doe her friend. Also, she searched the woman's habit, and it looked like she found something then put it back. I'm sure she knows who she is. I just don't know why she's lying."

"Okay, Michael, let's wrap this one up real quick." Vicky waves the roll of tape in front of Mike's face.

"I get it. Crime scene tape, wrap it up. Everyone's a comedian." Mike is relieved Vicky had called him Michael; all is well.

The drive back to the hospital is a quiet one. The events of the day are being processed, cubby holed, and stored. The information will be retrieved for future reference or will be relived in the throes of a haunting nightmare. A teenage boy has been found lying dead in an alley stripped naked, save one red Nike. Twelve bullets are lodged in the young boy's torso. Another two are in his head. The rats, the roaches, and the homeless who live in the alleys and in the abandoned warehouses are the only witnesses, and none of them are talking.

Hospital visiting hours will soon be over. While Mike parks the cruiser, the old nun leans over the young woman's bed. As she quietly speaks, the woman opens her eyes.

"My name is Sister Theresa Marie. I have been directed to help you." The young woman listens as the sister speaks. The R's roll from the old woman's tongue. The voice sounds like it belongs to her friend, Theresa Marie, but the aged and wrinkled face is not the face of the woman she knows.

"*You will always find the truth in the eyes.*" Familiar words echo in her memory. She looks into the old woman's sad eyes.

"How can you be the woman I have prayed for these many years? It is impossible," the sister whispers.

Unconsciousness overtakes the young woman once again. Mike hurries to the elevator. He hopes he will get a minute to question the old woman he watched earlier in Sister Jane Doe's room. A minute to question the nun is all he needs. That is all it will take. Then he will know for sure if she is lying. Mike and Vicky step off the elevator, they see a commotion at the nurse's station. Doctor Knowles runs past them.

"What's going on?" Mike hurries to catch up with Knowles.

"It's Jane Doe. Looks like she's in shock. Wait here." He shakes his head. "No, go talk to that nun in the ICU lounge." Mike and Vicky make their way to the ICU lounge. The sister is sitting quietly twisting her rosary ring.

"I'll take this one, Vicky, if you want. You can just sit and watch me do all the work."

"Go ahead. I could get used to this." Vicky laughs as Mike walks over and sits next to Sister Theresa Marie.

"*Buona sera*."

"I speak English," the sister says.

"My name's Mike De Augustino. I'd like to ask you some questions about the young woman you visited today."

"Yes, I understand," Sister Theresa Marie speaks quietly.

"Do you know the woman?" Mike continues.

"She bears a strong resemblance to someone I knew many years ago, but of course; it cannot be her."

"If you don't know her, then why did you call her your friend when you were here earlier? Why did you offer to come back to give her Holy Communion?"

"I am a sister of the Order of Saint Benedict. I offer my prayers to all who are in need."

"Sister, this woman is in serious condition. We don't know who she is or who her family is. If you really want to help your friend, you must tell us anything you know about her."

Sister Theresa Marie looks into Mike's face. "There is nothing I can tell you. I am sorry, but I cannot help you. I must return to the Holy Trinity. It's getting late."

"How old do you think she is?" Vicky whispers as the old nun slowly made her way down the corridor.

"Older than God's shoelaces," Mike answers.

"Hush, Michael. She'll hear you."

"She's around the corner. She can't hear me. She probably doesn't even remember me."

"You're kidding yourself, Michael. She's sharp."

"Yeah, damn it, she is. Well, I know she's lying."

"Lying? Think about it. She's not lying. She just gave you simple answers to your simple questions. How can she be lying?" Vicky laughs.

"Simple questions, really? What did you want me to do pistol whip the old gal? C'mon, let's go." Mike heads toward the commotion.

"What happened here tonight?" Mike asks Knowles.

"All we know is that she went into shock after the old sister came back to visit her. She's stable now, but the next seventy-two hours are going to be crucial. It's strange, though. The monitors are showing she's not responding to anything, just that bird that keeps tapping at the window."

"She's so young, poor girl, and she's been so badly treated," Vicky says.

"Calm down, Vic. You can't save all the ladies of the night."

"She's not a prostitute," Doctor Knowles interrupts.

"She's not?" Mike is strangely disappointed and relieved.

"We examined her for rape when she first came in, and the results from the exam showed that this woman has no signs that she's sexually active, so I think we can rule out your little nun *boutana* theory. Sorry, Mike, check back in a day or two. Maybe you can come up with a better theory by then." Doctor Knowles sits in the chair beside the woman's bed.

"I'm going to take my break in here. She needs the company." David Knowles yawns.

Tap, tap, tap.

Jane Doe moans.

"Don't worry, bird buddy. I'll take good care of her."

❧

Jane Doe sleeps. Her dreams bring forth sorrowful moans. However, her cries are hopeless, not one familiar soul comforts her. She is alone. Nothing is recognizable, save for her dreams.

THE GROTTO

Tap, tap, tap.

"Come in." Miriam wiped the tears from her eyes as the heavy wooden door to her convent room opened. A tiny woman entered the room.

"My name is Sister Theresa Marie. I have been directed to help you." Sister Theresa Marie's German was influenced by an Italian accent. The young sister stood a little more than a meter and a half tall. Her round dark eyes peered from behind gold-rimmed glasses. Her olive complexion was accentuated by the stark white linen coif that framed her face and the contrast of the black wool veil that hung past her shoulders. Theresa Marie held a large package neatly wrapped in brown paper. "This is for you. It is a habit. I made it for you." Theresa Marie smiled warmly.

"Thank you." Miriam took the package. "What do you mean directed to help me?"

"Mother Mary Gertrude, our superior, has charged me with helping you. Besides me, Mother Mary Gertrude, and the mother superior at the monastery in Düsseldorf, no one knows about you and your father. We will be the only people who knows your secret. You will be safe here. Do not worry. But now, you must put the habit on. I will take your clothes to the furnace," Sister Theresa Marie spoke quietly.

"What about the other sisters? What will they think?"

Miriam asked as she undressed.

"We are under a vow of obedience to the mother superior. No one will question her." Sister Theresa Marie neatly folded Miriam's clothes and wrapped them in the brown paper.

"I understand. I am also under a vow. I gave an oath to God that I will stay here and accept my existence, whatever it may be. I am bound to that oath now until I marry." Miriam hung her head and averted her eyes. What will the mother superior tell the sisters?" Miriam lifted her head, took a deep breath, and forced a smile.

"Mother Mary Gertrude has told our community that you are her niece from Düsseldorf and that your family has died in a house fire. She said that you came from our sister convent for a time of seclusion and recollection. That means you will be away from the others and in silence. No one will talk to you or look at you. Since the other sisters will not be paying attention to your business, you will have time to learn how to act like a sister. After I have taught you what you need to know to pass as one of us, Mother Gertrude will announce to our community that you have broken your silence. She will also tell them that you have asked to be allowed to enter our community. The sisters will be thrilled." Sister Theresa Marie smiled as Miriam struggled with the habit.

"Why do you call the prioress Mary Gertrude? Her name is Emma Herder. She and her brother, Wilhelm, are friends of my father and uncle." Miriam continues to struggle with the yards of dark material. Sister Theresa Marie helped her fidget with it until it was arranged properly.

"When we become sisters, we take the name of a saint, and we take the name Mary for the Blessed Mother of Christ. So many questions, you don't have to learn everything on your first night." She stepped back and looked at Miriam.

"Good, it fits. I had to guess at the length, but it looks good. Well, now you look like one of us, *Buono*."

"My mother was Italian," Miriam answered in flawless Italian.

"Mother Gertrude told me that beside German, you speak Italian and English. How did you learn English?" Sister Theresa Marie smiled.

"My mother taught me and my father. Her family traveled throughout Europe and England. They spoke many languages and dialects. I learned Italian and English before she died."

"Where is your mother's family now?"

"Switzerland."

"Good. It is safe there. I am from a small town on the Italian-Swiss border called Terre Rouge," Sister Theresa Marie's smile widened as she spoke her native language.

"Terre Rouge, that means 'red earth'. It must be close to the mountains?"

"My, you are clever. It is."

"Why are you here? Was there no monastery for you in your town?" Miriam looked into the sister's sad eyes.

"There was only a small convent. We were a very poor little town. There were very few sisters, so we were all reassigned to larger monasteries. This is where I was sent. That was seven years ago. I was sixteen years old.

"I am sixteen years old, but only two weeks from now, I will be seventeen. My father will come for me before then."

"Miriam, it may be a long time before your father is able to come back for you," the sister conceded. "I will teach you, so you can appear as one of us until he does come for you. You do understand how important it is that everyone believes you are a sister, right?" Miriam's thoughts race back to the night that her father found her reading his journal. She was afraid he would be angry.

∾

"I should not have read your journal, Father," she said. "But I have learned much. However, I know that now I have to accept the result."

"Yes, daughter, now you must accept the result. You have gained knowledge, and with knowledge, there must be understanding."

"Will it be difficult, Father, the result?"

"Yes, it will be difficult. However, you have set in place a strength that will sustain you."

"I understand," Miriam answered.

"Good, it is almost time for vespers. I will be back soon with your dinner. We will talk more then." Sister Theresa Marie turned back before she opened the door. "Oh, and Mother Gertrude suggested that we speak only Italian while I am teaching you."

"Why not English?" Miriam asked.

"My English is poor, but with your help, I shall improve. Some of the sisters speak a little English. We are the only two who speak Italian." The sister's smile widened. Miriam smiled in return. "My English is certainly not perfect either."

"Your English is fine, so you will be the English teacher. Good luck." Sister Theresa Marie chuckled as she turned to leave Miriam's room.

"Wait. What?" Miriam tripped on the generous black fabric as she hurried to the door. Sister Theresa Marie peeked around the door and whispered,

"I am late for vespers. I will be back soon. Practice walking."

"Practice walking? I have been walking for sixteen years. Now, I have to practice?" Miriam grumbled as she tripped once again on the abundance of material that draped her small frame. She maneuvered around her tiny room, trying to mimic the ethereal walk of Mother Gertrude and Sister Theresa Marie.

"This is going to take a lot of practice," Miriam spoke to the ceiling as she fell onto the cot, which along with a Lilliputian bureau, a straight-backed chair, and a small writing table, graced her new living accommodations.

"Oi." Miriam closed her eyes. She was tired, but sleep would not come. Instead of sleep, she watched as cheerless images projected themselves onto the deep sepia of her closed eyes.

Tap, tap, tap.

"Come in."

"I have brought you a dinner tray and a few cookies for later." Sister Theresa Marie set the tray on the writing table. She sat on the edge of Miriam's cot and nibbled on a cookie she took from her deep pocket.

"Thank you." Miriam was not sure what she was being served, but she was hungry. She decided it was stew and did not ask particulars.

"That was very good. Thank you." Miriam studied her dinner tray. The rosebud and vase were the only things left uneaten.

"I love roses; they remind me of my mother. She loved flowers, especially roses."

"I thought you might like one for your room." Sister Theresa Marie's smile came easily but did not light her eyes. Miriam searched Theresa Marie's sad eyes. Although her sadness was intense, it had not touched her soul.

"I know you said that I am supposed to be in seclusion, but will I be allowed to go outside? I would love to see the rose garden."

"Of course, you may go outside. Tomorrow, I will take you to the grotto. It is a private garden. We go there for quiet reflection. No one will bother you there."

"Thank you, Sister. You are very kind."

"Please, call me Theresa."

"All right, Theresa. Thank you."

"I have one more thing for you." Sister Theresa Marie withdrew her hand from her pocket and hesitantly placed a silver rosary worked with amethyst beads in Miriam's hand. "This was mine when I was a young girl, it means a lot to me. I am sorry, Miriam. I know this is not part of what you believe, but you must learn to pray like a sister."

Miriam looked in horror at the image of a crucified man. She had never touched a graven image, much less prayed to one. Now with everything else, she would be unclean. A cry lumped in her throat. Tears welled in her eyes but did not fall.

"I am sorry. I am so sorry, Miriam." Sister Theresa Marie wrapped her arms around Miriam.

"The days of sorrow shall renew themselves." As a storm threatened, Miriam comforted Sister Theresa Marie with her father's words.

Miraculously, the dawn broke, turning the sky from the dark thunderous heavens of the night into the radiant firmament of morning. The world was washed fresh by the storm that had raged during the night. Miriam had been up for hours. From her window, she could see the courtyard beyond the iron gate and the stonewall that secluded the monastery. Two sisters stood at the gate as children filed through with their books in hand; ready to face another day of academia.

Tap, tap, tap.

"Come in," Miriam welcomed Sister Theresa Marie into her room again.

"Are you hungry? I have brought you breakfast." Sister Theresa Marie put the tray on the writing table and uncovered Miriam's breakfast of fruit, cheese, bread, and hot tea.

"Thank you, Sister. It looks wonderful."

"Theresa, remember? Most of the sisters will want you to call them by their name. Some of the sisters are a little hard to get along with and will be more formal." Sister Theresa Marie began the day's instruction. "It is good to have someone to speak Italian with. I have missed my home and my language since I have been here," Sister Theresa Marie admitted to Miriam.

"This is a wonderful breakfast. This cheese is very good. Where is it from?"

"We make it here. It *is* very good. We even make enough to sell. We sell some of our produce and dairy at the market. It brings in a little money to the house.

"Miriam, last night I explained to you why we call your father's friend Gertrude instead of Emma. Do you remember?" Sister Theresa Marie began.

"Yes, I remember."

"Now, you must have a new name. Mother Gertrude has chosen Mary Katherine. Saint Katherine is the protector of young women and guards against being burned, and of course, Mary is the name of the Blessed Mother of Christ.

"I understand." Miriam swallowed the lump that welled again in her throat. "Will you take me to the grotto this morning?" Miriam put her unfinished breakfast aside.

"Yes, but there are a few more things to do before we go out. You must learn what I am going to tell you. Do not write it down. Memorize it. Your given name is Kristen Herder. You are eighteen years old. You are Mother Gertrude's niece from Düsseldorf, the daughter of her brother, Elmer, and his wife, Hilda. Your parents were killed three months ago in a house fire. You have come here from our sister convent there in Düsseldorf, where you have recently taken your vows as a sister. You are under a special dispensation for a time of seclusion. You have no family other than Mother Gertrude and her brother, Wilhelm."

"Eighteen? Who's going to believe that?" Miriam forced a smile.

"It is difficult to judge a sister's age because we are so covered by the habit. A sister's weight can be illusive too." Sister Theresa Marie giggled at her own joke.

Miriam mumbled the facts of her invented life as she followed Sister Theresa Marie through the corridors of the monastery, down the stairs, and past the courtyard. Finally, they reached the grotto, a garden with such a heavy canopy of trees that it seemed cave-like.

A large rock sat in the middle of the clearing, worn smooth from years of being sat upon in quiet contemplation.

"Here we are," Sister Theresa Marie said.

"It is so quiet here." Miriam felt the need to whisper, so as not to break the grotto's silent spell.

"You may come here to be alone. No one will come into the clearing if they see you are here." Sister Theresa Marie left Miriam quietly sitting on the smooth rock. As the morning sun fell through the trees, Miriam listened to the rustle of the leaves. To Miriam's ears, the songs of the birds were sad laments that wafted from somewhere beyond the trees.

Miriam sat in the grotto in silence save for the deafening sound of her heart breaking. As she sat wondering how she would ever bear her life, a raven landed at her side. Startled, Miriam jumped to her feet, but the raven stood where it had landed. Miriam returned to her seat and turned toward the large bird.

"You are a pretty one." Miriam leaned closer to the bird. The raven did not move. Miriam bent slightly forward to see the shiny object it held in its beak.

"What do you have?" The raven dropped his prize, a small silver vial at Miriam's feet. Miriam studied the vial.

"The essence," she whispered and held tightly to the vial. The raven moved toward her; she could see a band encircling the bird's leg. She scooped the bird into her hands and examined the band. A woman's wedding ring had been placed on the bird's leg. Miriam removed the ring. Engraved on the front in Hebrew letters was the inscription: "I am my beloved's." Miriam slipped the treasure into the pocket of her habit.

"Hello!" A voice came from the edge of the grotto. "Is that your bird?" Miriam shaded her eyes against the glare of the morning sun. She looked in the direction of the small voice.

"Who is there?" Miriam called out.

"Stephen." A young boy stepped from the shadows. "My name's Stephen. I always come here at recess. I am sorry, Sister. I guess I should not have disturbed you. But I saw you, and I wanted to see your bird. He sure is big!" Stephen hesitantly advanced. "Is he tame? What is his name? What is your name?" Stephen's cherub-like face shone, and his blue eyes danced.

"My name is Sister Mary Katherine." Miriam nervously tried her new name. "The bird's name is... umm... Sandalphon." *That was not too bad. He believed me. But he is probably only eleven or twelve years old. Well, it is a start,*" Miriam thought.

"Sandalphon, good name. I guess most people would have named him Blackie." Stephen squatted to have a closer look at the bird. Miriam laughed at Stephen's assessment of most people's idea of a creative epithet. The tolling school bell brought Stephen to his feet.

"I have to go back to class now. I will see you tomorrow if that is okay," Stephen called as he raced back to his studies.

"That would be nice, Stephen," Miriam called back. Miriam silently walked back to the monastery, ever aware of the large black bird that flew above her. Sister Theresa Marie met Miriam at the monastery door.

"I am on my way to the chapel. I will see you after lunch." Theresa Marie hurried along. Miriam was hungry by the time Theresa Marie brought her lunch.

"Sorry, we had leftovers," she said.

"Thank you, Theresa. It looks good." Miriam sat at her writing table prepared to enjoy her lunch.

"Yesterday, you said my job would be being the English teacher. What did you mean?"

"All of the sisters have a job. Some of the sisters work in the garden, some keep the house, some have missions outside of the monastery, and some are teachers. Since you have knowledge in English, you will be the English teacher in the convent school."

"What is your job, Theresa?"

"I am the mistress of the archives. Also, I keep the daily records."

"Will a record be kept of me?"

"Yes, a detailed record is kept of each sister from the time she enters the convent until the day she dies. Mother Gertrude and I have already created your records. As mistress of the archives, I am also in charge of preserving the religious icons. While you are learning, you can help me. Can you use a typewriter?"

"I was just learning when I came here. There was only one typewriter in our class, so we all had to take turns."

"You will learn quickly while helping me with the information in the archives."

"I have not practiced my typing as much as I should." Sister Theresa Marie's calm manner put Miriam at ease.

"Do not worry. I will give you plenty of opportunities to practice. Typing is something that you will always be able to use, and I can really use the help." Sister Theresa Marie walked to the heavy door, and then turned back to Miriam. "It is nice to have you here, Miriam. It is like having my little sister here. I did not realize how much I missed my home and my language until now. Thank you, Miriam." Sister Theresa Marie gave Miriam a quick hug before she left the room.

The weeks trudged along for Miriam. Although Sister Theresa Marie has shown her immense kindness and patience, much more than

Miriam had expected. Stephen and Sandalphon's antics are her only cheer. However, Miriam would keep the promise that she swore to her father. She would go on, she would force a smile, and she would continue to live as one of the sisters. She would learn their ways, pray their prayers, and then when her father returned for her, she would thank The One in heaven for concealing her in this unlikely crevasse.

❧

"Open your hand and close your eyes and I will give you something to make you wise," Stephen recited the children's singsong verse as he approached Sister Mary Katherine in the grotto.

"What are you up to?" Sister Mary Katherine asked as Stephen stood in front of her with his hands hidden behind his back.

"Open your hand and close your eyes. It is a surprise, Sister," Stephen insisted.

"Okay, but I hope this is not something crawly." Mary Katherine closed her eyes and held out her open hand. She felt Stephen place something in it.

"You can open your eyes now." Stephen giggled.

"Stephen, what a lovely gift!" Sister Mary Katherine was surprised to see a chocolate candy beautifully wrapped in shiny colored foil.

"My mother sends them to me. She is a confectioner." Stephen sat on the ground next to Sister Mary Katherine and opened his candy.

"Does she have a shop in town?" Sister Mary Katherine asked.

"No, her shop is in Düsseldorf." Sister Mary Katherine thought about the city that is contrived to be her home—a city she had never seen. "That is where I am from. I helped my mother in her shop before I came here to the monastery's school."

"Will you tell me about it?" Sister Mary Katherine thought it could not hurt to borrow some of Stephens's memories from his home.

Stephen beamed as he spoke of his home, his mother, her candy shop, and his desire to become a priest. "I'm an altar boy now, but Father Ignatius says I can start clerical work soon to prepare for the priesthood… Hey, he took my foil!" Stephen jumped to his feet, pretending to be annoyed at Sandalphon, who had taken the piece of shiny foil from his lap.

"That is what ravens do. My father had a raven when he was a boy that brought him every shiny thing that he found," Sister Mary Katherine said as Sandalphon dropped the foil into her outstretched hand.

"Then I guess your father was foil rich."

"Yes, I guess he was." Sister Mary Katherine smiles.

THE GIFT

Tap. Tap. Tap.

Sister Mary Katherine tapped the ruler on her desk to gain the class's attention. "Good morning, children."

"Good morning, Sister Mary Katherine." The children stood next to their desks and greeted her with the first English phrase they had learned. In three months of study, the students had learned enough English to confound completely anyone they might try to communicate with.

Sister Mary Katherine turned to the chalkboard and picked up a fresh piece of chalk. "Today is December 20, 1940." She spoke the words in English as she printed them across the chalkboard. As she wrote, a paper airplane sailed across the classroom, crashing into the chalkboard. Sister Mary Katherine dropped the chalk into her deep pocket and turned to face her class as they disintegrated into giggles.

"Airplane." Sister Mary Katherine held the object of hilarity in the air. She turned back to the chalkboard and picked up a piece of fresh chalk. Sister Mary Katherine wrote the word in large letters across the chalkboard.

"Airplane. Repeat after me." Sister Mary Katherine sailed the paper airplane across the room and continued her lessons. After class, Stephen came to Mary Katherine's desk.

"I will come after school and clean the board and erasers if you like, Sister." Stephen was always eager to please.

"That would be nice. Thank you, Stephen." Sister Mary Katherine was preoccupied with grading the stacks of students' papers that lay on her desk. She looked up from her desk to find Stephen studying her.

"Yes, dear, is there something else?"

"You are not like the other sisters."

"What? Why do you say that?" Sister Mary Katherine sputtered.

"Well, most of the other sisters would have been angry about the airplane, but you were not angry. You used it to teach us."

"Stephen, we must always learn from our mistakes, or our destiny will be to repeat them." The words of her father's instruction echoed in her ears.

"I hope I will be as good a priest as you are a sister."

"I am sure you will be a wonderful priest."

"I will come back right after school. I have to hurry now to boys choir practice for the holidays. See you later, Sister," Stephen called. Sister Mary Katherine watched her precious cherub turn into an impish little boy as he ran to catch his classmates.

Tap, tap, tap, tap, tap.

Mary Katherine's fingers flew across the typewriter's keyboard.

Tap, tap, tap.

"Your boyfriend is on the sill, Mary Katherine." Theresa Marie opened the window of her archives office and allowed Sandalphon to step in.

"Sandalphon. Yes, he is my boyfriend." Mary Katherine laughed. "I think I shall marry him. Then he will release me from my vow, and we will fly away together."

"Oh, no, Mary Katherine, you will not. I will not allow you to fly away from me."

"Do not fear, Theresa Marie. Alas, I have no wings, nor can I fly."

"Sandalphon has brought you something." Theresa Marie studied the shiny foil the bird held in his beak.

"It is probably a note from Stephen." Mary Katherine stopped typing and turned toward the window.

"A note?"

"Yes, one day while we were in the grotto, I told Stephen that ravens will bring any shiny thing they find to their person. After that, he started writing notes to me wrapped in candy foil."

"That is clever of him. Oh yes, and you too, Sandalphon." Theresa Marie stroked Sandalphon's broad chest. As Mary Katherine and Theresa Marie stood at the open window, they could hear angry voices from the office next door. The two young nuns listened quietly as the men argued. "You know I have finished construction of the Holy Trinity Monastery. Karl, come to the States with me. It will not be good for you to remain here."

"The Holy Trinity? I know that you finished it years ago, and I am sure Mother *thinks* she knows where all of her aristocratic money has gone."

"What are you saying, Karl?" Klaus roared.

"Do you think that I do not know, Klaus? You must think of me as a complete imbecile. I have access to Mother's accounts, and I have seen them dwindle considerably by your signature. You have misappropriated the lion's share of our family fortune, and yet Mother holds you in high regard while I have always been nothing more than an encumbrance."

"I do not think you of as an imbecile. No, you are more than an imbecile, Karl. You are a fool and an imbecile. I have enough for all of us in America. Come with me to the States. Mother has finally agreed to leave Düsseldorf." Klaus sighed.

"Karl, leave your past, start anew in America, as I have. Come with us when we leave. We will be sailing for the States in two days. Travelling to Europe from the States is becoming more difficult, so I will not be able to come here again for a long while."

"Klaus, you really should call me Father," Father Ignatius hissed.

"I see, you are determined to have your way as always, Karl." Klaus Duetzman ignored his brother's request. He had been ignoring his younger brother since the day he was born.

Almost fifteen years Karl's senior, the responsibility of keeping the family fell to Klaus upon the premature death of their father. Young Klaus had little time and even less patience for Karl, the hellion of a child, and now no patience at all for Karl, the malignant young man. Klaus turned his back from his brother. He would not speak to him again about coming to America.

Fourteen-year-old Richard Duetzman sat awkwardly in the corner of his uncle's office. He had learned very little of the German language that his father and uncle spoke, but he knew they were arguing again. Richard was sorry when his father and uncle argued. Richard loved his uncle, and his father was…his father. Richard's father had not taught him to speak German and was unable to teach him any social graces or proper human interaction of any sort. However, he had learned, under his father's tutelage, to straighten ten penny nails and that Jews were less than human. They were responsible for most, if not all, of the problems of the world; worst of all, they were the Christ killers.

"I am offering mass at the monastery this evening. I must prepare. Will you and Richard be at the mass, Klaus?"

"Yes, we will be there."

Father Ignatius turned his attention to his young nephew.

"Red, tomorrow, when the schoolchildren play in the courtyard, you may join them. A young sister from Düsseldorf who speaks English will be out with the children. You might enjoy talking with her."

"All the sisters look alike. I wouldn't know her from any other sister," Richard whined.

"You will know this sister. She and her raven will be playing tag with the children in the yard."

"Tag? How can a bird play tag?"

Father Ignatius rumpled Richard's bright red hair. "I think you will have to see that for yourself, Richard."

"Hey, stop it. I'm not a little kid anymore, you know."

"No, you're not. I miss that little boy."

❧

A light snow had fallen during the night, coating the ground with white. Young Richard Duetzman stepped out of the warmth of his room and grumbled,

"Snow! I hate this stuff! Glad there's no snow in Florida." He could hear the sounds of the children playing. He trudged toward the schoolyard. "I can't wait to get home and see Mother." Even though Richard enjoyed the company of his Uncle Karl, no one could take the place of his mother. His mother made the hours he had to spend with his father seem a bit more tolerable.

"Straighten those nails, boy. Do I have to show you again? Can you ever learn? Mama's boy, that's all you are. You are a good-for-nothing mama's boy." Richard mocked his father as he walked, as he often did. He could feel the power behind his father's words lessen with each one he repeated aloud. Richard followed the sound of children playing as he made his way to the schoolyard. In the yard, screams of laughter rang out. The children ran and jumped into the air, trying to tag a large raven that taunted them as it flew only inches from their reach. A young nun stood laughing as she watched the children's antics.

"That must be the sister from Düsseldorf," Richard grumbled as he approached Sister Mary Katherine. As he drew nearer, Sandalphon swooped down, causing Richard to lose his balance and tumble into the soft snow. The children continued their game, laughing all the more at the added bonus of seeing someone fall in the soft snow.

"What's so funny?" Richard's green eyes flashed, and his temper flared.

"Let me help you, young man." Sister Mary Katherine offered her hand to Richard.

"Naw, I can get up. I don't need help." Richard refused the sister's hand but slipped backward twice before finally making it to his feet. "Well, good morning, young man. I am Sister Mary Katherine. The children should not have laughed at your misfortune. I will speak to them about this matter."

"Just forget it." He brushed the snow from his pants.

"You are an American, correct?"

"Yes, I'm from Florida. My name is Richard Duetzman, but everyone calls me Red. I'm not used to the snow. I guess that's the problem."

"You came a long distance from home. What brought you here?"

"My father and I come almost every year to visit my uncle, Father Ignatius, and my grandmother who lives in Düsseldorf."

"Oh?"

"My uncle said you are from Düsseldorf. What part?"

"*Children*, it's time to go back to class. Richard… Red, it has been nice to meet you, but I must go now. I hope you have a nice visit and a safe trip home." Sister Mary Katherine gathered the children and hurried them back into the classroom before Richard could bid his farewell.

"What an odd duck," Richard said to himself as he made his way back to the guest quarters.

"Richard, did you go out to the school yard today?" Richard did not reply. He laid a gift next to Father Ignatius's plate. Richard hoped his uncle would like what he had brought him. He had thought long and hard about an appropriate gift for the priest. He had finally settled on the gold bookmark. Richard even spent the extra fifty cents to have it engraved with, To Father Ignatius. Love, Richard.

Father Ignatius picked the gift up and studied it. "Oh, is this for me, Red?" Ignatius pretended to be surprised although Richard brought a gift each time he visited.

"Yes. Open it." Upon Richard's eager words, Ignatius ripped open the gift. He smiled as he saw his present.

"A bookmark, and it is engraved! Thank you, Red."

"You're welcome," Richard beamed.

"Richard! I believe your uncle asked you a question that you rudely ignored," Klaus scolded.

"I asked you if you went out to play today. Did you?" Ignatius said.

"Yeah, I went out," Richard snarled, as he pushed his food around on his plate.

"Did you get a chance to chase the raven?"

"*No*, that stupid bird knocked me down. Then the dumb kids laughed at me. When I asked the sister about where she lived in Düsseldorf, she took off like her hair was on fire." Father Ignatius waited until Richard took his next gulp of water before speaking.

"Her family was killed in a house fire." Water and uncontrolled laughter spewed from Richard's mouth.

"I guess their hair was on fire." Richard fell from his dining chair and rolled on the floor in throes of exaggerated laughter.

"That's enough, boy. I would like to enjoy the rest of my dinner." Klaus glared at Richard and then his brother. Karl had not been a good influence on his son.

Father Ignatius smiles.

❧

Sister Mary Katherine sat in the grotto with Sandalphon as he preened his feathers, which shined iridescent in the warm spring sun.

"The best part of spring is that it comes right after winter." Sister Mary Katherine smiled into the face of the sun. She looked down.

"I think you missed a spot, Sandalphon." Sister Mary Katherine crooked her finger and scratched the bird's large black head.

"Good morning, Sister." Stephen found Sister Mary Katherine and Sandalphon in the grotto.

"Good morning, Stephen. Soon, it will be Easter. Are you enjoying the Holy Days?"

"I suppose so."

"You suppose so? What does that mean? The rest of the children are all happy to be excused from class. What is the matter?" Stephen slumped down beside Sister Mary Katherine. She ruffled his blond curls.

"I still have my altar duties and clerical studies." Stephen crossed his arms over his chest.

"Stephen, what is wrong? Is something bothering you?"

"No, Sister, I will be all right." Stephen dropped his head. His tears fell into the grotto's deep carpet of leaves and moss.

"Come here." Sister Mary Katherine pulled Stephen to herself. She held him as he cried. "Stephen, I will always help you if I can. Do you know that?"

"Yes, Sister. I know." Stephen pulled away and forced a smile. He stuffed his hand in his pocket. "Look, Sister, my mother sent us a holiday treat." Stephen produced two large chocolate bars.

"It is so nice of your mother to remember me."

"I think these candies are the most beautiful she has sent." Sister Mary Katherine admired the gold foil. The wrapper was delicately embossed with bouquets of pastel spring flowers.

"I will save mine. I think I will just look at it for a while." Stephen studied his candy. His eyes welled again with tears.

"Stephen, tell me what's wrong."

"Oh, Sister, I want to be a priest more than anything. It is all I have ever wanted. But I cannot." Stephen began to cry again.

"Stephen, you should speak to Father. I am sure he will help you."

"No, not Father Ignatius! He…" Stephen was suddenly quiet.

"What about Father?" As Sister Mary Katherine searched Stephen's eyes his tremendous sadness overcame her.

While the shadows lengthened in the grotto, and the sun set, Sister Mary Katherine read the sorrow in Stephen's eyes, the sorrow that had touched Stephen's very soul. As the months passed and spring gave way to summer, Stephen became increasingly distant. He no longer came to the grotto to find Sister Mary Katherine and Sandalphon.

ABSOLUTION

"Bless me, Father, for I have sinned," the man slurred. Father Ignatius waited, but the man did not continue. He merely sat in the confessional and quietly sobbed.

"How long has it been since your last confession?" Father Ignatius asked, although he did not care how long it had been or if, in fact, the man had ever been to confessions, nor did he care that the man reeked of alcohol and women.

"I don't know. A year or two? Maybe more," the man belched loudly.

"Why have you come, my son?"

"I'm drunk."

"Have you come to the house of God to seek forgiveness for the sin of drunkenness?"

"Drunkenness? If that were all I am guilty of, I would be at the beer garden now with a woman on each knee," the man sneered.

"God will also forgive the sin of lust."

"Lust, ha. That is a very bad sin, Father." The man laughed bitterly.

"Confess your sin, and the Father will forgive you." Father Ignatius was becoming annoyed.

"There is no forgiveness. Not for me." The man leaned his head against the heavy screen that separated the priest and the parishioner.

"Unless you confess your sins, there is no forgiveness. Only with confession will there be forgiveness and peace."

The man's quiet sobbing rose to a loud wail as the man broke under his burden.

"Father, I have been drunk for almost two years now. It is the only way I am able to live with what I have done."

"Continue, my son."

"At first, the drinking helped, but now there is not enough beer in all of Germany to drown the cries and pleading," the man said.

"What cries, my son?"

"November ninth of thirty-eight. I was there... they call it *Kristallnacht*, the night of the broken glass."

"*Kristallnacht*?" Father Ignatius' heart skipped a beat. He leaned on his hand to partially cover his face. With his ear pressed to the screen, Ignatius listened intently determined to extract the specifics from this tortured soul.

"Yes, it was in a small town in the countryside, we came through on motorcycles ;we smashed up the town. We saw a woman running into an alley. We beat the man she was with and then, we went after her. We were like savages, like wild animals. We were Hitler's youth league, the master race, showing our superiority over a crying, helpless woman. We ignored her pleas. When it was my turn to have her, she was badly hurt as she lay beneath me, dying, she looked into my eyes and said, 'We are going to have a baby, Jacob.' By the time we were finished with her, the poor woman was out of her mind. She thought I was her husband; I can only imagine." When I reported to my captain that the woman was dead and that she had been with child, he laughed and said, 'This is not a bad thing. Now, we have rid the world of two Jews instead of only one. I hear her cries every day. Please help me." He held his head in his hands and sobbed.

"Do you have remorse for your actions?"

"Yes, Father, but remorse will not restore that woman."

"If you are truly remorseful, you must make an act of contrition." Ignatius tried to see the face of the man who sat on the other side of the heavy screen that separated them in the confessional.

"You must pray three Hail Mary's for the purity of the Blessed Mother and ten Our Father's for the sanctity of the trinity. Then, you may go, and you are forgiven."

"Is that the worth of that woman's life?"

"God forgives those who repent, my son. Before you go, will you tell me the name of that heartless captain? So, I can pray for his immortal soul."

"Yes, Father. I will never forget him. His name is Karl Deutzman."

"So, he remembers me," Father Ignatius whispered as he watched the man stagger through the chapel door.

~

The summer breeze found its way through Sister Mary Katherine's open window. This particular evening, the sky was spectacular. In her darkened room, as she watched the stars, it seemed like a lifetime since she had shared the summer sky with her father.

"You are capable of doing whatever you wish," he had told her as they sat gazing into the starry night.

"I wish I could dance on the stars. Can I even do that, Father?" she had asked. *"Yes, child, you can even do that,"* he answered.

The stars seemed so close that Sister Mary Katherine thought that this night would certainly be the night in which she could dance on the stars.

The courtyard was quiet, save for the occasional parishioner leaving the chapel after confession—the forgiven on the way home to start anew, never to sin again, or more realistically, to just start again.

One man caught Sister Mary Katherine's attention as he stumbled out of the chapel. The sister watched as another figure stepped from the night's shadows. Now, two men walked in the darkened courtyard. As the man stumbled toward the gate, the second man quickened his step. Under the light of the torch that illuminated the gate, Sister Mary Katherine saw the face of the second man. Drawing a cord from beneath his robe, Father Ignatius absolved the man of his life.

❧

More than a month had passed since that starlit night. Sister Mary Katherine walked through the courtyard in the cool mist of the summer evening. The courtyard was quiet and deserted. The shadows grew larger as she hurried to her room. As she passed the gate, a dark figure stepped from the shadows.

"Sister, I would like to speak with you," Father Ignatius approached Sister Mary Katherine.

"Yes, Father." *Does he know that I saw what he did? Did he see me?* The sister's heart raced.

Father Ignatius took three quick steps. He now stood only inches from Sister Mary Katherine. He is too close. *Stay calm*, she thought. She wanted to run, but she was riveted by fear to the spot where she stood.

"I have something for you." Father Ignatius looked into her frightened eyes. She saw nothing in his eyes—only darkness. Her panic rose. Sister

Mary Katherine tried to scream, but no sound came from her throat as Father Ignatius tightened a cord around her neck. *I cannot breathe! I am dying*!

Mary Katherine struggled, then she floated into darkness. *I am dead. This is what it's like. I am dead…* Sister Mary Katherine awoke. The bed covers were the only foe that she had struggled against. The nightmare plagued her sleeping and also her waking hours. She wanted to escape the confines of the monastery and return to her father, but the oath that she had sworn to stay with the sisters would not allow it. She wanted to tell Theresa Marie about the murder in the courtyard and about her plan. However, fear of the harm that could befall Theresa Marie if she were made privy to Ignatius' deed kept Sister Mary Katherine silent. Her journal was her only confidante.

Tap, tap, tap.

Sister Mary Katherine worked at the typewriter in the archive office as Theresa Marie researched an ancient icon.

"You're getting pretty good on that typewriter." Theresa Marie took two cookies from her deep pocket and passed one to Mary Katherine.

"My speed has improved greatly thanks to you, Theresa Marie."

"What is your name?" Theresa Marie often quizzed Mary Katherine on the invented facts of her life as they worked in the archives.

"Kristen Herder."

"What is your father's name?"

"Elmer Herder."

"Where were you born?"

"Düsseldorf."

"Quick, tell me your birthday."

"June 19, 1923."

"1921, Mary Katherine, 1921. That makes you nineteen. You keep forgetting."

"1921. I will not forget again."

Tap. Tap. Tap

"Someone is looking for you." Theresa Marie brought Mary Katherine's attention to Sandalphon on the windowsill.

"Oh, he has a note from Stephen. I am worried about him; he has not been himself lately." Mary Katherine took the foil from Sandalphon.

"Maybe he is just having growing pains. Pretty foil," Theresa Marie said as Mary Katherine read the note.

"Oh! No. God, please, no!" Mary Katherine ran from the archives, along the halls of the monastery, through the courtyard, past the chapel, and into the boys' dormitory. Theresa Marie tried to follow but fell behind before Mary Katherine reached the boys' dormitory. Mary Katherine gasped for air as she ran into the dormitory's parlor and to the dorm mother.

"I must speak to Stephen Hunsberger!"

"Certainly, Sister, you could speak with the boy if he were here, but Stephen has been out all afternoon," the dorm mother said.

"Where is he?"

"I assume he is playing ball with the other boys."

"Where? Where do they play?"

"In the field, behind the dormitory."

Sister Mary Katherine ran from the dormitory to the field where the boys were playing. She saw the back of a familiar head as she ran.

"Stephen, thank goodness. Are you all right?" Sister Mary Katherine spun the boy around, only to see that he was not Stephen.

"Have you seen Stephen Hunsberger?" she asked.

"No, not since this morning, Sister."

"Where was he?"

"He was going to the attic. He said Father told him he was supposed to clean it for his penance."

Sister Mary Katherine could see Sandalphon perched on the peak of the dormitory's highest gable. Mary Katherine ran back to the dormitory, past the dorm mother, through the parlor, and bounded up the stairs, clearing two stairs with each stride. Her heart pounded.

"Stephen! Stephen! Where are you?" Mary Katherine called as she neared the attic door. "Help me! Please help me!" she cried to the curious boys who had followed her to the attic. Sister Mary Katherine stood on a stool holding Stephen's lifeless body. Her precious friend hung from the rafters.

∼

Sister Theresa Marie found her way to the stairwell and pushed through the boys who had gathered there. The older boys who had helped Sister Mary Katherine bring Stephen down from the rafters stood silently beside her as she cradled Stephen's body.

"Mary Katherine, the priests have come. They have to take Stephen now," Theresa Marie whispered as she knelt beside Mary Katherine who was still holding Stephen.

"No, they cannot have him." Mary Katherine glared at Father Ignatius as he stood with the other priest. Mary Katherine refused to leave her friend. She rocked Stephen in the cradle of her arms and quietly hummed a lullaby. She whispered, "I will help you, Stephen. I will not let him hurt you again. I promise." Sister Mary Katherine ran her fingers through Stephen's curly blond hair. "He looks like an angel, Theresa." Mary Katherine gently kissed Stephen's forehead and returned to the comfort of her lullaby.

"Mary Katherine, let me help you." Theresa Marie took Sister Mary Katherine's arm and gently helped her to her feet.

"I would like to go to my room now." Sister Mary Katherine turned from Theresa Marie to Stephen. Sister Theresa Marie gently took her hand and led her from the dormitory. In the screaming quiet of her room, Sister Mary Katherine took Stephen's note from her pocket. She read the note once again:

Dear Sister,

What I have done is called a mortal sin. It is at that cost that I will be free, and Father Ignatius will no longer be able to force the unspeakable acts of his desire upon me. I am unsure of what is to come after this life. Perhaps, however, it is only life that has been my torment and pain, and in death there will be a quiet nothing. Pray for me, Sister.

Stephen

Sister Mary Katherine opened the journal her father had given her and placed the folded note between the pages. "Stephen," she whispered. She laid her head on the journal, tears spilled down her cheeks and onto the blank page of the open journal.

Writing appeared under the wet tear stain that had made the page somewhat translucent. The writing was in her father's own hand. She examined the book and found that each page was an envelope that could be opened by loosening the ties that bound the journal together. Each envelope contained one page that her father had copied from his own journal. The remainder of the night was spent reading her father's thoughts and gaining insight into Kabbalah.

"Mother Gertrude?" Sister Mary Katherine approached the prioress in her office after the morning prayers.

"Yes, child?"

"When I was walking by the river one afternoon, I noticed a deposit of clay." Sister Mary Katherine studied Mother Gertrude to see if she was listening.

"Yes, go on. Clay by the river?" Mother Mary continued studying her notes.

"I would like your permission to bring some of that clay to the basement."

"Why do you want clay in the basement, child?" Mother Gertrude looked up from her reading.

"I want to create a monument, a sculpture, for the monastery in memory of Stephen."

"How much time do you imagine it will take to complete this sculpture?"

"I plan to work steadily for two months, with your permission, of course."

"Your own mother was quite an artist. She was truly a talented sculptor. I had the privilege to see some of her work, and if you have inherited any of her talent, I am sure your tribute to Stephen will be beautiful and most appropriate. You may have the clay. I will ask the gardener to bring it to the empty storage room in the basement. You may work in privacy there. If you need anything else, tell him."

"Thank you, Mother Gertrude."

"Two months, Mary Katherine. That is until the end of October. Theresa Marie will not want to do without you for longer than that." Mother Gertrude was trying to be stern, but her eyes betrayed her.

The storage room in the basement was small, but it was large enough for Mary Katherine's purpose. Mother Gertrude had even given her the key to the room so that her work would remain a mystery until the unveiling. Each day after class, Sister Mary Katherine worked in the privacy of her basement studio until vespers. Then after supper, she began again. She was often in the basement until the time came for

Morning Prayer. When she grew tired and could no longer work, she would study her father's journal. Day after day, week after week, Mary Katherine worked. Finally, she finished, and the next day would be the long-awaited unveiling. Sister Mary Katherine would spend one more night with her creation.

Tap, tap, tap.

"Mary Katherine, it is beginning to storm," Theresa Marie said through the door. "Are you going to come out? I have made tea for us, and I have four nice cookies, one for each of our hands, just as we like. Will you have tea with me finally, Mary Katherine?"

"I will, Theresa Marie, but not now," Mary Katherine called. "I will be all right. I will see you in only a little while, and we will have tea and cookies before bed. I promise. I will be finished soon," Mary Katherine politely dismissed her friend.

"You should be in your room during such a storm, not in this damp basement, Mary Katherine!" Theresa Marie insisted. She would not be easily dismissed.

"I will be up soon. I promise."

"You are a stubborn child, Mary Katherine."

Theresa Marie left the basement for the safety of her room. A thunderous boom and a lightning flash filled the basement as Sister Mary Katherine admired her work.

"Yes, there you are, Eliakim."

❧

The morning sun finally rose on the day of the long-awaited unveiling. The sisters were gathered in the courtyard, anxious to see what Mary Katherine had created.

"And it shall come to pass that I will call my servant Eliakim...and the key to the house of David, I will lay on his shoulder; so, he shall open, and none shall shut, and he shall shut, and none shall open." Mother Mary Gertrude read from the book of Isaiah. After the dedication ceremony, the sisters all commented on the beauty and realistic features and of his handsome face. Mary Katherine's Eliakim was a wondrous creation. The sisters crowded around Mary Katherine.

"He looks so real, Mary Katherine."

"Every muscle and every feature is so defined." Eliakim stood more than two meters tall. Muscles bulged beneath his robe and cloak. Eliakim's face was the image of a handsome man looking to the heavens. One of his muscular arms was raised to the heavens while the other held a key in a clenched fist at his shoulder. He was magnificent to be certain.

CONFESSION

"Duetzman!" The SS officer leaned over Ignatius's desk. "Perhaps you have forgotten why you were posted here." The officer leaned closer and snarled into his subordinate's face, "It is not so you can enjoy the company of young boys. I know the sisters are hiding children of the Jews here. You, Duetzman, are here to seek out the offspring of the vermin who has infested our country and report to me. I know the sisters are hiding children here." The officer spat his words. "Be well advised, Duetzman, you will find yourself serving the Fuehrer in the ranks if I find that you are not diligent in your search!" The officer turned on his mark and left Ignatius in his study.

"Father?" Sister Mary Katherine stood at the threshold of the open door.

"Yes, Sister Mary Katherine?"

"Mother Gertrude asks if you will join us for dinner after mass next week on All Saints' Day?"

"Yes, I will be joining you. Thank you for the invitation." Sister Mary Katherine silently left his office.

Ignatius wondered how long she had been standing there before she made herself known. These women skulk up and down the halls of this place like ghosts. A person never knows where they are lurking. The niece of the prioress could cause trouble for him. Ignatius was determined to guard his purpose.

Preparations for the All Saints' Day feast began early. Every sister who was available had a responsibility, and they worked diligently to complete their tasks before the evening mass.

"Potatoes! I need potatoes. Nobody brought the potatoes up from the cellar!" Sister Mary Francis called out to whoever was in hearing distance. Sister Mary Francis was the undisputed queen of the kitchen. In truth, she was the saint of the kitchen.

"I will get the potatoes and maybe a rutabaga or two if we have any," Mother Gertrude said. Escaping for a few moments to the root cellar was Mother Gertrude's guilty pleasure. The cool air and the earth's musky perfume rose from the root cellar and lightened Mother Gertrude's head. Mother Gertrude made her way up the steep wooden stairs with her apron full of potatoes and a few nice rutabagas. She could see a dark shadow of a man standing at the cellar door.

"Mother Gertrude, may I have a moment of your time?" Father Ignatius stood at the top of the steps. Mother Gertrude's exit was blocked.

"Father, may I pass please? They are expecting me in the kitchen with these vegetables."

"I asked for a moment of your time, Mother." Ignatius stepped forward.

Mother Gertrude tensed. "I really need to get these vegetables to the kitchen," she said, moving up a step.

Father Ignatius took Mother Gertrude by her shoulder and pulled her to himself. The vegetables spilled from Mother Gertrude's apron and bounced down the steps.

"Father, what do you want of me?"

"I want to know what you know." Father Ignatius gripped Mother Gertrude even tighter.

"I do not understand, Father." Mother Gertrude winced as Father Ignatius dug his fingers into her shoulder.

"You, worthless old woman, I want the truth. Tell me what you know now! What has Sister Mary Katherine told you?" Father Ignatius was determined. He stepped alongside Mother Gertrude.

"The only truth that I know comes from our Lord's Holy Word, Ignatius. Do not be deceived. God is not mocked, for whatever a man sows, that he shall also reap," Mother Gertrude spoke the words only seconds before one forceful push sent her tumbling down the stairs.

"You disgust me, Mother!" Father Ignatius called down the dark staircase. He spoke as much to his own mother as to Mother Gertrude. Father Ignatius opened the cellar doors and walked into the fading light of the late afternoon. As Mother Gertrude's broken body lie on the cold stone floor of the root cellar, Ignatius returned to his study to prepare his sermon for the evening mass.

Sister Mary Katherine finished setting the dining tables just as Sister Mary Francis began shouting for potatoes once again.

"If I do not start the potatoes soon, there will be none! Will someone see what Mother Gertrude is doing?" Sister Mary Francis said as she put pies into the hot oven.

"I will go to help, Mother," Sister Mary Katherine said. The afternoons were cooling quickly, and the days were growing shorter. Mary Katherine pulled her cloak close and hurried to the root cellar. It has been more than a year since she came to live at the monastery. During that time, Mary Katherine had learned the beliefs of the sisters. She had lived by her understanding and the oath that she had sworn to her father, and now she had a great respect for the sisters and their commitment to their beliefs. The sisters' dedication to one another and Mother Gertrude's unwavering gentle kindness had made her realize how much she had grown to love them.

"Mother? Are you down there? Mary Francis is still calling for potatoes." Mary Katherine started down the steps. A low moan rose from the dark cellar.

"Mother Gertrude?" Another moan, almost inaudible, ascended the staircase. Mary Katherine hurried down the dark stairwell, alarmed by the sound of the quiet moaning.

"Mother Gertrude, where are you? Are you all right?" Mary Katherine stumbled in the darkness that was relieved only slightly by the waning afternoon light that struggled through the cracks in the cellar door. Her hands searched the dark wall for the lantern.

"Matches, matches. Light the lantern. The lantern, light the lantern." Mary Katherine's words directed her frantic hands. She broke two matches before she succeeded in lighting the lantern. "Mother!" Mary Katherine knelt beside the Mother Superior and placed her ear on the old woman's chest. "Breathing, she's breathing. I must get help. The other sisters will help me take you upstairs, Mother. I need help." Mary Katherine rose to her feet. Mother Gertrude grasped the hem of Mary Katherine's habit. "Mother let me go. I must bring help."

"Ignatius…" Mother Gertrude whispered her last word.

⌒

"This is the last time we will come to the grotto for a while Sandalphon. It is becoming too cold. The trees are bare, and everything has gone to gray. Are you cold, Sandalphon?" It was not as much cold as it was of the overwhelming sense of loss that will keep Sister Mary Katherine from her quiet respites in the grotto. Her thoughts were of the afternoon in the root cellar and Mother Gertrude's last words. She was certain that Mother Gertrude had not whispered Father Ignatius's name in her final moment because she wanted his final absolution.

"Sandalphon, I must make confession tonight." The shadow of the large black bird that circled above the sister as she walked back to the monastery lent a somber shade of contrast to the winter day.

Mary Katherine closed the door to the confessional.

"Father?"

"Yes, child?" Ignatius was confused. She did not begin her confession with the words "Forgive me, Father."

"Do you believe the Holy Scripture is true?"

"Are you questioning your faith, Sister?" Father Ignatius recognizes Mary Katherine's voice.

"No, Father. I am not."

"Then what is your confession, Sister?"

"Father, do you believe the priests and prophets are held to a higher standard, just as the Holy Scripture states?"

"If the scriptures are true, then certainly it is of no consequence what I believe."

"That is true, Father. So, consequence must be in relationship to one's action."

"I suppose that is true, Sister."

"According to the Holy Scriptures, Father, if a man causes harm to come to one of God's own, his fate would be better if he were tossed into the sea with a millstone bound around his neck."

"Is there a point to your cryptic questions, Mary Katherine?" Ignatius snarled.

"Yes, Ignatius. Stephen and Mother Gertrude will be your millstone. I bid you good night." Sister Mary Katherine quietly left the confessional. That night, Sister Mary Katherine's words and dreams of young boys who cried out to be returned to their innocence haunted Ignatius's bed.

November 9, 1941

The SS officer appeared at the door to Father Ignatius's study.

"Your report, Duetzman."

"Good morning, sir. I did not expect you to be so early."

"I want your report, Duetzman, not whining excuses." The officer sat on the edge of Ignatius' desk and lit a cigarette as Ignatius leafed through papers. The opportunity to rid himself of the odd Mary Katherine sat before him.

"I don't believe the sisters are hiding any of the Jewish children. None of the children here seem out of place. Although…" he paused. "There is one young sister I have concerns about."

"Her name, Duetzman?" The officer demanded.

"Her name is Mary Katherine. She came here not long ago."

"Take me to her."

The sound of the small troop echoed through the monastery halls and across the courtyard as they marched. Father Ignatius led the troop to the convent school and finally into Sister Mary Katherine's classroom.

"Sister Mary Katherine, I would like to speak with you," Father Ignatius said.

"Children, continue to quietly work on your English conversation." Sister Mary Katherine turned from the chalkboard, dropped the chalk into her pocket, and addressed Father Ignatius.

"How may I help you, Father?" Sister Mary Katherine's eyes found the soldiers at her classroom door.

"The officer has come to question some of us. I am sure there is nothing to worry about." Father Ignatius's words were for the benefit of the sisters who had followed the troop to Mary Katherine's classroom.

"What is your name?" The officer was a formidable presence. He towered over the frightened Mary Katherine.

"Sister Mary Katherine." She trembled as she drew her strength to speak.

"What is your birth name?"

"Kristen Herder."

"No middle name?"

"Emma. It is Emma."

"Father's name?"

"Elmer Daniel Herder."

"Mother's name?"

"Hilda Ingra Herder."

"Where were you born?"

"Düsseldorf."

"How old are you?"

"Nineteen."

"When is your birth date?" The officer recorded each answer into his note pad.

"June 19, 1923." Sister Mary Katherine's eyes found her friend. Theresa Marie's breath caught in her throat. Mary Katherine had answered with her actual birthday. The officer continued his questioning, seemingly unaware of the age discrepancy.

"Your mother's maiden name?"

Sister Mary Katherine opened her mouth, but her mind would not give up a name.

"Your mother's maiden name, Sister." The officer stepped toward Sister Mary Katherine as he repeated the question, "What is your mother's maiden name? That is not so hard a question, Sister."

"Schliemann, Schliemann. Her maiden name was Schliemann."

"Schliemann? You seem uncertain, Sister. Was your mother's name Schliemann or was it not, Sister?" The officer circled Sister Mary Katherine like a hyena as he fired the barrage of questions.

"Yes, it was Schliemann." Sister Mary Katherine's eyes rimmed with tears.

"You are crying. Is something wrong?"

"My parents were killed in a house fire only recently. I am still sad when I think of them."

"Where is your faith, Sister? Were they not good people? Surely, you trust that they are in heaven with your God. I would like to see your room now."

"My room?"

"Yes, your room. I see no problem with that, do you, Sister?"

"No, sir, no problem." Sister Mary Katherine led the troop back into the monastery, through the priory halls, and to her room. Sister Mary Katherine's cot was neatly made. A large crucifix, the room's only adornment, stood on the bureau. Her writing table was clear.

"Search the bureau and the bed," the officer ordered his troop.

The soldiers ripped Sister Mary Katherine's mattress apart and searched her bureau drawers. The officer opened the drawer of her writing table.

"What is this?" The officer held the gold ring—that Sandalphon had brought her at their first meeting in the grotto.

"I found it on the ground," Mary Katherine said.

"This ring has a Hebrew inscription. It must have belonged to a Jew. Why would you keep this piece of trash?"

Sister Mary Katherine remained silent. She could not say the initials engraved inside the band identified the ring as belonging to her mother, Sara Rosa Davidson.

"I am waiting for an answer, good Sister."

"I thought it was pretty," she whispered.

"No. I think there is another reason you kept it, and be assured I will find that reason." The officer joined the three soldiers who now stood at the door to Mary Katherine's room. He spoke quietly to his troops and then turned to Sister Mary Katherine.

"It is fortunate for the children that you do not teach mathematics, Sister, as a simple calculation would put your age as eighteen, not nineteen. Take her!" The officer barked the order to his troop. Sister Mary Katherine was led through the halls by the officer. She was flanked on both sides by a soldier, the fourth soldier closed ranks behind.

"Where are you taking me?" Sister Mary Katherine asked. The officer pushed her into the back of a transport vehicle.

BOOG

The stench of urine, feces, vomit, and musty clothing emanated from the detainment center. The interrogation room held one chair that was positioned directly beneath a solitary light strung by a single cord from the low ceiling. The room smelled of fear. Sister Mary Katherine smelled of fear.

Early morning grew into afternoon, and Sister Mary Katherine still sat alone in the interview room. There were rumors she had heard, rumors of towns where the entire Jewish population had been detained. Some of the rumors told of camps where the Jews had been taken and of the unspeakable horrors that had awaited them there. However, there was no proof of the truth to these rumors—no proof at all since no one who had been taken had ever come back to attest to the atrocities. No one had ever come back.

The SS officer burst through the door in a matter of two long strides he stood towering over Sister Mary Katherine.

"What's your name?"

"Sister Mary Kather–" A loud crack rang out as her head hit the back of the chair with the force of the officer's blow. The stinging of her cheek and the taste of blood in her mouth was the officer's statement of intent to Miriam.

"I want your birth name."

"Kristen Emma Herder." Another hard slap. Sister Mary Katherine's cheek burned with the impression of the man's hand. Tears fell from Sister Mary Katherine's eyes, but she did not cry out. A closed fist blow fell to her opposite cheek.

"Do you see the papers in my hand? They tell me that Kristen Herder, the daughter of Hilda and Elmer Herder, never existed in Düsseldorf or anywhere else, as of that matter."

"Miriam Ruth Davidson. My name is Miriam." As the *result* of a sustaining strength, Miriam fearlessly looked into the face of the officer.

"A Jew."

"Yes, I am." Miriam did not break her gaze.

"One of the chosen?" the officer sneered. "Well, chosen one, take the habit off. We can't have you sitting around looking like a Catholic now, can we?" Miriam removed her habit. She stood in the mound of black wool and white linen, facing the leering officer wearing only her black cotton slip and leggings.

"Turn around," he ordered. Miriam turned her back to the officer. The air split with the sharp sound of a rod repeatedly hitting her tiny back. Miriam fell to her knees, but she still did not cry out. The officer pulled Miriam to her feet and threw her across the room.

"Tie her to the chair."

Two soldiers crowded into the small room. The soldiers tossed Miriam into the hard chair. They bound Miriam's feet to the chair's legs while the officer bound her hands to the chair's arms.

"Where are you from?"

"Tuttinger," Miriam whispered.

"Tuttinger? What is your father's name, child?" The officer's tone suddenly changed. "Jacob Nathaniel Davidson? Jacob Davidson. We have been looking for him and his comrades for more than a year." The officer squatted in front of Miriam. His enormous hands encompassed her head. He pulled her face within an inch of his own "Where is your father and his friends? Tell me where they are now, and it will be easier for you later." The officer lit a cigarette and waited for an answer.

"I do not know where they are. I swear. I do not know." The officer smothered his cigarette on Miriam's bare shoulder and left the room. Miriam could not determine the number of hours she had been tied to the chair. The sting of the officer's fist had left her cheek, replaced by a dull throb. The welts across her back wept, and her shoulder burned. She did not cry, but her bladder screamed. The dread of humiliation could not control her bodily functions much longer.

"We begin again, Jew." The officer leaned over Miriam. She did not acknowledge the officer. He wound his fingers around a handful of her hair and yanked her head back until they were face to face. Miriam winced. The officer dropped a handful of hair to the floor. "That is better."

I like to see your pretty face. Your…pretty…Jew…face." The officer traced Miriam's features with his finger, spat in her face, and then wiped the spittle from Miriam's cheek to her lips. "Where are your father and his friends?" Miriam spat. The officer simply knelt in front of Miriam, balancing on one knee.

"Take your time, think about it. I have time, you see. I can come and go as I like. I can eat and drink. I can do what I care to. I am not tied to a chair. So, please, think about your answer. Take your time." He stared into Miriam's eyes. Miriam stared into the abysmal darkness that was the officer's soul.

"You filthy bitch!" The officer jumped to his feet. His boot, the cuff of his pants, and his knee were wet with urine. The chair Miriam was bound to hit the floor as a result of the force of the officer's blow to her head.

The officer left the room again; the soldiers righted Miriam in the overturned chair. Miriam sat motionless in the chair until the officer and the two soldiers returned sometime later with a fourth man.

The man stood in the corner of the room. He held a small wooden box in his hands; his eyes searched the room. The man mumbled incoherently as he shifted his enormous weight from foot to foot, the wooden box tightly pressed against his protruding stomach. Even though the setting of the sun had cooled the room considerably, the man's bald head shone with beads of greasy sweat. His once white undershirt was wet with perspiration, and a ring of black filth encircled the neckline and dipped down to a point in the middle of the man's chest, drawing Miriam's eye to the man's dandling, ruptured navel. A bombastic sound escaped the man's buttocks, followed by a noxious odor. Miriam glanced toward the man.

"Pay no attention to Boog. He's just waiting." The officer smiled.

"Yes, sir." Miriam's head swam. She did not recognize her own voice. Miriam floated above herself.

This is not happening to me. This is happening to someone else. He cannot hurt me. He cannot hurt me.

"Your father, I want to know where your father is. Can he create a golem?"

"I swear, I do not know," Miriam mumbled. Her own voice was foreign to her.

"Can you create a golem?"

"I don't know what you mean." The enraged officer lifted the chair that Miriam was bound to and flung it across the room. The chair and Miriam miraculously landed in an upright position. The officer sighed.

"I have lost my temper again. I am sorry. I never know where it will take me. I think you are a very pretty little Jew. If you cooperate and begin to answer my questions, I will consider keeping you for myself. I have always wanted a Jew of my own." The officer lifted Miriam's face with the end of the rod that he had beaten her with and studied her.

"You would make a delicious little pet." He lit another cigarette. "How rude of me. May I offer you a cigarette?" The officer flicked a burning ember onto Miriam's shoulder.

"How many men left with your father?" Another ember fell to Miriam's shoulder.

"I do not know." Another ember burned deep into Miriam's soft flesh. Miriam closed her eyes. "It is not me," she whispered. She peered down at herself from the ceiling as the officer doused the remainder of his cigarette on the side of her neck.

"We are not finished with you yet, but now, it's Boog's turn." Boog moved toward Miriam, still tightly clutching the wooden box to his substantial belly. Muttering to himself, he searched the light cord hanging above Miriam's head and found an electrical outlet. The apparatus he took from the box made a high-pitched squeal when plugged into the outlet. Boog manipulated the instrument, which alternated between a high-pitched squeal and a steady hum. One of the soldiers pushed a stool under Boog's ample hindquarters as he sat. Miriam watched the top of Boog's bald head. Pores expelled tiny rivers of glistening sweat that dripped down his forehead and into his heavy brow. Boog touched Miriam's hand. She gasped in fear. A drop of sweat reached the corner of Boog's eye. He cocked his head upward to brush the salty drop away. As Miriam looked into Boog's soft blue eyes, crystal white flashes of light shone from his soul.

Boog sadly mouthed, 'I am sorry,' as the officer handed him a piece of paper. Boog gently untied Miriam's hand and retied it palm side up. She quietly allowed him to tattoo the inside of her forearm. Boog's eyes darted between his work on the tattoo and the officer while he spoke quietly to the soldiers.

"What about him?" one of the soldiers asked.

"Boog? He is deaf and addle-brained. Ignore him," the officer continued instructing the soldiers. Upon completion of his work, Boog, returned his tools and the scrap of paper to the box. He received a few cents from the officer and, still muttering, left the room. Boog shuffled through the streets and alleys, moving closer to the sound of laughter and music, but he heard nothing on his way to the Rathskeller.

Three men of the Miter Stand, the brave German freedom fighters, sat at a table in the corner of the crowded tavern. One of the men motioned to Boog.

"What did you see?" the man turned toward Boog as he spoke. "Young girl, a nun. They have been rough with her." Boog wrote these words on a notepad he took from his jacket. Boog watched the man's lips as he spoke.

"How many soldiers? Could you see what they said? Where are they taking her?"

"Au, but first, detainment center for questioning. They look for her father and the Kabbalah. They move her tonight, soon. Two soldiers and captain." Boog scribbled the words on his notepad.

The leader of the group spoke to the band of men, "Au, Auschwitz. Detainment center. Her father must be a Kabbalist. They will not take her to the camp yet. They want more information. She will go to the other center tonight. We can intercept them at the crossroads just beyond the forest. There will be only two or three of them. We will take the girl easily."

～

Miriam no longer ached from restraints that held her much tighter than necessary. She had lost all feeling in her hands. She could not recognize her own fingers; once alabaster they were now the blue-grey shade of sculpting clay. The officer returned to the chair where Miriam was bound. He placed his enormous foot in the center of her chest and with a swift push sent her forcefully crashing to the floor. White light exploded in Miriam's eyes as her head hit the floor. The officer untied Miriam's hands, leaving her feet bound.

"You have one more guest. He has been waiting patiently to speak with you." The officer nodded to the soldier, who opened the door and allowed the 'guest' to enter.

Ignatius stood over Miriam. The uniform that he wore identified him as an SS officer. Ignatius' heavy boot found Miriam's ribs several times as she lay on the floor. Still tied to the overturned chair, she struggled to no avail to right herself in the chair. Ignatius laughed, righted the chair, and crouched in front of her. Miriam gasped for air.

"Father Ignatius," Miriam moaned.

"I have been curious about one thing for some time now. I wonder how you knew of Stephen's death so quickly. How were you alerted?"

"A note. Stephen sent me a note telling me everything." Miriam looked into Ignatius's eyes. Ignatius turned away.

"And did you keep this note?" Ignatius paced, he did not know the exact contents of the note that this woman held, but he feared that if in actuality the boy had sent an explicit note, he certainly would no longer be able to hide himself in the church.

"Yes, I did." Miriam held her gaze on Ignatius. She did not blink. She had won this game many times in the schoolyard.

"Tell me where the note is," Ignatius demanded. Miriam's gaze remained fixed, but she was silent.

"Tell me where the note is. Tell me!" Enraged, Ignatius's hands flew to Miriam's tiny neck. The chair fell back to the floor. Ignatius fell on top of Miriam and continued to squeeze. "I will kill you. I will kill you and I will find the note."

"Ignatius, stop!" the officer in charge demanded. "She has to go to the detainment center for further questioning. You will not have the pleasure of ending her."

The officer pulled Ignatius to his feet, breaking the chokehold he had on Miriam's neck. Ignatius leaned close to Miriam.

"I will find that note. I will certainly find that note," Ignatius hissed.

"No, Ignatius, you will never."

"Enough, Jew. Untie your feet and get dressed." The officer turned to the soldiers. "We will process her here, and then we will deliver her to the center. They will transport her to the camp when they finish questioning her."

"But, sir, you said we could have her first," one of the soldiers reminded the captain.

"Not here…somewhere on the road. If we leave now, you will be back to your post before dawn." The soldiers marched their prisoner down the narrow hall.

November 9, 1941.

Against the light of the full moon, Miriam could see Sandalphon perched on top of the transport vehicle. A sharp thrust from one of the soldiers sent Miriam wheeling into the back of the truck. As the soldiers were closing the door, the raven swooped through the darkness and into the back of the vehicle.

"What was that?" The younger soldier stepped back from the vehicle.

"It looked like a bat," the second soldier said, he nudged the younger soldier toward the back of the vehicle.

"You should flush it out." The soldier nudged the younger soldier again.

"No, I will not. The bat will bite my arsch while I am having my way with the Jew. Let the bat have her for all I care."

"He's right. She's not worth getting rabies. Come, forget her. We will get a whore in Düsseldorf," the captain assured his men of their reward. The observation light dimly lit the back of the vehicle. Miriam found Sandalphon in the shadows and pulled herself closer to him. She used the last bit of her strength to reach him. She held him close, breathing in his comfort.

"I am hurt, Sandalphon. I need help. I cannot go where they are taking me." Miriam coughed, blood pour from her mouth. She wiped the blood from her mouth onto her sleeve, and gathered her strength. She pulled herself up and leaned against the bench attached to the wall of the vehicle, she perched Sandalphon on her lap. Her eyes rolled like marbles inside her clouded head. Her world spun in slow motion. Miriam closed her eyes. When she opened them, Sandalphon was still perched on her lap. She did not know if a minute or an hour had passed.

"Did I sleep, Sandalphon? Time… I dreamed of father, the spirit realm, time is not kept. The spirit realm… time. Jacob's ladder, father, the door, ladders, many doors…" Miriam closed her eyes again. A moment later, she reopened them. Metatron… "I dreamed, Sandalphon. I dreamed that I spoke with father. Then I climbed Jacob's ladder I could see time traveling in all directions. I saw time spiraling around and jutting out and then connecting to another spiral—repeatedly spiraling, jutting out, and then connecting. There was no backward or forward, no up or down or sideways. I then saw a being. He shone like the sun. I thought, *'If this is God and I look into his face, I will surely die.'* I looked into his face, but I saw no features. Instead, I saw everything. I saw all of existence, everything. Everyone who has been or ever will be on Earth made up his countenance. He did not speak words, but he told me he would take me somewhere. He reached out to me, and I to him. We touched. Then, I awoke."

Miriam's crucifix glinted in the dim light. Miriam lifted it from the floor where it had fallen and returned it to her deep pocket. A piece of broken blackboard chalk touched her finger. Miriam retrieved the crucifix and the chalk.

"Jacob's ladder," Miriam whispered, and she slid to the black floor of the vehicle and began to draw.

"Circles, circles, circles. Lines connect circles… lines, lines, lines." A supernatural strength sustained Miriam as she began to scribble on the floor of the vehicle. The night air grew heavy with the impending storm. Thunder rolled, in the distance, lightning lit the night sky. Each flash of light drew closer to the vehicle.

"Where did this storm come from?" The young soldier asked. He struggled to see the road through the torrential rain.

"It was not on the horizon when we left. Perhaps it will pass. Look in the back and see what the girl is doing." The captain closed his eyes to sleep while the storm raged. "She is on the floor. Maybe she's dead."

"Jacob's ladder. Now, I will go into the spirit realm, Sandalphon," Miriam whispered as she took in Sandalphon's essence in one last comforting breath. Miriam had scribbled the rungs of Jacob's ladder across the floor of the vehicle. She sharpened the end of the silver crucifix on the gritty floor. With one deliberate move, she cut deeply from the bottom of her palm, across her entire wrist. Upon Jacob's ladder, scrawled in chalk on the floor of a prisoner's transport vehicle, Miriam's life passed, and Sandalphon returned to clay.

At the precise moment of Miriam's escape into the spirit realm, lightning split the sky above the vehicle. The brilliant flash contrasted the dark night, momentary blinding the driver and sending the vehicle down the embankment.

"Are you all right?" The young soldier shook his head, trying to regain his vision.

"Yes, I am. But we better check the girl," the older soldier said.

Four men of the Miter Stand are crouched at the edge of the forest, hiding in the deep thicket. The men watched as the soldiers climbed out of the disabled vehicle.

"Shit, the door has flown open," the older soldier cursed.

"What the hell happened here?" the officer bellowed.

"A lightning strike, a direct hit, sir." The soldiers peered into the back of the truck.

"She must have escaped when the door flew open. This will not go well for us if we do not find her. She could not have gotten far. Come, hurry, we must find her," the captain said.

"Look!" The young soldier pointed to the roof inside the vehicle.

"How can that be? What would cause the roof to explode out?" Neither soldier had an explanation for the officer. The men of the Miter Stand watched the soldiers begin their search. They whispered among themselves.

"She was not in the truck."

"She has escaped."

"What about the SS?" one of the men asked.

"We have a marksman. He will take them easily." With three quick shots from his rifle, Boog ended the soldier's search.

"We will push the truck and the bodies down into the ravine. It will go unnoticed there. At daybreak, we will, without a doubt, find the girl."

THE PHILOSOPHER'S STONE

"Cold mutton, bread, and cheese—a very fine breakfast indeed. My stomach could not be any more satisfied if I were a king." Alden pushed back from the table, jiggled his sizeable belly, and laughed. The entire table toasted the spectacle with a cup of goat milk.

"Today, Jacob, Auvil, and I will begin on the Philosopher's Stone." Alden took a very large emerald brooch from his trouser pocket and laid it on the table for the men to see. "This is a donation from our host, Lord Smithe." The men gasped at the size of the jewel. "We all know the traditional accounts of the philosopher's stone and the emerald tablet. It is told that the secret of the elixir was written on an emerald tablet. The secrets of the emerald tablet have been handed down to us from generation to generation. However, the tablet has never been found. I believe the tablet is a myth, but an emerald *is* the key. An emerald must be distilled to its pure essence, and that will become the Philosopher's Stone. I am certain of that, and I am certain that using Auvil to carry out the process will finally enable us to extract the pure essence from the emerald. I understand that some of you are reluctant to delegate this responsibility to the golems, but this distillation must be carried out with no greed or avarice."

"Auvil will perform the process without such qualities. Thus, the principals that have been taught to us will finally allow us to extract the pure essence from the emerald. While Jacob, Auvil, and I begin with this process, the rest of you will work together. You will create two more golems like Auvil. You will grow the essence that we use to create the Homunculi. That will take forty days as you know. However, after the forty days, the essence will be built into the Kabbalists' golems. If we are successful in our endeavors, we will have all the specialized lab assistance we need. The men left the laboratory to begin their combined task.

"I have learned much from you, Jacob," Alden said.

"And I from you," Jacob acknowledged.

"Before our acquaintance, I thought that Alchemists were interested only in the quest to change lead to gold." Alden smiled.

"Regrettably, that's the thought most have about Alchemists. They imagine maniacs adding concoctions to lead to form gold or dripping solutions on rocks and pebbles to change them to diamonds and rubies. The truth is that the Alchemist works to better the plight of mankind, but the human avarice has always interfered with attaining that goal. However, now we have Auvil, who has no avarice for precious metals or gemstones, giving us the great success we will soon see and will continue to see. Jacob, my friend, Auvil is more valuable than all the gold in England; unfortunately, the madman across the channel is also aware of his value."

"Where shall we begin, Alden?"

"We will ready the retort for the distillation, and then we will have Auvil begin the process."

Many hours passed with Auvil working as he was instructed. Beakers were filled, emptied, and filled over again. The retort hissed as steam traveled through twisted tubes, the highway that would eventually lead to the success that the Alchemists and their predecessors have sought for centuries. Finally, the retort yielded the precious elixir. Jacob and Alden examined the liquid in the tiny bottle, but they did not remove the bottle from the clutches of the retort.

"What shall we do with it?" Jacob asked.

"Nothing," Alden replied. "It's still in Auvil's purpose." Alden directed Auvil to retrieve the tiny bottle from the retort. Jacob and Alden stood riveted to the sight as their creation obeyed. With utmost attention, Auvil turned the retort's latch. He carefully retrieved the precious elixir, the elixir that they believe will be the most powerful solution known to man: the Philosopher's Stone! Immediately as Auvil bore the magic into the world, Jacob and Alden were in the midst of a force not completely unlike an electrical storm. Jacob and Alden stood surrounded by a fantastic crackling, swirling light show of static electricity. The men turned in all directions. They were engulfed in the energy. Finally, Alden turned to Jacob and unexpectedly burst into laughter.

"Jacob!" Alden laughed. "You should see yourself."

"The hair on your head is standing straight up. And if you had any hair on the top of your head, it would be on its ends also." Jacob laughed and continued, "As it is, only that bit of fuzz around your face is standing out like a lion's mane. What do you suppose this phenomenon is?"

"I am not completely certain, but it seems to be a wall or a cocoon of energy," Alden said, running a hand down his face.

"Now, we must harness it," Jacob remarked as Alden studied the arcs of static that were displayed around him. "Auvil, now place the stopper lying next to the retort into the neck of the bottle," Jacob said. Auvil again obeyed precisely, and the maelstrom of static electricity dissipated immediately.

"We must go now to gather our men," Alden said. "This is splendid! There will be a great deal of discussion before we continue."

"Yes, Alden, in the council of many, there is great wisdom." Jacob, Alden, and Auvil left the laboratory and sought out the others. As the men sat in their quarters deep in discussion of the events of the day, the vendor's daughter, Lydia, walked from her home. Her rickety pull cart clacked on each roll of its wooden wheels. As Lydia neared the edge of the village, a familiar woman stepped beside her.

"Where are you going so late in the evening with your wagon so laden? What do you have there?" the woman said.

"Oh, good evening, Mistress Clarisse," Lydia greeted.

"Well, I say evening, but I think it's really only late afternoon. Either way, it's lovely. How are you today?" Lydia smiled hoping that the woman would think her addled and question her no more

"I say you have grown into a fine young woman Lydia. That seems quite a heavy wagon. Where are you headed?" Mistress Clarisse insisted.

"I'm going to the Vicar with a pot of mutton stew and these clothes for the poor box."

"That's quite a large pot of stew for one lonely Vicar."

Lydia twirled one long, dark curl around her finger as she spoke, "My mum thinks the Vicar has a guest."

"I see. Well, you better get on your way." Mistress Clarisse turned and walked back to her home. She unlocked the three locks that secured her privacy and opened the door. In the quiet seclusion of her dimly lit room, she pulled a suitcase from beneath her bed and fashioned the odd parts that lie inside into a radio transmitter.

"Lydia is traveling to the outskirts of the village," she reported.

"Watch her closely."

Lydia continued to the barn her destination and her mission.

The long walk to the cobbler gave Jacob and Alden the chance to revisit the discussion of the day before. Auvil followed Jacob and Alden as they left the cobbler and walked toward the edge of the village.

"I think that Seth was right about the lodestone." Jacob thought out loud.

"Yes, he is absolutely correct," Alden said. The natural magnetism of lodestone is exactly what we need. When we get back, we will start distilling it. Imagine how powerful it will be in its pure essence. How does that boot feel, Jacob?"

Jacob smiled. "It feels as good as new. I cannot even imagine the power we might unleash, but we will soon see."

"AUVIL, FIRE! JACOB, TURN AROUND!" Again, Jacob heard Aaron's voice from within the village. Jacob turned around; Auvil had also turned around and now stood motionless. A woman walked a few meters behind them. Upon Jacob turning, the woman hastily crossed to the opposite side of the pebble-strewn road and scurried into the alley.

"Who was that woman?" Jacob asks.

"Mistress Clarisse. She teaches the children," Alden explained.

"I don't know her well, even though she grew up here. She's either very shy or just standoffish. I could never decide. Her family was well respected for the fact that her father was a war hero from The Great War."

"The Great War…" Jacob looked wistfully at the sky.

"I have heard it called that. Also, it has been called The War to End All Wars. I fear what is coming will dwarf the dreadfulness of that war. Do you think she knows you're an Alchemist Alden?"

"Only a handful of trusted friends and family know, and they would never betray our trust."

"Do you think she's a Nazi sympathizer?" Jacob asked.

"There has been speculation," Alden said. "Only because her mother was a German war bride her father brought home with him, but her mother was a good woman."

"I ask because I heard Aaron warning me again. We must beware,"

"My fear, Jacob, is that you are correct. but let us not worry except that we do not make it back in time for dinner."

More than three months had passed since Auvil extracted the essence of the Philosopher's Stone. Jacob and Alden have worked tirelessly directing Auvil in the continuing process and their men in the labor of obtaining enough lodestone to extract a sufficient amount of its pure essence.

"This has been slow going, I must say," Alden spoke.

"Yes, it has," Jacob said, not wavering from his task of sorting out the magnetic rocks from the large pile the men had collected.

"I believe now we have enough lodestone, Jacob. Or should I say I believe I have lifted enough lodestone for a lifetime."

"Jacob, Alden. May I speak with you?" Bertram, the eldest and most respected of Alden's company, asked.

"What is it, Bertram? Have you a quandary?" Alden said.

"No, I require your opinion. Please come." Bertram turned quickly and left the laboratory. Jacob and Alden exchanged a quizzical glance and suspended their endeavors. They followed Bertram to the barn. In the barn, all of the men stood naked in a semicircle facing Alden and Jacob as they entered. Alden was the first to comment.

"Yes, Bertram, they are defiantly naked. Is that all?" Alden stated without wit or smirk.

"Ah, but look, Alden, our men have invited guests to their festivity," Jacob added.

"Why, yes, they have. Bertram, introduce these newcomers." Alden laughed he could no longer hold back his amusement with the men's frivolity. Bertram, Alden, and Jacob crossed the barn and stood in front of the two naked golems.

"This is Belenus," Bertram introduced, the first of the two. Belenus was the smaller of the golems. However, his fierce countenance shrouded his smaller size. "Belenus is the ruler of fire. It is a strong Celtic name, well befitting a golem. Do you agree, Alden?"

Alden laughed heartily. "That's a fine name. And the next, what do you propose to call him?"

"This is Gideon," Bertram said. " Do you accept that name, Jacob?" Gideon was quite large. He even topped Auvil by a few centimeters.

"Gideon is a superb name. His own mother could not have named him more appropriately. They are both magnificent and will serve us well." Jacob patted Bertram's back. The men cheered as they pulled their pants back on.

"Tonight, make merry. Tomorrow, we put them to work," Alden called out to his men, who had already begun the congratulatory merriment.

Before sunrise, Jacob and Alden returned to the laboratory and lit one lantern. Each held one corked bottle. Jacob held the Philosopher's Stone as Alden held the essence of the lodestone.

"I believe you must open the Philosopher's Stone first. When we are safely enclosed in the field it creates, I will open the lodestone essence. Are you ready?"

"Yes, I am." Jacob unleashed the Philosopher's Stone. Once again, Jacob and Alden stood amid an electric storm, safely cocooned in the middle. Alden then opened the bottle he held.

The storm intensified. Between the flashes of light, they watched as every piece of metal in the laboratory flew into the wall of energy with such force that the metal was completely demolished.

Alden and Jacob corked their bottles. They stood in the now quiet and completely dark laboratory. The force they had created had ransacked the cellar. There was not one piece of metal left. All had been destroyed. However, Alden and Jacob remained untouched by the rubble that had flown around them. They had been safely shielded inside the cocoon.

"Just as we thought, Jacob, we have created an extraordinarily strong electromagnet. We did not lose any of our elixirs, only the metal objects. Certainly, the retort will be missed, but we will bear up. I could not have done it without you."

"This is good, very good, Alden. We have worked together, and we have succeeded. We will be able to protect the channel."

"Yes, Jacob, we have been successful. But we must not be too hasty. We first must test the boundaries and the strength before we can know its true power." Two days later, all of Jacobs's and Alden's men stood in Lord Smithe's hayfield one hundred meters from where Alden, Jacob, and Lord Smithe stood. Each of them held a large and very heavy piece of scrap metal, Alden began speaking.

"Thank you, Smithe, for joining us and for allowing us to use your field for our final test of the force."

Lord Smithe laughed. "Righty-o, Alden, I wouldn't miss this for all the gold in the king's crown! Keep calm and carry on."

Jacob opened his bottle, and the three men were immediately cocooned. Alden then opened his. Straight away, a storm of metal hit the cocoon with such magnitude that the ground measurably shook. Once again, every piece of metal that slammed into the wall of energy was obliterated, but the men were left unscathed.

"This is certainly impressive, but pieces of scrap do not equate to the Krieg marine. The German navy will certainly be a more formidable foe than a few scraps of rubbish." Lord Smithe said. "I say, old chap, impressive nonetheless, but what say you tell your men to harness six of my draft horses to the reaper and lead them no farther than fifty meters from the point where we stand." The men did as Smithe said. Once more Jacob opened the Elixir of the Philosopher's stone and then Alden followed with the elixir of loadstone. The force surrounded the three men, the reaper rumbled, and the horses spooked as the reaper, and the horses left the ground. The reaper and the horses hopelessly entangled in their harness were swiftly and assuredly dashed to their destruction. Not one piece of the horses' carcass or a scrap of the reaper remained.

"Well, I dare say that was a bloody surprise. I never expected the force would move the reaper, much less the reaper *and* the horses." Smithe looked to Alden and then to Jacob. "I say chaps, had you an inkling the force was this stalwart?"

Alden's face had paled, his mouth hung open he stuttered. "We… We knew it would be formidable, but we could not have known the extent."

"I am sorry for the loss of your magnificent animals.

Lord Smithe." Jacob hung his head.

"Yes, yes, sad indeed. Jacob, but stiff upper lip you know." Smyth drew on his personal strength and carried on. "I say Alden; all that is left of this endeavor will be to establish when the Krieg's marine is moving. I have a contact; I will get back to you, chaps, when I have news. Keep calm and carry on."

Smithe left the men and returned to his manor. The men spent the rest of the day in the hayfield combing it for scraps of metal that had escaped complete destruction. None were found the men finally retired to the barn. The tired and hungry men congratulated one another on the day's work well done as they enjoyed the pot of stew Lydia had left them.

The sound of dogs barking in the night alerted Clarisse to activity in the street. From her window, she could see someone walking toward the edge of the village. Clarisse quickly dressed and rushed from her home, past the edge of the village, and into the forest. Yet, she was unable to catch the person before they disappeared into the shadows.

She turned back toward the village and walked only a short distance when she caught sight of a sudden bright light. Clarisse turned and ran through the brush toward the light; smoke caught her breath as she neared the source. She found herself standing in front of Lord Smithe's barn. A fire was blazing around the foundation and leaping up the walls.

She looked to the roof of the barn. The bay window was open. The huge, silent man who accompanied Alden and Jacob to the market stood at the bay, his eyes fixed on her.

She called out to him, "FIRE! WARN THE OTHERS!" Then, she disappeared into the forest.

Auvil knelt beside Jacob. "Fire," Auvil spoke. The word resounded as if it echoed back from the uttermost regions of the earth.

Jacob sprang to his feet. Smoke filled the barn. The men called out in search of their comrades as the flames engulfed the lower level and now threatened the supports that held the loft. Alden gathered the elixirs from the chest they were hidden in. He secured the precious elixirs on his person then he called to the men who were still in the burning barn.

"The bay window! The rope!" Alden yelled over the roar of the flames. The men escaped certain death as they dropped to the ground. Once on the ground, Jacob and Alden accounted for all of their men, save for Bertram the elder and Belenus the golem.

The fire hissed and writhed before them. Flames slithered up the sides of the barn and threatened to sting even the night sky. Then, from the belly of the blazing serpent, Belenus arose, Bertram cradled in his massive arms. Belenus gently laid the old Alchemist on the ground at Alden's feet.

"Thank you, Belenus. You have done well. We will see to him now." Alden knelt beside Bertram's body and wept the loss of his elder and cherished friend.

With his water wagon, Lord Smithe was able only to prevent the fire from spreading to the forest. The barn was lost. However, the laboratory deep underground beneath the stone foundation of the barn still held its secrets. Jacob stationed Belenus in the dark cellar to guard the contents of the laboratory. Jacob then instructed the golem, "Belenus, listen and obey. This laboratory is in your keep. Watch and protect it. Act only if there is a threat."

Jacob left the cellar and joined Alden, Lord Smithe, and the rest of the men as they laid Bertram to rest beneath the large evergreen that has long stood between the forest and the edge of the road. The grand and aged tree has marked the countryside for so many years that it has become a journeyman's point of reference.

"Alden, you and the men will come and stay in the manor until this is over. You may set up a makeshift laboratory in my basement," Lord Smithe said. The exhausted men trudged into the breaking dawn to Lord Smithe's manor. There was no argument the men would be the guests of Smithe for the duration.

From the forest's deep shadows, a figure appeared. Lydia stood among the smoldering ashes. She muttered as she poked through the ruins.

"I must make certain that all is destroyed for the Fatherland." As she searched, she discovered a secreted set of stone steps that led to a room hidden deep beneath the barn. Lydia used her flashlight to light the steps that led into the darkness. There in the cellar, she discovered the Alchemist's laboratory, the object of her destruction was still intact. Lydia did not notice the fierce guardian that stood in the shadows. She placed her light on the table, and it afforded enough illumination for her to act. Lydia picked one beaker from the shelf and threw it against the wall and then another followed by a corked bottle. Lydia reached for another bottle. A vice-like hand gripped her arm, shattering her bone. Lydia screamed. Belenus had silently crept behind her. Belenus picked her up by the back of her jacket and smashed her against the stone wall. The power with which he forced her into the wall was such that his massive hand penetrated through her thorax. Most of Lydia fell at once, but bits and pieces of Lydia slowly followed the slimy visceral trail down the wall to finally join her on the cold cellar floor.

Lord Smithe sat in his library with his guest. They whispered as they sipped their afternoon tea.

"You remember Lydia, the young woman from the village? We found her dead in the laboratory," Smithe said.

"Lydia? What happened?"

"Do you fancy the truth or the official story?"

"I would like to hear both, Smithe."

"We charred her body and told her father that she was somehow caught up in the fire. However, the truth is that the golem that was guarding the laboratory killed her. She was destroying the laboratory. We found some papers on her. Seems she was following orders."

"So, she was a Nazi."

"Yes, and a dangerous one at that. Now, I must ask you a favor. The men have finished their work. We need information from your contact in the Krieg's marine."

"What information do you need from the Nazis' war navy?"

"We need to know when the warships are moving toward the channel. Upon that information, the men will boat into the channel and set the force of our resistance."

"They think this force they have will be effective?"

"The Nazis' entire war navy cannot penetrate the force they have created."

"Very well, Smithe. You will have your information."

"Thank you, Clarisse. Would you care for another spot of tea?" Clarisse smiles.

"Why, yes, Smithe, I certainly would."

❦

More than a year has passed since Jacob and his men reached England. It was more time than Jacob cared to mark. The full moon has drawn him out of his slumber. On this cold November night, he sat in the hushed meadow. It was November the ninth, the night of Jacobs's fitful remembrances. The night of the broken glass, the night he last held his precious Sara Rosa. This night, he held a small bottle and Sara Rosa's silver box; he whispered, "Why do I go on mourning because of the oppression of the enemy?" A few drops of the Philosopher's Stone lay at the bottom of the corked bottle he held. He spoke to Auvil, who was sitting behind him.

"Tonight, Auvil, I open the elixir on my own." He held tightly the bottle in one hand and the silver box Aaron had saved was securely in his other hand. Jacob opened the bottle; inside the whirling cocoon, his thoughts were of his precious Miriam. He implored the God of the universe for their protection.

November 11, 2015

Only one salesperson has ever gotten past Denise, Doctor Sam's office manager. Denise now keeps a skimpy hospital gown in her desk drawer.

If a persistent vendor or sales representative is willing to don the hospital gown, they may have a ten-minute consult with the doctor.

"Paul Linder is here to see you, Doctor Rubinstein,"

"Good, send him in, D."

"I'm Paul Linder. We spoke on the phone yesterday."

"You got here quickly, young man. Where did you say you are from? Ohio?"

"Indiana, sir."

"Yes, of course."

"Our computer spit out the police report on your Jane Doe. I'd like to see her." Paul's attention is focused on the two large watercolors on Doctor Sam's office wall.

"Longfield-Smith," Doctor Sam says.

"Pardon me?" Paul turns his attention back to the doctor.

"The artist, Longfield-Smith."

"They're very colorful, Doctor."

"She lived in Barbados in the early 1900s. She tried to capture the bright, carefree island life. When I was a boy, I dreamed of living on a lush tropical island. I guess that's what drew me to these two watercolors." Doctor Sam's memory lingers in the bleak days of the camp and his dreams of escaping to a better place.

"I like them. My grandfather was an artist, not famous, but he left some nice work behind."

Doctor Sam stares at the brightly colored pictures for a moment longer. Still to this day, he plans his escape to a tropical paradise, but now his plans include Leah, the wife of his youth.

"Yes, yes." Doctor Sam returns to the present and the mystery at hand. "The girl, what is the nature of your curiosity, young man?"

"Our computer monitors for any reports of crimes or activities that could be neo-Nazi or Aryan-Nation-related," Paul began, "The tattoo on her arm is what the computer picked up on. We investigate what comes up, and sometimes it leads us to old Nazi war criminals, the old ones who got away."

"I believe most of them are gone by now, young man. However, if there are any left, I hope you bring them to justice."

"That's the plan, sir."

"I'm curious, Paul. What made you become a Nazi hunter?"

"My father and grandfather were Nazi hunters. My grandfather died in South America chasing some pretty notorious ones. My father chased Nazis all around South Africa. I guess it's just what I'm wired for."

"Let's go down to the ICU so you can see the girl, Paul." As they walk, Paul is very much aware of the nurses who follow him with their eyes, admiring his ruggedly handsome looks, while desiring his chiseled body, to consume upon their lust.

"She's not awake, but she's stable," Doctor Sam says as they enter the woman's room.

"Have you found out anything about her?" Paul steps to the woman's bedside.

"No, we have put out pictures. *The Trib* even did a human-interest piece, but no one has come forward—just one old nun from Europe—but that turned out to be nothing."

Paul makes notes, studies the woman's tattoo and commits her face to memory. "Thank you for your time, Doctor. I want to get to my hotel now and see what will come up on the web. Might be a pattern or something, you never know. Thanks again, Doctor. *Auf Wiedersehn.*"

"Do you speak German?

"Only a little, I learned it in school. My father was German. Tryin' to keep in touch with my heritage, ya know." Paul chuckles, his soft blue eyes sparkling.

"Very good." Doctor Sam accompanies Paul to the elevator. "Keep me posted, Paul. We can use your expertise."

"I'll be back." Paul does his best Schwarzenegger impersonation as the elevator doors close. Curious about a trinket that he noticed on Jane Doe's bed table. Doctor Sam returns to the woman's room. He studies the trinket, a silver box. The configuration of the grid that was engraved on the box was very familiar. He dropped the box into his pocket.

Doctor Sam heads to the cafeteria, where he meets Doctor Knowles in the hall.

"David, do you have time to join me in the cafeteria?

"Sure, Sam, I have time."

"Have you checked in on Jane Doe yet today, David?"

"I was in there earlier. It's a strange case."

"Well, you won't know anything for sure until you get the blood work." Doctor Sam wouldn't really deceive his friend, but leaving something out isn't lying, it's omitting. Until he knows what happened to this young woman, the lab reports which will confirm the woman's drug-free status will remain locked in his drawer.

"What do you think, Sam?"

"I think she will wake up tomorrow or the next day. But I've been wrong before." Doctor Sam smiles.

"I'll watch her closely. What's with the guy who was in the girl's room?"

"Big boy Nazi hunter. Not much to tell. We'll see. It was crazy last night. It must have been a full moon." Just as the doctors reach the cafeteria, Knowles' pager sounded.

"Guess we'll have to catch up another time. I got to go."

"Wait a moment, David."

"Sure, Sam. What is it?"

"I was just wondering if Jane has had any visitors?" Doctor Sam clutched the box. He wonders who left it in the woman's room.

"No, none at all. I guess no one knows or cares about her. People, huh?" Doctor Knowles hurried to the call box.

"Yes, David, people. I'll see you tomorrow, be safe."

"Good afternoon, Doctor." Paul lays a manila folder on the doctor's desk.

"Please, sit down."

"I researched Jane Doe's tattoo on the web last night. It turns out that it was actually given to a girl in 1940." Paul makes himself comfortable as he sits in the chair in front of Doctor Sam's desk.

"That is very interesting, Paul. But it could be a coincidence."

"There's more. The girl's name was Miriam Ruth Davidson. She was the daughter of Jacob Davidson; some kind of mystic Kabbalah person, the Nazis were looking for. The girl escaped from the Gestapo when the vehicle she was being transported in was in an accident. She was lost in the forest and was presumed to be dead." Doctor Sam raises his eyebrows.

"How do you know all of this?"

"The Nazis kept records of everything. It can be found on the web if you know how to get it. But there's more. The forest she was lost in was near the town that my grandfather was from in Germany, so I got online with my father. He, in turn, searched my grandfather's records and came up with this." Paul takes a copy of a hand-drawn sketch from the folder that he had laid on Doctor Sam's desk. A sentence is printed in German across the top of the paper.

"We are searching for this woman.'" Doctor Sam reads the words out loud.

"Don't you see the resemblance, Doctor? I think the girl in Germany didn't die in the forest, and I think this woman is a relative of that girl."

"Tell me how your grandfather came across this paper."

"My grandfather made this sketch. He was a member of the German resistance, the Miter Stand. He went undercover and gained the Nazi's trust. They thought he was just a big deaf fool, so they were never careful of what they said in front of him."

"They were brave men, the Miter Stand. May I keep this copy?"

"Yes, of course. I had hoped to be able to talk to Jane Doe, but something has come up at home, something we've been working on for a while. I'll be leaving this afternoon, but can I come back?" Paul asks.

"We will look forward to it, and I'll let you know if I find anything more. Sam locks the sketch in his desk drawer along with the lab reports. The events of the last few days have flooded Doctor Sam's mind with memories of hiding from the Gestapo. Memories of moving with his mother from one cellar to the next, hiding in attics, secret rooms, churches, or monasteries, trying to escape Nazi Germany and of traveling the underground until they could reunite with his father, a "mystic Kabbalah person", as Paul had put it.

"Doctor Sam, Doctor Knowles is in line one."

"Thanks, D. put him through. What can I do for you, David?"

"I'll be down in the ER for a while. Can you check on
Jane Doe for me?"

"Certainly, David, I was just on my way down there."

"Thanks, Doc."

"Miriam?" Doctor Sam tries the name that Paul left with him. "Miriam Davidson?" The woman's eyelids flutter. Doctor Sam takes her hand; she opens her eyes. The young woman stares at the old doctor sitting next to her bed but says nothing.

"You're in the hospital. You have been badly hurt, but you're going to be all right," Sam says quietly. He wets the corner of a clean cloth with cold water and gently touches it to her lips.

"You have a visitor." Doctor Sam smiles. He points to the raven at the window.

"Sandalphon," she whispers as she closes her eyes.

Doctor Sam quietly leaves the young woman sleeping. He stops at the nurse's station and gives explicit instructions.

"Jane Doe is awake. I want you to check on her every twenty minutes. No sudden movements or loud noises. She's fragile. Do not wake her if she is sleeping. Quietly reassure her if she is awake. Do not question her. If she says she is hungry, give her clear liquid. Thank you, nurse." Doctor Sam returns to his office and dials his home.

"Hello, Leah. I won't be home tonight. Jane Doe woke up. I want to talk to her as soon as she is able. I love you, darling. Good night."

~

"I thought this was your day off, David." Doctor Sam looks up from studying the nurse's notes. Morning rounds seldom found Doctor Sam on duty, but this morning, he has been in the ICU since dawn.

"I'm not officially here. Just thought I'd check on Jane before I take off bicycling today." David grins.

"Not much changed since she woke up last night. I stayed in case she woke up. I'll let you know if something happens. Go, David. Go and enjoy your day."

"Okay. I really need this day off. I need to ride. Thanks, Sam."

"Enough. Go ride your bicycle before I change my mind."

"You have my cell number, right?"

"Yes. Now, for the last time, go." With that, David Knowles hurries from the room.

The woman opens her eyes and stares at the ceiling.

"Good morning, young lady. We've been waiting for you. I'm Doctor Rubinstein."

The woman glances at Doctor Sam and then returns her gaze to the ceiling.

"How are you feeling this morning?"

"You are German," she whispers.

"Yes, I am. I suspect by your accent that you are, too. Your friend, Sandalphon, is still at the window. He's been looking for you. He has been your guardian, just like the spirit."

"You know of Sandalphon?" the woman asks.

"The bird or the spirit, my dear?"

"The spirit."

"I only know what I have read in my father's Kabbalah."

"Your father's Kabbalah?" The woman winces as she attempts to move closer to the doctor. She looks around the room and leans closer.

"Do they force you to work here?" she whispers.

"Force me? Who? I don't understand, dear."

"I apologize. I have used the wrong words."

"It's all right. Tell me about yourself." Doctor Sam holds the woman's hand as he speaks.

"They have not told you?"

"No, no one knows anything to tell about you."

"Of course, they know. They brought me here. They must have told you." The woman pulls her hand away.

"Who are 'they'? Who are you afraid of?"

"The Gestapo," she whispers as she closes her eyes.

"Gestapo." Even now, after all the years, the word returns Samuel Rubinstein to a little boy's world of fear. He sees that same fear reflected in this woman's eyes.

"My head hurts," she mumbles.

"You have a concussion. You've been unconscious for four days."

"Did a very old sister come to my room, or was I dreaming? Four days? Then, it is the thirteenth of November?"

"Yes, the thirteenth. Is there someone you would like me to call?"

"Call?"

"Call. Contact your family or a friend."

"Do you mean my father?"

"Yes, can I contact him?"

"I told them I do not know where he is and that I do not know what he can do. I will tell you the same. You can send me back, but I cannot tell you what I do not know."

Suddenly, Paul's words come back to Doctor Sam. Miriam believes she is the daughter of a Kabbalist.

"I'd like to show you something." He pushes the sleeve of his lab coat far enough up his arm to reveal his tattoo.

"This tattoo was my identification. The tattoo on your arm was given to a young girl. Her name was Miriam Davidson. Are you related to her?"

"Why do you say you know nothing of me and then say my name?"

"So, your name is Miriam Davidson also?"

"Is there another Miriam Davidson here?"

"No, I'm referring to the Miriam Davidson who was presumed dead after an accident that occurred while she was being transported to a detainment center."

"I am Miriam Ruth Davidson. I am not dead. I do not know where my father and the others are. I do not know about the Kabbalah or what my father can or cannot do." Her eyes fluttered. "I am tired." The woman closes her eyes and gives in to a medicated sleep.

Doctor Sam studies the young woman. She is convinced that she is Miriam Ruth Davidson, the young girl who died more than sixty years ago. Miriam Ruth. How does she know the woman's middle name? Doctor Sam is sure he had not used it. It is very possible she had gotten the name and the other information from the web, just the same as Paul Linder had, but a small quiet voice whispers, "Listen with your heart."

THE WEB

Doctor Sam helps Sister Theresa Marie to a comfortable chair.

"Thank you for coming, Sister. You must be very busy setting up the display of religious antiquity. There's been quite a write up about it in *The Trib*."

"We have been *very* busy. We have only two months to get the religious treasures and the icons ready for the seventy-fifth anniversary celebration of the Holy Trinity, so I don't have much time to spend."

"Would you like a cup of tea?"

"Tea would be nice. Thank you. Now, tell me, how may I help you?" Doctor Sam sets the cup in front of Sister Theresa Marie.

"Sister, you told the officer that you don't know the young woman you visited. You said she reminded you of someone. Can you tell me about that person?"

"That was so many years ago in Germany. It was a dark time in our history." The nun sips her tea.

"Yes, a dark time, Sister, a very dark time indeed. It was only for the courage of many like you that some survived. Tell me what you can about that woman, Sister."

Sister Theresa Marie is quiet for a moment, she removes her glasses and dries the corner of her eyes. "A day has not passed that I have not said a prayer for her. The person I knew was just a young woman, no more than a girl really. She was brought to our monastery by her father. He hoped to hide her with us from the Gestapo. We were successful in hiding her for more than a year, and then she was discovered and taken away. I never saw her again. It was rumored she had escaped, but I assumed she died in a camp."

"Can you tell me anything about her?" Doctor Sam asks. "Do you know if she had family or friends, or maybe you remember her family

99

name? Can you remember anything about that girl? Anything, even if it seems insignificant."

Sister Theresa Marie searches her memories. "Yes, a pet. I remember she found a bird while she was with us, a raven. She called him Sandalphon. It was so long ago. This is all that I recall. I am very old you know," Sister smiles. "The memory fades." Sister Theresa Marie shakes the memories from her head. "Doctor, I must return to the monastery. I have much to do. I'm sorry I could not help you."

"Thank you again, Sister." Doctor Sam escorted the sister to the door and then turned to Denise.

"D, get me Paul Linder on the phone, please."

"You got something?"

"I think so." Sister Theresa Marie's words— "rumored she had escaped, a raven she called him Sandalphon"—are racing through Doctor Sam's head when the phone rings.

"Hello, Paul. It's Sam from Tampa. I have a quick question. Are there any details about Miriam Davidson online, anything about a pet?"

"I didn't see anything about it when I was going through it, but let me look. I'm right by a computer. Can I put you on hold for a few minutes?"

"Great. Yes, I can hold."

"I'm sorry, Doctor Sam, there's nothing that I could find. I can look again for you next time I search."

"No, that's probably good, Paul. Anyway, it was just a hunch." Sam walked out to D's office.

"I'm going down to Jane Doe. Hold my calls please, D."

∾

"Are you hungry?" Doctor Sam pulls a chair next to Jane Doe's bed.

"Yes, hungry."

"I'll have the nurse bring you something to eat. Does your head still hurt?"

"Not as much."

Tap, tap, tap

Doctor Sam looks to the window. "Sandalphon tapped for you the whole time you were unconscious. I have never known anyone with a pet raven. Did you find him?"

"He found me."

"Sandalphon…you named him after the spirit on Jacob's ladder."

"I know nothing of Jacob's ladder."

"I didn't know very much about the spirit world or the Kabbalah when the Gestapo took me. I was too young to study Kabbalah, but of course, the Nazis didn't know that. I survived because I told them the little that I knew in bits over the years and made up the rest."

"What do you mean you were too young?"

"I was only six years old when the Gestapo found us and took me from my mother. I'll never forget that day. The soldiers separated me from my mother, but I ran away from them and fought my way back to her. As the soldiers pulled me away again, she whispered in my ear, 'it is better to be a living dog than a dead lion'. I did not see her again until the camps were liberated in forty-five."

"Forty-five, forty-five what?"

"In 1945, I was eight years old. I was in the camp from 1943 to 1945. Two years."

"Doctor, what you are telling me is nonsense. You could not be eight years old in 1945 when it is November 13, 1940, today!"

"1940? My dear, this is November 13, *2015*."

"Time! Jacob's ladder…" she whispers, "Sandalphon, the spirit. Doctor, my father was right. The ladder is a door." Miriam's eyes widen as she speaks.

"Don't be afraid, child."

"I am not afraid, Doctor. I gained knowledge from my father's journal, and with knowledge must come understanding. Sandalphon, the spirit has allowed me passage me through a spirit door, through time, and so may it be." Miriam closes her eyes and envisions Jacob's ladder and time spiraling through the spirit realm.

"Mike DeAugustino is here, Doctor. He's asking to talk to the patient." The nurse has been true to her word and alerted Mike when Jane Doe awoke.

"One minute, nurse." Doctor Sam leans close to Miriam and whispers to her in German.

"Listen to me, child. My heart tells me that you are telling the truth and you have somehow come here upon Jacob's ladder. I will help you, but you must say that you don't remember anything. You must say that to anyone who questions you. Can you do that?"

"Ja, I will," she whispers. Mike knocks on the side of the door and enters the room.

"Doctor, can I talk to her now?"

"Yes, but she seems to be suffering from amnesia. She's still weak. You can have only a few minutes."

"How are you feeling? You look better than you did when we found you." Mike smiles.

"My head hurts."

"You found me?"

"Yeah, me and my partner found you."

"You are police?"

"Yes, can you answer a few questions for me?" Mike opens his note pad.

"What is your name?"

"I do not know."

"Can you tell me who did this to you?"

"No, I do not know. I do not remember."

"Where do you live?" Miriam looks to Doctor Sam and then to Mike.

"I do not know." Tears clouded her eyes.

"Mike, I think that's all for now. She's had enough for today," Doctor Sam interrupts. He walks with Mike into the hall.

"Do you think she's faking?" Mike asks once they were in the hall.

"I don't think so, Mike. I've seen this before. Severe trauma, whether physical or emotional, can cause the mind to shut down. We'll have her evaluated in a day or so if she doesn't snap out of it."

"Thanks, Doc. I'm going to close this case for now. I can't prove a crime was committed if she doesn't remember. Call me if she remembers anything."

❧

"He's real scared, Vicky."

"He's all I got." Joniqua is talking quietly with Vicky in the hospital's parking garage. Mike and Vicky are in agreement that a certain amount of contact with the street people is helpful, but Mike is not supportive of her involvement with Joniqua. He has tried to explain to Vicky that although Joniqua is probably harmless, the people she hangs with certainly are not. At the sight of Mike, Joniqua stops talking and watches him get into the patrol car. Mike sounds two short blasts of the siren, and grins at Vicky.

"I'll see what I can do. I promise." Vicky glares at Mike as she walks to the car.

"Click it or ticket. Buckle up. I'd hate to ticket you. What were the scrubs about, some new hook?"

"Joniqua said she's been off the streets for months. She's been going to the annex for some nursing courses. She'll be finished soon. She's interning now. And, Mike, you better never sound that siren at me again, hear?" Vicky will not have to tell him again.

"Sorry. What did you promise?" Mike mumbles.

"Joniqua's son knows something about the boy who was murdered over on Channel Side."

"Did she say that?"

"She said some stuff about drugs and gangs. No details. She wants help, protection for her son in exchange for information." Vicky pinches the soft skin behind her ear and worries as she watches the streets of Tampa whiz by.

"Don't worry, Vic. We'll keep your promise. It'll be okay."

"Thanks, Mike. What happened with Jane Doe?"

"Amnesia, according to the doctor."

"Amnesia? Baloney skin on the pump handle," Vicky declares.

"Well, Knowles says so. I closed the case for now, but you know it as well as I do, something just isn't right."

~

"Miriam, can you tell me the last thing you remember?" Doctor Sam whispers.

"I was in the back of a truck. The soldiers were taking me somewhere. My head hurt. I dreamed of my father and Jacob's ladder spinning in time and I remembered what my father had written in his journal. He thought the ladder was a door to the spirit realm. He thought that there are many doors that open to the spirit realm. In my dream, my father gave me my mother's amulet a tiny silver box. My head hurt so badly I could hardly think.

I wanted to escape, so I drew in chalk on the floor of the truck. I drew Jacob's ladder as it is drawn in the Kabbalah. But I knew that I could not escape, so I decided that if I could not escape, I would rather die than go where they were taking me. I sharpened the crucifix from my pocket then cut deep into my wrist and laid myself on the chalk ladder. When I woke up, it was morning, and I was sitting on a bench. Where am I, Doctor?"

"Somehow, Miriam, you did open a door or ladder," Doctor Sam says. "You're in Tampa, Florida, my dear, America. But I don't know why you are here, or why you came at this time."

"America?! I have been brought across time and distance to be here."

"I wonder why your bird is here."

"He was next to me when I was brought up. I suppose he was carried along. There is a purpose, Doctor. Although I do not know it yet, this existence shall be revealed in its time. What will we do until the reason is known?"

"Between your guardian Sandalphon and me, your friend, we'll think of something. Try to get some sleep now."

"Doctor?"

"Yes?"

"You did not answer my question. Did an old sister come to my room?"

"Yes, she did."

"Will she come back?"

"If you like, I will see to it. Rest now, child."

"Yes, I would like that." Miriam closes her eyes.

Doctor Sam sits at the computer in his office. He is not a computer genius, but he has skills. He can scan a document, alter it, print it, and then he can fax it. Yes, the old doctor has skills. Doctor Knowles will have Jane Doe's bogus lab reports on his desk in the morning.

BUREAUCRACY

The telephone is ringing as Doctor Sam unlocks his office door.

"Doctor Rubinstein here."

"Good morning, Sam."

"Good morning, David."

"I got the labs you faxed over. Rohypnol, a big dose!"

"She's lucky to be alive." *Not a lie*, Doctor Sam thinks.

"Strange that there was no alcohol involved."

"Hmm, yes, I didn't think of that."

"She might have been the designated driver. She could have gotten it in a soda or something," David said.

"A lot of unanswered questions, David."

"Have you had a chance to talk to her?"

"This morning, I talked to her a little. I didn't get anywhere. What do you think, Doc?"

"I think we'll get a specialist in a day or so."

"Shouldn't we get someone in sooner?"

"No, David, I think we need a little more time. I'll go down this afternoon. I promised her that I would help her."

"Who are you going to ask to see her? Kline? He's the best."

"I was thinking about Boyd. Kline's too opinionated."

"Boyd? He's a moron." David is surprised at Sam's choice of residents.

"Boyd's a good man. Give him a chance, David. Oh, and have her transferred to a private room tomorrow." Sam knows David's assessment of Doctor Boyd's medical skills is more than accurate, but Boyd will suit his purpose.

"Okay, Sam, if you think he's the man, it's all right with me. I'll talk to you later."

"David, wait, will you do a favor for me?"

"Sure. What is it?"

"I need you to get with maintenance and give them a work order to remove the television from the room you put Jane Doe in."

"All right, Sam, but why?"

"The woman is fragile, and I don't want her exposed to any excess stimuli."

"Good call."

"Thanks, David." Doctor Sam's good call also covers the fact that he does not want Miriam exposed to any information that might begin to bring her up to speed with the twenty-first century before her sessions with Doctor Boyd.

The hospital room is lit only by the streams of light that shine through the partially closed mini blinds. Sandalphon remains perched on the ledge, guarding his keep.

"Good afternoon, young lady," Doctor Sam says.

"Doctor, what is going to happen to me now?" Miriam asks.

"I told you that I will help you. Don't worry. I have a plan. All you will have to do is play dumb."

"Excuse me? Play dumb?"

"Just an expression. I'm going to bring a specialist in to examine you."

"What is a specialist?"

"A doctor who is an expert in a certain field."

"What will this doctor do to me?"

"The doctor I am bringing will ask you questions about yourself," Doctor Sam explained. "You must remember to answer that you do not remember anything to each of his questions."

"I must tell the doctor that I do not remember?"

"Do you think you can do that; just like you did with the police officer?"

"Ja, but then what?"

"Then I will suggest to the doctor that he hypnotize you."

"Hypnotize? I have never been hypnotized. Will it hurt?" Miriam is puzzled.

"No, child, I won't let anyone hurt you. He will just talk to you until you relax. Then he will ask you questions. It will be all right, just answer his questions. Trust me, it will all work out."

"I know it will work out, Doctor. I have been brought here for a reason. Thank you."

The intercom sounds, "Doctor Samuel Rubinstein, will you please go to the nearest call box?"

"I'm being paged. I'll be back soon. Just remember, don't worry, child." Doctor Sam hurries to the call box.

"Yes, Denise?"

"I'm sorry to bother you, but there are some men here. I think they're from the government," Denise whispers into the phone.

"It's all right, D. Tell them I'll be right there." Doctor Sam knew that there would be an official investigation, with all the safeguards that have been put in place in the years since 9/11, but the doctor's plan covers Homeland Security, too. If it all goes as planned, Miriam will be deemed an amnesiac, not a threat to national security. She will be monitored for a time, and eventually, her case will be filed away and forgotten. The Feds are waiting in his office; now he has to pull this plan together.

"This is it," Doctor Sam whispers as he opens the door to his office. "You can do this."

"Good afternoon. I'm Doctor Rubinstein."

"Good afternoon, Doctor. I'm Agent Broadstreet, and this is Agent Giles." Giles stands a few inches behind Broadstreet who almost eclipses the smaller, baby-faced man. Their stance is reminiscent of an offensive player protecting his quarterback in the pocket.

"How can I help you?" Doctor Sam asks.

"We need to fingerprint your Jane Doe and take some pictures so that we can run a background on her."

"The girl is very fragile right now. I can't allow you to stress my patient."

"We respect that, but this woman has just appeared from nowhere with no identification of any kind and supposedly with no memory. We must be allowed to investigate her." Broadstreet's finger ringed the size-eighteen collar of his starched, white shirt, trying in vain to relieve the pressure that the collar and the double-knotted black necktie bear on his size-nineteen neck.

"She could be a citizen, and if she is, she has rights whether she remembers those rights or not. I'm certain you will also respect that possibility."

"Of course, Doctor, we're here to protect the citizens. All we want to know is if the woman has any terrorist connections."

"I can allow you to do this, but I only ask that you do not interrogate her at this time. If you find something during your investigation that is deemed a threat though, of course, I understand that you will have to act. Come, I'll take you to her."

The men follow Doctor Sam to Miriam's room where they take her fingerprints and photographs. Broadstreet pays special attention to the tattoo on her arm. When they are done, Broadstreet and Giles keep their word to Doctor Sam and quietly leave.

"Who were those men?" Miriam asks.

"They're from the government. They are trying to find out who you are."

"How can they know?"

"They can't know, they'll find nothing, don't worry." Doctor Sam reached into his pocket. "I found something that I'm sure is yours. Close your eyes and put out your hand." Miriam closes her eyes and opens her hand. The doctor places a silver box in her hand. Miriam looks with great surprise at what Doctor Sam had given her.

"Where did you get this?" Miriam's eyes well with tears and her voice cracks. "It's like the one my father gave me in my dream."

"I found it in your room soon after you came here. I knew it was Metatron's box by the engraving. I took it for safe keeping. Also, I wanted to study it." Doctor Sam smiled.

"My mother had a box just like this. She always told me it would be mine when I turned eighteen." Miriam turned the box from side to side as she studied it.

"My mother told me that she wore it on a ribbon around her neck when she rocked me to sleep. She said she only quit wearing it when I teethed so hard on it, she thought I would break my teeth." Miriam laughed and continued examining the beautiful silver box. On the bottom corner, she discovered a tiny dent, no larger than a baby's tooth.

"Thank you doctor for this."

"You are very welcome, young lady. It's an important part of your heritage."

"Doctor?"

"Yes?"

"Will the old sister come back?"

"Yes, child, she will. Rest now." Doctor Sam walks to the door.

"Doctor?"

"Yes, dear?"

"Thank you." Miriam closes her eyes.

Doctor Sam's office is quiet, Denise is on her lunch break. She is a good office manager, and over the years, she has become a good friend. Denise watches over her friend Sam like a gruff, temperamental mama bear. However, if the brusque bear mantle were stripped away, a beautiful, fragile, and delicate bird would be revealed to the world. Doctor Sam has a few minutes to himself before the caseworker's appointment; Social Services will be the last hurdle to mount before Miriam is out of the woods. "I have a good plan. All my *I*'s are dotted, and *T*'s crossed. This will work. You've been doing this long enough to know how to work it," Doctor Sam mumbles to himself. He answers the knock on his office door.

"Doctor? I'm Ms. Johnson from Social Services."

"Good afternoon, Ms. Johnson." Doctor Sam greets the young woman. Ms. Johnson has the most beautiful, biggest brown eyes that Samuel Rubinstein has ever seen. Although she may not be considered stunning by the world's unrealistic standards, Doctor Samuel Rubinstein is certain Ms. Johnson holds many young men's attention.

"Ms. Johnson, please come in sit down." Doctor Sam directs her to the chair in front of his desk.

"Thank you, Doctor. I would like to address the Jane Doe case. I need some information for our review."

"Yes, Ms. Johnson, the young woman was brought in by the EMTs four days ago. As you know, HIPAA does not allow me to disclose anything about her medical condition."

"Of course, Doctor, but I need to get a sense of how long she will be in the hospital on state-provided assistance. I also will have to place her if she is unable to care for herself."

"She will be examined by one of our staff psychiatrists tomorrow. I assure you we will have a report for you within a day or two, Ms. Johnson."

"All right, Doctor, that sounds good. We're so swamped down at the department. There are so many cases and just too few case workers. Your help is really appreciated."

"I'll get in touch with you when we have a report, Ms. Johnson. Like I said, probably a day or two."

"Thank you, Doctor. I will expect your call then."

"Yes, thank you, Ms. Johnson."

Doctor Sam sits at his desk and considers what needs to be accomplished in two days to satisfy Social Services, Ms. Johnson, and the government. Two days is not much time, but it seems to the doctor that time is certainly on Miriam's side."

"D, I'm going down to the ICU, and then I'm going home."

"Okay, Doctor, see you tomorrow.

"Yes, see you tomorrow."

A Matter of Importance

Boyd Douglas Boyd waits at Doctor Sam's office door. Boyd Douglas Boyd? What were his parents thinking? Certainly, the young man had entered the mental health field to find the answer to that question and a myriad of other personal idiocy's. He knocks softly on Doctor Sam's door.

"Ah, Boyd, just the man I want to see. Come in, sit down."

"Sam, I just went down to the, uh, ICU to see your Jane Doe, but she wasn't there. Uh, what should I do?"

Doctor Boyd tries to keep his distress from reflecting in his voice, but the pitch, cracks, and stumbles make him sound like either a very distraught thirty-year-old or a lovesick adolescent.

"David put her in a private room this morning. Usually, the nurses have that kind of information." Now, Sam is sure he has chosen the right man for the job.

"I know. Uh, they were all busy. Figured I'd take this time to come up and get your thoughts. What's going on with her?"

"Well, I'm glad you asked me. I've talked to her a few times. She's very young. I don't believe she is even twenty. I would guess eighteen or nineteen. There's physical trauma: cuts, bruises, broken ribs and burns—look like cigarette burns. She has a concussion, which could be the major factor of her memory loss, but there could be psychological factors also. I think that if she were my patient, I would ask her some questions and then I would hypnotize her to see if anything that she's blocked comes out," Doctor Sam slyly advises.

"Should…should I do that right away?" Boyd is clueless.

"You might want to see her a few times. You know, form a trust bond with the patient." Doctor Sam is spoon-feeding the young Boyd. This is working out perfectly.

"I would like to start soon, maybe today. What do you think, Sam?"

"Excellent. That is exactly what I would do. You're a good man, Boyd."

Doctor Sam stands and shakes Boyd's hand, gives him a hearty pat on the back, and walks him to the door. Sam sits back down at his desk. He is tired.

The events of the last week have exhausted him, but he will continue. Doctor Sam has the vision to see this young woman through the immediate future. Then the distant future will have to take care of itself. Sam doesn't know why or exactly how this woman has come to him, but he knows it was not a mistake. There are no mistakes.

"D, I need to talk to one of the police officers who came in with Jane Doe. Her name is Vicky. Do you think you can get her on the phone for me? Please ask her to come into my office at her earliest convenience."

"No problem, Doctor. I'll get back to you with that. Doctor Knowles just walked in. Do you have time to see him?"

"Of course, always. Send him right in, D."

Doctor Knowles takes the seat directly in front of Doctor Sam's desk.

"What brings you here, David?"

"Boyd." David is concerned about the choice Doctor Sam made.

"What about Boyd? He just left here a short time ago." Sam sits down at his desk.

"Has he seen Jane Doe yet?"

"That's where he was heading when he left."

David leans toward his old mentor.

"Do you really think Boyd can handle this, Sam? I know you're usually right about things, but I'm concerned about this one."

This is the first time David has ever questioned Sam's judgment.

"I see that you're concerned, David, but don't worry, I spoke extensively to him. He is a brilliant hypnotist, and we agree completely on his plan of treatment."

"Sam, I've seen amazing hypnotists in nightclub acts and carnival side shows. I don't know, but that says to me that one doesn't have to be a brilliant physician to make someone think they're a chicken. "

"Don't worry, David. I'll be there observing. Nobody will think they're a chicken." Sam chuckles.

"As a matter of fact, I was just going down there when you came in. Come with me if you like."

"No, I can't, but I feel better knowing that you will be there. I have to run now. Thanks, Sam."

David hurries out of Sam's office, slightly embarrassed that he questioned his old friend.

Doctor Sam stops at Denise's desk.

"When you get Ms. Knight on the phone, will you ask her to please come into my office? I must speak to her about a matter of great importance.

"Yes, Doctor. Anything I should know about? "

"Soon, Denise, soon."

∽

"Hello, Doctor," Vicky says as she takes a seat in front of Doctor Sam's desk.

"Your secretary called and told me that you have an important matter to discuss with me."

Doctor Sam smiles and nods. "I'm glad you could come right away."

"Well, I had the day off, so I came right in. What do you need to talk to me about, Doctor?"

"Our Jane Doe. You know that I fully support you and your efforts with the women who are occasionally brought here, and I wanted to talk to you about that."

"I don't understand what that has to do with Jane Doe, Doctor."

"I know that the ladies that you have been involved with, often because of your hard work, leave the streets and go on to more acceptable employment. You know that on your request, I have even given a few of the women you help my recommendations for their employment in this very hospital."

"Yes, I do know that, Doctor, and I'm very thankful to you for what you've done. I know you wouldn't have called me here without a good reason, but I still don't know what that has to do with Jane Doe."

"Our Jane Doe, yes, yes. I know. I know I must come to the point." The doctor paces as he speaks.

"She is here because… she came… it was a force." Doctor Sam continues pacing. Vicky looks confused as the old doctor paces about. "There is a point, but I can't really tell you anything about her except that *I know that I know you can help her*. Honestly, Ms. Knight, I don't know why she's here or how exactly she came to be here. All I know is that she is a young girl who desperately needs help."

"Wow, I can't believe that you said *I know that I know*." A smile stretches across Vicky's face. "I haven't heard anyone use that expression since my grandmother passed. Whenever she said, 'I know that I know,' well, no one questioned her after that. What do you need me to do, Doctor?" Vicky's mind races back to her grandmother, a mild unassuming woman, who in Vicky's estimation knew the secret of all the secrets.

"I'll tell you, Ms. Knight, if any young girl ever needed your help, this one certainly does. She needs a friend and quick. I know it's a lot to ask, and I understand if you can't help."

"I don't know how I would be able to help, and what about her memory? Does she remember anything, Doctor? Anything at all?"

"I can't tell you that she has any recollections, and Social Services want to place her since no one has identified her and she can't identify herself. What I can tell you is that I am sure an institution is the wrong place for her."

"What do they expect?"

"They want her to have a place to live and employment when she is able."

"Well, that's not unusual."

"What I'm trying to tell you is she will be placed in an institution until they feel she is able to take care of herself if she doesn't have work and family or a friend to help. I'm going to give her a job, filing in my office, but I have no place for her to live and no guardian." Doctor Sam takes a breath and continues, "My hope is that you can help with that. There's not much more that I can tell you about this girl except I promise you that she's not a danger to you or herself. For the time being, I will just say she is lost in this world, and if you can accept that, I know that we will be able to help her find herself. Can you accept that?"

Doctor Sam stops pacing and looks at Vicky. He has said what he had to say, and now he hopes for the best. Vicky looks back at him, long and hard.

"Let me say, Doctor, I heard of you and your reputation as an excellent doctor and a good man even before the first time I ever came here, and then after I got to know you, I knew what I heard was true. You're a good man. And Doctor, please call me Vicky."

The doctor chuckles lightly. "Thank you Vicky, You're very kind." The doctor took a chance. He put bet on Vicky's character, and now he hopes that she will not disappoint him, but she has not agreed just yet.

"Hold up a minute, before I say anything let me see if I understand exactly what you are asking of me. You want me to take guardianship over this young woman and bring her into my home—a girl who showed up out of the blue with no known family and no one coming forward to identify her or claim her as a friend or even an acquaintance. And you want me to commit to this for an unspecified amount of time, and the reason being for this is to keep her from going into a state institution because you know that you know it's the wrong place for her. Is that correct, Doctor?"

"Yes, I suppose that sums it up pretty well."

"I wouldn't be inclined to agree to this proposal, but I do have a nice guest room, and you and I have worked together a time or two before. So yes, I'll agree, but I need some time to get things ready." Vicky's mind wanders home to her guest room. "Hmm, peach would be nice. Yes, I think I'll paint the guest room peach."

"Yes, peach, very nice, my dear. Thank you so much, Vicky." Doctor Sam steps from behind his desk and vigorously shakes Vicky's hand. "You're a good woman."

"Oh, okay then, I guess it's settled then. When do I get to meet her?"

"I have another meeting with the social worker, and then I will explain to our Jane Doe what will happen. She will have a few more sessions with our resident psychiatrist, and then she'll be ready to be released to your custody. Give me a few days. Thank you, Vicky. Thank you. You're an extraordinary woman. I will call you in a few days."

"I will be looking forward to your call, Doctor."

❧

"Doctor Boyd, I see you're getting along with my favorite patient."

"Yes, Doctor Knowles. We're just finishing for today. We'll have another session in the morning," Boyd calls over his shoulder as he leaves the room.

Doctor Knowles sits on the stool next to Miriam's bed and studies her chart while the young lady eats.

"Well, little lady, looks like you have your appetite back. You're doing very well. How do you feel?"

"Better, I think."

"That's good, I'd rather hear 'better I think, 'than awful, I think." Doctor Knowles peeps over the chart at Miriam she smiles.

"Ha, I knew I could make you smile."

Miriam points to the door and grins as Doctor Sam walks-in pushing a wheelchair.

"Well, there you go, I get a faint smile, and he gets a full-out grin. What do you make of that, Doctor Sam?"

"I think you and Doctor Boyd are monopolizing this young lady's time, so now I'm taking her out. We're going to the atrium right now. Will you join us Doctor Knowles?" Doctor Sam knows his offer will be declined.

"Sorry, wish I could say yes, but duty calls." Doctor Knowles continues his rounds.

Doctor Sam parks Miriam's wheelchair next to a bench in a shady spot.

"I've brought you a surprise." Doctor Sam waves across the atrium and then excuses himself.

A small figure of a woman makes her way through the courtyard and stands in the shady spot where Miriam sits.

"Theresa Marie!" Miriam beckons her to sit.

"Mary Katherine," Theresa sits on the bench. "Is it really you? Are you really the girl I prayed for all of these years? How is this even possible? Where have you been? What has happened to you?" Theresa Marie tries to bring some logic to this completely illogical situation.

"Theresa, Yes, it is me. I am the girl you ate cookies with so long ago. One cookie in each hand. Just the way we like."

"Mary Katherine it is you." The old sister holds the young woman as she weeps tears of joy and confusion.

"Yes, it is and there is so much I must tell you, but first tell me, how did you find me?"

"I did not find you, Mary Katherine. The saints have brought us together. I am here only by chance to accompany a display of religious treasures that have been brought here to be displayed at the Holy Trinity Monastery."

"The Holy Trinity Monastery? The one Ignatius's brother, Klaus, built?"

"Yes. Ignatius will be here also. He will celebrate mass for the anniversary of the monastery. He's a cardinal now."

"Ignatius! Theresa, he is a very evil man!"

Theresa averts her eyes from Miriam. "I know. I have always known."

"How could you know? Tell me how you knew, Theresa."

"It was when Ignatius first arrived at our monastery," Sister Theresa Marie began. "He was a new priest. We passed in the halls as I went to the archives, and he went to his office. I was always cordial to him, but never anything more. One morning, he followed me into my office. He said he had something he thought that I would like to see. He asked me to come to the window. I could not imagine what I would see there that I had never seen before. I went to the window. Suddenly he clasped his hand over my mouth and pushed me to the floor. And then…he raped me. Afterward, he told me if I told anyone, I could be assured that he knew men who would gladly make the same thing, or worse, happen to my little sister in Italy. I have remained silent to this day."

"Oh, Theresa, I'm so sorry."

Sister Theresa Marie remained emotionless. "It was a long time ago, Miriam. I have come to terms with the truth that because of his action, I will never be worthy."

Miriam searches her friend's eyes, and the sadness overwhelms her. Although Miriam can see that Theresa Marie has suffered much, she can also see that her friend's soul is unscathed.

"Theresa, I have known you as a friend, a sister, and a confidant. I would champion your character even to the highest heavens, if need be, but there is no need, as your love and your dedication to your beliefs are your magnificence."

"Miriam, I should have told you before, but I feared that Ignatius would be true to his word, so for the sake of my little sister, I remained silent until now.

"Tell me, Theresa, what made you tell me of all this now?"

"I am surprised you asked me such a question."

"Why are you so surprised?"

"Just think, Miriam, think of what has happened to you and look at the outcome. I see that fate has done its worst for you, but because you do not serve the blind god of fortune your God has given you a new life. You have been given a special gift, like the saints."

"Well, Theresa, I do not think I will be canonized anytime soon, but that is a kind thing for you to say."

"I wish you could see yourself as I see you now. You are not the girl I knew, yet you are. I don't know how, and I can't explain it, but you are different…remade."

"I have been changed. You are right I have been changed." Miriam's thoughts go to the moment that she crossed into the spirit and the gift that the first spirit bestowed upon her. Miriam smiles. Theresa will never know, at least not in this life, the extent of that special gift.

"Tell me, Theresa, when will Ignatius celebrate mass at the Holy Trinity?"

"Ignatius will be there the Sunday after the Thanksgiving celebration. That is a little more than a week from now."

"Good, I will attend, but tell no one about me. If anyone asks, say only that I have come from your convent in Germany to help you with the treasures. Do you understand?"

Sister Theresa Marie nods. "I understand. I will say nothing. Now, I have a surprise for *you*. Miriam, you have another old friend here... Eliakim. He came with the rest of the antiquities."

Miriam's smile widens. "Eliakim...perfect. We have much to talk about before that mass."

~

Miriam's room is dimly lit. The blinds are drawn to block the late afternoon sun. Doctor Boyd speaks to Miriam in a quiet, metered tone as Doctor Sam observes.

"Listen to my voice. You are standing at the edge of a beautiful pool. Do you see the pool?"

"Yes," Miriam says.

"I will begin to slowly count backward from ten. As I count, you will descend the steps into the pool. When I reach one, you will be totally immersed in the water and be completely comfortable. Do you understand?"

"Yes."

"Ten, you step into the pool. Nine, a warm tingling sensation covers your feet. Eight, you take the next step. The warm water rises past your ankles. You are relaxed. Seven, the warm water has passed your knees, and the sensation travels up to your abdomen and lower back. Six, you take another step into the warm pool. Your chest relaxes. You breathe deeply. Five, the warm water of the pool covers your hands and arms. Four, your neck and shoulders are now immersed in the pool. Three, you are now effortlessly floating in the pool. Two, you breathe deeply and exhale as you float. One, you are completely relaxed. "It is November ninth, where are you

At the monastery."

"What are you doing?"

"Teaching"

"What are you teaching?"

"English."

"What do your students call you?"

"Sister Mary Katherine."

"What time of day is it?"

"It's morning, ten o'clock."

"Go forward in time to the evening of November ninth. Where are you?" Miriam becomes visibly uncomfortable. Doctor Boyd continues.

"You are safe in the water, you are comfortable."

"Where are you now?"

"Detained."

"Where are you detained, Sister Mary Katherine?"

"Not Sister Mary Katherine, Miriam Davidson."

"Where are you detained, Miriam?"

"I do not know."

"Who detained you?"

"The Gestapo."

"What is the date, Miriam?"

"November ninth, 1940."

"Go to the moment that you escaped. How did you escape?"

"Death." Miriam begins to flail. Doctor Boyd ends the session.

"It appears to me that something so horrific has happened to her that she cannot bear it, so her mind has put this fantasy memory of the Gestapo in place." Doctor Sam offers the analysis that he had readied on the very afternoon that he had decided that Boyd would suit his purpose. "So, you think that this fantasy that she has created is easier for her to accept than the truth, whatever that may be?" Boyd questioned. "Yes, Boyd, that's exactly what I think. I think, she will eventually remember. But who knows how long it will take?"

"Yes, you are right...I will put that in my report."

"Very good Boyd. I expect your report will be finished tomorrow. I am meeting with the social worker soon. The girl must be placed somewhere."

"Uh, yes. Of course. Tomorrow."

"Thanks, Boyd. I knew I could count on you." Doctor Sam pats Boyd on his back and returns to his office.

"You look like the cat that swallowed the canary." D looks up from her computer.

"D, how would you like a helper?" Doctor Sam has mischief in his eyes.

"I won't say no to help, but you have something up your sleeve, and I don't know if I like it."

"I want to give Jane Doe who came in last week a job."

"Jane Doe? Are you kidding?"

"No, D I'm not."

"Do you know anything about her?"

"No, I don't." Doctor Sam knew Denise would bluster. He is enjoying this little chat.

"Are you kidding?"

"No, not kidding."

"Can I at least talk to her first?"

"Of course, you can." Doctor Sam walks to his door then turns back to D.

"Will you get the social worker on the phone? Give her the message that everything is set for tomorrow. She can come anytime. Thanks, D. You're a dear."

"Don't 'Thanks D, you're a dear, me. If that girl doesn't hop on one foot, she'll be out of here."

Doctor Sam chuckles as he closes his office door and dials Vicky.

"Hello," Vicky answers.

"Hello, Vicky, this is Sam Rubinstein I'm glad I caught you at home."

"I'm just leaving for the station. What's up Doc?"

Vicky snorts into the phone as she tries to stifle her giggle.

"I was wondering if you might have some time tomorrow to come in and meet our Jane Doe. We call her Miriam, that's all I can tell you so far though."

"I can be there tomorrow around lunch. See you then?"

"Of course."

"Goodbye, Doctor. See you tomorrow."

"Thank you, Vicky."

Vicky is incredibly anxious to officially meet Jane Doe. Mike, of course, is not at all anxious about this turn of events. Mike does not share her enthusiasm toward the ladies of the night; he has certainly tried to dissuade Vicky from her decision to take in the young woman.

However, Vicky has made up her mind and will not be moved. Miriam will become a part of her life.

Mike has not been very supportive of Vicky's selfless efforts until recently, when Joniqua's son gave information to Mike about the murdered teenage boy found on Channel Side. He also gave information about the Vicente family's involvement with the Mexican drug cartel in Kumquat. The information was enough to put the boy and his mother in the witness protection program. There is a good chance that Vicky might never see Joniqua again, but she has kept her promise.

THE BOOKMARK

The bungalow is nestled under a giant mimosa tree and sprawling live oaks in Hyde Park, a quiet and historical neighborhood a few blocks from the beautiful Bayshore Boulevard. Vicky parks her car in the driveway.

"Is this your home Vicky?"

"Yes, Miriam, this is your home too now."

"It is very pretty." Miriam can see Sandalphon perched high in the mimosa tree, watching her through the feathery leaves.

"Thanks. It was a mess when I got it, but I worked at it. It's nice and comfy now.

"Comfy?"

"Oh, that's short for comfortable. Don't worry, I'll teach you. Soon, you'll even have a southern accent." Vicky laughs. She is at ease with her decision to allow Miriam into her home. She trusts old Doctor Sam, besides when she was painting the guest room for Miriam, she realized that she is not only alone, but also lonely.

"A southern accent, ja?"

"Come on in. I think you'll like it." Miriam winces when Vicky touches her back as she helps her to the door. Most of Miriam's visible wounds are healed, but she is still tender. She also suffers headaches from her head injury, but she never complains.

"This is very close to the hospital. It took only a brief time to drive here, this is good. I will walk to the hospital for my job."

"Hold up there sweetie. We're not talking about you walking anywhere just yet. Let's get settled in, and then we can take care of the details, okay?"

"Ja good, Vicky."

"I'm glad you're here. I hope you'll be happy here as well." Vicky gives Miriam a gentle hug.

"My father always said to me, 'Happiness is a choice,'
and you have made an easy choice for me. I will be happy. Thank
you. Vicky, do you hear a noise?"

"Oh, I forgot about Rocky."

"Rocky?"

"Come with me." Miriam follows Vicky through the house to the
back door. Vicky opens the door and in bounds a gangly red dog with
ears disproportionately large for her head. Vicky taps her chest, and the
dog stands on her hind legs and gently rests her front paws on Vicky's
shoulders. Vicky kisses the scraggly dog's black nose.

"Miriam, this is Rocky. Rocky, this is Miriam. Miriam lives with
us now, so you have to take care of her too, okay?" Rocky's ears rotate
like satellite dishes searching for a signal as Vicky speaks.

"I am pleased to make your acquaintance, Rocky." Miriam kneels
as the big dog enthusiastically greets her.

"She likes you, and she's not easily impressed."

Vicky is also impressed. Rocky isn't just Vicky's dog; she is Vicky's
best friend and an impeccable judge of character.

"Then I am honored. I am sure we will be great friends."

"I put some clothes in your room for you, let's go look." Miriam
and Rocky follow Vicky to the guest bedroom. Vicky has chosen a few
things from her wardrobe that she thinks Miriam might be able to wear.

"This will be your room, Miriam. Do you like the color?"

"Ja, peach is my favorite color. It is very nice."

Miriam nods her approval as she speaks.

"I hope you can wear some of these. I think we're almost the same
size. Anyway, these will do for your new job until we can go to the mall."

"Mall?"

"Yes, shopping."

"Oh, shopping. This is good. "

Vicky smiles. "Yes, this is good, very good, Miriam."

~

"Hi, what's up, girl? Boy it was wild at the station today. Must be a
full moon." Vicky sits on the edge of Miriam's bed.

"Vicky, I feel this is not right." Miriam turns to Vicky.

"What isn't right? You've only been with me a couple weeks; something can't be wrong already."

"You have been so good to me, and I have kept things from you because we thought you would not understand." Miriam sniffles and wipes her eyes.

"Are you crying? What do you mean 'we?'"

"Doctor Sam, but it's not all his fault. It is all so strange."

Vicky puts an arm around her new friend. "Miriam, sugar, it's okay. You can tell me. We'll figure this out, whatever it is."

Miriam cries as she takes the rest of the evening to account to Vicky how it happened that she came to be here. Vicky had taken the old doctor's word that Miriam had no family or friends here. Now, Vicky knows that was true enough. She believed the doctor when he said that Miriam was not a danger. Well, the truth of Miriam's story didn't change that either. She is lost as the doctor had said, that's for sure. Doctor Sam had been truthful. Vicky holds Miriam as she sobs.

"So, Doctor Sam figured this out? Who you are and everything? He said he knew that he knew. Just like my grandmother, I guess he did." Vicky shakes her head. She has a newfound respect for the cunning old doctor.

"Ja. He is the only one who knows about me, and now you know."

"I knew you didn't have amnesia. I knew it was bull."

Vicky smiled a big self-satisfied grin.

"Bull?"

"Yeah, bull—not real."

"Bulls aren't real now?" Miriam questions.

"Sure, bulls are real, Sugar, but… well. It's okay. You're a brave girl. Go to sleep now, don't worry. We'll talk about this more later.

Vicky is tired but she will be awake most of the night processing everything that Miriam has told her.

~

"Is this your first Thanksgiving Sister Theresa Marie?"

"Yes, it is, Vicky. Thank you for inviting me."

"Please Sister, take the seat across from Miriam." Vicky welcomed her guest.

"My first too," Miriam giggled.

In the time Miriam has been living with Vicky, she has experienced quite a few firsts. Some were odd and quite jarring, like her first ride in hectic interstate traffic and some were pleasant, like watching movies on the flat box that hangs on the wall they call television and now this wonderful big family meal they call Thanksgiving.

"Vicky, you know I am quite fond of your friend." Sister Theresa Marie smiles.

"So am I, Sister. Now, make sure to save room for dessert," "Dessert? Are there cookies?" Theresa Marie winks at Miriam.

"Yes, cookies and even pie!" Miriam smiles back at Theresa Marie. Rocky races to the front door, as the doorbell chimes.

"That must be Mike. He always comes for dessert on Thanksgiving." Vicky opens the door, and Mike greets Rocky with the expected vigorous pat on her head and rub on the belly. The bouquet of flowers and a bottle of wine he holds are, like always, the gifts for the hostess.

"For you, Vicky. Happy Thanksgiving." Mike hands the flowers and wine to Vicky and gives her a quick hug.

"Thank you, Michael."

Mike pulls a chair to the table between Vicky and Miriam. He leans over and gives Miriam a one-armed, big brother-type of hug.

"Good to see you girl. How's the job coming?" Mike is warming to this new living arrangement. He is actually beginning to like Miriam.

"It is good, Mike. I do not work too hard." Miriam smiles.

"É bello vederti di novo, Sorella Theresa Marie." Mike greets the sister in Italian.

"It is good to see you again, young man," Sister Theresa Marie says.

Mike fixes himself a plate of pumpkin pie, heavy on the whipped cream, and watches Vicky and Miriam as they laugh and talk. He is sure Vicky is keeping something from him. As much as Mike is beginning to like Miriam, he knows something is fishy. His father had always said, "The fish stinks from the head down." Although his father's stinky fish quote is quite colorful, Mike has learned to rely more on his mother's words, "It will all come out in the wash dear." Mike guesses he will have to wait for the wash. After the meal is over, Miriam clears the table and Vicky loads the dishwasher.

"This is a very good thing, this dishwasher. I think I am able to do this by myself. I have watched you often now."

"I think you can give it a try." Vicky smiles.

"On Sunday, I would like to go to the Holy Trinity. There is going to be a special celebration of mass for the religious treasures display. I know you are on duty, but Theresa Marie said that she could arrange for someone to pick me up and bring me home. I feel well, Vicky, and I would really like to go. Do you think that would be all right?" As she speaks, Miriam keeps her eyes on the dishwasher puzzle she is trying to solve.

"Try fitting that platter on the other side," Vicky suggests. That might work. I don't see any reason why you shouldn't go, that will be a nice outing."

"Yes, it will be."

His Excellency Ignatius Duetzman stands in the vestibule of the chapel at the Holy Trinity Monastery. He peers down the long hall. He can see two nuns engaged in conversation. He has known one of the nuns, Sister Theresa Marie, for more than sixty years. The other sister he does not recognize, but she has an air of familiarity. Cardinal Duetzman walks toward the sisters. The young sister glances at the old cardinal, and then she turns and walks away. The cardinal's old eyes, or perhaps the shadows of the dimly lit hall, had played a trick on his mind. *"Of course,"* Ignatius thinks, *"That could not be the young Jew, the sisters had called Sister Mary Katherine. No, that would be impossible."*

"Sister Theresa Marie, may I speak to you for a moment?"

"Certainly." Theresa Marie does not bow.

"Is everything ready for the opening of the exhibit? It's only five days from now. Who was that sister you were talking to?" Ignatius strains to watch the young sister.

"Yes, everything is ready, Ignatius. That was a young sister from my convent. She will be helping with the artifacts. I must go now. Excuse me."

Sister Theresa Marie walks the dim halls of the monastery to her room in the private quarters for visiting sisters. Miriam waits there.

"Mary Katherine, I mean, Miriam that was perfect, just as we planned. Ignatius is not sure of what he has seen. Tell me, what's next?"

"I want to see Eliakim. We can talk on the way." As they walk through the monastery's dim halls, Miriam tells Theresa Marie about the night she saw Ignatius murder the man in the courtyard.

"Miriam, I fear there is nothing we can do. That was so long ago."

"You are right, Theresa. It was a long time ago, but I have not told you the complete account of that night. I was certain Ignatius did not know that I had seen what he had done. I quickly crept to the courtyard, keeping to the shadows so I would not be discovered. I followed Ignatius as he dragged the man's body into the grotto and buried him under the trees. When I knew Ignatius had left the monastery for the night, I went to his office. The door was locked, but I knew that his balcony door was always open. I went through the archives room and then out onto the balcony. I climbed over the rail that separated the two balconies. I went to Ignatius's desk in hopes of finding something. I wanted something that I might be able to use against him, a note a journal, anything. I did not know what I was looking for until I came upon a book with a gold marker in it. Engraved on the marker was the inscription: 'To Father Ignatius, Love, Richard.' I put the bookmark in my pocket and hurried back to the grotto. I then dug with my hands into the dirt that covered the man and placed the bookmark there. I planned to expose Ignatius. The bookmark would be the evidence, but the opportunity never arose. But now, I have a plan."

"We shall see, Miriam. Now, we shall see," the older sister says.

"Mass will begin soon. I must take my place." Sister Theresa Marie hugs Miriam and leaves her in the treasures room with Eliakim.

"I will be in soon, Theresa." Miriam studies Eliakim. His plaster finish is very much intact, and he has only a few slight scratches. He is none the worse for wear.

Cardinal Duetzman begins the consecration of the cup. His Eminence is miraculously changing the wine to blood. With all parishioner's eyes closed, he lifts the cup.

"Take this cup of the New Testament, the blood that was shed for all, for the pardon of all your sins." The cup in Ignatius's hand has not become the elixir that would save their immortal souls. It remains merely a sacristan's concoction of mixed dregs of wine. It would, by no means, save anyone's soul. Ignatius watches Sister Mary Katherine enter the chapel. She quietly takes a seat next to Sister Theresa Marie.

His Eminence doesn't notice the exact moment that the wine from the cup he holds in his shaking hand splashes onto his white robe. Moreover, for his life, Ignatius cannot see the distinction between the splash of wine and a stain of blood.

~

"Shake, shake, shake your booty. Shake your booty." Vicky sings along to the music that blares through her house as she and Rocky dance. Rocky jumps and hops, following Vicky as she gyrates around the kitchen.

"Is this a private dance?" Miriam giggles.

"Oh, I didn't hear you come in. How was work? Are you hungry? I'm thinking about pizza. How's that sound?"

"Ja, pizza would be good. Very good," Miriam calls to Vicky as she changes from her work clothes. Miriam emerges in sweats and flip-flops, her first purchases from her first paycheck, and flops onto the couch.

"What do you want on your pizza? I'm ordering now."

"Black olives and salty fishes."

"Anchovies? *Yuck!* Only on your half."

"Vicky, do you think you can drive me to the Holy Trinity?"

"Probably. When do you want to go? Do you want a salad with your pizza?"

"ja, salad please."

"Tonight."

"Wait, what? Hold on." Vicky quickly finished the pizza order.

"Tonight what?"

"Tonight, go to the monastery."

"It's getting late. We'll have to hurry!" Vicky stands next to the couch where Miriam has flopped.

"No, not now. I do not care to go so early. I think about one o'clock is good."

"One o'clock in the morning? No, not good! What in the world do you want to do at that hour in the morning at the monastery?"

"There is something there that belongs to me. I will sneak in and take it back."

"Miriam, you can retrieve your own property that's at the monastery. It's the law. Just ask for it." Vicky looks down at Miriam, wondering what on earth is going through this girl's head.

"Ja that is good. I will go in and ask them for my property. Then they will ask me, 'How is this something yours?' Then, I will answer that I made it when I lived in Germany in 1940. Then, they will say, 'Go home, crazy girl!'" Miriam rolls her eyes. Vicky doesn't argue she could see that Miriam's thinking is based on irrefutable hypothetical logic.

"I don't know, Miriam. How long do you think it will take you to sneak in and out again?" Vicky then shakes her head. She can't believe that she is actually considering being a part of breaking into the Holy Trinity Monastery.

"Only a short time. I will be in and out quickly, I promise, I think. Please, Vicky, this is important."

❧

"I can't believe I'm driving you to the monastery in the middle of the night so you can break in. God help me. I think there is a special place in hell for me now." Vicky drives toward Kumquat to the Holy Trinity Monastery. Miriam sits in the passenger seat with a large Mickey Mouse beach towel folded in her lap, another one of her first purchases. Rocky sits in the backseat with her head out the window, her jowls flapping in the salty breeze. Vicky turns the lights out and parks the car in the alley behind the monastery.

"I'll be here for five minutes and only five minutes, no longer," Vicky cautions.

"I'm not fooling, Miriam. I'll leave you after five minutes if you aren't back by then, so you better be in this vehicle buckled up and ready to go in five minutes, you hear me?"

"Ja, Vicky, five minutes. This is good. I understand." Miriam knows that Vicky won't leave her, but five minutes is all the time she needs. She opens the car door and sprints toward a stand of unkempt bushes.

"Rocky girl, this is not good. What am I doing?" Vicky asks her companion. Rocky's ears rotate. She sticks her nose in Vicky's face for a kiss. Vicky sighs, rubs Rocky's ears, and watches the bushes that Miriam had disappeared into. She looks at her watch. Only two minutes have passed.

"Damn, Rocky, that girl doesn't even have a watch. What was I thinking? Damn, damn, damn." Rocky sticks her cold nose in Vicky's face again. Vicky checks her watch. Three minutes have gone by.

"Rocky, Rocky, Rocky. I can't go to prison. A police officer in prison. Oh Lord." Rocky paws Vicky's shoulder and lays her nose on the back of Vicky's seat. "Alright, one kiss and then you sit back and settle down, Rocky." Vicky kisses Rocky's nose, and the big red Dingo settles into the back seat. Vicky checks the time again. Four minutes have passed, but it seems like hours. Vicky watches for any sign of Miriam. A huge flash illuminates the night sky, and Rocky jumps into the driver's seat with Vicky.

"Get off me, you big chicken." Vicky pushes Rocky, who stubbornly resists, back into the rear seat. Another flash is followed by a loud, booming sound. Rocky shivers in fear in the backseat.

"You're right, Rocky. That was thunder, it was not an explosion." Even as she says it, Vicky knows that it isn't true. Vicky knows in her heart of hearts that Rocky actually isn't right and it *was* very much an explosion. She hates it when she has to lie to the dog.

"It was thunder. Oh God, oh God, oh God. That wasn't an explosion. Thunder, it was just thunder. Oh damn, damn, damn, damn." Just as Vicky is in the middle of her breakdown, she sees Miriam running through the bushes, followed closely by a night guard who is wearing only Miriam's Mickey Mouse beach towel tied around his hips.

Of course, he is. Why not? Nothing about this night has made any sense anyway. Vicky's mind is boggled. She starts the car and spins around to the place where Miriam will come out of the bushes. The guard is close behind her. Vicky leans over and opens the passenger door.

"Get in, hurry!" Vicky has the motor revved and is ready to speed off. To Vicky's surprise, Miriam opens the rear car door and pushes the half-naked man into the backseat and slams the door.

"Drive quickly." Miriam jumps into the front seat. Vicky speeds away, fishtailing her way down the narrow alleyway. Vicky speeds down the alley behind the monastery.

"What are you doing? No, who is that? What's going on? Why do I have a half-naked guy in my car?" Vicky speeds down the alleys behind the houses, races across city streets, and turns back to Bayshore Boulevard. She heads toward Hyde Park; she is almost home.

"It is the law, Vicky. He is my property. I have retrieved him." Miriam tries to reassure Vicky.

"Oh God, oh God, oh God."

"Are you praying, Vicky?"

"Hell yes, I am!"

"Oh, I was not sure. I have never heard a Baptist pray before. Was that a stop sign?"

"Stop sign, where? Crap! Maybe no one saw." Red flashing lights fill the car. "Crap, crap, crap!" Vicky pulls the car over.

"Act natural, Miriam." Vicky rolls down her window as the officer walks up.

"Hey, Vicky, I didn't know it was you." The rookie leans into Vicky's window.

"You would have if you had run the plates. You still riding with Zamboni?"

"Yeah, as long as I'm a rookie, I guess that's the program."

"What's the old man doing back there?"

"He's just sittin', I think. Waitin' to retire, you know."

Zamboni nudges the rookie aside and sticks his head in the car window.

"Where you goin' so fast, Vic?"

"We're just out for a ride."

"Hey, I just heard on the radio. There's been an explosion at the Holy Trinity. You came from that way. Did you see anything?

"No, Zamboni. I didn't see anything. Did you see anything, Miriam?"

"Ja, no, I did not. Did you see anything, Vicky?" Vicky purses her lips and squints her eyes at Miriam.

Zamboni shines his flashlight around Vicky's backseat, illuminating a curious red dog that is cautiously sniffing a very well-proportioned, muscular man who is wrapped only in a Mickey Mouse beach towel.

"You're out kind of late, Vic." Zamboni chooses to ignore the bizarre scene in the backseat of his colleague's car.

"Yeah, when Rocky can't sleep, I like to take her out for a little ride," Vicky says. "She loves to stick her head out the window on Bayshore."

"I imagine she does. It smells a lot like garbage," Zamboni retorts as he walks back to his patrol car.

"Vicky needs a break. She's been working too hard lately." The rookie declares. Zamboni nods in silent agreement.

ELIAKIM

Vicky locks her front door. A half-naked man stands in her living room, and Miriam has some explaining to do.

"Okay, Miriam, *if*—and that's a big if—if I accept your explanation that you created him and then animated him with some sort of ancient mystic recipe, or something, why would you bring him from the monastery? Wouldn't it have been enough to know that he was there safely on display? Why did you want him?"

"It wasn't him that I wanted, but I had to animate him to get what I did want." Miriam pulls a book from under her sweatshirt.

"This is what I wanted."

"What's that?"

"This is the journal my father gave me. In this book are all of my father's notes about the Kabbalah. I used what he had written in it to create Eliakim."

"Why would you create him?"

"I created him to have a place to hide my father's journal from the Gestapo," Miriam started.

"And because I thought there might be a time that I could use the protection of a golem. When I was taken away, Eliakim was left with the journal hidden under his robe. When I found out that he was here, I knew that I had to animate him to retrieve the journal, and then I had to take him with me. All that is left at the monastery are some pieces of clay that were his robe and cloak. His robe and cloak would not animate, of course. Miriam examines her creation. "Oh, there is a small amount of plaster dust. You see, I put a plaster finish over him for protection. That was my own idea. That was good. See, he looks fine."

"I can't believe I helped you break into the monastery. There's a big hole now in the side of it!" Vicky's voice squeaks, Rocky cocks her head toward Vicky and rotates her ears.

"That, I am sorry for, but really, Vicky, we broke out of the monastery, not in. We could not leave through the door Theresa Marie propped open for me, so Eliakim walked through the side of the building. He is very strong." Miriam announces proudly. She continues studying her golem.

Vicky cradles her head in her hands. She looks at Miriam, then Eliakim, and finally Rocky, who has returned to again sniffing Eliakim. She doesn't know if she is going to laugh or cry or both. Miriam admires her work.

"No one would believe that this is my first golem, ja?" Vicky snickers. The snicker turns to a giggle, and then the giggle turns to laughter. Tears fall as she laughs.

"You're right about that, Miriam. No one would believe it. Now, what are you going to do with him? Hide him in your closet? Oh okay, actually that's a good idea. He can hand you your sweaters." She laughs all the more.

"That is a good idea, Vicky. Watch," Miriam puts her fingers into Eliakim's mouth and pulls out a small piece of paper. Eliakim immediately turns back to clay. Vicky stops laughing. Miriam returns the paper to Eliakim's mouth, and he becomes animated once more. Miriam, Vicky, and Rocky escort Eliakim to his new quarters, deep in the back of Miriam's closet.

It is almost ten o'clock the next morning when the telephone rings. Everyone is asleep.

"Hello," Vicky answers sleepily.

"Vicky, you're not still in bed, are you?"

"What is it, Michael?"

"Just wondering if you heard about the break-in at the monastery last night?"

"Yes, I heard, Michael. That's really something."

"What are you up to today?" Mike hopes that Vicky doesn't have plans so he can drop by later.

"We're cleaning today and then run errands." Vicky says. She is really planning to sleep most of the day.

"That's probably what I should do."

"I better get started if I'm going to do what I have planned. See you tomorrow, Michael." Vicky hangs up the phone and puts the pillow over her head.

"Why yes, Michael, we do have a golem hidden in the closet. Thank you for asking," Vicky whispers into her pillow as she falls back asleep.

～

"Please sit. It's been a while." Doctor Sam offers Paul Linder a chair.

"Was that Jane Doe out there filing papers?" Paul points toward Doctor Sam's outer office.

"Yes, we call her Miriam now."

"She looks good. I know it's been more than a month since I've been here, but I didn't expect her to be fine, I mean, look so good. I mean, healthy." Paul struggles to find the appropriate words to describe the beautiful young woman he has just seen. He blushes.

"She's doing very well." Doctor Sam smiles. He recognizes the look on Paul's face. He, himself, had been smitten by his beautiful wife Leah so many years ago.

"I would like to talk to her, you know, just about what happened."

"I can tell you now that she doesn't remember anything. Her picture has gone out nationwide and even to Europe. No one seems to know her. Homeland Security has nothing on her. It's as if she fell out of the sky."

"I'm planning to stay in Tampa for a while. A working vacation, sort of. If she has time, I'd still like to get with, ah, talk to her while I'm here."

"That sounds like an excellent idea. I'll speak to Miriam and call you as soon as I have something worked out. Paul, I am curious about something."

"What's that, Doctor?"

"You seem so apt in your profession. I just wonder how long you have been doing this sort of work."

"After I graduated high school, I took a few years of drafting and then switched to criminal justice. I graduated three years ago and started working with my father. Now, I have taken over the family business. So, I guess I've only been doing this officially for three years, but I've been involved since I was a teenager."

"I see. I will get with you as soon as I speak to Miriam. You are a dedicated young man, Paul. Very good, very good."

Paul shakes Doctor Sam's hand. "Thanks, Doctor. Hope to hear from you soon." Paul really hopes to hear from the doctor very soon. Doctor Sam's calculations put Paul in his early twenties. He considers

Paul Linder. He thinks that Miriam's friend, Sister Theresa Marie, might be interested in Paul Linder and this turn of events too.

Doctor Sam begins devising a plan, a good plan, a plan with which he would need Sister Theresa Marie's assistance.

Miriam agrees to meet with Paul Linder in the hospital's atrium. Doctor Sam is surprised at how quickly Miriam had approved of the meeting. Now, Doctor Sam will speak to Sister Theresa Marie about the smitten young man; his plan is coming along nicely. Little does Doctor Sam know that for Miriam's purpose, the meeting with Paul will fit into *her* plan quite nicely. She will conspire with Sister Theresa Marie before the day of her meeting with Paul. Miriam will give her a map to the murdered man's grave and verse her on the particulars of Ignatius' crime. Sister Theresa Marie's meeting with the young Nazi hunter will certainly suit Miriam's purpose.

Paul spots Miriam across the atrium. The sunlight streams through the trees, transforming Miriam's hair into a mesmerizing halo.

"Hello, Miriam. My name is Paul Linder." Paul offers his hand.

"Hello." Miriam extends her hand. His incredibly good looks are not lost on her. Paul takes her hand.

"I guess the doctor told you why I'm here?"

"Yes, he told me you came earlier, before I was awake." Miriam looks into Paul's soft blue eyes, and her heart skips a beat; crystal white light shone from deep within his soul, a kind heart that she recognizes from a life long ago. *Boog!*

Paul covers her tiny alabaster hand with his free hand and gently turns her palm up.

"Then you know this tattoo on your arm tells me that what happened to you might have been at the hands of the Aryan Nation, the neo-Nazis, or some other group that is hate driven." Paul lightly traces the tattoo as he talks.

"Ja, I know. I am sorry that I cannot tell you anything." Miriam gently pulls her arm back to herself. Paul sits on the garden bench, next to Miriam, stretches his long legs in front of himself, clasps his hands together behind his head, and gazes into the brilliant blue Florida sky. He isn't ready to leave Miriam's company yet.

"I've never seen a sky so blue or so high." Sister Theresa Marie suddenly appears.

"Hello Sister Theresa Marie! What are you doing here today?" Miriam feigns surprise. Their plan is on track, now, all Theresa Marie has to do is make an excuse to speak with Paul in private.

"I'm visiting a friend. How are you today Miriam?"

"I am fine thank you. Sister this is Paul Linder. Paul, this is Sister Theresa Marie."

"I see, it's very nice to meet you Paul." Theresa Marie smiles at Miriam.

"It's nice to meet you Sister." Paul stands to greet the sister.

"Will you sit with us for a minute?" Miriam asks.

"Oh, no, I can't. I have much to do. You, young people, please continue to enjoy your afternoon. I must return to the monastery. The relics don't take care of themselves. Actually, you should bring your friend to the monastery to see the display of treasures. I'm certain he would enjoy it." Theresa Marie smiles.

"Thank you, Sister. You're right, I would enjoy it." A slight smile creases Paul's lips. I think Miriam should give me the guided tour of the monastery. I would love to go to Kumquat and see it."

"Good. Then I will see you soon." Sister Theresa Marie leaves Miriam baffled. This did not go the way that they had planned. Theresa Marie had not followed the plan. How will they ever reveal Ignatius evil deeds unless Theresa follows the plan? Miriam decides to go over the details once again with her.

The holiday lights reflect in the dark waters of the Tampa Bay. Green and red lights wrap the palm trees that line the Bayshore Boulevard. Each house that they pass in the quaint little town of Kumquat seems to outshine the one before. It is Christmas Eve, and Paul has asked Miriam to give him his guided tour of the monastery this evening. To Paul, the time that passed since he met Miriam in the hospital's atrium has seemed to grind slowly on. Miriam looks beautiful tonight. She is worth the wait. Paul offers his arm to Miriam as they walk from the parking lot to the entrance of the monastery.

The candlelight mass is proudly attended by the Duetzman family. Cardinal Duetzman does not offer mass but rather holds a position of honor at the altar. After mass, Paul and Miriam stroll around the halls of the monastery, admiring the architecture, the antiquities, and the display of relics. They whisper as they walk.

"I'm glad you came this evening. Merry Christmas, Paul, Miriam." Sister Theresa Marie says as she meets Miriam and Paul in the vestibule.

"Merry Christmas, Sister Theresa Marie. Thank you for the invitation. The service was beautiful." Paul bows ever so slightly.

"Please, come to the banquet room. We have set out refreshments." Paul and Miriam follow Sister Theresa Marie into a large room warmed by a fire set in a massive fireplace ornately mantled with carved angels and cherubim.

Sister Theresa Marie understated the holiday feast that was prepared. The tables groan under their burdens. Cookies, cakes, freshly baked pies, and breads are displayed alongside fresh fruits and a variety of nuts, crackers, and pate. Fresh pine branches lay on each table as festive table decorations. A tall evergreen stands in a corner, angels and sparkling white lights decorating its boughs. The crèche sits beneath. As Paul, Miriam, and Theresa Marie enjoy the banquet and each other's company, Ignatius and Richard inch closer to them. Miriam pretends not to notice. Theresa Marie does not notice, and Paul notices only Miriam. Soon, Ignatius and Richard are standing next to Sister Theresa.

"Ah, Sister, you have made a beautiful holiday celebration." Even as he is speaking to Sister Theresa Marie, Ignatius keeps his eyes on Miriam.

"Thank you, but I had a lot of help. I could not have done this by myself."

"No, certainly not, and you have invited friends. How nice."

"Yes, your Eminence. This is Paul Linder. Paul, this is His Eminence, Ignatius Duetzman." Theresa purposely excludes Miriam from her introduction.

"Pleased to meet you." Paul extends his hand.

"And I'm pleased to meet you, your Eminence." Ignatius introduces, Red. "Paul this is my nephew, Richard
Duetzman."

"Good to meet 'cha." Richard runs his hand through his disobedient, aging red hair before he offers it to Paul. Paul's six-foot stature towers over Richard's spindly frame. Richard is a small man by any standard.

"Good to meet you. Merry Christmas, Mr. Duetzman."

Ignatius turns to Theresa Marie. "Sister Theresa Marie, you may remember Richard. He visited the monastery often when he was young."

"Yes, I remember Richard. He was a quite petulant child." Theresa Marie smiles.

"Thanks, Sister. You're a good old gal." Red is inappropriate as usual.

"Richard, will you accompany me across the room? I would like to introduce you to His Grace, the Bishop." Ignatius and Richard make their way back across the room.

"I know I've seen that woman before, but I just can't place her." Red studies Miriam from across the room. He tries to put a vague remembrance in place.

"She's the spitting image of Sister Mary Katherine.

Remember the sister with the raven?"

"Yeah, she is! You should ask her if she's related.

She's a dead ringer, that's for sure."

"Don't be a dolt, Richard," Ignatius snaps. "Do you not understand the danger of that? For all these years, I have thought that Mary Katherine had died. If she somehow survived and this is one of her offspring, then why has she come here? She could cause trouble for me. I'm certain I saw her at mass recently. She looked different then, but I am sure it was her." Ignatius is shaken. He wonders if this woman is simply taunting him, or does she have some information that might be damning? Ignatius cannot afford that possibility.

"Richard, I know you have friends who can make this problem go away.

"Take care of it" Richard nods.

"I'll speak to Joe."

⁓

"Ricardo, to what do I owe the pleasure of this visit?" Joseph Vicente welcomes Duetzman into his Davis Islands home.

"I need a favor Joe, for my uncle."

"What can I do to help His Eminence?"

"There's a young woman who might have information about him, some damaging stuff. He can't take that chance. She needs to disappear."

"Ricardo, the last time you came to me with woman problems, I had to turn you down. I was sorry. I could have easily had the problem 'taken care' of for you. Unfortunately, because your daughter-in-law's family name is involved with my family name through the sanctity of

marriage, I couldn't get involved or I would cause *vendetta famigliare*—
family feud." Vicente punctuates his words with his hands.

"I understand."

"I owe you this time, Ricardo. I'll take care of this problem."

"Thanks, Joe. We'll talk later." Richard stands to leave.

"No, no, Ricardo, sit, sit. You must stay. My beautiful Christina is
cooking."

∼

"I hate to leave you on New Year's Eve, but it's a tradition. Mike
and I have always done New Year's Eve together." Vicky primps in the
bathroom mirror while Miriam watches.

"You look very nice, sexy."

"Sexy? Where did you learn that?" Vicky laughs.

"On the television," Miriam answers. "That is where I learn about
everything like sexy and germs and that mouthwash kills ninety-nine
percent of the very bad germs and panties that are just my size. It is
strange, ja, Vicky? How do you imagine they know my panties size?"

Vicky rolls her eyes but continues her mission in the mirror.

Miriam continues, "And do you know that most people do not have
enough fiber in their diet?" Vicky giggles.

"Oh no, Vicky, you must not laugh. This is very serious. It says this
on the television often."

"Maybe you watch too much TV, sugar."

"And did you know that people will pay to have food that will make
them thin sent to their home? Oh, and Vicky, dog food with corn is bad,
so don't ever feed it to Rocky. That is important. And a rubber bone
will keep her teeth clean. A rubber bone, imagine that? Does Rocky
have a rubber bone? Does she have one of those dog jackets that looks
like a ladybug?"

"No, she doesn't." Vicky shakes her head at Miriam's chatter.

"Good. I will buy her one. She will look nice in a ladybug jacket,
ja?" "Wow, now I'm sure that you've watched way too much television."

Miriam smiles. "You do look very pretty tonight. Mike will be
pleased." She playfully bats her eyes at Vicky, who is taken aback.

"Mike? Why? Mike and I are just friends. Partners,
that's all."

"Mike loves you, Vicky. You can see it in his eyes if you look."

"See it in his eyes? Don't be silly, Miriam." Vicky shakes her head yet again, this time at this newest preposterous suggestion.

"Where are you and Mike going?"

"Dinner at the Columbia. What are you going to do?"

"Paul's coming over tonight. He said he must speak to me about Sister Theresa Marie."

"What do you think that's about?" Vicky applies one more coat of mascara.

"They have been talking a lot lately. Maybe she knows something." Miriam suggested.

"Maybe, or maybe you know something, sugar."

"Me? I just got here. I do not know anything yet. Remember?" Miriam crosses her eyes and leans into Vicky's mirror view.

"Right, just don't tell me anything. I haven't recovered yet from ya'll's last scheme." Vicky takes one last look in the mirror before walking out of the bathroom.

"Don't wait up for me. I'll be out late." Vicky gives Miriam a playful pat on the cheek as she passes. Miriam follows her to the door. Vicky opens the door and jumps back. She is surprised to see Paul standing on the porch; she places her hand over her heart for emphasis. Miriam giggles behind her.

"Paul! You startled me. Did you just get here?"

"Yeah, I just got here. Didn't Miriam tell you I was coming?"

"She did. I'm just leaving. Y'all have a nice time. Goodbye. Oh, and Miriam, save your money. No ladybug jackets."

"Ladybug jackets?" Paul repeats.

"For Rocky. Too much TV," Vicky calls out on the way to the driveway.

"Rocky, the dog?"

"Yes, Rocky is the dog." Miriam explains.

"Vicky thinks she's been watching too much TV. I think she drinks too much coffee."

"Vicky drinks too much coffee?"

"No, Rocky." Miriam smiles. "I hope you like to watch fireworks."

"Rocky?" Paul wants to understand, but his critical thinking skills are baffled, so he gravitates towards the familiar.

"Yeah, I do. I love fireworks." Paul does love fireworks, but he would have said he loves pearl diving if that was what Miriam had planned.

"Good. Vicky says that we can see them from the backyard."

"Before the fireworks though, I need to talk to you about Sister Theresa Marie." Paul says.

"What about her?" Miriam asks as she closes the door behind Paul.

Paul waits until they are seated in the living room before speaking again. Miriam's plan is back on track.

"She told me that she witnessed the Cardinal murder a man when he was a young priest. She gave me a map to the location of the man's grave."

"Sister Theresa Marie told you this?" Miriam asks.

"Yes, and she also gave me a suicide note from a young boy who references the Cardinal abusing him. She says that she always suspected that he was secretly a Nazi, but she never had the opportunity to expose him."

"What will you do, Paul?"

"That is why I'm telling you this. Even if you don't remember there's a chance that you are a nun because when you were found, you were dressed in a nun's habit. I like you, Miriam, but I have to turn this information over to the FBI. I can't let my friendship with you stop me from doing what I do."

"It does not matter what I remember or do not remember. Do what you must, and please do not be sorry for seeking justice."

"I just want to say that if sometime you remember that you are a sister, please don't hold this against me. I'm sorry. I would never hurt you, but this man must be exposed."

"I know you would never hurt me Paul. You must do what you know is right, just like your grandfather did. I am certain that he did not like what he had to do for the Nazis." Paul hugs Miriam and nuzzles her soft hair, but what she said about his grandfather sticks in his mind. He can't remember talking to her about his grandfather's work. He holds Miriam at arm's length as he searched his memory. Paul is certain he has never spoken of his grandfather or his work.

"How do you know anything about my grandfather? I need an explanation."

"You have his beautiful eyes." Miriam's mind goes to the horrifying night so long ago in Germany. She remembers Boog. She can see in her mind's eye the crystal white light that flashed from his soul and shone out through his eyes that night she allowed him to affix two letters and a string of numbers on her arm.

"We have to talk girl."

"Ja, I will tell you everything…" With Miriam's explanation, that night not only begins a new year for Paul Linder, but it also begins a new reality.

~

The last person Mike expects to see eating alone in the Columbia on New Year's Eve is Victor Duetzman, but there he sits…alone. Mike wants to speak to his old friend, but this is his special night with Vicky. She looks up from her plate.

"What is it Michael?"

"Victor Duetzman's at the table in the corner. I haven't seen him in years."

"Go say hi to your friend, Michael." Mike is unsure about this. "He's eating alone on New Year's Eve." Mike whispers.

"All the more reason to go over." Vicky nudges Mike.

"I'll be fine by myself for a little while. Go say hi, Catch up."

"You're right." Mike lays his napkin next to his plate and goes over to his old friend.

"Victor, hey!"

"Mike, I thought that was you." Victor stands, shakes Mike's hand, and then bear hugs him.

"It's been a long time." Mike grins.

"Sit down for a minute."

"How are Cooper and the kids?" Mike takes the seat across from Victor.

"The kids are great. They're growing up, they're six and ten now."

"Six and ten! No, that doesn't seem possible. How's Cooper?"

"She's good, but Coop and I aren't together anymore."

"I'm sorry to hear that. What happened?"

"She couldn't take it. It's my own fault. I wasn't strong for her. I would still have my family if I had been the man I should have been."

"She seemed like a nice girl."

"She is nice, too nice. My family made her life a living hell. My brothers and sisters were ruthless. My father especially hated her. It was disgraceful. You know, my family has everything money can buy. They want for nothing, but they hated my wife because she has something that they do not have, something they could not buy, and they couldn't take from her. Do you know what that one thing is Mike?"

"What, Victor?"

"Virtue Mike, It's virtue.

GASPARILLA

"I'll never get used to Eliakim. He scares the beejesus out of me when I come home and he's awake." Vicky tosses her car keys onto the entry table.

"He only does what I tell him to do, so, ja, I guess you better be careful then." Miriam laughs.

"Not funny. What if he got mad and went crazy or something?"

"That cannot happen. There is nothing in his head. You know, poor thing, if I only had a brain." Miriam makes circling motions around her temples with her fingers as she sings the scarecrow's refrain. Miriam had recently taken the opportunity to watch *The Wizard of Oz,* each and every time it had been shown on the movie channel.

"Way, way too much television, Dorothy!" Vicky calls from her room. Miriam continues humming as she puts the finishing touches on Eliakim's fresh attire. Now, instead of the Mickey Mouse beach towel tied around his waist, Eliakim sports black spandex biking shorts, a gray tank top, and a Tampa Bay Rays baseball cap.

"There, done. Come see how nice he looks, Vicky."

"That's better than the towel." Vicky returns to her room.

"Is something wrong? Did I tease you too hard? I promise Eliakim will never hurt you."

"No, it's just, I've been thinking about what you said about Michael, that he loves me, seeing it in his eyes and all. I think you're right, and I don't know what to do about it."

"Vicky, maybe there is nothing for you to do. Just let love take care of itself." Vicky gave Miriam a tight hug.

"Miriam, why are you so smart?"

"Because I only have a brain, "Miriam squeaks.

"Well, Sugar, I've got Gasparilla duty I'll see you this evening."

"See you later. I'm going to watch it on the television."

"I imagine you are."

Gasparilla—the celebration of the taking of Tampa by the bloodthirsty pirate José Gaspar. José Gaspar, as legend tells, raped, sodomized, and murdered men, women, and children and then pillaged and burned the city until it fell into submission. Of course, the celebrants will tell you, "It's only a legend. Pure myth. No truth to it whatsoever." This leaves them celebrating the idea and spirit of plunder, rape, sodomy, and murder.

The Tampa elite, in all probability, are generally good and civilized people, merely with a dedicated sense of style and an over exaggerated penchant to be well put together. Oddly however, in drunken revelry, the Tampa influential have dressed themselves in garish costumes to celebrate Gasparilla for more than a century. The Gasparilla celebration has begun. The pirates have invaded Tampa. The keys to the city have been surrendered to the pirate captain. The mayor and the police chief are in the dungeon, and chaos rules. Pirates and scantily clad wenches parade down Bayshore Boulevard. Rowdy pirate men, pirate women, pirate children, and pirate dogs and cats mill through the crowds. Mike and Vicky work crowd control. Mike works the east side of Bayshore Boulevard, and Vicky works a few blocks farther north on the west side of the street.

"Vicky, Vicky!" Joniqua runs toward Vicky, waving her arms desperately, trying to get her attention. She fights her way through the throng of revelers and stands in front of Vicky and blurts out her horrific message. "Vicky! I had to come. I had to warn you. Vicente put a hit on your friend Miriam." Vicky's eyes widen.

"Are you sure?"

"Vicky, yes, I'm sure. One of Vicente's girls told me to warn you. There's no time. The guy's been sent today. I just found out. You have to hurry. There's no time."

Vicky pulls her cell phone from her pocket and dials her home.

"Pick up, Miriam. Pick up, pick up," she murmurs to herself.

"Hello?"

"Oh, thank goodness, Miriam. Are you okay? Are the doors locked?"

"Yes. Are you still at that Gasparilla thing?"

"Hush, Miriam. Listen to me."

"What's wrong?"

"Is Eliakim awake?"

"Yes, he is. You are frightening me. What is wrong?"

"Someone has been sent to our house to kill you! Get out of the house! Get out quick! Run toward Bayshore. I will find you; I promise. Just run fast, Miriam!" The phone falls from Miriam's hand. Vicky can hear the sound of glass breaking and Rocky barking wildly before the phone disconnects.

"Eliakim! Protect me," Miriam shouts. She points to the man dressed as a pirate who has broken the glass and is trying to push open the kitchen door. Without a backward glance, she runs out the front door and heads toward Bayshore. The hit man pushes open the door just as Eliakim reached the kitchen. He fires two shots directly into Eliakim's head, but Eliakim keeps walking toward him.

"What the hell?" the man says. He fires one more shot and then turns and runs back through the kitchen door. Eliakim follows while Sandalphon circles above. Certain that he did not miss his target, the hit man was unsure of exactly what had just happened, but he is determined to catch up with his intended mark. The hit man, dressed as a pirate, appears to be one of the celebrants as he runs through the crowd. When he catches the girl, he will finish his job, and the happy crowd of revelers, thinking that he and the girl had been part of the festivities, will be none the wiser. Vicky radios to Mike.

"Code 2! Code 2! Mike, watch for Miriam. She will emerge on to Bayshore from West Bay Street or thereabout. Advise on her location and the direction she is heading. Copy?"

"Copy. I see her and Rocky now. She's running through the crowd on the west side of Bayshore, heading toward the Platt Street Bridge. They're a block north of you." Vicky runs toward Miriam, and Mike runs to back up his partner. Miriam and Rocky continue running toward the Platt Street Bridge.

The hit man is catching up to Miriam when Rocky turns and jumps, hurling herself into the path of the hired killer. With one powerful movement, the assassin catches Rocky in midair, flings her to the pavement, and continues running. Vicky is heartbroken as she runs past Rocky, lying motionless on the pavement; she pushes herself forward to catch up. Vicky can see Miriam. She can also see the assailant getting closer, but he has been slowed down a bit thanks to Rocky's bravery. Now, Vicky can catch up to him before he catches Miriam. Exhausted, Miriam reaches the bridge, the hit man following close behind. She tries to continue running along the sea wall, but her aching body fails her. Miriam stumbles and falls, the gunman takes aim.

"Police, drop your weapon! Turn around, and drop your weapon!" Vicky holds her gun on the hit man. He drops to the ground, firing shots. Eliakim walks through a firestorm of bullets. The hit man turns his gun toward Miriam, but a crushing grip prevents him from firing. Eliakim lifts him from the pavement by the throat and effortlessly holds him over his head. One sharp snap and the assassin grows limp. Eliakim effortlessly tosses the dead pirate over the sea wall.

The crowd engulfs Eliakim and Miriam as they cheer the Gasparilla hijinks. As the celebrants shout with delight and the pirate floats into the bay, Miriam and Eliakim disappear into the crowd.

Mike cradles Vicky's body as he makes a frantic cry into his radio.

"Officer down! Officer down! I need an ambulance!

My partner is down! I need assistance! Please! Platt Street Bridge! Officer down!"

≈

Miriam sits beside Paul. Mike and David Knowles sit silently at her other side. Paul tenderly holds her hand to comfort her. The words that Miriam hears— "suddenly taken", "loved by many", "will be greatly missed"—make no sense to her. They bring no comfort; she grieves the loss of her friend. After the service, when all the condolences have been given, Mike excuses himself. Only Paul and Miriam remain seated.

"Will you go to the monastery today?" Paul speaks in hushed tones.

"Ja, I will," Miriam says. They will meet again very soon.

≈

Miriam opens the front door. Vicky's house is quiet. Eliakim stands in a dark corner. Miriam crosses the room. She takes a small piece of paper from Eliakim's pocket, and puts it in his mouth.

"We are going to the monastery, Eliakim, as soon as I change."

Miriam walks the quiet hall to her room and opens her closet. With each item of clothing that she puts on, she once again becomes Sister Mary Katherine.

Miriam kneels at the altar with her back to the confessional and waits for the parishioner to leave. A few moments pass, and the confessional door opens. The parishioner thanks His Eminence and hurries away. The parishioner glances back as he reaches the chapel doors. Ignatius walks to the altar. When Miriam feels Ignatius standing behind her, she stands and turns to face him. His eyes widen as he steps back. "What do want from me? Who are you?"

"I think you know who I am." Miriam steps toward Ignatius.

"No, I have never seen you before."

"You have, but perhaps you have forgotten."

"No, no," he whispers, "Why do you haunt me?"

Ignatius stumbles but does not fall.

"Only a ghost can haunt. Do you think I am a ghost? Look at me. I am flesh and blood. I am alive." With each step Miriam takes toward Ignatius, he takes one back toward Eliakim, who stands in the shadows.

"Will you hear my confession again, Your Eminence?" Miriam takes another step.

"Again? No, I have never heard your confession before. You have mistaken me for someone else, young woman." Ignatius steps back.

"I make no mistake, Ignatius. You must have forgotten," Miriam says. "It was so long ago when last you heard my confession, so let me remind you. The Holy Scripture teaches that anyone who does harm to one of God's own will have a better fate if a millstone is hung around their neck and they are cast into the sea. Mother Gertrude and Stephen will be your millstone. I bid you good night, Father." Miriam turns away.

"Tell me where the note is!" Ignatius screams. The old cardinal lunges toward Miriam. His flailing arms grapple Miriam's waist, and the two fall to the floor.

Eliakim steps from the shadows, grasps Ignatius by the back of his neck, and lifts him from the floor. Eliakim dangles a squirming Ignatius by the throat. Ignatius digs at Eliakim's hand, struggling to loosen its hold. Slowly, Miriam picks herself up from the monastery floor and stands beneath the writhing old Nazi.

"Do not kill him yet, Eliakim. I must introduce you first, Eliakim, this is Cardinal Duetzman. Cardinal Duetzman, this is my golem, Eliakim. He is the creature that you and your Nazi comrades sought, the prize you desired. He is the statue that stood in the monastery for decades, holding beneath his robe, Stephen's note. Do you think you can take the note from him, Ignatius?" Ignatius struggles to speak but makes only desperate rasping sounds.

"I created him, and I control him. I can have him crush you." Miriam hesitates. Ignatius squirms.

"Eliakim, now," Ignatius's plea is nothing more than a whimper. "Release him."

Eliakim releases his grip, and Ignatius falls to the floor. Miriam and Eliakim walk down the long hall, through the monastery doors, and down the steps to the waiting taxi.

"Are you going back to the same place, Sister?" the driver asks.

"Yes, but wait for a few minutes please."

Miriam waits in the parked taxi. A few minutes later, a car pulls into the monastery parking lot. Four men in dark suits meet a fifth man at the monastery door. The five men enter the monastery. A short time later, Miriam watches Paul Linder and four FBI agents escort His Eminence in handcuffs from the monastery to the waiting car.

❧

"How's Rocky?" Vicky's breath is labored. Mike has been at the hospital every day since Vicky was shot. The hit man's bullet went in at an angle under her vest. It did a lot of damage, but she will recover.

"I told you she'll be fine. Don't worry." Mike gently brushes Vicky's matted hair to the side. Vicky closes her eyes.

"You're not just telling me that, so I don't worry, are you?"

"I'm not just telling you that. She has a few broken ribs, but she's recovering at the animal hospital. She'll be jumping around in no time."

"How was the memorial service for Doctor Sam?"

"It was nice. There were so many people, some had to stand in the hall."

"A massive heart attack." Vicky shakes her head. "It was so sudden. He was a good man. I'll miss him, how's Miriam taking it?"

"Hard. So is Doctor Knowles, and the secretary is a mess."

"What about the detective exam, Mike?"

"Well, Vicky, I don't know. With everything and you in the hospital, there hasn't been a lot of time."

"Michael! I can't believe you! You wanted that so badly."

"Wanted what? This?" Grinning Mike flashes his shiny new detective badge.

"Michael, you did it! I'm so proud of you."

"We won't be partners now though. You'll probably get the rookie." Mike laughs.

"Not partners…Now what?"

"Now I tell you that I love you. I have always loved you; I will always love you, Vicky."

"I know." Vicky smiles.

"How do you know?" Michael tenderly kisses Vicky.

"I looked into your eyes."

GRACE LOVE STANDARD

Grace Love Standard, that's what my mama named me, but my daddy always called me Gracie. I'm not sure now if I still have a name since there's no one around to call me to dinner or get me up in the morning. "Gracie it's time to eat." "Gracie wake up, rise and shine." No, I can't say that I hear much of that lately.

I have two things to say right off the get go. I'm dead and I'm not a whore. That's pretty much all that I have on my mind these days, but I don't really remember much since that last day. You're probably thinkin', 'what are you still doin' here, bein' dead and all? Oh, I know all about that go into the light, move on stuff, but I'm kind of havin' a good time here in Kumquat, now. They can only kill you once, I've heard. And yep, it's true.

Kumquat is a sleepy little town of five thousand residents, soon to be five thousand and two. Jerri Thompson is pregnant again, twins this time. I think that three thousand five hundred of the five thousand residents are in the witness protection program. The fifteen hundred remaining folks don't have a clue. The town takes its name from the kumquat that grows in abundance there. The kumquat is a small citrus fruit with a sugary sweet outside and an inside that is bitterly unpalatable, much like the townspeople. Well, that's just my opinion, but as in life, so in death an opinion doesn't really count for much, it's just an opinion.

My first day in Kumquat, is when I realized what a small town I had moved to. It was brought to my attention, by no less than the mayor of the sleepy little hollow, that my dog, Spider, chased a flock of chickens into town. Really now, I'm not kidding. Well, I will admit that was my fault, because my daddy said you can't fault a dog for being a dog. Anyway, it wasn't only the fact that the town's people knew it was my dog that chased the chickens into the Piggly Wiggly Store; they also knew that the flock of chickens belonged to old Miss Wallace. Well, that was my first insight into the comings and goings of Kumquat, but the true grasp came upon me two weeks later.

I'll tell you honest right now that I'm not opposed to guns, nor, do I have anything against snakes, but they are right up on top of my squish list. That cotton mouth that slithered out from underneath my house should have waited for me to go back inside. My mama always said dynamite comes in small packages. I figure she was referring to me. Well, maybe that snake thought that my five foot two and a half inches didn't pose a real threat. Better think again, Bubba. Of course, I don't really know what snakes think, at least I didn't then. Anyway, two shots from Lyle, my thirty-eight, and the snake was headless. It was what happened right after the snake showdown that *really* set me straight about Kumquat. My telephone that was installed only the day before, rang. As I live and breathe, or don't live and don't breathe. Guess I gotta' get used to that. This is how the conversation went.

"Hello." I answered.

"Hello little lady." The deep voice of a southern gentleman greeted me.

"This is the sheriff. What you shootin' at darlin'?"

'Crap!' I thought. 'I don't even know my phone number yet, but the sheriff does. This isn't good.' Not that I have anything to hide from the law, but one would just generally think, this isn't good.

"A snake." I answered.

"Did ya get 'em?"

"Yes sir, I sure did." I was pretty proud of my shootin. Daddy taught me to shoot, one Sunday morning before church, whilst we were sittin' on the back porch waitin' for Mama.

The sheriff chuckled and then said. "There were two shots."

"The first shot was a warning shot." I answered. I heard the sheriff chuckle again. He must be bored,' I thought.

"Whatcha' usin'?" He asked.

'Yeah, he's bored,' I decided for sure.

"Lyle, my thirty-eight." I was startin' to kinda' like the sheriff.

"You call your gun Lyle?"

"Sure do, 'cause he sings so good." I said, wishin' that Lyle was my cowboy man.

"I call mine Horace 'cause I bought him from Horace."

"Horace? Well, I haven't had the pleasure." I cooed.

"You use rat shot?" The sheriff asked.

"No, just bullets." I knew he'd be impressed.

"Well, little lady if you'd used rat shot, you'd got 'em on the first shot."

"Where do I get me some rat shot, around here?"

"Horace's Guns and Ammo."

"Thanks for the tip, sheriff."

"Sure enough little lady. Hope to see you at Horace's."

"I really did like the sheriff."

I'm still at the house where I lived when I lived. The house is a ramshackle old roadhouse. That's polite talk for whore house. I'm really not surprised that I'm still here at the old house, even with being dead and all.

You know, I had a suspicion from the beginning that the house was spooked, but I didn't care much. My whole family carries on with ghosts, especially mama did. Mama went on ahead many years ago. I'm pretty sure that when mama saw the light, she didn't walk into it, she ran and never looked back. I always thought she would be there to lead me over when my time came, but I haven't seen her around any. I did see an old cowboy one day, but that was while I was still amongst the living.

It was late one afternoon; I hadn't slept well the night before. The sound of laughter, music and dancing had kept me awake pretty near most the night. The sounds were bothersome, but I had made a deal with the spirits that shared their home with me. It was settled. They would leave me alone; I would look after the place, and they would have a hi oh time at night while I slept. Not the best deal I've ever struck.

It was the dancing I was mainly thinkin' about that afternoon. I was wondering if Lyle Lovett liked to dance. I was hopin' he didn't. You see I've never been much of a dancer. I have trust issues, so the thought of being led around backwards with my eyes closed doesn't really appeal to me. So, I was thinkin' that there should be some kind of dance intervention clinic. Just in case Lyle did like to dance. I had the notion that the clinic would be run by a dance intervention professional.

The clinic's therapy would consist of falling backwards, blindfolded into a trusted partner's arms. I figured I'd begin my dance therapy by falling to a nice waltz, then move on to falling to a samba, and finally graduate to falling to a spirited rumba. Well, I was just thinkin'.

Anyway, just when I was getting ready to fall backwards into Lyle's arms, I heard a ruckus coming from the chicken coop. I ran out the back door. I was determined to get that fox that was studying for my chickens. I ran past the old-abandoned bath house to the chicken coop that sits at the edge of my property. Surprisingly, I found the chickens just doing their regular chicken stuff. Bitty, Dot, Bertha, and Penelope were playing pinochle. (Kidding about the pinochle, they were really shooting dice.) Powder was chasing down a big, yummy roach, and Clementine and Penny were arguing over bits of lint. It was *always* something with those two. Anyway, the whole lot was normal; I started back to my house. As I passed the old bath house, I heard a noise coming from inside. I thought it was probably a possum making a home in the junk that I had stashed in there, so I picked up a big stick and opened the door. Taken aback, I stood in the open door and stared at a weathered cowboy, wearing a ten-gallon hat, bathing in an old copper tub.

"Close the door. You're letting in a draft." He called out in a gravelly voice.

I ran back to my house, like there was no tomorrow. A few days later my curiosity got the best of me. I went back to the bath house, opened the door a crack and peeped in. The cowboy was there, just like before.

"Are you in or out, Missy?"

"Ii-in I guess." I sputtered.

I sat on a stool in the corner of the dusty bath house and regained my composure.

"Wha, - wha, what are you doing here?" So much for composure.

"Bathing. Are you blind, girl?"

I didn't want to be rude and just blurt out, "You're a ghost!" in case he didn't know. So, I thought I should ask him again very slowly.

"No, what - are - you - doing - here?"

"Bathing. Are - you - blind - girl?"

"Why are you here?" I thought I'd better just start over.

The cowboy leaned forward and pushed his hat back.

"I'm dancin' with Miss Fancy tonight, and I paid an extra nickel for this bath. Miss Fancy's expecting me, so if you'll excuse me now, Missy…" With that the cowboy disappeared.

I walked back to my old roadhouse. That night I slept well, knowing that the sound of laughter and distant music was just the weathered old cowboy leading Miss Fancy around the parlor backwards with her eyes closed.

THE CONCERT

"Look what came today." Miriam held up the shiny new dog tag for Vicky to approve of. The engraving across the front of the tag reads, 'Rocky, My Hero.'

"Rocky sure is your hero, Miriam. If she hadn't of jumped in front of that hit man that was chasing you, well, I'd hate to think, but we'd probably both be goners. What are you cooking?" Vicky leans over Miriam's shoulder to get a look at her brew.

"Soup." Miriam stirs the steaming cauldron. 'We'd probably both be goners Miriam doesn't need to dissect that phrase to understand it. She continues with the preparation of her latest batch of chicken soup.

"Smells good." Vicky leans in for one more sniff.

"Ja, good." Miriam nudges her back.

When this fresh batch is finished it will go into the freezer with the rest of the quarts upon quarts of soup. The soup then sits in frozen suspended animation, awaiting its future steaming hot reanimation. Miriam adds another ingredient to the latest pot of broth and offers Vicky a steaming spoon full.

"Taste this. How is it?" Miriam dribbles the spoonful of soup into Vicky's open mouth.

"Geez, Miriam, hot!" Vicky exaggerates as she fans her mouth with her hand.

"Mm, ja, good." Miriam tries a spoonful for herself.

"What have you got girl, Teflon lips?"

"What came today, Vicky? Is it the make-up you ordered? Did my lipstick come?"

" No make-up Sugar."

"Fiddlesticks."

"Fiddlesticks? Where did you learn that expression?"

"From the old movie channel. People say fiddlesticks. I think it means; I am sad. It is best to learn the expressions from the beginning. I learn everything at TV." Miriam smiles.

"At TV?" Vicky smiles. "On TV, not, at TV, sugar." Vicky corrects. Miriam pouts she doesn't like to get her words wrong.

"Mike's got three tickets to the concert at the Forum this Friday?"

Vicky is excited at the prospect of finally leaving the confines of her home. She spent six weeks in the Tampa General Hospital recovering from a bullet wound; she spent another month in rehab and months languishing on her couch. Miriam has hovered over her friend, and guardian, all the while, making certain there will be no shortage of chicken soup, earmarked especially for Vicky's recovery.

Rocky sat on the floor next to Vicky. She pays close attention since her people have mentioned her name. She is certain the next familiar word will be cheese since they *are* standing in the kitchen. Miriam attaches the tag to Rocky's collar. Rocky sniffs it. It doesn't smell like cheese, but as soon as she can get to it, she will taste it just to make sure. Her people seem happy though, so Rocky is happy. She jumps back up on the couch and curls up.

Rocky is Vicky's American Dingo, she has ears that are too big for her head, gentle, soft brown eyes and a scraggly red coat that hangs on her svelte body. Vicky picked Rocky out of a backyard litter. When anyone asks Vicky, "What kind of a dog is Rocky?" Vicky just smiles and answers in her lovely southern drawl, "She's a lucky dog."

"Are you sure you're strong enough to go out?" Miriam stirs the simmering broth.

"I'm good, I'm sure, and Doctor Knowles even says so. He said I can start doing things. Mike got us tickets and we're going." A night out sounds like just the thing to Vicky. She doesn't want any more chicken soup, she wants to go out, and now being out in the world again finally seems to be a reality.

Vicky has made up her mind; she flops onto the couch and slides her feet under the sleeping Rocky foot warmer. She easily tires these days, but she will never let on to Miriam.

"I've never been to a concert, not even when I was at home. Do you want dumplings?"

"Sure, dumplings are good. Vicky doesn't want any more chicken soup or dumplings she wants a night out.

"You're going to enjoy the concert sugar. I know, I am. Oh, and Mike called he'll be here soon."

Vicky looks over at Eliakim. Eliakim, Miriam's protector, stands quietly in the corner of the room. Eliakim, Rocky, and Vicky had surely saved Miriam from the hit man who had been sent to silence her. It was the hit man's bullet that had sent Vicky to the hospital's intensive care unit.

"I will take care of him." Miriam walks Eliakim back to her closet.

"We need to talk to Mike about everything. You know that, don't you sugar?" Vicky followed Miriam to her room.

"I know, but where will we begin? The trip here? The Monastery? Maybe we should start with Eliakim." Miriam hangs her head. She trusts Mike but telling him about Eliakim and her past is another matter. Miriam's presents is unquestionably another matter. It is going to be tough to come clean to Mike.

"We'll figure it out, sugar. Come on, I hear the door." Already at the door, Rocky is barking and turning in circles, her usual greeting for Mike.

"Hi, Michael." Vicky kisses Mike hello. Every time they kiss Vicky feels a spark.

"Hi, sweet pea." Mike feels the spark too. As a matter of fact, he felt the spark the first time he laid eyes on Vicky. That was six years ago on the day she became his partner. Vicky will not be Mike's partner when she returns to work. He recently passed the detectives exam, and now most of his work would be done in the station at his desk. Mike heard, by the station grapevine, that when Vicky returned to the department, she would be taken off the street and put on desk duty permanently. Vicky won't be anyone's partner; she will be devastated.

It is said that virtue is its own reward, Mike's virtue is patience, and it has finally rewarded him. Mike stayed in the hospital at Vicky's' bedside as she struggled for her life. It was during that time, as Vicky was slowly recovering, that he finally declared his love for her.

"How are you feeling, sweet pea?" Mike sat on the couch; Vicky snuggled in next to him and laid her head on his shoulder. "Got any sweet tea?" Mike nuzzled Vicky's hair.

"Yeah, I just made a fresh batch." Miriam called from the kitchen.

"I feel great, Michael. What time are we leaving for the concert tomorrow?" Vicky snuggled a little closer. Miriam set Mike's tea on the coffee table, took a seat in the armchair, and started flipping through the channels. "I'm going to meet you there. I have to talk to the kid in witness protection. He remembered something about the Vicente family." Mike's fingers gently twirled Vicky's curly blond hair as he spoke.

"Oh Michael, not tomorrow." Vicky pulled back and frowned.

"Sorry, sweet pea, tomorrow is the only time we have." Mike pulled Vicky back.

"Don't worry, I'll meet you there." Mike kissed her temple.

"How long is the boy going to be here?" Vicky wasn't satisfied.

"We have a three-hour window, then he's gone. We'll need to get him in and out before anyone even knows he's here."

Mike leaned forward mostly to change the subject, but also to give Rocky a real proper greeting. He took the loose skin of Rocky's neck in his hands jiggling it back and forth as he spoke to her.

"Yeah, eebees, good girl. You like those eebees don't you, Rocky girl?" Rocky obviously liked it; she was smiling her biggest dog smile ever.

Miriam stopped flipping through the channels and looked from Vicky to Mike and Rocky and then leaned over to Vicky.

"Eebees?" She whispered. Miriam wasn't the only one who was confused by Mike's display of affection. Vicky just shrugged.

"Look, Vic, she really likes this." Mike continued jiggling Rocky. "Come on try it she likes it," Mike grinned.

"It's okay, Michael I'll pass on the eebees. Just make sure you make it on Friday." Vicky leaned her head back on Mike's shoulder and rolled her eyes.

❧

The Tampa Forum is crowded with fans. Vicky and Miriam made their way to their third-row seats.

"We'll leave the aisle seat for Michael we'll switch around when he gets here. Don't let anyone take that seat. Hear Miriam?" Vicky raised her voice to be heard over the crowd.

"It's so noisy." Miriam covered her ears.

"It'll calm down once the lights go out. Until then, you can whoop and holler all you want." Vicky instructs Miriam on proper concert etiquette and continues her text with Michael.

"Oh. Okay, whoop and holler." Slang is confusing to Miriam, so she isn't really sure what all whoop and holler consisted of.

The world which Miriam once knew, and this unfamiliar world have recently collided; Vicky is doing her best to help Miriam bridge the gap between those two worlds. Now circumstances, which are outside of Miriam's control *and* beyond her wildest dreams, are continually redefining her. Miriam turns to the woman who has taken Mike's seat.

"That seat is taken." Miriam leans close to the woman, so she doesn't have to holler.

"I'm so excited. I've never been to one of his concerts. I just love that man; I can't believe I'm really here." The woman keeps her eyes on the stage.

"I'm sorry we are expecting someone to come and sit here." Miriam leans a little closer to the woman in case she hadn't heard her and expands her previous statement in case the woman didn't understand.

"He's not coming," The woman states as if she knows it to be a fact.

Vicky tugs Miriam's arm; she is still texting with Mike.

"Michael's not coming. He can't break loose. He's going to miss the concert." Vicky is disappointed.

"Really, I wonder how she knew."

"Who knew, sugar?"

"The woman that's sitting in Mike's seat." Miriam rolled her eyes toward the woman and bobbed her head in the direction of Mike's seat. Vicky leans forward and looks past Miriam. All she sees is Mike's empty seat.

"What woman would that be, Miriam?"

"There was a woman sitting there just a second ago."

"It's okay, sugar. I believe you. When I was a little girl, I had a broken arm and a tiny little man in a three-piece suit, peeled my banana for me then disappeared."

No one ever believed Vicky's story about the strange, smartly dressed, banana peeling, little man, except her strange little grandmother.

"She was sitting right there." Miriam insisted.

"Hush, Lyle's coming on."

∽

"Mike, are you riding with us this weekend?"

"I don't think so, David, I missed a concert with Vicky last week. I think I'll spend some make up time with her this weekend. By the way, David, what are you doing here? Did you quit your day job?" Mike looks up from the mound of paper he is searching through and grins at his friend.

"Had to! That last month with your girl was too much." David laughs.

"Yeah, she can be a handful." Mike teased. The day Vicky was shot Doctor David Knowles saved Vicky's life.

Mike continues to search through the files on his desk. His attention is on the Vicente crime family. The meeting with the boy in witness protection had not been as rewarding as Mike had hoped. He doesn't know exactly what he is looking for, but he will continue going through the files until he finds it. He feels as if he owed his father that and so much more. He is determined that he will close the case that cost his father his life.

"I saw Miriam on the way in here. How's she working out? Has her memory returned? Has she remembered anything at all?"

"She's doing good. Vicky and I had to pull some strings to get her here, but she's doing a great job. I don't think she remembers anything yet. Vicky would know more about that, they're pretty close you know."

"You think it's okay if I stop and say 'hi' on my way out?

"I think she'd like that, David."

"Good, I will then. There's a ride next weekend, Mike. Hope you can make that one."

"I'll try," Mike returns to studying his files.

"Catch you then."

"Sure, see you later, David."

Miriam is poring over the stack of papers that she's filing when David crept up behind her.

"How's the best patient in the world?" He whispers over her shoulder.

"Doctor Knowles, are you trying to frighten me?" Miriam giggles; she is glad to see the young doctor.

"I just wanted to say hi. I haven't seen you since the memorial service." David's eyes reflected his sorrow.

"I miss him too." Miriam shares the sadness of the passing of their friend Doctor Rubenstein.

Samuel Rubenstein consulted with David during Miriam's stay in Tampa General, unbeknownst to David the sly old doctor had discovered Miriam's secret and devised a complicated plan to help her navigate her life. David suspected that Doctor Rubenstein and Miriam had put together some sort of elaborate plan, but he had acquiesced to the doctors' wisdom and experience, and never let his suspicions be known, nor will he ever. David would probably never know exactly what the doctor and this charming enigma had conjured up, but he accepted it without question or reservation.

"So, how's the old bean?" David Knowles gently taps Miriam's temple with his finger and changes the subject.

"What bean?"

"Brain, brain." David clarified.

"So, bean and brain are the same ja? That's interesting." Miriam knows what he is asking but she would rather play dumb than deceive her friend.

"Yes, bean and brain are the same. You're silly girl." David laughed. "Are you taking good care of Vicky?"

"Vicky who?" Miriam giggles again.

"Okay, now *you're* pulling *my* leg.

"It wasn't me." Miriam holds her hands up for David to see and laughs.

"You're impossible girl." David's pager buzzed, he hugs Miriam goodbye and hurries on his way.

Miriam returns to filing. It is the same thing that she did for Doctor Rubenstein before his death. The old doctor had created the job for Miriam in his office, to satisfy social services. Then, he persuaded Vicky to take Miriam into her home and act as her guardian to prevent her from being placed in an institution. She misses her friend, Doctor Rubenstein.

Miriam is almost finished filing the last stack of folders when a paper fell to the floor. Miriam picks up the paper. Reward for information about the death of this woman, is printed in bold letters above the top of the picture of the woman. Below the picture was printed the contact information and the woman's name, Grace Standard.

"You look familiar, Grace. Where have I seen you before?" Miriam whispers. She puts the paper on top of the filing cabinet and continues filing the last of the folders; she would insert the wayward paper when she came across Grace Standard's file.

"Are you almost done? It's five o'clock, Miriam." Mike is anxious to leave the station. He plans to take Miriam home, and then he and Vicky will take off for a long weekend on St. Petersburg beach.

"I'm almost finished I only have this one last paper." Miriam reaches for the paper that she had placed on top of the filing cabinet. It wasn't there. Miriam looks on the floor and behind the cabinet for the missing paper. The paper is nowhere to be found.

"Don't worry about it. You'll find it on Monday. Come on, let's clock out."

∾

St. Petersburg, Florida is a trendy beach community, famous for the green park benches that line the city sidewalks, and the throngs of widowed seniors that have retired to the balmy tourist town. The sunbaked retirees flitter around the green benches like squawking flocks of seagulls, looking for the perfect green perch on which to land, a sign to other old seagulls of their availability, and desire to attract a mate. The benches of St. Petersburg are the answer for many of the lonely hearted who find a second or maybe even a third chance at romance.

The beautiful white sandy beaches of Saint Petersburg are a frequented getaway spot for the locals and tourists alike, but the Tampa natives avoid the streets of Saint Pete at all costs *and* the sunbaked retirees of the balmy tourist town who mindlessly drive the streets of that trendy beach community. The Tampa natives laughingly refer to Saint Pete as 'the town of the newly wed and the nearly dead,' who are often one in the same.

"We'll be back on Sunday, sugar. Don't do anything crazy while I'm gone." Vicky is pretty sure that Miriam wouldn't do anything crazy . . . again.

"Don't worry Vicky. Since Sister Theresa Marie went home, I no longer have a partner in crime." Miriam whispers so Mike won't hear. Vicky really can't admonish Miriam too harshly for breaking into the Holy Trinity Monastery, since she is somewhat complicit. As one of Miriam's only friends at the time, Vicky aided Miriam in the nefarious deed of freeing Eliakim, from the cloister of the monastery. Vicky acted as the getaway driver and still struggles with the recollection of that wicked deed and night of unabridged transgression. Miriam picks up Vicky's overnight bag.

"Give me that bag. I can carry it, I'm not helpless!" Vicky reaches for her overnight bag. Miriam gave her a playful slap on the hand and carries the bag from the room.

"Ja, I know you can carry it, and Doctor Knowles even said so." Miriam teases as she carries the overnight bag to the door.

"You're getting pretty sassy girl."

"I know I am impossibility!" Miriam smiled.

"Impossible Miriam you are impossible." Vicky shakes her head. Mike quit playing a game of tug of war with Rocky, greets Miriam and meets Vicky at the front door.

"All ready to go?" Mike takes Vicky's bag and walks to his car. Vicky turns to Miriam.

"Make sure Eliakim is out while I'm gone. Keep the door chained. "Hear?" she whispers.

"I will as soon as you leave. Go now, have a good time. See you Sunday." Miriam chains the door. Miriam has every intention of following Vicky's instructions to the letter, and she certainly isn't planning to do anything crazy. She and Rocky are heading back to her closet, to wake Eliakim when the doorbell rings.

"Maybe Vicky forgot something. I'll beat you to the door, Rocky."

Miriam's challenge sent Rocky running down the hall. Rocky is sitting at the door, smiling a happy dog smile when Miriam catches up. Miriam peeped through the peep hole, just as Vicky taught her.

"No one is here, Rocky." Miriam looks down at Rocky who is cocking her head from side to side, intently studying Miriam.

"You're such a good dog, Rocky. How long have you been a dog?" Miriam patted Rocky's head and turned back toward her room. Vicky has often heard Miriam ask Rocky how long she's been a dog, but she dismisses this odd query, holding to the belief that it's some turn of phrase, from her first language, that has lost meaning in translation.

"Let's go get Eliakim." Miriam and Rocky race to her bedroom.

Miriam goes to the closet, and wakes Eliakim. Her golem lumbers out of the closet. Rocky jumps onto the bed cocks her head from side to side, again closely scrutinizing Miriam.

"Why are you looking at Eliakim so hard, Rocky. It's alright, you know him. Come on, you silly girl." She calls Rocky to follow her from the room. Rocky does not follow. Instead, she paws a crumpled piece of paper lying on the bed.

"What have you got?" Miriam lifts the paper from under Rocky's paws and smooths it. Reward for the information about the death of this woman is printed above a picture.

"Grace Standard! Rocky, how did you get this?" Miriam looks at Rocky and then over at Eliakim who stands at the door where she left him.

"I will figure this out later. I'm hungry now Rocky, let's get something to eat. Come on, girl." Puzzled Miriam puts the paper in her pocket and heads to the kitchen. Miriam takes a few cartons of left-over Chinese takeout from the refrigerator.

"Maybe we should make scoodle, you like that. Ja, Rocky?" Scoodle is Miriam's specialty, Rocky loves it! Vicky won't touch it. Miriam puts a large skillet on the stove and begins scoodling, a large spoonful of margarine, egg foo young, and sesame honey chicken with garlic green beans.

"Ja, good, yummy, but I think it needs something else." Miriam searches the condiments lining the fridge door. Finally emerging with her ultimate and favorite choice she pours a generous helping of ketchup into her concoction.

"There, that is good now. Are you hungry, Rocky?" Rocky cocks her head and rotates her ears. Miriam heads for the couch. Eliakim stands in the corner of the room. Rocky sits next to Miriam on the couch and savors the aroma of scoodle that hung in the air. Miriam would save the last bite of scoodle for Rocky. Rocky knows that she always gets the last bite, so she never begs, but she does watch the bites very closely. Rocky is satisfied with her last bite; she snuggles up to Miriam on the couch. Miriam starts clicking through the TV channels; she will lie on the couch with Rocky and watch old movies until they both fall into the arms of Morpheus.

"Wake up. Rise and shine."

Miriam looks at Rocky, sleeping at the end of the couch. It is late, the television has turned itself off. She must have been dreaming, Rocky can't talk, at least she hasn't yet. Miriam closes her eyes.

"Wake up. Rise and shine."

Miriam sits straight up. Now she is wide awake, so is Rocky. Miriam looks around the darkened room. She can make out the shadowy figure of a woman standing next to Eliakim. The woman moves toward Miriam.

"Eliakim help me." Miriam calls out to her protector. Eliakim does not move. Miriam looks from Eliakim to the woman who is now standing at the end of the couch.

"Who are you, what do you want?"

The woman remains silent; Miriam struggles to see the woman's face through the darkness. The woman sat on the end of the couch. The dim light in the kitchen cast enough light on the woman for Miriam to recognize her as the woman that she had seen at the concert, and the dead woman, Grace Standard.

"Do I smell scoodle? Mmm, my favorite." The woman speaks.

"Ja, scoodle. You like scoodle?" Miriam is trying to act nonchalant as if this isn't the first time she has ever spoken to a ghost.

"I'm teasin' you, hon. I heard you earlier. I never had any scoodle." Grace smiled.

"Oh, that's funny, Grace." Miriam laughs nervously.

"Call me Gracie. Did you like the concert? I sure did."

"Yes, I did, Gracie. What are you doing here? If you don't mind me asking."

"No, hon, I don't mind you askin', but I sure don't have an answer, I can't even make one up. You know, I'm not exactly sure yet how this dead thing works but I'll figure it out, that's a fact."

"Oh, good, you know. I wasn't sure if you knew you are dead." Miriam is strangely relieved.

"Well, why wouldn't I know? I lost my life not my mind, child."

"Yes of course, I apologize. How did you get here?"

"I followed you home after the concert."

"Why?"

"I saw you at the concert, and then when you saw me and spoke to me, I had to figure this out. I've been watchin' you at work this week, but you didn't notice me again, so I took my picture from the files. I was tryin' to get your attention. Guess it worked, since here we are havin' a sleep over. Nice, huh? Want me to paint your toenails?"

"Uh, no thanks." Miriam looks down at her feet.

"No one has seen me since I passed 'cept you and animals. Rocky's been gawkin' at me all week. What's the fella's name in the corner?" Gracie keeps up the conversation.

"His name is Eliakim." Miriam hopes Gracie will move on to another topic.

"What's with him? He's pretty quiet."

"He does not talk."

"What's wrong with him? He looks okay." Gracie circles Eliakim.

"He is okay. He's a Golem."

"Pardon me, hon. He's a what?"

"He's a golem, he is a creature. I made him out of clay. I brought him to life, and now he obeys me." Miriam decides she might as well satisfy Gracie's curiosity and get it over with, since the dearly departed soul probably isn't going to be spreading that secret around anyway.

"He's a mighty good-lookin' golem. Can't say I've ever seen any other golem, but he sure is right pretty."

"You say you have been here all week, why haven't I seen you before now?" Miriam is puzzled.

"I don't know, but I'm bound and determined to find out."

"You can be invisible if you want?" Miriam is trying to figure exactly how this works.

"No, hon, I'm guessin' I can be visible. I'm always invisible. Come here, you'll see." Gracie glides over to the wall mirror and Miriam follows. They stand in front of the mirror, but only Miriam's reflection appears.

"So, you are still invisible, but I can see you. How do you do that?"

"Don't know that either, hon." Gracie shakes her head.

Miriam returns to the couch and tries to take a mental inventory of what is unfolding. Gracie glides over to where Eliakim stands and studies him. She leans over and appears to sniff him.

"Are you sniffing him?" Miriam's foreknown suppositions are muddled.

Gracie laughs. "No just remembering." Gracie closes her eyes, for a moment. "Mm, Eau de clay, my favorite fragrance, so earthy." Gracie turns her attention back to the conversation with Miriam but keeps her eyes on Eliakim.

"Why you're seein' me. I can't honestly say, because I don't really know. I think it has more to do with you than me. Don't worry, I'm workin' on figuring that out too." Gracie returns to circling Eliakim.

"Where are you when you aren't following people home?' Miriam is curious especially because of her own *unplanned* trip up and back from the unknown.

"I stay pretty close to my house; I wander around some, but actually this is the first time that I've really left Kumquat since well . . . I passed."

"Gracie, can you remember the day that you 'passed'?"

"Oh, sure, I can recall it like it was yesterday. Well, I recall some of it anyway. Ole' Miss Wallace had come by; she's my neighbor and a big ole' busybody. We had a piece of cake and a cup of tea to celebrate her birthday. I had thought she was getting a little daffy lately, but that proved it, since we had celebrated her birthday last year in January and this was November. Well, she had just left, it was early, but I was tired, so I went to bed and fell right to sleep. I woke up in the night and I thought I was dreaming 'cause I saw a figure standing in my room, then I thought, well it must be one of the spirits that share the house with me. It didn't look like any specter that I'd seen before, so I sat up in bed to get a better look. I tried to see its face. Now, you're probably going to think I'm off my rocker," Gracie continues. "But the thing didn't have but one face. It had a jumble of faces, but I wasn't scared. He reached out his hand; I took it and got out of the bed. I felt very safe and loved, you know, the warm fuzzies." "Ja, so where did you go with that specter?" Miriam does not know exactly what the warm fuzzies means, but she does know exactly what the specter with the jumbled-up faces mean.

"I didn't go anywhere, and when I turned around to go back to bed, I saw that I was still lying there looking for all the world like I was sleepin."

"I could just hear that ole' Miss Wallace, what she would be saying in the morning . . .. "And did you hear about Gracie Standard? Well, she woke up dead this morning!" But I fooled them all 'cause I don't feel dead at all, as a matter of fact I've never felt so alive. Go ahead hon, touch me I'm real."

Miriam touches Gracie's arm a small jolt of electricity shot through Miriam's fingers. Miriam pulls her hand back, but the tingling continues.

"I have seen that spirit, Gracie. That spirit somehow helped me get here."

"Get out. You mean you've seen the same spirit with all the faces that I've seen? Well, I'll be. That's really strange. Where'd you get here from, hon?"

"I was brought here from Germany."

"I thought that you must be foreign, with your odd accent and all."

Miriam stares in disbelief at Gracie. She is sure that Gracie is the only one in the room with an 'odd' accent.

"The fact is, when I was taken from Germany and brought here, it was more than sixty years that passed in an instant. I saw that spirit right before."

"My stars and garters, girl, that's really strange." Gracie and Miriam are redefining strange by the minute. "Girl I'm not bein' judgey and if you say so; but damn, sixty years or *more* you say? My land, my, my, my. What on earth were you doin' there in Germany?" "I was a prisoner of war."

"I was hiding in a monastery, but the Gestapo found me. I was taken to a detainment center but then I escaped.

I believe that spirit you saw, is the spirit, called Sandalphon who is charged with guarding all humans."

"Sandalphon, why do you think that's the specter's name?"

"My father was a Kabbalist he taught me about the spirits and things before we became separated.

"A Kabbalist, haven't heard about that."

"He was a Jewish wise man." Miriam kept the explanation simple for Gracie.

"Also, what I learned from my father is what helped me when I created Eliakim."

"Eliakim, yeah he's good lookin'. Good job girl." Gracie went back over to Eliakim, she ran her hand across his shoulder, and then up the side of his neck.

"Nice, can he see me?" she cooed.

"Ja, I think not, since he didn't respond when I asked him to protect me from you." Gracie's obvious infatuation with Eliakim was making Miriam a little uneasy. She could not nor did she want to even try to wrap her mind around a golem / ghost relationship.

"So he does whatever you ask him to?"

"No, obviously not. Are you going back to Kumquat?"

"Well, I want to, but I'm not sure how to get back. I came here with you from the concert; maybe you can take me back to Kumquat." Miriam studies Gracie. Gracie is floating back over toward Eliakim again.

"Okay, come on, Gracie, I'll call us a taxi."

"Is Eliakim coming?" Gracie perks up.

"No, Gracie, I don't think so!"

"Well, all I know is what it says on that paper in your pocket, about me being dead and all. Lord knows I could have been murdered. I don't know but it sounds like there's some pretty tough characters around Kumquat. I'm just sayin' might be smart to have a big handsome golem along for protection you know what I mean?" Gracie grins.

～

"10801 Sweet Blossom Road." Miriam directs the taxi driver to the address that Gracie had given her.

"That's in Kumquat ain't it?"

"Yes, on the east side, out toward the orchards."

"Not orchards, groves." Gracie corrects Miriam.

"Quiet. Do you want him to hear you?"

"HEAR ME?" Gracie screams. Miriam covers her ears to muffle the deafening sound. I CAN SCREAM AT THE TOP OF MY LUNGS AND HE CAN'T HEAR ME A BIT!" Gracie laughs.

"Stop it. Stop it. Quiet down Gracie or I *will* put you out right here, or I will make him take us back then you won't ever get home!" Miriam is tired and feeling a little cranky.

"You know it's kinda' tight in here, I could sit up on his lap." Gracie offered. "Gracie, you are not going to sit on anyone's lap, settle down. I'm not telling you again," Miriam can't believe she let the ghost talk her into bringing Eliakim; Gracie's tomfoolery is wearing thin. The taxi driver watches through the rear-view mirror as the drama is unfolding in his back seat. The young woman is covering her ears shaking her head and threatening to put her silent companion out of the taxi, if he doesn't quiet down. The driver isn't quite sure what the sitting on the lap is about. The woman continues threatening the man as they ride toward Kumquat. The driver after taking into consideration the obvious insanity that is taking place in the backseat of his taxi and the size and stature of the woman's companion opted not to comment on the fact that he has never known a man to be named Gracie. Yes, that is one comment that he will definitely forgo.

"Here we are. That's fifteen dollars and seventy cents ma'am."

"Will you please wait? I'll be right out." Miriam digs in her pocket for a twenty.

"I have another fare waiting." The driver gruffly made an excuse.

"Then can you come back in about an hour and pick me up?" Miriam pays the driver, while the passengers seen, and unseen piled out of the taxi.

"Sure, lady I'll come back. Yeah, sure, about an hour." The taxi's tires squeal as the driver speeds away.

Miriam, Gracie, and Eliakim stand in front of the old roadhouse that Gracie has called home for so many years; she hoped to spend her entire natural life in the old house that she loved so dearly. Gracie had thought she would grow old and die quietly in her sleep there. Well, she was partially right she did die in her sleep.

"You can get in the back door; it never did lock. Come on, I'll show you." Gracie led Miriam and Eliakim through the tall weeds to the back door. Miriam turned the knob, the door opened.

"See, I told you, come on in. It's okay." Gracie invited her guests in. They stood in Gracie's kitchen it was antiquated. It looked as if it had not been remodeled since the turn of the century. The light of the full moon illuminated the old house. Miriam noticed a cowering spirit sitting in a corner next to a small door that looks like a pantry door, it's secured shut by a large heavy pad lock.

"Who is that sitting in the corner Gracie?"

"That's Elizabeth ignore her." Gracie glides from the kitchen into the living room. Miriam and Eliakim followed.

"Okay, Gracie, you're home now. I suppose that is all you needed from me." Miriam is interrupted by a sound coming from the porch; she hides in the shadows and crept to the window. Through the dusty lace curtains, she can make out the figure of an old woman sneaking around the porch trying to peer through the windows into the darkened house.

"That's Ole' Miss Wallace she probably saw the taxi." Gracie stands at the window that the old woman is peering into.

"But it's three o'clock in the morning." Miriam whispers as she watches the old woman try each window.

"I swear, she sees everything night or day." Gracie follows Miss Wallace from one window to the next. There is a quick burst of light, and Miss Wallace turned and ran home.

"Boy howdy, she really high tailed it. I'd split my sides laughing if I actually had sides that would split."

"What was that flash?" Miriam asks.

"It was me. That scares people away."

"How do you do that?"

"It's kind of a reflex, like when you get scared, and your hair stands up on edge. Well, when I get scared or excited, I make a flash of light. Easy like this see." Gracie squinches her eyes tight and grunts. Nothing happens.

"I haven't got all the bug's worked out yet, but I've got time to work with it." Gracie squinched her eyes one more time, still nothing. Miriam chokes back a giggle.

Gracie begins searching through a desk and then a pile of papers that lie on a table beside her couch. She pulls papers and pictures from drawers and cubby holes and drops them where she stands. Miriam follows Gracie from the living room into her bedroom. Gracie searches the bedstands and the bookcase in the room. Miriam notices that the whole house had been completely ransacked.

"Gracie what are you looking for? You've made a big mess here."

"I'm looking for something. I didn't make all this mess, but I guess I didn't make it better."

"Who made this mess if you didn't? You are the only one here."

"I don't know."

"What is it that you are looking for?"

"I don't know. I can't remember, but it's important. I have to find it." Gracie sat on the bed and began to cry. "Really, I don't remember much about my last day except bits and pieces. I don't know what happened to me. I don't know why I'm still here. I don't know why you see me or hear me. I don't know why I went to the concert and saw you. I don't know why anything. I just don't know anything." Gracie sobs.

"Gracie how did you get to the concert? Do you remember how you got there? Did you follow someone like you followed me?"

"That is the strange thing," Gracie began as if this whole evening has been the norm.

"I was here at my house when a raven landed right over there outside my bedroom window. I went to the window and looked out and low and behold if that raven didn't have the same faces as that spirit that I saw the night I passed; you know it was all that jumbled up mess of faces.

Well, I guess I don't have to tell you what a surprise that was, seein' that bird with all those tiny little faces floating around its head. I opened the window and the bird hopped in. Then, I was there at the concert sitting next to you and you were tellin' me that the seat was taken."

"Tiny faces are you sure?"

"Yes, hon, tiny faces."

"Sandalphon." Miriam whispered.

THE TRUTH IS…

"Thank you for bringing us home, officer." The officer opened the back door of his cruiser and let Miriam and Eliakim out in Vicky's driveway.

"No problem. Tell Vicky we hope she's back to work soon."

Miriam is tired; she just wants to clean herself up and go to sleep. It has been a long walk in the wee hours of the morning, from Gracie's house to the highway where finally she and Eliakim had been spotted and picked up by a Tampa police officer as they walked along a deserted highway toward Bayshore Boulevard.

"Miriam! Where have you been? I've been so worried!" Vicky flung the front door open.

"I thought you were coming home tomorrow. What happened?" Miriam is surprised to see Vicky.

"Mike was called to go in this morning, but we're going to meet for lunch." Vicky smiles a dreamy smile. "NO! Where have you been? I've had the police out looking for you since five o'clock this morning. Where were you?"

"Kumquat." Miriam is so tired she can hardly stand. She sat on the couch; Vicky sat down next to her.

"Geez, no! Miriam, not the monastery again!"

"No, Vicky. It was this." Miriam takes the crumpled paper from her pocket and shows it to Vicky.

"A reward flyer? That's what you went to Kumquat for?"

"Ja, but no, the flyer came from the files at the station."

"Why did you take a file from the station?"

"I did not take it. She did." Miriam points to the woman's picture on the flier.

"This is a dead woman, Miriam."

"I know, I know. Vicky, it sounds cuckoo, but she came here, and she needed to go home, so I took her home in a taxi last night, well this morning. Ja, it was about two or three this morning." Miriam yawns and laid her head on Vicky's shoulder. "I'm so tired. The taxi didn't come back, so we walked, I got lost. Gracie flashed an old woman in the window." Miriam closes her eyes, exhaustion overcame her.

"Flashed an old woman in the window? Goodness, Miriam what is going on with you? Well, sleep now sugar. Sounds like you had a big night. We'll talk about it later." She kisses Miriam's forehead and makes her comfortable on the couch. Miriam holds the crumpled flyer as she sleeps. Vicky gently takes the paper from Miriam's hand and studies it.

"Grace Standard, I need to find out about you." Vicky dials Mike.

"Hi Michael."

"Hi, sweet pea, I heard that Miriam was escorted home. The officer says she was walking a lonely stretch of highway east of Kumquat with some guy. Is she okay?"

"She's just tired she's sleeping now."

"Who's the guy she was with?"

"Oh him, yeah, uh. He's an old friend from college."

"Should I be worried?" Mike teases he doesn't really want to have to deal with the possibility of a competitor, but he would.

"No, Michael don't worry. He was just passing through and took a chance to stop by. He's leaving on a flight back to Atlanta this afternoon. Sorry you missed him. I think you'd like him." Vicky knew that the truth is sometimes more dangerous than a lie; she has learned that a small detail in a lie is always good, but she will work on a backup lie in case this one falls through. That's because she also knows that if a person is caught in a lie the best thing to do is admit that you lied, beg forgiveness, and say, "the truth is" . . . and then offer the backup lie. Not that she is a big ole' liar but it is useful knowledge when a 'save yourself' situation comes along.

"What were they doing out in Kumquat?"

"Not really sure Michael. I think they were sightseeing."

"Sightseeing in the middle of the night?" Mike is slipping into detective mode.

"I guess they were just kickin' up their heels. Anyway, Eli's a good guy. Whatever they were up to, Miriam was safe. I'm going to go start getting ready for our lunch date. I'm thinking maybe we can take a road trip over to Tarpon Springs and have some Greek food on the sponge docks."

"That sounds really good. We can spend the rest of the day there." Michael is not ready to give up his plan to spend the entire weekend with Vicky.

"Alright, I'll meet you at the station. We'll leave from there; I'd like to say hi to everyone anyway. See you in a bit, Michael. Goodbye." Vicky hangs the phone up and walked back over to Miriam asleep on the couch.

"You sleep now, sugar." Vicky gently comforts her friend. Miriam moans as she often does in fitful sleep.

~

The officers are a tight knit family. Everyone on duty came over to hug Vicky, pat her back, or shake her hand.

"Vicky, it's good to see you."

"You look great."

"When are you coming back to work?"

"We need you."

"You're our hero you know." The officers gather around Vicky like she's a rock star.

"Ya'll stop now. I didn't do anything any one of you wouldn't have done." Embarrassed by the attention, Vicky's eyes plead Mike to rescue her. Mike joins Vicky.

"Yep, don't let her kid you she's a hero alright. Why, you should have seen her run that hit man down. The guy didn't have a chance. Yep, that's my girl a real hero." Mike chuckles. Vicky purses her lips, wrinkles her nose, and squinted her eyes at Michael.

"Okay now, ya'll just back away from my girl. Nothin' to see here, move along." Mike laughs as he rescues Vicky.

"Are you done, Michael?" Vicky takes Michael's arm. "Thanks,' sweetie." Vicky whispers as they walk toward the door.

"Yeah, I'm all ready to go. Did you park in the employee's lot?"

"Yes, I did."

"Good, we'll take my car."

"Mike, I remember that you looked in on the case of that woman in Kumquat that was murdered. Do you remember about it?"

"Yeah, the chief wanted me to tag along after work that day since I was working toward this detective thing. It was ruled a suspicious death not officially murder. Why?"

"I was just wondering if it was ever solved."

"No, it hasn't been."

"What happened to her?" Vicky asked.

"She died in bed. She was stabbed, but that didn't kill her. The autopsy report says she was dead before she was stabbed. Oh, and her nose was broken, also postmortem, strange. No motive for murder. It could have been a robbery gone bad, but it didn't appear that anything was taken. It's a hard case you know there's no rhyme or reason."

"How did she die then, drugs?"

"The only drug found in her was in the sleeping pills she had taken. The bottle was on her bedside table."

"So, it was suicide?"

"No, the coroner found only a trace of Doxylamine it's a sleep aid, not enough to kill anyone. He says possibly she died of an allergic reaction to the sleeping pills."

"Why would she take sleeping pills if she was allergic, and then why was she stabbed, and her nose broken after she was dead? That's odd."

"Why are you asking about that case, Vicky?"

"Oh, I don't know I guess I just got spooked when Miriam showed up in Kumquat and then my thoughts got away from me. I'm glad we still have time to spend together this weekend." She will not bring up Kumquat or Grace Standard again.

❧

Miriam begins to stir; she slept on the couch all afternoon. She opens her eyes. Eliakim stands where she left him earlier. Rocky snoozed at Miriam's feet, off and on, all day. Vicky left a note to Miriam on the coffee table explaining that she will be home in the evening, maybe late and not to wait up for her.

"Come on Rocky. We'll put Eliakim to sleep now." Miriam isn't quite awake yet; she stumbles down the hall listing to the left as she follows the wall to her room. Eliakim follows to his spot in the back of her closet.

"I'm hungry, let's eat." Miriam yawns and tries to shake the sleep from her head.

"I hope Vicky's not too mad with me Rocky. I guess she's not since she put X's and O's at the end of the note, she left for me. She says that means hugs and kisses."

"Do you think the O's mean kisses, or the X's? Three X's mean poison, don't forget that Rocky, it is important." Miriam scrambles two eggs and put a bagel in the toaster. "

"You know, Rocky, the bakers in Germany used to cook bagels in oil, but the oil was taken away from the Jewish bakers, so they started boiling them then baking them. Vicky says if someone gives you lemons make lemonade. Ja, Rocky?"

Rocky just cocked her head and rotated her ears. She listened carefully to Vicky and Miriam when they talked to her, because somewhere in all the blah, blah, blah, they always said "Rocky" and that is the high point of the conversation.

"Let's eat on the deck." Miriam takes her breakfast outside. Rocky watches as Miriam takes a sip of her coffee.

"Don't worry, girl, I didn't forget yours." Miriam puts a cup of coffee on the deck in front of Rocky.

"There you go, Just the way you like it, cream and sugar and it's in your favorite cup. See it's the kitty cup." Miriam makes a tiny meowing sound and Rocky happily laps up the coffee.

"You're such a good dog, Rocky. How long have you been a dog?" Miriam takes another sip of her coffee. Then she puts her cup down and stared into the bottomless darkness of her drink.

"I had a really strange dream, Rocky. But it seemed so real." Miriam held the gaze into her cup. Rocky cocked her head. "Would you like to hear it?" Rocky rotated her ears again. "Alright, since you're interested, I will tell you. It was when I was sleeping on the couch this morning. In my dream, I stood in a dark forest. I could see Sandalphon perched on a limb above a large flat stone that lie on the forest floor. Then a man in a black robe came to the stone with a young woman in a purple robe. The man drew a dagger from his sleeve and pointed to the stone. The woman positioned herself down onto the stone and opened her robe. Then, three more men appeared from the forest and took their places around the stone. Then the first man made a mark on the woman's middle with the point of his dagger. I was very frightened for this woman, but it seemed that she was completely unaware of what was happening. Suddenly, my attention was drawn to Sandalphon. He had spread his wings and was preparing to fly. That is when I became frightened. Then I woke up."

Miriam reached into her pocket and pulled out two black feathers. "I found these next to the couch when I woke up. It's very strange. I'm sure Sandalphon could not have left them, but I have no idea where they came from. What do you think Rocky girl?" Rocky put her head down, stretched out in the sun, and closed her eyes.

"You're right, girl. I'm not going to worry Vicky about two stray feathers. It'll be our little secret for now. At least until I have it all figured out. Ja Rocky?" Miriam leans back and sips her coffee.

She searches for Sandalphon between the feathery leaves of the Mimosa tree, that hung over the deck. Since she has arrived here, there has been quite a lot going on in her life. Starting from the time that she spent recovering, and then there is the time that she spent with Vicky as she lingered in the hospital. Now, her new job at the police station takes a lot of her attention. Miriam feels that she has neglected her feathered friend. What's more, something that Gracie said about a raven on her windowsill stuck in Miriam's mind. Still tired from her night out with Gracie she relaxed on the deck in the shade of the Mimosa. She closed her eyes, but her pause was suddenly interrupted.

"Sandalphon, there you are. Where have you been? I have missed you!" The large raven lands on Miriam's shoulder. Miriam scratches her raven's head. He closes his eyes and enjoys the attention.

"Where are you going, you funny bird?" Sandalphon has suddenly taken back to the sky. Miriam watches him as he flew away.

"He'll be back, Rocky. Don't worry"

❧

Vicky and Mike poke through the curiosity shops that line the sponge docks of Tarpon Springs. A tourist to Tarpon Springs can find anything they can hope for that's made of beach sand or shells, or made of a combination of beach sand and shells. If a person can't find exactly the souvenir that they are looking for, that doesn't mean, it's not there. It's probably just covered by a giant mound of sponges. The mounds of sponges have been gleaned from the floor of the gulf, by the incredibly good-looking Greek sponge divers, and don't they know it.

"There's a little cafe around the corner. It has pastry and the best Greek coffee that you'll ever taste. I think you'll be surprised" Mike led Vicky down a narrow side street to the tiny cafe.

"*Veeky!*" Zoe threw her arms around Vicky. "Oh, I'm sorry did I hurt you? Please sit." Zoe motions for Vicky to sit at one of the bistro tables on the sidewalk in front of the cafe.

"Zoe, what are you doing here?" Vicky is surprised.

"This is my family's other place. I haven't seen you Veeky since before you were hurt. I have missed seeing you come into the Tampa restaurant with Mike." Zoe lowered her voice and leaned toward Vicky. "He's been like a lost puppy. I'm glad you're back."

"Hey, am I invited to this reunion? I *am* the one who brought her. Remember?" Mike pulls a chair up beside Vicky, and grins. "See? I told you that you might be surprised."

Mike and Vicky sat at Zoe's Cafe eating Greek food and pastries; they drank sweet Greek coffee until the sun began to set. Music streamed from the tavern across the street.

"The poster on the window says belly dancers." Vicky drew Mike's attention across the street. "Let's go in there. Have you ever been there, Michael?" Vicky is feeling especially emboldened by her caffeine buzz.

"Yeah, Zorbas, I've been in there. Me and my friends used to sneak in there with fake ID's when we were in high school. It's not a bad place, just a noisy local tavern. I'll tell you though, it does get a little rowdy, but the good thing is if you drink too much ouzo you won't have a hangover in the morning. You just won't be able to make a fist."

"Come on, Michael. Let's go, this'll be fun." Vicky is out of her seat and already to the curb. Vicky snaps her fingers over her head, twirling and gyrating her interpretation of a belly dance as she crosses the street to the tavern.

"Whew, hot, sweet pea, wait for me!" Mike left cash on the table and called out to Zoe.

"Girl gone wild, gotta go!"

～

"Good morning, Vicky I didn't hear you come in last night." Miriam pours herself a cup of coffee.

"We got back really late. You were out like a light. You must have still been tired from your adventure." Vicky looks over the top of the morning paper and raises her eyebrows.

"Did you and Mike have a nice time?" Miriam pretends she didn't notice the eyebrow thing. "Will you pass the sugar?"

Vicky tried to pick up the sugar bowl, but her hand failed her. She pushes the bowl across the table to Miriam.

"Did you hurt your hand, Vicky?" Miriam spoons a large teaspoon full of sugar into her cup.

"No, I just can't seem to make a fist this morning."

"*Oh, my goodness, Vicky!*" Miriam bolts from her chair to the other side of the table and grabs Vicky's hand.

"We need to go see Doctor Knowles, maybe you had a stroke or something maybe worse we have to see Doctor Knowles *now*! He will know what to do." Miriam tries to pull Vicky out of her chair she doesn't budge.

"*Oh no, you're paralyzed!*"

"*Miriam* calm down. I'm okay. Sit down and drink your coffee." Vicky rolls her eyes and shakes her head. Miriam sits back down and picks up her coffee, she peers over her cup to see if Vicky's eyebrows were still doing that scary thing.

"Vicky?"

"Yes, Miriam?"

"I have a very important question to ask you."

"What is it sugar?" Vicky focuses her attention on Miriam.

"It's this . . . do the X's or the O's mean kisses?"

"Sugar, you *are* impossible. What am I going to do with you? We still have to talk about whatever it was that happened the other night."

"I know, and I am really sorry that I made you worry, but I had Eliakim with me." Miriam tried to give the outing a positive spin. "Well, taking Eliakim that was Gracie's idea. I think she likes him."

"Gracie?"

"Ja, you know, Grace Standard."

"Oh, right the dead woman, she likes the golem. I understand perfectly now. Miriam listen to me! Wandering around in the middle of the night is dangerous, you have to realize that. If you get hurt or get into trouble Social Services will take you away from me and put you in another home. I don't want that to happen." Vicky tried her diluted version of scared straight on Miriam.

"Gracie is home in Kumquat now. I think all she needed was a ride; she won't be back, don't worry Vicky, I think she's a little you know. . ." Miriam made a goofy face and circle motions around her temple.

"I don't know Miriam; she sounds like a scam artist ghost to me. I don't know much about ghosts, but from what I've seen in movies ghost don't need to be taken around in taxis. Anyway, I'm just thankful you're alright." Vicky can't believe she has actually used the phrase 'scam artist ghost', she is sure that it is the first time in spoken history those words have been strung together into a sentence.

"Vicky?"

"Yes, sugar?"

"What's a scam artist?"

"It's someone who is really, really, good at tricking someone." Vicky's eyebrows scare Miriam again for just a moment.

"How does that make them an artist?"

"Miriam, too much. I have to get ready to go to the station now. I'm talking to the chief about coming back to work on Monday."

⌒

"Vicky, how do you feel?" The chief got right to the point.

"I feel good, Chief. I'm ready to come back."

"We're glad you're coming back, but you were hurt pretty bad. There was one point when it was doubtful that you would make it. I'm thinking that I'll put you at a desk for a while. Just to see how you do."

"But Chief, the doctor said I am ready to start back."

"You'll have another review in six months then we will reevaluate." The chief closes Vicky's folder and laid it on his desk. The decision is final.

"We'll see you Monday morning, Vicky."

"Yes, sir. Monday Morning." Vicky forces a smile as she walks from the chief's office. Vicky's coworkers avoided her eyes. It is obvious that they heard the gossip that she will be on desk duty. Six months, well it wasn't like it would be forever. Vicky stops at Mike's office.

"Hi, sweet pea. Have you been to the chief's office?"

"Yes. You don't have to pretend that you don't know that I'm on desk duty." Vicky sulks.

"It won't be so bad. We'll all be here. Miriam and you, and I'll be here too. I'll tell you what, you can bring me my coffee, pick up my laundry, and then you can sit on my lap. Won't that be fun?" Mike grins, Vicky raises her eyebrows; that scares Mike as much as it does Miriam, maybe more.

"I'm just teasing you. It'll be good, really and anyway I'm in my office doing paperwork most of the time."

"I know and it's only for six months."

"Six months, huh?" Mike tries not to act surprised. He heard that it will be a permanent assignment, but time will tell.

❧

A huge bouquet of roses greet Vicky on Monday morning. The entire department got together and chipped in to buy the bouquet from Ted the I.T. guy. Ted, the station's head nerd can fix anything and grow a mighty fine rose.

"Very pretty, Vicky. Your coworkers love you. You are very fortunate to have such good friends."

"They are beautiful, and you are so wise, Miriam. Thanks for the perspective. Now get to work. I'll see you at lunch."

Vicky settled in at the desk. After the first rush was over Vicky took a quick break. Cold drink machine, for a bottle of spring water, ladies' room to powder her nose, and lastly, to the cold case files for some reading material. Miriam has already returned the flyer to Grace Standard's folder. Vicky returned to the front desk and began to study the woman in the picture.

"What's going on, Grace? I think I'll have to find out." Vicky speaks to the dead woman's picture; it is a professional photograph. Vicky pored over the information in the folder, but she kept going back to the woman's photo. Dark hair, green eyes, olive skin, five feet two inches tall, slight frame but not thin. The woman would never be considered heavy, but she was curvy. She really was a striking woman. Mike said that there was no apparent motive for murder. Vicky knows better. She knows that a pretty *and* single, middle aged woman who could pass for a woman half her age, could have unknowingly driven any frumpy, saggy boobed, unhappy housewife to murder and mayhem. Now, all she has to do is just find that housewife. Vicky laughs to herself. Vicky wishes she had snapshots of Grace Standard. Pictures that aren't professional might give Vicky a better insight into her life. Vicky glances over the crime scene photos.

"Are you going to lunch, Vic?" Vicky's lunch relief arrived.

"Oh, thanks, I lost track of the time." Vicky sticks the file in her purse and meets Miriam in the cafeteria.

"Miriam, tell me more about the woman."

"What woman, what do you mean?"

"I mean tell me what happened in Kumquat. Tell me everything you remember. Miriam recounted to Vicky exactly what had happened.

"So, it looked like the house had been ransacked and she was tearing it up even more? Strange, very strange," Vicky repeated part of the story.

"Yes, but she didn't know what she was looking for, and there was a pantry in the kitchen that was pad locked. She never even looked in there."

"Miriam, if there was a door that was pad locked that lock would have been opened during the investigation." Vicky pulls the file from her purse and takes another bite of her sandwich.

"Here look. Is this the door that you saw?" Vicky shows Miriam the crime scene photo, which was taken in the kitchen.

"Yes, exactly, but it's open. It was pad locked shut when I was there." Miriam said.

"Yes, and it's open now. If you look closely, you can see that it's not a pantry it's a staircase."

"Ja, it *is* a staircase. I wonder what's up there." Miriam glances through the rest of the crime scene photos.

"I wonder why the door was pad locked, and who relocked it after the investigation. I'm going to show this to Mike. He was there." Vicky planned *not* to talk to Mike again about Kumquat, but she has to know what is upstairs in Grace Standard's house. She will question Mike tomorrow one last time and hope that she doesn't raise his curiosity. Vicky studies the files the rest of the afternoon. When five o'clock rolls around, she put the file in her purse and took it home, she would go over the file once more before she returns it to the cold cases. Vicky reads and rereads the case. She reads into the wee hours of the night. Then finally, she turns her light out and falls asleep.

Six o'clock came early. Vicky starts a pot of coffee; Miriam joins her at the kitchen table.

"I'm so sleepy this morning. I stayed awake way too late reading that file. She died in her sleep, sugar. She was stabbed, and her nose was broken but both injuries happened after she was dead."

"Why would someone stab someone after they are dead? That does not make sense. Well, at least she didn't know." Miriam spooned a mound of jam onto her toast.

"The autopsy report says she died around seven o'clock in the evening. I wonder why she went to bed so early or was that usual for her?" Vicky was thinking out loud trying to sort out the details of this woman's strange demise.

"She was tired." Miriam garbled through a mouthful of sticky toast. She took a sip of coffee.

"*What?*"

"She was tired. She told me she was tired."

"You didn't tell me that before."

"Ja, I forgot." Miriam takes a big gulp of coffee.

"Are you just about ready to go?" We have to leave for the station in about ten minutes.

"Ja, let's go.

~

"Michael?"

"Yeah, sweet pea, what'cha need?"

"Have you got a minute?"

"For you always. But make it quick." Mike looks up from the stack of folders and papers on his desk and grins.

"Stop it, Michael, really."

"Okay really. For you, always."

"I want to know something about the Standard case."

"Sure, what?"

"What was upstairs? And was the door locked?" Vicky laid the photographs on Mike's desk.

"Why do you have these photos?"

"I was looking at the file yesterday and I was just wondering."

"The door was padlocked but the key was in the lock. There was nothing upstairs, just a dusty old sitting room and two bedrooms." Mike twirled a pencil between his fingers and studied Vicky.

"Why are you so interested in that case?" Mike asks.

"I don't know it's just so sad I guess, and I keep thinking about how that poor woman died in her house all alone and no one even cares." Vicky sighs for affect; she decides she *is* becoming a big ole' liar, and that she better start working on her back up lie now.

"Well, we might never know what happened to that poor woman." Mike patted Vicky's hand. Any other time he would have comforted his sweet Georgia peach, but at the station of course, Mike is all business.

"We might not." Vicky picks up the file and starts for the door, then she turns back. "What time are you coming over on Friday?"

"Five o'clock, we'll have an early dinner." Mike winks and returns to his paperwork.

Vicky has just enough time to get a bottle of water from the drink machine and return Gracie's folder to the file before she returns to her mind-numbing job at the front desk.

"Six months and I'll be back on the street." She mutters.

DRIVING MS. CRAZY

"Happy birthday, happy birthday, happy birthday to you!" Vicky sings at Miriam's bedroom door holding a cup of coffee in one hand and a bagel with a burning birthday candle stuck in the middle, in the other hand. Vicky is surprised to find that Miriam is already awake and sitting on the end of her bed.

"It's your birthday, hon? Why didn't you tell me?" Gracie glides around the end of the bed and inspects the burning birthday bagel.

"Burr. It's cold in here sugar, we should shut those vents some."

"Ha, that's all she knows. It's not cold, it's me." Gracie ridiculed.

Miriam is trying to ignore Gracie, since she promised Vicky that Gracie will not return. Miriam doesn't want to upset Vicky with the news that Gracie has indeed returned. She has come back to tell Miriam that she remembered what she is looking for at her house. Gracie has been troubling Miriam most of the night about a letter that she is searching for. It is a letter from Henry, the old hermit, who was the previous owner of the roadhouse. The letter has come up missing... Gracie insisted that the letter held his will and the deed to the property that Henry claimed over to her before his death.

"I have a big day planned for us, and a surprise for you." Vicky announced.

"Oh, hon. There's nothing better than a birthday surprise. Wonder what it is." Gracie is excited, she glides over to Miriam and sat next to her on the bed. Miriam tries to squeeze Gracie out by sliding over into the spot where Gracie sat.

"Yeow! Ouch" Miriam falls from the bed onto the floor.

"Hon!" Gracie howled with laughter.

"Are you alright, sugar? Do you need help?" Vicky helps Miriam back up on the bed.

"Ja, I'm alright, Vicky. It must have been static electricity." Miriam's body tingled; she will remember to keep her distance from Gracie. But she suspects that Gracie has some control of that phenomenon.

"Yeah, I even saw a little spark."

"That was my spark, thank you, ma'am." Gracie proudly announced. Miriam gave Gracie the stink eye.

"You better blow out this candle before it melts all over your bagel." Vicky holds the bagel toward Miriam.

"Thank you, Vicky. How nice, a birthday bagel." Gracie moves next to Miriam and puckers like she is going to blow. Miriam looks at Gracie and mouthed, *stop it, Go Away!* Miriam blew out the candle.

"Did you make a wish when you blew out the candle, sugar?"

"No, I didn't know I should."

"You didn't know you should? hon! How could you not know?" Gracie continued to interject herself into the conversation. "Oh yeah, I forgot you're not from around these here parts. Sorry. Ask her again, what's the surprise." Gracie laughed.

"I'm not from around these here parts." Miriam repeats Gracie's comment.

"It's okay. You can still make a wish since it's your first time. Close your eyes and go ahead, make a wish."

I'm not from around these here parts, is a strange thing for Miriam to say, but Vicky is endlessly amused and often surprised by what comes out of Miriam's mouth. Miriam closes her eyes and quickly reopened them, mainly, because she didn't want to take her eyes off of Gracie for too long and also because her wish is the same wish that she has been wishing for months.

"What did you wish for, hon?" Gracie asked.

"I wished that. . ." Confused by the two conversations that have been going on simultaneously, Miriam began to answer Gracie's question.

"No, never tell your birthday wish or it won't come true!" Vicky interrupted Miriam before she finished telling her wish.

"Well, every party has a pooper." Tired of being ignored, Gracie disappears.

Vicky put the waxy bagel on the nightstand and pulls a box from the pocket of her robe.

"Happy birthday, sugar."

"A present! Thank you, Vicky." Miriam hugs her friend.

"Open it."

Miriam found a cell phone inside the small box. Miriam is not familiar with the cell phones, although she has been curious about these tiny little telephones that everyone everywhere has plugged into their ear. This is certainly a wondrous time. Although she is not familiar with cell phones, she knows all about telephones. There had been a public telephone near her home, only twelve kilometers away in Düsseldorf.

"A cell telephone! Thank you, Vicky. This is a surprise."

"That's not your real surprise.

"That surprise is from Michael."

Mike, the good Tampa man that he is, has been raised in a traditional Italian family. The man provides for his family and the sons always, always watch out after sisters, female cousins, nieces, aunts, mothers and grandmothers. Occasionally a friend, a girlfriend or a girlfriend's friend are included under the watchful mantle. That would be only under special circumstances of course. Mike's gift is the product of his heritage and of the fact that Miriam's disappearance had scared the hell out of him.

❦

"Where are we going?"

"It's a surprise." Vicky drives toward downtown Tampa.

"Are we going to the mall?" Miriam is excited, she is becoming a passionate consumer. Miriam and Vicky's consumer marathons usually begin at Publix grocery market. Much to the delight of the stock boys, Vicky and Miriam wander up one aisle and down the next, filling their cart with incredible delicacies. Anchovies are one of Miriam's favorites. Vicky on the other hand hates anchovies and made Miriam promise that she will never again fry them in the middle of the night with onions and garlic as a late snack.

"No shopping yet, Miriam." Vicky turns the car into the DMV parking lot.

"What is this place?"

"It's the DMV. We're going to get you a learner's permit for your birthday."

"Really?" Miriam didn't have a clue what that meant, and she didn't like to bother Vicky all the time with the endless questions that ran through her mind, which mostly she asked anyway. She knew that Vicky didn't mind the questions, but Miriam didn't want to appear to be a complete dolt, so she silently followed Vicky into the building. If the truth be known, she didn't want to speak in case this was a solemn occasion. Vicky takes a number and sits in one of the chairs that stand in a long line of hard chairs, Miriam sat next to her.

"Hey hon, so you're getting your learners permit?" Gracie stuck her head in between Miriam and Vicky from the chair in the line behind. Miriam winces, but otherwise ignores her.

"You okay, sugar?" Vicky turns to Miriam as she is texting with Mike.

"Michael says good luck with your learners' permit."

"Tell him thank you. Ja, I'm alright. Something I ate, I think."

"Good luck, hon. Boy you'll need it. You'll have to learn a lot of stuff now that you're getting *the* permit to learn. Better you than me I guess." Gracie laughs.

Miriam is getting worried. Gracie continues kibitzing from behind.

"I don't know Vicky. Maybe we should just go shopping."

"You don't want to learn to drive a car, sugar?"

"It's a permit to learn to drive a car?" Miriam is relieved. Gracie grins.

"Vicky, I have to go to the lady's room. I'll be right back." Miriam looks back and discreetly motions to Gracie. Gracie got the hint and follows Miriam to the lady's room.

"Hurry back there's only one number ahead of us." Vicky warns Miriam.

Miriam locks the stall door and turns to Gracie.

"Will you please leave me alone? You are ruining my birthday."

"Oh, hon, I was just havin' some fun with you. You know it's been a long time since I joked around with anyone. I'm sorry I didn't mean anything." Gracie frowns.

"Listen I promise, I *will* help you but could you pleeeese just leave me alone for now?"

"Sorry, sugar" Vicky stands at the stall door; she is surprised by Miriam's tirade.

"I didn't mean to disturb you, but they called our number, they're waiting for us."

Miriam opens the stall door slightly and sticks her head out. She whispers to Vicky. "I didn't mean you Vicky." Miriam pulls her head back into the stall and locks the door. Vicky can hear Miriam mumbling.

"Who are you talking to?" Vicky knocks on the door. She is beginning to worry about Miriam.

Miriam came out of the stall and leaned against the door to hold it shut. "It's Gracie. She's in there." Gracie walked through the wall.

"She's out." Miriam looked helplessly at Vicky.

"One of the perks of being vaporized. That was a good one. I've got a million of 'em." Gracie laughed at her joke.

"It's okay sugar just get a hold of yourself, ignore her, and pretend she's not here. They won't give you a learners permit if they think you're not firing on all your sparks. Oh, and fix your lipstick they're going to take your picture." Vicky and Miriam left the ladies' room.

"You better fix your hair too; hon. Looks like you combed it with an eggbeater." Gracie follows along.

"Sorry it took me so long. We had girl problems in there." Vicky tries to smooth it over with the woman behind the counter.

"It's okay, I took a break, I needed it. Crazy up in here today." The woman shakes her head.

"You should have been in the toilet with the one with the crazy hair." Gracie stands next to Miriam, joking to the woman behind the counter as if the woman can hear her.

"How does my hair look, Vicky?" Miriam caught a stray lock and twisted it behind her ear. She isn't doing very well ignoring Gracie.

Miriam's heart pounds, her head is spinning, her mind is racing, and she is sure that any minute she was going to die. She is certain all of her sparks aren't firing, and that the woman behind the counter will surely notice and deny her the learner's permit.

"Okay, let's go over and get your picture and your permit."

"It's done?" Miriam suddenly felt better.

"Sure girl. I've been working on this for more than a week. Ms. Johnson from social services helped me. Now all you have to do is smile and sign."

Miriam admires her learners permit all the way to the car.

"My hair looks okay, ja, Vicky?"

"Beautiful, sugar. We can start driving lessons as soon as we get home you can drive around the block."

"I'll teach you to drive," Gracie offers.

"Vicky will teach me, Gracie." Miriam is relieved that she doesn't have to hide her conversation with Gracie.

"What did she say, sugar?" Vicky asked, determined to get to the bottom of the ghost thing.

"She said that she would teach me to drive."

"Miriam, it's about time I meet your little friend. Don't you think so, Gracie?" This is the first time that Vicky has actually addressed Gracie.

"*Little friend*! Who does she think she is? What kind of a crack was that anyway?" Gracie might be dead, but she can still recognize smarmy.

"I think she means that you are, well, were petite." Miriam doesn't know what Vicky meant, but that is her best guess.

Vicky smiles, she can't hear the conversation, but she can tell that she has struck a nerve. "Introduce us, Miriam."

"Vicky Knight this is Gracie Standard. Gracie Standard, Vicky Knight."

"Nice to meet you, Gracie dear." The words dripped from Vicky's lips like honey.

"Gracie says.' 'The pleasure is certainly all mine, sweetheart. I've heard so many nice things about you.'" Miriam relays the conversation verbatim.

"Bless your heart, Gracie dear. It's my pleasure to meet you of course. Miriam speaks so highly of you."

The women are being viciously nice. It is the southern lady's version of a throw-down. Miriam is understandably confused; the fact is, only another southern lady would understand the implications of the 'sweethearts' and 'dears' that are being thrown on the mat. The added 'bless your heart' means this has the potential to get really ugly.

Miriam looks from Vicky to Gracie and back to Vicky. They have identical looks on their faces. They each have a fixed smile, that indicates that they are either suffering from a severe case of indigestion, or they are paralyzed from the neck up. An evil glaze, that belies their smiles, has cast over their eyes. Miriam averts her eyes and hopes she hasn't caught anything.

"Gracie, Vicky is a police officer where I work."

"I've never seen her there. Are you sure?" Gracie jabs.

"What did she say?" Vicky asks.

"Hmm, Gracie said how interesting." Whatever is going on Miriam thought that repeating Gracie's comment might make it worse. She doesn't know what is worse than what she has already witnessed, nor does she want to know.

"I did not!" Gracie protests. Miriam ignores her protest.

"Yes, it is interesting Gracie. I've been looking at your case as a matter of fact." Vicky says.

"Good Lord." Gracie huffed.

"Ja, Gracie says thank you."

"Your nose is going to grow girl. Those are some whoppers you're tellin'. Mama would have washed my mouth with soap by now if I was telling whoppers like that. Shame - on - you." Gracie sat back and sulked.

"It's not right what happened to you. I'd like to help." Vicky guessed maybe Gracie isn't really bad, just misunderstood. "There are no bad ghosts just misunderstood ghosts." She mumbles." Vicky laughs she feels like the Father Flanagan of Ghost town.

"What?"

"What?" Miriam echoes Gracie.

"Nothing, sugar. Gracie did you take any prescription drugs?"

"No. I never took anything. Just aspirin, never had a sick day in my life. Why is she asking me that?"

"No, she says she didn't take anything except aspirin."

"What about sleeping pills?" Vicky continues.

"I told her *no,* what part of *no* does she think means yes?" Gracie is getting exasperated with the questions.

"She says no, and she wonders why you keep asking about pills?"

"The coroner found a trace of Doxylamine in your blood Gracie. It's an ingredient in over the counter sleeping pills, and a package of Sleep Aid was on your nightstand."

"I don't know anything about that. I only remember that I'm lookin' for the deed to the old house, and Mama's gold watch pendant it's been handed down for generations but now I can't find either one. I know she's tryin' to help but that's all I remember. I just can't remember much else. Thank your friend for me hon." Gracie disappears.

"Gracie doesn't remember anything about sleeping pills. She just remembers about a will, a deed, and a watch pendant. She's gone now, but she said to thank you for trying to help. Are we going to the mall now?"

"That's the plan. A will, a deed, and a watch pendant? Interesting." Vicky mulled the questions that this odd phantom has brought to mind.

Miriam and Vicky headed over to the International Plaza where they can find anything that they want, some things that they don't want and everything in-between. Vicky is planning makeovers and new dresses all around. Then Michael will take them out for a birthday extravaganza. Miriam has consented to the makeover, only after Vicky assured her it is just lipstick and powder and such. As far as the new dress went, Miriam is hoping for red.

Yes, a red dress would be just what would make the birthday celebration almost perfect. To Miriam, absolutely perfect would have been if Paul had agreed to celebrate with her. Miriam misses her young hero, Paul. The young Nazi hunter who helped Doctor Sam in his quest to discover Miriam's identity.

"Let's go to Macy's, I always find something nice there." Vicky hooks her arm into Miriam's, and they headed to Macy's.

"Ja, I like Macy's, let's go."

"You like all the stores." Vicky laughs as they sashay toward their destination.

"Our make-over is at three o'clock. That gives us plenty of time." Vicky checks her watch when they reach Macy's.

"Now if we get separated you can call me on your phone like I showed you. Okay, sugar, let's shop!"

Vicky is in a dressing room with as many articles of clothing that she is allowed to bring in. Miriam is no slouch and occupies the dressing room across with equally as many articles of clothing, all red. Vicky's phone rings.

"Yes?"

"I can see your underwear." A scratchy gravelly voice whispers.

"I know it's you, Miriam." Vicky laughed and hung up.

"How did you know?" Miriam snickers. She stood in front of the mirror in the most delightfully chic red dress she has ever seen.

"I have caller ID, and I think I should check out what you're looking at on TV." Vicky exited her own dressing room and gasped. She is stunned when she sees how lovely and grown-up Miriam looks.

"Miriam, you look gorgeous."

"Ja, not bad for eighty-seven." Miriam twirls then curtsies.

"Sugar, ladies never tell their real age. I think Michael's going to love this one" Vicky stood in front of the mirror in a sexy little black dress that definitely accentuated the positive.

"Mike doesn't care if you wear anything."

"I think you mean he doesn't care what I wear!"

Miriam looks puzzled, it seems the same to her. Vicky giggled.

∼

Dressed up and made over the two women are ready for the big birthday extravaganza as Mike has been promoting it. They will begin with dinner at Donatello's and then the last surprise. Mike has not confided even to Vicky what the big finale will be; Miriam and Vicky will both have to wait.

Miriam wowed Vicky and Mike as she spoke Italian to Donatello's maître d'; thanking him for the long-stemmed red rose he gave her, a gift from the establishment to each and every lady who graces the restaurant with their presence.

"You speak Italian, Miriam! We knew you speak German but fluent Italian too, wow. That's great. Learn a little Cuban and you'll fit right in around here." Mike teases.

He wonders about this new revelation but will ask Vicky sometime later. Sometime much, later. Vicky, is very protective of Miriam even to him. Vicky, it seems has an over developed sense of fair play. She decided early on that Miriam has been fouled in the game of life, and Vicky has thrown a flag on the field. From what Mike has seen he can't dispute that call.

∼

The valet brings the car around, and they are on their way to the grand finale of the evening. Mike parks his car at the docks on Channel Side and escorts the ladies up the gang plank of the party boat. It is sunset, the Tampa sky is streaked with every color imaginable and some that are not. The horizon looks, as if it has been finger painted by Picasso's giant love child. Miriam can hear the band playing, as she boards for the sunset cruise. She can see couples sitting at small tables with their heads together and other couples dancing on the deck.

"Do you dance?" Someone has whispered from behind her. She turns to see who it is.

"*Paul,* you came!" Miriam's hero took her hand and leads her to the dance floor. Paul gently held Miriam as they dance the night away. It *is* an absolutely perfect birthday celebration after all.

THE LOVERS STONE

"Can I get anyone a cup of coffee?" Vicky is tired, from the evening's celebrations, a cup of sweet Cuban coffee would take her through the rest of the day.

"I'd love a cup." Paul acquired the taste for the Tampa brew on his last trip to the Big Guava. "So, Paul, you're here for a seminar at USF?" Vicky calls out from her kitchen.

"Paul is the main speaker." Miriam gushes. Paul entwines his fingers with Miriam's. He is glad that Mike hatched this birthday surprise.

"How long will you be here?" Vicky handed Paul a steaming cup.

"Thanks, Vicky. I'll only be here for a few more days. The seminar started today but my part starts tomorrow. I came early just for Miriam's birthday."

Mike and Paul have been planning Miriam's birthday surprise for weeks. They became friends when Paul first came to Tampa to try and determine if she had been the victim of a hate crime.

When Paul Linder, the rugged young Nazi hunter, had finished his investigation he returned to his office in Indiana, besot with thoughts of Miriam. These thoughts left no room in his handsome head for thoughts of bad guys and catching old war criminals. It seemed that his willful thoughts were impeding his ability to be the champion of all things helpless. Finally, Paul came to terms with his thoughts and gave himself over to the object of his emotion. Now, he is the official champion of Miriam, all things wonderful, and he is helpless. "Are you staying over by the university?" Mike asked.

"No, I got a place in Seminole heights. It's closer to town, so I can visit." Paul winks at Miriam. Miriam blushes.

Seminole Heights was once a Tampa suburban show piece. The red brick streets were lined with stately homes. The trolleys ran the red brick streets carrying the suburban residents south to downtown Tampa. The trolley tracks have long been taken up. Many of the beautiful stately old homes are gone now; fallen victim to real-estate carpet baggers. Shame on the city planners.

"Seminole Heights, that place has quite a history." Paul is familiar with Tampa's mob connection."

"Yeah, the head of the south-east crime syndicate grew up there." Mike said.

"Isn't that Joe Vicente?" Paul asked.

"Yeah, he lives in South Tampa now, Davis Islands. He's been watched for decades, but the locals love him, so nobody talks. They call him pop; they think that his handouts are worth their silence. Maybe they're right." Mike is frustrated. He is not making any progress with the case against Vicente; the same case that his father was working when he was murdered.

"Maybe they're just scared; by the way, Michael did I see Victor Duetzman in your office last week?" Vicky remembers seeing him and is curious.

"Yeah, he's worried. One of his distant cousins was hit."

"So, there's more than just the Red Duetzman family here in Tampa?" Paul asked.

"Yeah, there's a bunch of 'em. Seems they all followed old Klaus Duetzman over." Mike said.

"Why would someone hit Victor Duetzman's cousin?" Vicky asked.

"I heard that the Mexican cartel put the hit out on him. The only reason he would be hit is because he or his family ticked somebody off, and that's how it works. There's going to be war now with the Mexican drug cartel in Kumquat. Victor said that his father got in touch with him just to tell him that."

"Kumquat?!" Vicky and Miriam echoed.

Mike and Paul continue their conversation, but Mike noted the ladies' strong reaction, something is going on with them. Mike will find out; he will make it a point to find out.

"Do you know what set this off Mike?" Paul asked.

"Not yet, but I have a kid in witness protection. I should be able to get something from him."

"But Michael, you say that Victor Duetzman isn't mixed up with all that business." Vicky took the last sip of her coffee and snuggled up to Mike.

"Victor's not, but his father gets information from Vicente. Red and Vicente go way back. Red Duetzman knows that these wars can spill over. He's worried about his kids. Well, even a reprobate will give his child a loaf of bread." Mike shook his head.

"I've read about the mafia wars in Tampa. Seems they've been fighting over Tampa for a long time." Paul took his last sip of coffee.

"You're right, Tampa is prime real-estate. Location, location, location."

"But Mike, Red Duetzman has never been tied to any mob dealings.

"Yeah, but I do wonder what the old chums are up to." Mike shook his head.

"Alright, guys, enough shop talk this is Miriam's birthday." Vicky brought the group back to the celebration.

Mike turns the conversation to Zorbas. He teases Vicky and entertains the others with embellished stories of their night at the Greek tavern.

". . . and then she stood on the table and started dancing, she had the whole place going," Mike teased.

"Stop it, Michael! He's making this up. Y'all know that?" Vicky protested.

"I don't think so Vicky. Mike's a pretty stand-up guy." Paul laughs.

"Okay, I see y'all taking sides. I think I need another cup of coffee. What do you think Paul, sound good?" Vicky picks up Paul's empty cup and heads to the kitchen.

"You know what I think? We better go for a walk before I get into trouble." Paul takes Miriam's hand.

"Don't be out too long, we'll have birthday cake," Vicky calls to the young couple who have disappeared into the night.

❧

"I've wanted to get you alone all evening Miriam." Paul gathered Miriam into his arms.

"Why is that, Paul?" Miriam's first crush has grown, into a new deeper experience. She wants to be alone with Paul too. She wants to explore these new feelings.

"To give you, your birthday present. I wanted to give it to you when we were alone. Happy birthday, Miriam." Paul places an opal ring in Miriam's hand.

"Paul, it's beautiful." The ring's stone flashes brilliant blue and red, under the glow of the streetlamp.

"It was my grandmother's. My grandfather gave it to her when they were courting."

"An opal, the lovers' stone. They are very soft stones they break easily. The legend says that if your true love gives you an opal it will never crack, if it does, he is not true." The opal glowed. Miriam searched Paul's soft blue eyes. He looks back at her with the eyes of his grandfather, pure white light shone from deep within his soul.

"It will never crack, Miriam." Paul promised.

"I know."

A heartfelt chorus of Happy Birthday from Vicky and Mike greet the couple when they return. Vicky lights the candles on the cake.

"Okay blow them out, sugar and don't forget your wish."

"I already got my wish."

"Well make another, it's not midnight yet."

Miriam closes her eyes she can't think of anything to wish for, she opens her eyes. Gracie stands in the far corner of the room smiling; Miriam closes her eyes and made her wish for Gracie.

"What did you wish for, hon?" Gracie is standing beside her when Miriam opens her eyes.

"It's a secret." Miriam whispers. Gracie disappears.

"This has been great fun, but I have to be at the station early." Mike begins his farewells as he stands to leave.

"Miriam, happy birthday. Don't stay up too late."

"Thank you, Mike, it was a wonderful birthday you made for me." Miriam gets up and gives Michael a big hug and returns to her spot on the couch next to Paul.

"Good to see you again Paul. We'll get together again before you leave."

"Sweet pea, I'll see you at the station." Mike kissed Vicky's forehead and started for the door. Mike stops when he reaches the door; he turns around and walks back to Vicky and properly kisses her goodnight.

"There, that's better." Mike grins, turns, and leaves.

"I'm going to bed now. Y'all heard Michael don't stay up all night."

"Okay." Miriam promises.

⁓

"Well, I think they stayed up all night." Vicky laughed. "Oh, and I just signed Victor Duetzman in. He wants to see you."

"Sure, Vicky send him back." Mike has had a long friendship with Victor. They had been friends at the Sacred Heart Elementary School and continued their friendship throughout high school.

"Victor, what can I do for you man?" Mike hardly recognizes his friend. Mike noticed that Victor had lightened his hair and his usually clean-shaven face is sporting a stubbly shadow. Victor takes a seat and turns his back to the door.

"I'm really spooked about this drug war that's brewing. I' m thinking about taking my family and disappearing, until this blows over."

"What about Cooper? I thought you two split."

"We did, but we're working it out."

"Good, I like Cooper."

"Me too." A slight smile momentarily softened the concern that has creased Victor's face.

"Where are you going to go?"

"I have a houseboat up on the Chassahowitzka River. I figure we'll be okay there for a while. We'll keep a low profile and move around a lot. I'll keep in touch, Mike. You're the only one who I can trust. I'll give you my phone number. It's a prepaid so it can't be traced, and I've disabled the GPS. Don't give this number to anyone. Only call in case something happens. Remember don't give the number to anyone, not even my family. *Especially not my family!*" Victor slipped a folded piece of paper into Mike's hand as he left. Victor nodded to Vicky, but he averted his eyes as he passed the front desk. He did not know the woman that Vicky was talking to, and he wasn't taking any chances.

∾

"What? Fifty thousand dollars? Are you sure?" Vicky asks.

"Yes, Ms. Knight I have the check right here. You see, fifty thousand."

"My goodness. Wait a minute please." Vicky dials the phone. "Um, Mike, can you come to the desk? Yes, right now. It's urgent."

"This is my very good friend Detective De Augustino. You can talk in front of him." Vicky explains.

"What is it, Vicky? Is something wrong?" Mike has dropped everything and hurried to the front desk.

"No, nothing's wrong, I mean yes. No, I mean no. Michael, this is Ms. Johnson. She has Fifty thousand dollars for Miriam." Vicky lowered her voice.

"What? Are you joking?" Mike looks at the woman in disbelief. Ms. Johnson's smile widened.

"Not joking, Mike, she's from social services." Vicky explains.

Having grown up watching old reruns of Dragnet with his father, Mike wanted what Joe Friday wanted, 'the facts.' Mike wanted to say, 'The facts Ma'am, just the facts.' Instead, he politely asked.

"Will you please explain this, Ms. Johnson?"

"When Miriam was found the Trib ran a few articles about her, to try to find someone who might know her or recognize her." Miss Johnson began. "Anyway, there were a lot of people in Tampa that were touched by the story. A fund was set up to help her get back on her feet if she recovered. People started sending in donations, the money has been trickling in since then and as of today, it amounts to fifty thousand dollars."

"What happens now?" Mike asked.

"The money belongs to Miriam. It will be in Miriam's full control when she turns twenty-one. Until then as Miriam's guardian, Ms. Knight will control the disbursement of the funds." Ms. Johnson continues to explain what the papers that Vicky needed to sign mean, and then left Vicky with the cashier's check for fifty thousand dollars.

"I want to be there when you tell Miriam. I have to see the look on her face." Mike is giddy.

"Sure, Mike, come over tonight we'll tell her then."

⮐

Miriam feels that there is a certain something between Vicky and Mike this evening. Miriam made a list in her mind of reasons why her friends might be acting strangely. Maybe they had a lover's disagreement, maybe they would start throwing dinner plates at one another, as the angry lovers on the movie channel had. Miriam decides she should prepare to take cover under the table with Rocky if that is the case. Another reason could be that Vicky is tired. Even though Vicky tries to hide it, Miriam knows that she tires easily; Miriam decides to make a pot of chicken soup after supper, just in case. Maybe, Vicky wants to tell Mike everything about everything, and has decided this would be the perfect night for that. Miriam is sure there would not be a perfect night for that. Maybe she has already told Mike! No, plates would already have flown. She dismissed her third option.

"How are you feeling, Vicky?" Miriam didn't look up from her plate. She put words to her second option first, as chicken soup would be the easiest remedy.

"I'm feeling very well Miriam. Thanks." Vicky glances slant eyed at Mike.

"Are you happy tonight, Mike?" Miriam continues her questioning. Mike chokes on his meat loaf. Takes a gulp of water and smiles broadly.

"Yes, Miriam, I am thanks for asking. This is great meat loaf Vicky. Meat loaf is my favorite." That answer settled her first option. It also settled her third option, even though she dismissed it.

"Ja, Vicky, good." Miriam still isn't satisfied; her friends *are* acting oddly.

"Miriam, Ms. Johnson came to see me today."

"Really?" Social Services an option Miriam hasn't considered.

"Yes, she wanted me to give you something." Vicky hands Miriam an envelope she took from her lap.

"What is it?" Miriam is afraid it is bad news.

"Open it, Miriam. It's for you. Go ahead open it."

Miriam's hands trembled; Vicky's scared straight talk is flooding back. Miriam swore in her heart of hearts that she will be good and not get into any more trouble if only this once she will be spared bad news. She takes the paper from the envelope.

"Vicky, what is this? What does this mean?" Miriam cannot fathom what she held in her hand.

"Its real money, Miriam. It's a bank check for fifty thousand dollars made out to you. It's your money for when you turn twenty-one." Vicky explains.

"How did this happen?" Miriam's eyes fill with tears. Vicky brushes a tear from her own eye. Mike's eyes sparkled with his usual mischief and just a hint of moisture.

"This is because of a story that was printed in the Tampa Tribune about you. Many of the people who read the story sent donations to help you when you recovered because they felt so sorry about what happened to you. Ms. Johnson gave me this for you today."

"Smile ladies." Mike flashed a picture with his cell phone The doorbell rang.

"I'll get it." Mike opens the door to find Paul on the porch.

"Hi Mike. Miriam invited me over."

"Come in. We're just finishing dinner you should have come sooner." Vicky calls out.

"Thanks Vicky but the seminar went late. I caught a bite on the way over. Trang's, it was great."

"Oh, Trang's Yeah, it's good. Come on in. Sit down, relax." Mike and Paul sat on the couch. Vicky and Miriam whispered in the kitchen.

"Can I tell Paul?"

"Of course, sugar. He can be trusted." Miriam, Vicky, and Rocky piled on to the couch next to Paul and Mike. The troupe brought to mind Alice in Wonderland, as they were each one smiling like a Cheshire cat, except Rocky who would not smile like any kind of a cat; she would only smile like a Cheshire dog. Paul is slightly taken aback.

"What's up, guys?"

"This is what's up." Miriam shows the check to Paul and explains how she came to have it.

"Wow, Miriam! What are you going to do now that you're a rich lady?" Paul laughed.

"Buy a Fould."

"Buy a what?" Mike asked.

"Fould."

"Sugar, a what?" Vicky questioned.

"Fould. You know, have you driven a Fould lately?"

"Oh, Ford!" Paul exclaimed.

"Ja, Fould." Miriam grinned.

～

After much discussion, the group settled Miriam's finances. She will put a substantial down payment on a car and make small monthly payments, thus, establishing a credit history and keeping her nest egg mostly intact. On Monday Miriam and Vicky will go banking.

～

"As soon as we get done here, we'll go look at cars." Vicky and Miriam have taken the Monday off to take care of the banking after which Miriam will pick out her Fould.

"Here you go, Ms. Davidson. All of your banking papers are in this envelope and my card if you have any questions, be sure to call." The banker wishes them luck.

&

"Yes, yes." The banker smiles as he spoke. It had only been two hours since Vicky and Miriam left the bank and now the dealership has called. Miriam has chosen a jet-black Ford Escape. Just a little more information from the banker and the deal will be set.

"Vicky?"

"Yes, sugar?"

"I like my new car but . . ."

"But what?" Vicky is surprised at this unexpected 'but'.

"But Vicky, I can't drive it. How will we get both cars home now?" Miriam looks worried. Her brain is in overload she can't process any more information. This final quandary has brought her reason to an impasse.

"Sugar don't worry. I'll drive your car home. Mike will bring me back later to get my car. Come on let's go, the guys are probably waiting for us by now." Vicky pulls Miriam's new car into the driveway. Paul and Mike *are* waiting. Miriam bounds out of the car and hurries to Paul.

"How long have y'all been here? Have you got the picnic ready?" Vicky asks Michael.

"We just got here, and yep we got the fixin's." Mike opens the hatch and slides the picnic basket in.

"Come look at my Escape Paul. Isn't it wonderful?" Miriam pulls Paul by the arm to the driveway.

"Let's go to the end of the Island now, come everyone. Drive Vicky. Come let's go." Miriam is beside herself with excitement.

"No, let Paul drive. We'll sit in the back seat and make out, huh, Vicky?" Mike slips his arm around Vicky's waist and gives her a squeeze.

"Stop it, Michael, act right." Vicky playfully pushes Mike away, Mike grins. They all pile in, and Paul starts the engine.

"Wait, Wait!" Miriam ran back to the house and opens the front door; Rocky runs to the car and jumps into the back seat next to Mike.

"We have to take Rocky. She likes to ride too."

Down Bayshore Boulevard and across the Davis Islands Bridge the group rode to the end of the island. They sat on the sandy shore and watched the sun set, and the lights flicker on in the boats docked at the yacht club marina.

❧

"Rise and shine."

"Oh, nooo." Miriam turns over and pulls the pillow over her head.

"Are you asleep, hon?" Gracie leans over Miriam.

"No, I thought that if I ignore you, you will go away. I can sleep longer. I don't work today. Leave me alone, Gracie."

"Well, I guess you're just going to sleep right through your day with that handsome young man of yours." Miriam sat straight up.

"Wait! What time is it? Paul will be here at ten o'clock. Oh no, I overslept. Why didn't you wake me earlier, Gracie" Miriam ran to the bathroom and jumped into the shower.

"Well, I see how it is. Damned if I do, damned if I don't. I'll help you get ready, don't worry, hon." Gracie sat on the edge of Miriam's bed.

"You know he doesn't have to teach you to drive. I can teach you. I had a car once when I was your age. Daddy gave it to me when I graduated high school, he was so proud. A 1959 bug-eyed Sprite that's what it was. I reckon you're not familiar with that car. Well, it was a cute little car, all green and sporty. That's what daddy called it, a sports car. The headlights were sittin' up on top of the hood makin' the car look for all the world like a little green frog, that's what I named him Frog. I even painted the name on the side in little yellow letters. Well, his name turned out to be forg since sometimes I get my letters all mixed around." Gracie's soliloquy rambled on until Miriam reappeared, she slipped into a little pink sundress and headed for the kitchen.

It was nine forty-five, there was just enough time for a cup of coffee and a bagel before Paul got there. This would be Paul's last day in Tampa; he will give her a driving lesson, before they have lunch. Then Paul will catch a plane back to Indiana that afternoon.

~

"Well Miriam that wasn't too bad." Paul walked Miriam to her front door.

"Is, it wasn't too bad, good? Did I frighten you?" Miriam didn't want Paul to be disappointed with her. She knows driving is a small accomplishment, in the grand scheme of things, but still what Paul thinks of her seems to be strangely important.

"Yes, not, to bad is pretty good."

"Oh, Paul you are teasing me again ja?"

"Yes Miriam, you did good. I was hardly frightened at all." Paul chuckles. Miriam and Paul stand on the doorstep. Miriam takes a step closer to Paul.

"I will miss you, Paul Linder."

"I'll miss you Miriam, but not for too long."

"Paul, you should miss me for more than too long."

"Calm down girl. I will miss you. That's why Mike and I are planning a trip for all of us very soon."

"A trip? Where?"

"To the mountains I have a cabin there. It's beautiful you'll love it."

"I will, Paul, I will love it." Miriam held back tears. Paul put his arms around Miriam and pulls her close. She can hear his heart pounding; Miriam looks into Paul's soft eyes.

"I will miss you until then." Miriam whispers,

Paul kisses Miriam goodbye. Miriam mindlessly opens the front door and walks into the kitchen. Vicky sat in the armchair. She put the magazine down that she was leafing through.

"Hi, sugar I made sweet tea if you like. Miriam, I want to ride over to Kumquat."

"Kumquat?"

"Yeah, I want to go to Gracie's house."

"That's alright with me. When do you want to go?" Miriam pours a big glass of sweet tea and squeezes half a dozen lemon slices into it.

"Tomorrow."

Vicky eyed Miriam's lemon spiked tea. "That's a lot of lemons, girl."

"Ja, if you put a lot of lemons in then when you are finished, and the ice melts, you have lemonade, just like you say, 'make lemonade when you get lemons', have you heard anything about a trip that Mike and Paul are planning?" Miriam plops down on the couch.

"Haven't heard anything about it. Do you think Gracie will mind if we drop by?" Vicky walks into the kitchen.

"Paul just told me about it. . . Vicky?"

"Yes?" Vicky is digging through the freezer for something to fix beside chicken soup.

"Do you like Paul?" Miriam asks.

"What do you mean, sugar?" Vicky pulls her head out of the freezer, walks back over, and sits next to Miriam on the couch.

"I mean, I like Paul." Miriam blushes she studies the opal ring on her finger.

"Oh, sugar, that's alright. Its natural, and he likes you too." Vicky smiles, she hopes this will be as far as she will have to take this conversation.

"Vicky, I like him a lot."

"Well, you can like him a lot Miriam. He's a nice guy." Vicky patted Miriam's knee and began to stand, hoping that would signal the end of the conversation. Miriam pulls her back on to the couch. Obviously, it is not the end of the conversation. Vicky knew 'the talk' would have to happen eventually but she thought she had more time to study for it.

"I mean when he kisses me, I like it . . . a lot." Miriam sighs a deep sigh of relief; she feels better having gotten that off her chest and into the wind.

"Thanks Vicky, I love you." Miriam went into the kitchen, fixes herself another glass of sweet tea, then flops back onto the couch next to Vicky, and turns to the movie channel.

"I love you too, sugar. I guess, chicken soup will be good for supper." Vicky isn't sure why 'the talk' ended so abruptly but Miriam seems content. It will probably be the first of many, but Vicky is proud of their first 'chat' and decides it really went pretty well.

"I think Gracie will be alright if we come for a visit and yes, chicken soup would be nice." Miriam mindlessly flips through the channels.

"Good be ready to go first thing in the morning, sugar." Vicky takes a frozen block of soup from the freezer.

SUNDAY GO TO MEETIN'

"Here, it is. This is Gracie's house. You can park over there." Miriam directs Vicky to an area in front of the house that has been mowed by the county. The rest of the yard is completely overgrown. Vicky stands at the edge of the property. It is painfully obvious that the house is empty and has not been cared for in quite a while. Even so, the still remains of the dwelling; tells Vicky a poignant story of an old roadhouse, which obstinately stands taunting the powers that be; silently daring any soul, essence, or spirit, to add to the mayhem that has been unleashed upon it.

"Ja, this is it. We can get in the back door." Gracie is looking at them through the living room window. Miriam waves to her.

With an audible sigh, Vicky musters her courage, and the two ladies make their way through the tall weeds, spider webs, and on towards the back door of Gracie's house.

"Miriam, do we knock? I don't know what's proper." Vicky follows Miriam through the weeds to the back of the old house.

"I think it is only proper to knock Vicky." Miriam didn't really know what is proper either; she just said the first thing that came to mind.

"Okay, sure." Vicky rolls her eyes; she knows Miriam is full of beans.

"I saw that." Miriam didn't really see that, but she knows Vicky always rolls her eyes.

"Just keep walking. Yuck, daddy long legs." Vicky swats at the giant spiders as she walks.

"I think they are only garden spiders, Vicky."

"They look like daddy long legs to me."

"I am pretty certain they are only harmless garden spiders."

"Maybe they're harmless where you're from." Vicky madly swats as she fights her way through the spider snarl. Miriam and Vicky reach the back door. Miriam balls her fist to knock, before her fist hit the door it swung open.

"Hi, y'all." Gracie greets her guests. "If I'd known ya'll were coming, I'd have baked a cake." Gracie laughs.

"Hello Gracie, Vicky wanted to come by if it's alright with you." Miriam explains.

"Sure, hon. It's Okay. I don't get much company these days. Y'all come on in.

"She says come in."

"To what do I owe this pleasure?" Gracie really is pleased that Miriam and Vicky have come to call, even though she suspects Vicky is not at all too fond of her. Miriam shrugs she wasn't sure what that meant, she repeated it to Vicky.

"Tell Gracie that I'd like to look around in her things for something." Vicky Is still furiously brushing off imaginary spiders.

"She can hear you Vicky, she's dead not deaf."

"Geez, Miriam. I know she's dead, sorry Gracie no offense."

"None taken." Gracie excused Vicky's perceived insensitivity.

"I'm new to this. Give me a break, and I have Daddy Long Leg spiders running all over me. You know they're the most poisonous spiders in the world!" Vicky swatted another imaginary spider off herself as she spoke.

"Lord! Who tied a tin can to her tail?" Gracie joined the dithering, Miriam giggled at the image.

"Are you girls about done?" Gracie decided to be the responsible adult this time.

"Yes, we're done. Sorry, Gracie." Miriam apologizes. Vicky continues swatting.

"Can I look around Gracie?" Vicky is calming down a bit.

"Help yourself, maybe you can figure this mess out. Tell you the truth I haven't been able to make heads nor tails of it. And tell Vicky not to eat the daddy long legs that's the only way they might poison her."

"Gracie says we can look around. She hopes we find something. She says don't eat the spiders" Miriam is beginning to decipher Gracie's lingo pretty well.

Vicky shook her head in disbelief, she can hardly believe this conversation, and for that matter there have been many a conversation lately with which she has had similar difficulty. Certainly, she will admit that since Miriam came into her life there have been some very strange happenings, but all in all she would not take anything in trade for her newfound friend.

"I guess we should start in the living room." Vicky moves to the front of the house. Miriam and Gracie follow Vicky to the living room. Vicky picks up a box and sets it on the couch.

"Let's start looking through this mess of papers. We'll gather the pictures up and put them in this box." Vicky picks up another empty box and sets it on the coffee table.

"We'll put the papers in this box."

Vicky and Miriam just finished filling the boxes with pictures and papers that have been lying in piles on the floor, when they heard footsteps on the porch, and a knock at the front door.

"Yes?" Vicky opens the door.

"I'm Barbara Wallace, I live across the street. I keep an eye on this place for the owner."

"It's Miss Wallace and *that's* a big ole' fat lie." Gracie grumbles to Miriam who kept out of sight.

"Well, thank you Miss Wallace but this is an ongoing police investigation." Vicky flashes her badge.

"I'm sorry I disturbed you. Just remember I live right across the street; I was very close to the poor lady who lived here, if you have any questions."

"So, you knew Grace Standard well, Miss Wallace?"

"Land, yes, we were real close. She was like a daughter to me, poor thing. Remember me if you have any questions." Miss Wallace turns and leaves. She hurries over to Sondra Kinsman's to spread the word of the investigation.

"That woman is out of her ever-loving if she thinks we were close. My goodness my, my, my. I can't believe it 'like a daughter to me' humph, my grandma's big red toe." Gracie ranted.

"It looks like we got it all up. I think we should pick up the papers in the bedroom then go thru it all at home. I want to finish up and get back home before the whole town shows up and starts asking questions."

"Okay, Vicky. Is that all?"

"Yeah, but there is something about that old lady Wallace; she is quite off putting. I just don't trust her."

"Gracie says that she was not good friends with her, she said that's a big ole' fat lie."

"Good to know that Miriam. Let's finish up in the bedroom real quick."

Miriam and Vicky hurriedly scoured Gracie's bedroom gathering each and every piece of paper that they find, but nothing seems of much importance. Vicky searches under the bed and night stand, she pulls a few wrinkled papers from beneath the nightstand and put them in the box with the rest of the papers. Vicky glances over the bedroom.

"That looks like everything. Let's get back home and start going through all of this. I hope you will come with us, Gracie." Vicky stuns Gracie with the invitation; she is speechless, for once.

"Is she still here?" Vicky asks after an extended silence.

"Yes, but she is just standing there. I am not sure why she has not answered." Miriam watches Gracie who remains dumb struck where she stands.

"Cause I can't figure what came over that girl. That was the last thing I expected, to be *invited* over. That's why." Gracie said.

"Gracie says she can't figure why you invited her, as a matter of fact Vicky that took me quite by surprise myself." Miriam blinked a few times as she spoke, as if to clear her eyes in case Vicky had been secretly replaced with an affable doppelganger.

"What do you two think, I have no social graces? I'm certainly not uncouth. Anyway, we need you Gracie, when we go through this stuff; you can help us sort through it. Come on let's go. We haven't got all day." Vicky heads to the door.

"Of course, I know you're not uncouth you have plenty of social graces, *you* are all full of couth." Gracie begins another rant.

"I was just thinkin' this morning, about how 'couthful' you are. Yeah, I was thinkin, '*that* Vicky she really has couth's. My one friend Roberta, now she has couth. She is one smart woman with couth. 'Course she is crazier than an outhouse rat, but she knows what fork to pick up. Sure enough, she really has couth, no doubt!" Gracie rambled on, all the way back to Tampa. Vicky and Miriam dropped the boxes next to the kitchen table.

"Okay Gracie we're going to go thru the pictures first. I'm looking for snapshots if you see anything that sparks a memory speak up." Vicky instructs her unseen but invited guest. They look thru mounds of pictures. Many of the pictures were of Gracie's daddy. In most of them, he was holding a stringer of fish. There was a creepy picture of three stern looking women. The picture was Gracie's stern no foolishness looking mother, grandmother, and aunties. There were countless pictures of the pets. Then finally, Miriam handed a picture to Vicky.

"Gracie wants you to look at this picture; she says it's a picture of her high school graduation." It *was* Gracie. She was all dolled up posing in front of a fireplace.

"That's nice, I bet your parents were proud of you." Vicky dismisses the picture and continues looking through the box of pictures.

"Gracie said you missed something. Look at her closely she's wearing a necklace. It's the gold watch pendant! Her mother gave it to her the night of her graduation. It's the necklace she can't find."

"Gracie, this is great! Wonderful! Exactly what I need!"

"Gracie wants to know what you are going to do, Vicky."

"I'm going to have the picture enlarged and take it to the pawn shops and see if one of them has had this watch come in. If so, boom, we got our thief and probably the murderer."

"Gracie says thank you for everything you are doing, Vicky."

"You're welcome, Gracie. It's getting late. I'm tired, we can work on this some more tomorrow."

"I'm ready for bed too." Miriam yawns.

"Well, I reckon I'm going home. Goodnight. Y'all sleep tight." Gracie vanished.

～

Miriam found Vicky going through papers the next morning.

"Have a cup of coffee Miriam."

"How long have you been up?"

"Oh, awhile, sugar. I couldn't sleep."

"Vicky, do you want a cup of coffee too?" There was a coffee pot cooking on the coffee maker, a thick film of brown sludge was clinging to the bottom.

"No, I had some."

"Yes, I can see that." Miriam unsuccessfully attempted the raised eyebrows, scary, thing. She starts a fresh pot and put a slice of bread in the toaster.

"How about toast?" Miriam asks.

"Huh?"

"Toast? Would you care for toast?"

"Oh, yeah, sure. Sounds good." Miriam still isn't sure if Vicky has heard her, but she put another slice of bread into the toaster anyway.

"How long have you been awake?" Miriam peered into the toaster.

"A few hours, I guess. What time is it?" Vicky yawned.

"It's eight o'clock."

"A little more than four hours. I only have these few papers left, from Gracie's bedroom to look through." Vicky mindlessly answers as she continues searching. Miriam pours herself a cup of coffee, the toaster pops up the toast, and at that same instant, Vicky jumped from her seat.

"I found it Miriam. I found it." Vicky jumped for joy. She waived a piece of paper in the air and danced what could only be described as the 'I've overindulged in coffee and been up since four o'clock in the morning' victory dance.

"What did you find? What did you find?' Miriam joined Vicky in her kitchen dance of triumph.

"The deed, the deed! I found the deed to Gracie's property. The house is signed over to her. Just like she said, look here." Vicky lays out the paper on the table, the ladies study it.

"Part of the bottom is torn off. Does that matter Vicky?"

"No, it still has the notary stamp on it and anyway Henry had it filed. See there is the file number." Vicky points out a string of numbers in the upper corner of the paper.

"Can we go to Kumquat, Vicky? We have to tell Gracie right away she will be so happy."

"Tell Gracie what? hon." Gracie appears.

"Gracie! When did you get here?" Miriam is surprised.

"Is she here, Miriam? What got her here so early?"

"All the ruckus you two are causing that's what got me here, for pity's sake. You sound like a couple of banshees, you could wake the dead, not that the dead really sleep, funny expression. Tell Gracie what?" She repeats.

"Gracie says our ruckus woke her, but she doesn't really sleep. What is ruckus Vicky?" Miriam turns back to Gracie.

"Vicky found the deed to your house. Look its right here." Miriam held up the deed for Gracie to see.

"Gracie says it is the deed. She remembers she was looking at it the night she passed, she remembers now! She remembers taking it out of the envelope. There were some other papers in the envelope, the will and some papers about the taxes and legal things. She dropped the envelope on the floor next to her bed and was looking at the deed when she fell asleep. She remembers how happy she was that the old house was finally really hers." Miriam relays to Vicky what Gracie has told her. Miriam pauses and looks to Vicky. They stand in heart wrenching silence. Gracie's behavior up until now has distracted them from the sad truth of Gracie's bitter allotment in death, it was a harsh portion indeed.

"Ruckus is a lot of noise." Vicky chokes on her whisper. She wipes a tear from her eye, then recovers herself.

"That all makes sense. This stray piece of paper is all I found. It must have slipped under the bed when you fell asleep, Gracie. But the will and the rest of the legal papers in the envelope were not there. There is one other thing that hasn't made sense to me. Remember the crime scene photos, Miriam? They show that the house is tidy nothing is out of place. Yet, you said that the house had been ransacked when you took Gracie home. Where did the rest of the legal papers get off to and who took them? Do you have any thoughts on this, Gracie?" Vicky asked.

"Miriam, will you come to church in Kumquat with me on Sunday?" Gracie's brow is furrowed. It looks like she is cooking up a plan.

"I think I can do that, Gracie." Puzzled Vicky looks to Miriam.

"What does Gracie want you to do Miriam?"

"She wants me to go to church with her in Kumquat on Sunday."

"If you go, do you think you will be able to stay at the monastery like you did when Sister Theresa Marie was here? Michael and I are going on a day trip this Sunday." Vicky has long suspected that Gracie knew more than she was sharing. Now it seems that this bit of information has put her wheels in motion.

"Yes, I think I can, that will be perfect! Since Gracie's house is all closed up, Sister Mary Katherine will make another visit to the monastery. Yes, perfect."

"Good, I'll take you to the monastery later today. You can get a taxi to the church tomorrow, and then home after." Vicky has a feeling that Gracie is remembering more now, than she is saying. Vicky can respect that, she herself is no stranger to secrets.

～

"Have you got your duds all packed, girlie girl? I've been waiting all day long for this." Gracie is eager to put the plan she has been devising into action. Gracie indeed hatched a plan when the deed was found. Now, the forgotten pieces of her life are puzzling back together. She is ready to end this sad chronicle of her demise. Her grand plan is to have the last word after all.

"Yes, Gracie I'm ready. I just have to change." Miriam walks the hall to her bedroom when she emerges once again, she is Sister Mary Katherine; the young woman who had been hidden away inside the cloister of the Monastery so many years ago. Gracie is stunned, her friend is almost unrecognizable. The black and white fabrics of the habit covered every inch of her tiny body save for her face and her hands.

"Are you a nun? I can hardly recognize you. My, my. Mercy me, I guess I better start mindin' my p's and q's. Well, I *guess* that's a nun outfit if you say so. I'll mind my p's and q's anyway."

"No, Gracie, I am not a nun."

"Why are you dressed like that then?"

"Remember when I told you that I hid in a monastery in Germany before the Gestapo found me?"

"Yes, I remember. Is this what you wore back then? 'Cause I don't think they wear those kinda getups anymore."

"Yes, this is what I wore then, and some still *do* wear this." Miriam is a bit defensive of the habit that was made especially for her, in another place and time.

"Well, sugar, I see that you're ready to go." Vicky stands at Miriam's door.

"What are p's and q's, Vicky?"

"What? What do you mean, sugar?"

"Gracie says she will mind her p's and q's."

"Oh, that's a good thing. It means she's going to behave herself. You're lucky."

"As soon as I think I am learning, there is always something like p's and q's." Miriam shook her head.

"That's right, there is always something. So, Gracie's here?"

"Yes, she is."

"I surely am. Let's hustle bustle, girl!" Gracie hurries from the room.

"Okay then, let's get going. Hustle bustle, Miriam." Vicky walks to the door.

"What is hustle bustle, Vicky?"

"It's just an old expression it means hurry."

"Why did you say that?"

"I don't know it just came to me."

"Okay, then we shall hustle bustle." Miriam follows Vicky.

"You're catching on, Miriam."

"You are too, Vicky." Miriam smiles.

"Good afternoon, Sister Irma, do you remember me? I am Sister Mary Katherine."

"Yes, my dear, I remember you. You came when Sister Theresa Marie was here for the religious treasures display." Sister Irma welcomed her into the entry parlor of the Holy Trinity Monastery.

"I would like to speak with the prioress, if I may."

"Yes, I'll tell her you're here." The spry octogenarian disappeared into the Prioress's office.

"You may go in." Sister Irma escorts Miriam into the Prioresses' parlor.

"Thank you, Sister."

"Sister Mary Katherine, how nice to see you again," The prioress seems genuine.

"Thank you. It is nice to see you again also, I hope you have been well."

"Yes, very well, thank you. What can I do for you, Mary Katherine?" The prioress would not meddle but would *listen* if this peculiar sister had anything of juicy interests on her mind. The Holy Trinity sisters are nothing like the selfless sisters that Miriam had come to love in another lifetime. These sisters are more like the fairies that Miriam had read of as a child. Tiny beings that appear as beautiful gentle creatures, only to morph into dreadfully evil souls. Save for Sister Irma, if there *are* saints on earth, a belief that Miriam, as of yet, has not fully formed an opinion on, Sister Irma would certainly wear the saintly circlet.

"I would like to stay at the monastery, for a time of recollection and prayer." Miriam explains.

"Yes, Sister Mary Katherine you may stay. Sister Irma will show you to a room. Will you be in silence?"

"Yes, I will."

"I will advise the rest of the sisters. We will see you at dinner."

"Thank you, Mother Mary Francis." Miriam glided from the room.

Mother Mary Francis watched the young nun as she seemingly floated to the door. The disagreeable old sister could not understand why any woman would want to be burdened with the outdated habit that they had been relieved of by the Second Vatican Council. In truth, Mother Mary Francis felt nothing less than repulsion in regard to any of the sisters who chose to keep this archaic garb. It was a feeling that most of these modern sisters shared, that and the feeling of insufficiency, as they measured themselves by the standard of these outdated icons.

❧

"I know you will be in silence, but I will say a prayer for you tonight."

"Thank you for your prayers, Sister Irma." Miriam hugs the old sister and turns toward her room.

"Good night, my dear." After decades of faithful obedience, Sister Irma longed for genuine human contact, something that to the frail old sister has been unattainable. Sister Irma unlike many of the other sisters came to the monastery on her own volition. She was not forced into monastic life because there were too many mouths to feed in her home and too little money to feed them with. Young Irma's state of affairs were much different, she came from privilege. Young Irma was strong willed and independent. For her own concealed reasons, she left her home during the celebration of her return from boarding school. Then took a lonesome journey, to the monastery in Kumquat Florida and a new life.

When the dinner bell rang, Miriam waited before going into the dining room. She waited to allow the sisters to fill their plates and be seated. Miriam fixed herself a meager plate, and quietly ate her dinner, as Sister Theresa Marie had taught her.

❧

In the quiet of her room, Miriam sat on her tiny cot. Gracie appears and sits next to her on the edge of the bed.

"Well, hon are you fixin' to hit the hay? We got a big day tomorrow." Miriam doesn't think that Gracie thinks that there is really any hay to be hit; she decided that 'hit the hay' means something entirely different than actually hitting hay. She will remember to ask Vicky when she got back home. Miriam slipped into her night gown, crawled into bed, and adjusted her pillow. Miriam was pleased she thought that she was really starting to understand Gracie . . . maybe.

"Why do you want me to go to church with you Gracie?" Miriam sleepily whispered.

"I just want you to meet my friends, hon. They'll all be there. It'll be a real come to Jesus experience." Gracie grinned.

"Alright. Goodnight, Gracie." Miriam closed her eyes. She softly whimpered as she began to dream. Miriam was being taken back to the strange dream, of the dark forest. Miriam again stood in the forest. The robed men were there. Everything was the same. Again, her attention was drawn to Sandalphon as he spread his wings to fly. Miriam was frightened she wanted to wake up, but she could not. She watched as Sandalphon morphed into a huge raven. Then he glided to the ground. Sandalphon towered over the men as he stepped onto the flat stone. He took the woman in his talons and flew away. Miriam whined.

"Sleep now, hon. Don't cry. You're a good girl." Gracie leaned over and gently kissed the sleeping Miriam's cheek. Gracie remained with Miriam in her room. She quietly sang the lullaby that her mother sang to her.

Sleep the sleep of cherubs child.

Dreams will come all meek and mild.

Hush, a baby, hush, a baby, hush, hush, hush.

Angels fly to be nearby you.

Taking wing to guard you through.

Hush, a baby, hush, a baby, hush, hush, hush.

It was not the first time that Gracie comforted Miriam in the night as she struggled through her dreams.

~

"Where are you headed, lady?" The cabbie started his meter.

"To, the Open-Door Community Church please." Miriam gave direction to the cabbie; she was no longer Sister Mary Katherine.

"Isn't that a church that you just came outta? Wass up you don't like the seats?" Miriam could not understand how the seats in the monastery any bearing had on where she wanted to go.

"I will need a ride, after the service. Will you please come back and pick me up?" Miriam was a little concerned that there was a chance she would be left without a taxi ride back to the monastery. Miriam was slightly comforted by the fact that since she had the cell phone now, she could always call Vicky or Mike if she got into trouble. Not that she's expecting trouble. After all she's just going to church with Gracie, a dead woman, who, for all Miriam knew, could have been murdered by one of the church goers. Miriam is beginning to believe Gracie's words, 'It'll be a real come to Jesus' experience.'

The driver pulled into the church parking lot.

"Thank you. I'll see you after noon, then. Thank you, again. And don't forget me."

"Yeah, I'll be back a little after noon to pick you back up."

Miriam could see Gracie standing beside a huddle of people who were talking in the church yard Miriam was a little more than concerned. Gracie met Miriam as she walked to the church doors.

"Tell everyone that you are my cousin from Germany when you introduce yourself."

"Alright." Miriam agreed.

A sinewy, way too tan, woman greeted Miriam at the steps. Miriam noticed that three cats were winding themselves around the woman's leg, and a few dozen more were peering through the foliage that grew around the foundation of the church. The foliage camouflaged a dozen or more large bowls of cat food.

"Good morning. I'm Lee Ann Matthews, Welcome."

"Good morning, I'm Miriam Davidson."

"It's good to meet you, Miriam. What brings you to my, err our little church? Have you recently moved to Kumquat?" Lee Ann knew that Miriam didn't live in Kumquat. Lee Ann knew everyone who is living in Kumquat, beside that she knew everyone who had lived there for the last sixty years, and Lee Ann's mother knew everyone who had lived there for the last eighty years. And Lee Ann's grandmother... The story goes on and on.

"I have come from Germany to visit my cousin, but alas, I have not had good news. Perhaps you knew my cousin, Grace Standard?"

"No! I can't believe it!" Lee Ann quickly composes herself and continues.

"Gracie was your cousin? I'm sorry, I didn't mean to be rude, we all just never thought she had any family."

"I am her only family."

"I see. Will you excuse me? I have to go over a few points with the reverend about his sermon."

"Certainly, it was a pleasure to meet you, Lee Ann." Gracie looked like the cat that ate the canary as Lee Ann walked away.

"She's going over there to tell the preacher man what he can say or what he can't say from the pulpit and that just depends on which way she has her britches on today." Gracie was suddenly quiet; her eyes followed a red truck as it parked. A large black man stepped out of the truck and opened the passenger door for a white-haired, aged black woman. Gracie's eyes continued to follow the ebony masterpiece.

"That's the sheriff, Adrian Thomas, and his mother, Jessamine. She's a special lady. You'll like her. People call her the root lady, except a few of the white people. Those don't call her anything, they just stay away from her. They're mostly afraid of her, but she's a sweetheart. Adrian doesn't come here to this church. Must be something special goin' on today." Gracie smiles. Gracie pointed across the church yard. A horsey faced, big boned, (which is polite southern for mannish) woman was making a bee line toward the preacher and Lee Ann.

"That's Jean Louise, she thinks she's still the assistant minister, her and Lee Ann tangle asses all the time. Jean Louise is got her eye on the preacher, and so does Lee Ann. Jean Louise has carried on with most of the single men in Kumquat, and some of the not so single men. She has a number more, hear tell over in Tampa, she tips the bottle a bit. Lee Ann on the other hand, you see, is a teetotaler. I doubt she's ever carried on with any man. The preacher man over there, he's not interested in either one of 'em. He's got *his* eye on a stripper over at the Mons Venus strip joint." Gracie lost Miriam at 'root lady'. She hopes she can remember everything that Gracie is telling her because she was sure that Vicky was going to ask her a lot of questions.

"Gracie, what is the big brick building between your house and the church?

"That's the city hall. There's… I'd say fifteen or twenty people in the church and about half of 'em are on the city council. They're a bunch of old wind bags."

"There's only twenty people in this church?" Miriam is surprised.

"Well, honestly, I wouldn't really even call it a church, it's more like a private social club. New people try to come but they get run right off."

The steeple bell rings signaling the members that it is time to ante up their dues. After the service, the reverend Thane Colin Slice III greeted Miriam.

"I hope you enjoyed the service, Ms. Davidson. I'm Reverend Colin Slice but everyone calls me Tri." The minister smiled.

"Tri?" Miriam questioned.

"Yes, Tri, you know, three. I'm the third Colin Slice." Colin Slice seemed a bit aggravated that he had to explain to Miriam.

"I didn't know your cousin, but I've heard a lot about her."

"I bet he has! Jean Louise probably gave him an earful," Gracie added her two cents worth. "She had an abiding hate for me. She always thought that drunken mess of a two-legged snake boyfriend of hers was comin' around me. Disgraceful, the way he is, and him, a deacon and all." Gracie is giving Miriam a candid look into the church that she referred to as The First Community Open Door Church *of Hell*.

"Have you been the minister here long, Reverend Slice?" Miriam asked.

"Only a little more than a year. I was the assistant minister at another church for five years though, I was sent here when the last minister was transferred." The reverend attempted to qualify himself.

"Oh, I see. I ask only because I am confused. Given the closeness of my cousin's house to the church and your duties as a minister, I am surprised that you did not know her. Had you or the last minister never visited her? I was under the impression that Gracie attended this church. Since that must not be the case, I do wonder why she never visited. Did no one invite her?"

"There was only so much I could do, Ms. Davidson. Will you excuse me?" Reverend Slice hurried away.

"Girl, that was good! You really ran with that one. I'm proud of you." Gracie grinned with delight.

"There's my taxi, Gracie. I am going back to The Holy Trinity now. I will meet you there."

"Sure, hon, see you later." Gracie was focused on the sheriff and his mother. As Miriam approached the waiting taxi she turned. She could see Gracie standing near Jessamine Thomas. Jessamine nodded her head toward Miriam, appearing to acknowledge her or had she just acknowledged Gracie, Miriam wondered. "She's a special lady," Miriam repeated Gracie's words.

THE LETTER

The sisters are still in the dining room when Miriam arrived back at the monastery. She would sneak back into the building the same way she had snuck out through the basement door. Miriam had left a small stone in the threshold of the door so that it didn't close securely, she had learned to do this the last time that she had stayed at the monastery. It was a trick that the sisters used when they happened down to the basement without their key. It was also a handy way to sneak a par amour into your room as Sister Mary Magdalene had discovered, now that's irony at its best. Miriam would then take the freight elevator from the basement up to her room. She would change back into her habit and the sisters would never know that she had left.

Miriam sat on a wooden glider under a huge loquat tree on the grounds of the monastery. Her spirit was comforted by the beauty of the tropical foliage and stately oaks that enveloped her as she lingered within her thoughts. The neatly manicured Kumquat groves stretch down to the edge of the crystal clear water of a small lake.

The sisters languish in the lake's cool water on sultry summer days.

"Hey, hon, I found you."

"Oh, Gracie! My mind was wandering."

"What were you thinkin' about?"

"A little bit of everything, I guess. I saw you going over to the sheriff as I was leaving the church." Miriam changed the subject and raised an eyebrow for emphasis, something she had learned watching Vicky.

"Uh, yeah, I was going over to get close to Adrian," Gracie confessed.

"Adrian?" Miriam continued to dig; this might be something to know about.

"Yes, hon, the sheriff. We were quite the talk around Kumquat, you know."

"No, I did not know, Gracie. Tell me."

"Well, truth is, the sheriff was pretty fond of me and I kind of liked him myself. Oh, who am I tryin' to kid. I was in love with the sheriff, and he was in love with me. There I said it. It doesn't make much difference now anyway." Gracie looked down and flicked an imaginary piece of something from her sleeve. "I guess it wasn't meant to be." Gracie sighed.

"I'm sorry, Gracie." Miriam could feel Gracie's sadness. A raspy caw and a fluttering of wings ended the conversation.

"Sandalphon, you found me too. Come here." Sandalphon flew on Miriam's shoulder.

"Does that bird belong to you?"

"Yes, Gracie, this is Sandalphon." Sandalphon hopped from Miriam's shoulder to Gracie's.

"I think we've already meet!" Miriam is stunned not only by Sandalphon's action but also by his countenance. Sandalphon no longer wore the face of a raven. As he sat on Gracie's shoulder, countless small faces swirled around Sandalphon's head.

"This is the bird that landed on my sill the night of the concert," Gracie announced. Miriam took a moment to process what had just taken place, and then she acted on her thought.

"Sandalphon, come here." Miriam raised her hand. Sandalphon hopped to her hand then to her shoulder. She studied the raven; his head was again a normal bird's head. Miriam took Sandalphon in her hands and placed him on Gracie's shoulder, again his face changed to a swirl of tiny faces. Amazed by this, Miriam decided on one last trial. She raised her hand, Sandalphon flew to her shoulder then Miriam stepped beside Gracie and touched her. Suddenly, there was a storm of static electricity twisting around the three of them. Furthermore, Miriam had not been shocked as normally she would have been on touching Gracie. The electricity continued to swirl. Through the swirling wall, Miriam could see the world around her. As if she were looking through a ship's port hole.

"Welcome to my world, hon." Gracie appeared slightly more corporal in this strange electric cocoon. Two sisters passed. They did not speak. Either they had not spoken because of Sister Mary Katherine's silent retreat, or they did not acknowledge her because they had not been able to see her. Miriam wanted to follow the sisters. She found herself standing beside them as soon as the thought was fully formed in her mind.

"Good afternoon," Miriam greeted the sisters, but neither sister returned the greeting. Miriam giggled and waved her arms; she hiked up her habit to her knees and jumped up and down in front of the sisters. She stretched her lips into comical distorted shapes. There was no response from the sisters. They could not see her.

"Are you done? You are such a baby." Gracie laughs.

"I could have saved you all that trouble. I knew they couldn't see us. You have to be careful though, hon. Some people are like you. They can see in here, so try to stay out of sight until you know if there's anybody around who can see in. The good thing is mostly nobody believes them folks when they start going on about seeing things flash by or people peeking around corners at them. They usually end up in Chattahoochee."

"Chattahoochee?" Miriam looked confused.

"You know, the Booby Hatch." Gracie tried unsuccessfully to clarify. Miriam didn't know, she will definitely add Chattahoochee and Booby Hatch to her list of things to ask Vicky.

"Let's go back to my room, Gracie."

"Sure, hon. Do you want to walk back or just step back in the cocoon?" "Let's walk." When they reached the room, Gracie encouraged Miriam "Go on, Hon, try to walk through the door." Miriam stepped through the closed door. Gracie follows.

"Why am I able to go through the closed door, Gracie? I am not a spirit."

"I think it's because everything is different in the spirit realm. When you step in, there are different rules of time and material things. You're not the same in here, you aren't a spirit but you're not solid either. I don't understand it all and I'm certainly not an expert, but that's how I figure it."

"How do I get back out?" Miriam's eyes grew wide. As she spoke, Sandalphon flew from her shoulder and landed on the bed stead. Miriam followed him.

"Thank you, Sandalphon. I guess that answers that question." Miriam had one more test. She stepped back toward Gracie and touched her; the force of the shock knocked her to the floor.

"That was a hard lesson, but one you really needed to learn." Miriam picked herself up.

"Just remember, it works both ways. If you touch someone when you are enveloped in the cocoon, that is what happens to them. You might need to use that sometime." Gracie did not smile or even offer her usual roguish grin. Miriam packed her overnight bag and looked around the room to see if she had forgotten anything.

"Oh no, Sandalphon! I can't take him through the building, the sisters will see him and if I open the window to let him out, it might make the alarm go off." Before Miriam finished her sentence, Sandalphon flew toward Gracie and disappeared.

"Where did he go?" Gracie asked.

"Isn't he with you, Gracie?"

"No, he's not. My goodness, hon, this *is* a new wrinkle!"

"Yes, it is, Gracie."

"Let's go home." Gracie disappeared. Miriam called a taxi before she left her room. The taxi would be waiting for her by the time she finished thanking the sisters.

Miriam sat in the back of the cab and took a long, deep breath. She is exhausted. Miriam has learned a lot of extraordinary new things in the last twenty-four hours. Furthermore, she has also learned how to put some of the things that she already knew into working knowledge. Miriam *has* learned extraordinary things and she has discovered hidden things that now belonged to her forever. She is anxious to share her new-found knowledge with Vicky.

Vicky is frantically looking through the papers when Miriam arrives home.

"Hi, Vicky. I'm home."

"Good! You can help me look for that deed. I can't find it anywhere."

"You got a lot of 'splaining to do, Vicky. Did you know that was Ricky Ricardo?"

"Come on, Miriam, help me; I don't have time for TV trivia. I want to find that deed, so I can stick it in Gracie's file then discover it. Then ask Mike what he thinks about it."

"Good plan."

"Yeah, especially if we ever find it. Come on now, Miriam. Help me."

"Find what, hon?" Gracie popped in.

"The deed." Miriam said.

"Yes, sugar, the deed, that's what I said."

"Not *you*, Vicky, I'm talking to Gracie."

"Gracie? Don't tell her I lost it," Vicky whispered.

"Don't tell me she lost what, hon?" Gracie whispered.

"Don't tell you she lost your deed," Miriam whispers.

"I said DON'T tell her." Vicky squinted her eyes and pursed her lips at Miriam.

"Well, did you take it out with you when you went for a walk? Did you pass it around at the coffee shop?" Gracie giggles.

"Gracie wants to know if you passed it around the coffee shop."

"What? No, I haven't left the house since Saturday afternoon when I took you to Kumquat."

"I thought you went out with Michael."

"We stayed in." Vicky blushed.

"Well, then it's here somewhere. Tell Vicky not to worry, it'll turn up in a day or two."

"Gracie says not to worry, it'll turn up soon"

Vicky stops searching. It seems to Vicky that Gracie is acting mighty cavalier about this turn of events. Her nagging feeling that Gracie might know more than she lets on has suddenly morphed into the undeniable belief that Gracie definitely knows, way more than she is letting on.

"Hon, did you tell Vicky about what we did today?" Gracie asked.

"No, not yet. I'm going to tell her now."

"What's going on, sugar? One conversation at a time please." Vicky is picking the strewn papers up and stashing them back in the boxes.

"Gracie wants me to tell you what we did today."

"I'm afraid to ask, but what did you two do today?"

"I disappeared. I was invisible. Ja, this is good, what I did. Good, ja, Vicky?"

"You what?" Vicky looks up from her chore.

"Disappeared into another realm, you know, I was invisible."

"Yes, I know what disappear means, but in case *you* don't know, you are not invisible when you close your eyes, Miriam." Vicky wanted to laugh this statement off just in case it was going to turn into a long and complicated arduous account.

"I know that. Vicky, really, this is real. Sandalphon showed me!"

"Sandalphon, the crow in the backyard?" Vicky knew now that this was not going to be a simple explanation.

"He's a raven, not a crow. It is very insulting to a raven to be called a crow."

"Sorry, no offense intended. Sandalphon, the raven?" Vicky rolls her eyes.

Miriam gently put her hand over Vicky's eyes as she spoke, "Vicky there's something I never told you."

"Geez. Should I sit down?" Vicky swatted Miriam's hand away.

"No, it's not that bad."

"You mean compared to breaking and entering or grand theft, or what?"

"Yes, no. I don't know which one to choose." Miriam suspects that Vicky is trying to trick her.

"Just tell me, Miriam. I can take it." Vicky braces herself.

"Remember when I told you about the Gestapo and the night that they were taking me to the detainment camp. I did not tell you all of it. I was not trying to hide anything, there is just so much; I did not want to burden you with small details." Miriam sat down on the couch and began her tale.

"When I cut my wrist in the back of the prisoner's truck, I died. Sandalphon was on my lap, and he should have turned back into a clay statue because I died."

"A clay statue! You mean Sandalphon is a golem too? How many of those things did you make, sugar?" Vicky has been well versed on the principle of golem rules and regulations; she sat down for the rest of the account.

"Just Sandalphon and Eliakim. That is where I got confused, because as you know, when the person that creates the golem dies, the golem always turns back to clay. So, when I died, Sandalphon would have naturally turned back to clay. So, he should have been clay until I brought him back to life. Right?"

"Naturally, I guess." Vicky has no idea.

"Well, that is what I thought too, but it did not happen like that, and you can imagine my surprise when I found that Sandalphon was here with me and alive!"

"That must have been a real shocker."

"Ja, a real shocker. I decided that the reason Sandalphon did not turn to clay, was that although my father brought Sandalphon to life, since I was the one who originally created him, he was under some sort of special dispensation."

"I see how you would think that." Vicky shakes her head; she stands up hoping that signals the end of this elaborate explanation. Miriam pulls her back into her seat.

"No, that is what I thought, but that is not what happened either."

"Just tell me what happened, Miriam. The suspense is killing me." Gracie giggles. *She* appreciated the absurdity of the moment even if it escapes Miriam.

"When I died, Sandalphon and I were both pulled through Jacob's ladder by the spirit, Sandalphon who stands on the first rung of the ladder. I was given my life back and Sandalphon was given a portion of life from the spirit Sandalphon. That's why he has so many faces. He's an extension of Sandalphon the spirit. It was that simple."

"Wow, sugar! So many faces, I don't know how you missed that." Vicky didn't have a clue, but she would endure to the end of this saga.

"Ya, I know, but that *is* what happened."

"I believe you, even if that part about the crow faces is a little farfetched."

"Raven, Vicky. Do you want me to explain it?"

"The difference between a crow and a raven?" Vicky asked, she pressed her lips together to keep from smiling.

"No, the part about the faces."

"No! Please, I'm good. Let's just clean this mess up. Michael is coming over later."

"You're not going to tell Mike, are you?"

"Heavens, no!" Vicky walked away shaking her head.

This is the day that Vicky decided she will never tell Michael the truth about Miriam. It will be okay if she doesn't, Vicky rationalized. Michael knows that all ladies have their secrets. Curious little clandestine mysteries that keep the romance alive, like what color their hair *really* is or how old they are. That's not to detract from the titillating secret of how much they weigh or how many pairs of shoes they have hidden in the trunk of their car. Furthermore, everyone knows that the most desirable ladies are keeping the coquettish secret of the two golems and their creator that live with them. However, of course, they only live there when they're not disappearing into another realm. Well, she didn't have to actually be concerned with that last part. That's just absurd. *Of course,* they don't live there when they're in another realm! *Naturally, they don't!* Miriam gathers the papers and pictures into boxes. Vicky forced the boxes into the hall closet and quickly shut the door.

"Don't open that door, sugar. It'll be an avalanche." Vicky pushes her weight against the door to make sure that it's latched shut.

"I won't. I am going to my room now. I'm very tired."

"Good night, sugar. Sweet dreams."

"Sweet dreams," Gracie echoed.

"Good night, Vicky. Good night, Gracie."

∾

"I just can't figure it out, Miriam. I know I had that deed in my hand before I took you to the monastery, but now I can't remember what I did with it." Vicky is still obsessing over the deed as she drives to the station.

"Have you put it in a safe place like whenever you can't find your gold earrings?"

"No, I don't think so. At least I have the picture of Gracie's necklace. I'm going to enlarge it today."

"Can you take me to practice driving after work?"

"Sure, you're getting pretty good, you'll be ready for the driving test sooner than you think."

"Good." After work, Miriam drove her car around the back streets of Hyde Park. Then Vicky treated Miriam to Cuban sandwiches and devil crabs at Havana Village. Vicky and Miriam talked and laughed as they sat in the Cuban café.

"Has Gracie been around, Miriam?"

"No, she has not."

"I thought it's been quiet. What do you imagine she's been up to, sugar?"

"I think with Gracie, we will know soon enough."

"That's true. I dropped the photos of Gracie's necklace at a couple of pawn shops on my lunch break. No luck. I gave them my card and told them to call if it comes in."

"I hope we find it." Miriam parked her car in the driveway. "Let's watch The Princess Bride tonight." Vicky is ready for a relaxing night, and she guesses Miriam is too.

"Okay. I will make popcorn."

Vicky and Miriam have become each other's sister, that they never had. They have found that there is no stronger bond than the bond sisters share. Miriam took one end of the couch; Vicky took the other end. Rocky holds down the middle as the official foot warmer. The women snuggle their feet into the soft warmness of Rocky's belly; they each held their bowl of popcorn. A big glass of ice water sat on each of their TV trays. They are ready for the umpteenth encore showing of The Princess Bride. Vicky's most favorite movie of all time. This movie stands as Vicky's best boyfriend test movie. The Princess Bride is the movie that she insisted that Michael watch with her early on in their relationship. His reaction determined how their relationship would progress. He loved it.

&

"Good morning, Miriam." Vicky is feeling especially chipper.

"Look what I found." She pointed to Gracie's deed lying on the table next to her.

"Where was it?"

"It was in the hall closet. I saw part of a paper sticking out from under the door, so I pulled it out and there it was."

"It's good you found it." Miriam takes a sip of her coffee.

"Yeah, Gracie will be happy."

"Happy about what, hon? What will I be happy about?" Gracie also is bright-eyed, and bushy tailed this morning.

"Your deed, Gracie, Vicky found your deed."

"What are y'all doin' today?"

"What did she say?"

"She said what are y'all doing today."

"That's all? Doesn't she even care? I've been making myself crazy about this and that's all she says?"

"Ja, that's all she said." Miriam takes another sip of coffee and jellies her toast.

"Sheesh." Vicky finishes her breakfast in silence.

"Why's she so onry? Did she fall out of bed?" Gracie asks, Miriam shrugs and spreads a bit more jelly on her toast.

"I have to get going. Michael and I are taking off early today. Y'all have a good day." Vicky excuses herself.

"See you later, have a nice day."

"Yeah, see you later, alligator." Gracie chimed in.

"Alligator? What? Why did you say that Gracie? Vicky is *not* an alligator."

Vicky just kept walking. She will have plenty of time to primp if she just ignores them.

"Alligator," Vicky mumbles she shakes her head as she walks.

Gracie glides over to the kitchen table and sits next to Miriam.

"What are you doing today, Gracie?" Miriam asked.

"I have no plans."

"We should go somewhere." Miriam thinks that maybe she should spoon feed Gracie what she has on her mind.

"Go where?" Gracie plays along.

"I have been thinking, Gracie." Miriam looks at the ceiling and lays her finger on her cheek striking a thoughtful pose.

"What have you been thinkin' about?" Gracie copies Miriam's thoughtful pose.

"Time."

"Time!?" That is not at all what Gracie was expecting to hear.

"That's a queer thing for a young girl to be thinkin' about. Most girls are dreamin' about some handsome movie star. Or some ole' boy. But you, oh no, not you, your moonin' over time!" Gracie laughs.

"I been thinking that we could go somewhere in time.

"I reckon' we could, in time." Gracie purposely misconstrued the words.

"Not sometime, in time!"

"Not sometime, in time. Another time? Is that what you mean?" This in fact is bizarrely making sense to Gracie.

"We can go back," Miriam begins unfolding her thought.

"You mean back in time? Tell me what you're thinkin', hon." Gracie likes the sound of this, but she needs more information before she agrees to accompany Miriam on some half-baked time travel junket.

"I told you when I came here, a lot of time passed. The thing is that before I was brought here, I had a vision of time."

"You mean you saw time? Goodness, that's really somethin.'

"Ja, I saw it. It was spiraling all around me and connecting itself together like rungs connect a ladder. I think that is how I got here, in this time. I was taken across a time connection into another time spiral."

"Okay, hon. That's good enough for me. Let's go!" Gracie has never known to be overly cautious. Miriam felt like she could have given a little more information, but she is certain that her hypothesis is sound. Anyway, they will go on that assumption.

Miriam raises her hand and calls Sandalphon. Sandalphon appears. He lands on her shoulder. Miriam takes the bird in her hands and tosses him into the air toward Gracie, Sandalphon disappears. This is excellent. Her theory is holding true.

"I have one more thing to do before we go." Miriam hurries back to her room. She returns dressed as Sister Mary Katherine. She is again garbed in the dark clothes that she was brought here in.

"Now, I am ready. Where do you want to go, Gracie?"

"Well, I've been curious for some time now, about a closed meeting that the city council had. It was about a week before I passed. I think we should go snoop around there a little bit."

"Ja, that is where we go." Miriam lifts her hand and calls Sandalphon. Miriam steps beside Gracie and they are swept away. They are instantly standing in the parking lot between the city hall and the church. The clock set into the cupola of the city hall struck seven o'clock. The air is chilly; people are hurrying into the building.

"Dag gum. Here we are, that's the city council gong in right now." Gracie is flabbergasted.

"Let's go in, Gracie." They instantly stand in the council room. The council members sit around a semicircular table. The moderator calls the meeting to order.

"There will be no minutes as this is a closed 'unofficial meeting'. The topic of the discussion this evening will be the property 10801 Sweet Blossom Road, which as you all know is the property adjacent to the city hall," the moderator began.

"The property has come under scrutiny from some members of the community who feel that the age and somewhat deteriorating condition of the house make it unsafe for habitation. One member of our community in particular has voiced concern for the safety of the unfortunate woman who is living there."

"Some of the woman's many concerns, she has sent to the council in a letter. Her concerns are that the woman would fall through the floor, or the second story would fall on top of her as she sleeps. The person suggests that the house be demolished." The moderator read the letter that had been sent to the council, folded it then stuck it in his shirt pocket.

"What're we going to do, Miriam?" Gracie whispered.

"We can only watch. We can't change anything, Gracie. We must not meddle in the past, but we can gain knowledge for the future. You don't have to whisper; they cannot hear us."

The member of the community who had sent the letter to the council had made no suggestions as to where this unfortunate woman would go after her home was demolished. Furthermore, the writer seemingly had no concern whatsoever about what would ultimately become of the woman. It is obvious that this person, who cowardly signed the letter only, concerned citizen had no concern for anything but a certain agenda.

"I will now put this matter to the floor. Does anyone have any comments?" Rietta Kinsman raises her hand.

"Rietta, you have the floor."

Rietta stood to speak. Rode hard, put away wet, that is the phrase that's often used to paint a word picture of Rietta. She is a tall woman, gangly and awkward. She appears to be in her early sixties but was probably only fifty. Even as a young woman, it is unlikely that she turned many heads. It is not at all improbable that her suitors were few and far between, until after she had breast augmentation surgery. But alas, along with everything else in Rietta's pitiful life, her breasts have fallen from a lofty pinnacle to a lowly station.

"My husband and I moved here from Chicago. The first thing that we noticed was the eyesore that is 10801 Sweet Blossom Road. I agree the house should be demolished. The next thing that caught our attention was that the woman who lives there has male callers at all times of the day or night. There seems to be some kind of illicit activities going on."

Rietta is familiar with illicit activities since she and her husband, Mark, are in the witness protection program. Mark Kinsman and his brother, Wield, were Chicago thugs. Notorious wise guys who had decided to save their own skin by turning state's evidence on the kingpins of their Chicago organization. Now, instead of being touted as the infamous wise guys, as they were in Chicago, they are known in Kumquat as the loudmouth Yankees. Mark's 'connections' had set Rietta up in an influential career that over saw the charitable contributions to a state-run children's home. It was not complicated or tedious work. It was an endeavor at which Rietta could really excel. Her chief task in the organization was to funnel twenty five percent of all moneys from the donations to the children's home into a 'special' account. Rietta's skills in accounting and her propensity toward deceit made her assignment effortless. She was even clever enough to put away a little nest egg for herself, to the tune of two hundred thousand dollars. There's nothing like a government job.

Sondra Kinsman, Wield Kinsman's wife, was next to take the floor. Sondra bristles whenever anyone calls her Sandra; she insists that it's Sondra with an 'o'. But it is widely suspected that her birth certificate reads just plain Sandra with an a, born and bred on the seedy side of New York City. She will be next to offer comments. Sondra, compared to Rietta, Mark, and Wield, is a compassionate caring human being. Compared to the rest of humanity, she is completely unprincipled.

"Well, I can't stand to go out in my yard," Sondra begins her tirade. "I thought I was moving to a nice place with decent people, but then I find out that the woman across the street from me is running a whore house! Excuse my language, but that's what they're all saying." It's laughable that Sondra acts as if the word whore scandalized her, when she herself, being from the bustling, get the freak out of my way, pace of The Big Apple, thinks that a 'decent' person's proper greeting is to raise your middle finger into the air and shout out 'up yours'. Well, some colloquiums just don't translate well.

"Thank you, but that's just gossip." the moderator dismisses Sondra's charge. "None of those allegations have ever been proven. You can sit down now. Thank you. Sondra."

"Lee Ann, you have the floor." The moderator allows Lee Ann Matthews to comment, even though she isn't a member of the city council. Nothing ever happens in Kumquat without a Matthews knowing about it. Nothing ever has, nothing ever will.

"Well, I agree with Sondra." Lee Ann smiles at Sondra. "I always see men stopping and talking to her. I never see any women taking any time at all to talk to her, just men, always just men."

"Maybe that's because she's so nice and she's easy on the eyes too," a voice boomed from the back of the room. The men all snickered, every one of them. Gracie grinned. Adrian Thomas walked to the front of the room and faced Gracie's accusers.

"I'll just say my piece and leave. Won't we, Lee Ann? I haven't heard that you've been voted into the council." Adrian Thomas is a daunting figure of a man. He stood six feet and three inches high and almost three feet at the shoulders, and he loved Gracie Standard with every inch of his being. Adrian is a firm but just man; there would be no funny business in Kumquat as long as he is the sheriff.

"I have heard every piece of gossip about Miss Standard that the people in this town have ever come up with. By my mind, this woman has done nothing to warrant any of the cruel accusations that have been claimed about her. The only thing that any one of y'all have against her is that she is living on a piece of property that each and every one of you have designs on. Y'all couldn't weasel old Henry out of his land and when he let Miss Standard move there, it just stuck in your craw. Well, I can't do anything about it if y'all devise some legal scheme to get her off that property. But listen to me now. If in the course of your dealings with Grace Standard, she is harmed in anyway, I will use everything I have in my power in opposition to you. Mark my words, misery will be on you all. Now, continue if you dare. I'm done." The sheriff left the council hall. Lee Ann followed; she's one of the folks in town that's scared stiff of the sheriff's mother. Lee Ann would not cross Jessamine Thomas or her son. The council hall is silent for what seemed like an eternity. Not one of the council members raised their eyes to the face of another. Finally, the moderator spoke breaking the silent spell of the sheriff's ominous decree.

"We will now vote on the property at 10801 Sweet Blossom Road. All those in favor of starting eminent domain procedures on the property of 10801 Sweet Blossom Road signal by saying aye."

The room resounded with ayes.

"Those opposed signal by saying nay." The room fell silent.

"The ayes have it. We will begin condemnation procedures after our next open city council meeting in two weeks, that's November 15th. This meeting is adjourned."

Mark and Wield Kinsman stand outside the courthouse doors reveling in their success. 'The Brothers', that's what they were known as in the Windy City's mob circles. The Brothers could be depended on to resourcefully deal with situations that even the vilest of criminals could not.

"I wouldn't be counting my chickens if I were you. You don't have that property yet," Miss Wallace cackled, putting voice to the obvious.

"What are you talking about, old woman? That place is as good as ours," Mark sneers.

"I don't know. I just don't know." Miss Wallace doesn't particularly like Gracie, but she really doesn't like the Kinsman's. However, the crafty old lady will play both sides against the middle to her advantage.

"Get out of here, you crazy old bat. She's a nutty old broad." Wield studies the old woman as she walks away.

"Don't worry, Wield, she won't be a problem for the brothers," Mark promises.

Miriam and Gracie returned home.

STEP IN TIME

Vicky quietly stands next to Miriam as she sleeps; she touches Miriam's forehead to determine if she is feverish. Relieved, she quietly slips out of the room.

"I'm a little worried about Miriam, Michael." Vicky snuggles close to Michael. At his request, they would watch The Princess Bride again.

"Why is that, sweet pea?"

"She's been sleeping since early this afternoon. I hope she's not coming down with something. Well, if she is, at least we have plenty of chicken soup." Vicky settles in for the evening.

~

"Rise and shine, hon. Are you going to sleep your life away?" Gracie announces the breaking of the latest dawn.

"What?" Miriam is in a sleep stupor. "It's morning, wake up, sleepy head."

"Morning?"

"That's right. Get up, hon. There are some bits and pieces I want to talk to you about. Let's get this show on the road."

"All right, Gracie, but can you give me some time?"

"Sure." Gracie disappeared. Miriam staggers to the kitchen. She is not quite awake yet, but Vicky is, and has almost finished her breakfast. Miriam pours coffee.

"Good morning. I was wondering when you were going to get up. You've been up and down for the better part of the weekend, sugar. I was starting to worry."

"I was really tired. Gracie and I went to Kumquat before." Miriam puts a cup of coffee on the floor for Rocky and joins Vicky at the table.

"That's her third cup this morning; I think she should cut back." Vicky took the last sip of *her* third cup. Rocky contentedly laps up her morning brew.

"Back away from the coffee, Rocky, just back away," Miriam says in an exaggerated gruff tone of voice. Vicky smiles. She figures Miriam is watching police shows now.

"You and Gracie went to Kumquat, before, what, sugar?" Vicky pours herself the dregs that remain in the pot.

"Before she died."

"Geez, Miriam."

"No, we just watched." Miriam knows 'geez' doesn't mean good.

"What did you watch?"

"The city council meeting. They wanted to condemn Gracie's house."

"Why did they want to condemn Gracie's house?" Vicky put her paper down and began to pay attention.

"There was a letter from someone who suggested it."

"Really? That's very interesting. Who sent the letter?"

"They did not say a name, just a concerned citizen."

"Darn, that would be nice to know. Anything else interesting?"

"Yes, Gracie and the sheriff were in love. He was very angry with the city council."

"Hmm *that* bit of information might come in handy." Vicky smiles as she processes these latest bits of news.

"Gracie has something else she wants to tell me."

"I'm sure she does, sugar, but now we better get ready for work, or we'll be late!"

❧

"Hon, do you have time now? I've got somethin' I need to get off my mind before I forget it." Gracie materialized in front of Miriam at the station, disrupting her organizational efforts.

Miriam's stomach has been suggesting to her the importance of a Cuban sandwich and a deviled crab for the better part of an hour. She has strayed far and afield from the dietary laws that she has been raised by. Miriam rationalized that if neither a Cuban sandwich nor a deviled crab are kosher, ergo, when eaten together, it became a double negative, resulting in a positive. Thus, negating bad, not kosher, and becoming a yummy, good, Cuban sandwich and deviled crab lunch.

"All right, Gracie. I can have lunch now, and we can talk."

It is between mid-morning break and lunch hour in the food court at the station. It is a quiet time. Nothing like the free-for-all morning coffee grab-and-run, or the frantic, mid-morning, smoke-em if-you-got-em as fast as you can, first ten minute break of the day.

"What do you have to tell me?" Miriam unwraps her Cuban sandwich.

"Well, mainly, I want to tell you that I remembered I made some people mad soon before I passed, they were really mad. Yep, around the bend mad." Gracie seems pleased with herself even though whatever she had done may have resulted in her untimely demise.

"What happened?" Miriam is already interested in Gracie's latest tale.

"It was just a few days after the city council had their private meeting," Gracie began.

"I was sitting on my front porch, just rockin' in my grandpa's old rockin chair, and watchin' my chickens scratch in my front yard. That was my most favorite thing to do. I usually let the girls out of the coop in the afternoon and they always came home to roost before dark."

"I had just stepped inside to get myself a glass of sweet tea when I heard a frightful banging on my front door. I ran to the door. I declare I thought there must be a tornado headin' my way or somethin'. When I opened the door, it was no other than that no good rascal Jeffrey Roberts standin' there drunk as a skunk right on my porch."

"Now, that was twofold bad. First of all, I didn't want him anywheres near me, and second of all, Jean Louise already had some crazy thoughts that there was somethin' goin' on between us. Huh, not likely. Not even if we were the last two people on earth, and I was deaf, dumb, and blind. Jeffrey is a low life reprobate, but that's not the point. He's a deacon at the community church where Jean Louise is the assistant minister. At least they were, but I'll get to that later. First things first, I'm getting ahead of myself."

"Anyway, Jean Louise had broken off with Jeffrey soon after she became the assistant minister. Everyone in town knows that Jeffrey is a drunk, but they turned a blind eye to it because of Jean Louise. The old pastor is the one who made him a deacon. Well, but he's gone now.

I'll come back to that too, later on. The old pastor was glad to have Jean Louise as assistant minister for a while, anyway. They got real cozy, but he figured out right quick that Jean Louise was real cozy with a half dozen other fellas, so he put the brakes on. Well, then Jean Louise started to yearn for her old drinkin' buddy, Jeffrey. And so, she made some advances towards him. Of course, he was still lickin' his wounds from the ego beatin' she had just given him. So, he started playing hard to get and actin' like he had somethin' goin' on with me. He was always tryin' to come around on Sunday morning when I was enjoyin' my coffee on the porch. He knew good and well that Jean Louise would be passing by to get to the church, so there he'd be just so that Jean Louise could see him there with me. Well, I caught on to that foolishness and ran him off right quick. What a dick weed."

"Do you want me to tell Vicky all of this?" Miriam's head is spinning. She hopes Gracie does not want this story recounted verbatim.

"No, just the important stuff, hon," Gracie begins again.

"Where was I?"

"What a dick weed."

"Forget that. It's not important.

"Anyway, there was Jeffrey poundin' on my front door like a mad man. He was goin' on about the chickens. He was yellin' that the chickens bother Jean Louise, and she says that they should not be allowed to roam free, which is not in any kind of a violation in Kumquat as she well knew since she *is* on the city council. I figure that she just wanted Jeffrey to come over and give me a hard time. To her way of thinkin', that would prove that he doesn't care anything about me."

"So, there he was, standin on my porch swearin' a blue streak. I swanee the words comin' out of his mouth would have made a sailor blush. Then Jean Louise showed up, and then she laid into me about the chickens coming around the churchyard, and that my house should be condemned, then *she* started cussing me somethin' awful!"

"Well, I just stood there and listened, didn't even answer them back. All the while, Jeffrey was carrying on about tearing my house down, and Jean Louise was screaming about chickens. When there was a lull, I calmly and respectfully asked. Since when does the Church send a drunkard and a whore to deliver their messages? Well, you would have thought I insulted their character." Gracie laughs. "Oh, I guess I did, but I had just enough of them to set me off good. I thought I had seen and heard the last of those two when they drove away. But it wasn't over yet, I soon discovered."

"The next afternoon, I went into town. I had to go all the way to Tampa to get some paint that I had ordered. I got back home later on in the day. When I turned into my drive, I saw a pile of feathers beside my porch. I thought a hawk must have grabbed a hen, it's sad but it does happen on occasion. I would give the girl a proper burial and offer the survivors extra scratch to comfort them. To my horror, there were no survivors, every one of my chickens were dead on my porch and their blood was spattered all over my front door and windows. I was overtaken with sadness. I can hardly stand the thought of it even today. I gathered them from the porch and buried each one of my little friends. I couldn't even say any words in their memory. I was completely overcome.. Just as I finished washing the blood from my porch, Jeffrey stopped his truck in the road in front of my house. He just sat there in his truck and smirked at me. I turned my back on him. I guess he was expecting me to break down, as it was my one simple action of turning my back on him that seemed to make him hoppin' mad. He revved up the motor in his big ole' truck. I heard the wheels scratch in the loose gravel; I turned and looked in his direction. He was driving his truck full out straight for the corner of my house. His face was frozen in anger as he slid across my lawn. He would have gone right into the side of the house if he hadn't hit that big 'ole cherry laurel stump that's hidden under the guava bush. Well, that day, Jeffrey ended up against the telephone pole. Adrian came and took him to the drunk tank and his truck was impounded. Adrian warned him that he better stay away from me, but that didn't satisfy me. No, not one bit. I went inside and wrote a letter to the bishop of the Open-Door Community Churches and recounted exactly what had happened.

The next morning, Jessamine and I went into Tampa to the headquarters of that church and hand delivered the letter to the bishop's secretary. I figured even if the bishop ignores my letter, I had said my peace. I was satisfied, my anger was quieted. What happened next is the point of this whole story. The next day, I was sitting on my porch when an old man came up. He stopped at the steps to the porch and introduced himself as the bishop of the church. He asked if he could come up on my porch and sit with me and talk. The first thing that he told me was that he raised chickens as a boy in Puerto Rico and he understood how attached I must have been to mine. He apologized for the actions of his church. We talked about his chickens and then we just talked. Nothing was said about the letter I had written. Then he excused himself, I watched him walk back over to the church. Later, Miss Wallace told me that the bishop had called the minister, along with Jeffrey and Jean Louise to a meetin' where he read them out royally. Then he transferred the minister to another church, relieved Jeffrey from his duties as deacon and dismissed Jean Louise as the assistant minister.

That's it, hon. The whole story."

"Gracie, that is a terrible thing. I am sorry that happened to you." Miriam is not unfamiliar with human cruelty.

"Oh, hon, don't fret about me." Gracie vanished. Miriam quietly finished her lunch and returned to her work.

"I missed you at lunch, sugar. Where'd you go? I looked for you."

"Gracie came. I had lunch with her out in the courtyard."

"What did she have on her mind?"

"She told me about some people, Vicky. She made them really mad just before she died."

"Really, what happened?"

"They said bad things to her then he killed Gracie's chickens and put the blood on her door and windows."

"What? Who are they? Who did this? Who would do something like that?"

"Jean Louise and her friend, Jeffrey."

"Wasn't the sheriff called and a police report made?"

"Gracie said that Jeffrey got put in the drunk tank, whatever that is, and his truck was impounded. She says the sheriff told Jeffrey to stay away from her."

"Jean Louise and Jeffrey, huh? Well, we'll see about this. There must be some paperwork." Vicky already has a plan.

As soon as Vicky has a break, she dials the Kumquat Sheriff's Department. The deputy on duty puts Vicky's call right through to the sheriff.

"Hello, Sheriff, I hope I didn't catch you at a bad time. This is officer Knight at the Tampa Police Department," Vicky begins.

"Well, hello, Officer Knight, you wouldn't be the one who was poking around Gracie's place a few days ago." The sheriff chuckles.

"One in the same, Sheriff, but that was an unofficial visit," Vicky confesses.

"I thought that it might be, didn't bother me much, but Miss Wallace was all up in the air about it, though. So, what can I do for you?"

"I've been looking through the file on that case. I found Miss Wallace's statement. She stated that she went to Gracie's to have a cup of coffee with her because she thought she hadn't been feeling well the night before, that's when she found her deceased. She also stated that there was trouble between Gracie, Jean Louise and Jeffery, I'm wondering if you have any paperwork on that. I can't find anything about it here in the file."

"Yes, I do have paperwork about that day. I thought I sent it. I'll send it all right over."

"The detective that you gave the case over to here in Tampa has since retired and there is a new detective covering the cold cases. It's Mike De Augustino. Would you mind faxing copies of whatever you have over to him?" Vicky asked.

"Yes, attention, Mike De Augustino! Thank you, sheriff. Good bye."

Vicky loiters around the fax machine until the papers from the Kumquat Sheriff's Department came through. Vicky gathers the papers and heads back to the front desk, she has only one last loose end to tie up. Then, she will present this neatly tied bundle to Michael. She takes a piece of blank paper from the desk and types out a thank you note from Grace Standard to the bishop of the Community Church and put the note in an envelope. Vicky makes a point to pass the file room on her way to Mike's office. Miriam will have to deliver a few more pieces of paper to Gracie's file before Vicky delivers her package to Mike! And he will never be the wiser, she hopes. At the same time that Vicky is laying the fax from Kumquat on Mike's desk. Miriam is filing important papers into the folder, a deed, a thank you note, and a picture of Gracie all dolled up, went right into the Standard file.

"What's this?" Mike looks up from his paperwork.

"It's a fax from the sheriff in Kumquat."

"I hope he didn't send us another case I know that they don't have the resources to thoroughly pursue a case. But really, I'm swamped!" Mike looks the case over. Vicky stands in the door and watches, Mike's brow furrows.

"This is about that Standard case." Mike looks at Vicky.

"Strange that he would send this now, right when you've been asking about the case. What do you think is up with that, Vicky Knight?"

"Can't ever tell, Michael. I've got to get back to the front. See you tonight?" Vicky is afraid that Michael *is* all the wiser.

"Yeah, I'll see you later." Mike tosses the fax folder to the side and returns to what he had been working on. He really is none the wiser to Vicky's devious manipulation of Gracie's case.

A while later, Mike made his way to Vicky's desk. "I looked over that fax from Kumquat."

"What was that all about?"

"The sheriff sent a report that he made about a disturbance between the Standard woman and a couple of neighbors."

"She was fighting with her neighbors?" Vicky figures she should get an Oscar. The words 'and the award goes to Vicky Knight for her unforgettable performance as the double-dealing girlfriend' rings in her ears.

"No, she wasn't, but it seems like the neighbors were intent on causing trouble with the woman. She even alleges that the man killed her chickens, but the woman never filed a complaint."

"She never filed. That's strange. Maybe she was afraid," Vicky said.

"That could be, but it seems that she would have filed for something like that, if it were true."

"What do you think, Michael?"

"I think that I'll bring the two of them in and ask them some questions."

"Good idea, Michael. It might be a good lead."

"Call them in, their numbers are in the fax. Tell them it's important that they come in today!"

∾

"Jeffrey Roberts and Jean Louise Soto are here to see you, Michael

"Good, Vicky, send Ms. Soto back in about two or three minutes. Then send Roberts back as soon as you see Ms. Soto leave." Mike will let the tension mount for a few minutes before he begins the questioning. The fax that Mike received included arrest records, there was nothing on Jean Louise Soto. Jeffrey Thaddeus Roberts, on the other hand, has been a naughty boy. Jeffrey has racked up numerous D.U.I.'s, drunk and disorderly, and misdemeanor drug charges. Mike would save him for last. Given what Mike has discovered studying the Grace Standard folder, the cold case might be warming up, maybe just a degree or so, but that could be all it takes.

"Hello, Ms. Soto, I'm detective Mike De Augustino. Please sit down. Can I offer you a water or a cup of coffee?" Mike turns on the charm.

"No, thank you. I'm fine." Jean Louise is feeling pretty comfortable.

"I'm going over some cold cases. There is one case in particular I think you might be able to help me with. It's the case involving the death of a Grace Standard in Kumquat. Did you know Miss Standard?"

"Yes, I knew Grace." Louise is not quite as comfortable as she had been.

"I don't know what I could add to Gracie's case, Detective."

"Just a few questions, Ms. Soto." Mike smiles. "How long had you known her?"

"About twelve years."

"Would you say that you were a close friend of Miss Standard?" This is the question that would be Mike's marker.

"No, Detective, we were not close at all. As a matter of fact, we were not very fond of each other." Jean Louise knew that this is common knowledge in Kumquat, so she had better out with the truth. Jean Louise seems to be answering truthfully. Mike's gut is telling him that she was not involved in any harm done to Grace Standard. He has only a couple more questions for her.

"Do you know anyone who might have wanted to harm Miss Standard?"

"No, I don't."

"What about Jeffery Roberts, did he want to harm Miss Standard?"

"Jeffery?" Now, Jean Louise is really uncomfortable.

"Do you think he wanted to harm Grace Standard?" Mike repeated.

"No, I don't think Jeffrey wanted to hurt Gracie. He might be a hot head when he's drunk, but he never would have physically harmed Gracie. A bar fight is one thing, but hurting Gracie, I really don't think so."

"One last question, Miss Soto. Would you be willing to submit to a polygraph?"

"Yes, I will." Jean Louise knew that she had been truthful and would submit to about anything this handsome detective suggested.

"Thank you, Miss Soto an officer will escort, you to polygraph."

Mike went over his notes. He would be surprised if Soto flunked, he doesn't think she has fooled him. He did not assume that she is as innocent as a newborn babe, far from. Mike recalls a story that, years ago, was being passed around the station. The young officers, who frequented the same drinking establishment, had, on separate occasion, encountered a woman by the name of Jean Louise in that establishment. This woman had sexually harassed the young officers every time they sidled up to the bar for another round. Allegedly she pinched each and every ass that had seemingly presented itself for her drunken pleasure. Miss Soto's seedy behavior didn't carry any weight in Mike's consideration as to whether or not she is telling the truth. It was just a story. The officer returned, followed by Jean Louise. The officer hands the results of the polygraph to Mike.

"You're free to go. There will not be any more questions, Ms. Soto. You have been honest with your answers. Thank you for your time."

Jeffrey Roberts was escorted back.

"Take a seat, Jeff." Mike is gruff with the man. He will establish dominance right away. Jeffrey sat, his eyes searched every corner of the room, he twitched and blinked. Mike watches Jeffrey as he fidgets with his hands. Mike stood over him and began questioning.

"Are you Jeffrey Thaddeus Roberts?"

"Yes, sir I am."

"Do you know of a Ms. Grace Standard?"

"Kind of."

"Kind of, yes, sir, I do, or kind of, no, sir, I don't?" Mike steps into Jeffrey's space.

"Yes, sir, I do know Grace, but she's dead is what I meant." Jeffrey got the message.

"Yes, she is dead, Jeff. Would you say that you were a friend of Ms. Standard?"

"Yes, sir." Jeffrey's critical thinking skills aren't quite as honed as Jean Louise's are.

"Did you ever have an argument with Ms. Standard?" Mike already knew the answer to that question. But Jeffrey is unaware that Mike has a file brimming with documents reports and letters that answered all of Mike's questions concerning Grace Standard before they are even asked.

"No, sir." Jeffrey looked down at his feet; the happenings of that day were a vague blur in his alcohol addled mind. Jeffrey had not only been drunk on the day that he and Jean Louise had argued with Gracie, but he had continued his drunkenness into the next day. By the time he drove his truck into the telephone pole, Jeffrey was most likely unaware of a lot of things, but he does know that he's lying now. BINGO! Mike has made a breakthrough, Jeffrey is lying.

"Jeff, do you know anyone who wanted to harm Grace Standard for any reason?" Jeffrey's eyes darted around the room, everywhere except to Mike.

"No. No, sir, no one."

"Did you kill Grace Standard?"

"No! I did not." Jeffrey is emphatic.

"One more question, will you agree to a polygraph test?"

"Do I need a lawyer?" He mumbled into his hands as he tried to wipe the guilt from his face.

"I don't know. Do you?"

"Well, I didn't hurt Gracie."

"That's all we want to know."

"Okay, then. I'll take the test."

Mike paces in his office as he awaits the results of Jeffrey Roberts' polygraph. He knows that this guy is trouble and is certain that he is going down in flames as soon as he has those results. The officer and Jeffrey return to Mike's office. Jeffrey is smiling. Why would this man be smiling? Mike reads the results of the test. Jeffrey has been untruthful about every answer to every question except one. One question, just one question; did you kill Grace Standard? No, I did not, that is his *only* truthful answer. Mike is stunned. He dismisses Jeffrey but tells him not to go too far in case he had to bring him back in for more questioning. is not off the hook yet. Do you know anyone that might have wanted to harm Grace Standard? Mike keeps going back to the answer to this question. No, I don't know anyone who wanted to harm Grace Standard, was an untruthful answer. So, most probably Jeffrey *does* know someone who wanted to hurt Grace Standard, maybe he even knows someone who would have murdered her, but who? Mike will uncover the secret that Jeffrey Thaddeus Roberts holds. Kumquat is a small town and it's hard to keep a secret in a small town. The truth is that it's better not to try at all to keep a secret in a town like Kumquat. The reason being, if it is suspected in a small town that someone is hiding something, the speculation is usually much worse and far more damaging than the truth would ever be.

"How did it go, Michael?" Vicky hurries back to Mike's office as soon as she sees Jeffrey leave. "I had to cut them loose."

"Both of them? I didn't expect that."

"Yeah, neither did I, but they were not involved with whatever happened to that woman. It's still a big damn mystery." Mike is frustrated.

"What are you going to do, Michael? Is there a plan B?"

"I'm going to ask some more questions. There's something that I don't know yet."

"You're a good detective, Michael, you'll figure it out. It's five o'clock, are you going home now?"

"No, I'm going to make a few calls."

"Okay, I'll see you tomorrow, good night, Michael. Don't work too late."

"I won't. Good night, Vicky." Michael dials the Kumquat sheriff's department. Adrian Thomas answers the phone.

"Hello, Sheriff, this is Detective Mike De Augustino. I just interviewed Jeffrey Roberts."

"How did he do?"

"Well, he didn't have anything to do with whatever happened with Ms. Standard, but he wasn't completely truthful."

"What do you mean?"

"I had him polygraphed, and when asked if he knew of anyone who might have wanted to harm her, he answered no he didn't. That was an untruthful answer."

"Hmm, I'll watch him for a while, see who he's hanging with. He's been in some scrapes with the law before, maybe he's taken up with some riff raff."

"Thanks, Sheriff."

"No problem, Mike, glad to help. You know, there is one more thing. There was someone in town who wrote a letter to the City Council about condemning the house that Gracie Standard lived in. Whoever it was that wrote the letter could have wanted that property for themselves. I suspect whoever it was is pretty influential. But if I were you, I'd ask the moderator, he's the one who would know, if anyone does."

"Is that right, Sheriff? I'd like to talk to him. Can you give me the city hall number?" The sheriff looks up the number and gives it to Mike.

"Hey, Mike, I gotta go. I got a call coming in. Catch ya later.

"Sure, Adrian. Catch ya later."

～

"I hope you got some sleep last night, Michael." Vicky checked on Mike first thing when she got to the station.

"Morning, sweet pea. I didn't stay late, just made a call to the sheriff in Kumquat then went home."

"Did you find out anything?" Vicky hopes that the sheriff had not mentioned her unofficial visit to Gracie's house

"Yeah, he told me that the city council was going to condemn the property that the Standard woman lived on."

"Why? Did he say?" Vicky is relieved; looks like the sheriff kept her secret.

"Someone sent a letter to them about condemning the place, so they did. Sounds fishy to me."

"You'll get to the bottom of it, Michael, I'm sure. Are you coming over tonight?"

"I don't know, depends." Mike is back into Gracie's file.

"Okay, see you later, Michael."

"Later, sweet pea." At nine o'clock sharp, Mike dials the number that Adrian Thomas had given him.

"Kumquat City Hall."

"Yes, I'd like the city council, please."

"I'll transfer your call, hold please."

"Hello."

"Yes, hello. This is Detective Mike De Augustino. I'd like to speak with the head of the city council."

"Speaking. How can I help you?"

"I'm investigating the Grace Standard case. There have been some things that have come to light that you might be able to help me with."

"I will if I can. What do you need?"

"Just some information. The council was sent an anonymous letter about condemning the house that Ms. Standard lived in. The council read the letter and voted to condemn the property. Is this normal for the council to take such drastic actions based on one anonymous letter?"

"I can see how this would be a reasonable question, especially if a person doesn't understand the mechanism of a small town like Kumquat. If the truth were known, the council has had many complaints about that property. We were continually being stopped on the street by neighbors or friends who had concerns," he explained.

"I see. Did you know who wrote the letter?"

"No, it could have been anyone."

"That's all I wanted to know, thank you for your time."

"No problem, Detective. Call again if you have any more questions. Good bye."

"Who am I speaking to, if I call back?" Mike asked a dead receiver.

"I'm glad you came over, Michael. I miss your face. How did your day go?" Vicky led Mike to the couch.

"Not so good. I didn't get anywhere with the city council. That was my best lead."

"What do you think, Michael?" Vicky sensed Michael's frustration; she gently strokes his face and snuggles closer.

"I think that I love you, that's what I think. Besides, something might happen." Mike tenderly pulls Vicky to himself and kisses her passionately.

"Well, you're right. Something just might happen." Vicky matches Mike's kiss.

Vicky and Miriam have already determined that the next morning something would definitely happen. They will bring a new approach to the Gracie undertaking.

GOODNIGHT, SLEEP TIGHT

Before the dawn broke, Miriam clothed in the antiquated garb of a nun sat in her dark room. She stands, raises her hand to the darkness, and calls out to Sandalphon. The raven flew to her shoulder.

"We're going to Gracie's bedroom on the day of her death," Miriam whispers to Sandalphon. They are immediately standing in a corner of Gracie's room. Safely cocooned, they cannot be seen or heard, but they are now privy to the events of that evening. Gracie is sitting on the edge of her bed. The clock on her bed stand reads six o'clock, the evening shadows are growing. She holds an envelope in her hand, in the dim light of dusk, Miriam can read the return address on the envelope. The letter is from the Franklin Law Firm in Kumquat. Gracie takes only one of the papers from the bulging envelope. Then she lets the envelope fall to the floor beside her bed. She stretches out on her bed and studies the paper that she has separated from the rest.

"That must be the deed." Miriam spoke to Sandalphon. Gracie puts her hand to her head then to her throat, she holds tight to the precious paper in her hand. She switches off her bed light and pulls the covers up, she relaxes.

"She's dead." Miriam hears noises in the shrubbery in front of Gracie's window. She goes to the window and peers out; she stares into the face of Miss Wallace who has hidden herself in the foliage growing next to the window. As she watches, a dark figure approaches, a ski mask covers the trespassers face. The intruder stops in front of the bedroom window, no more than a foot from where Miss Wallace hides; she slinks back into the bushes. The sinister figure silently opens the bedroom window, climbs inside, and creeps to Gracie's bedside. Miss Wallace inches closer to the window just as the hooded figure plunges a large knife through the covers straight into Gracie's chest. Shocked, Miss

Wallace gasps, turns, and scurries from her hiding place. The sound of Mrs. Wallace making her hasty retreat frightens the interloper.

After pulling the knife from Gracie's chest, the intruder quickly climbs out of the open window and dashes away. Sandalphon takes flight behind them. Miriam now sees through Sandalphon's eyes. The masked figure disappears into the darkness. Miss Wallace runs toward her home. The frightened old woman is met by Sondra as she hurries on her way. They have a brief conversation then they continue each to their respective homes.

As Sandalphon flies, Miriam sees what he sees, Mark Kinsman and Jeffrey Roberts entering Kinsman's barn. Sandalphon returns to his perch on Miriam's shoulder. Miriam hears a loud noise in Gracie's living room, it appears to be the hooded intruder returning to finish the night's work. The masked figure quietly slinks into the bedroom. In the darkened room, the killer goes to Gracie's bed. Surprisingly, the assassin throws the covers over Gracie's head and begins to choke the woman that he no more than a few minutes before had stabbed. His strong and efficient hands wrap around Gracie's neck, and his vice-like grip tightens around Gracie's throat. While engrossed in the pleasure of exacting death, a cloaked figure enters the room, and went unnoticed by the murderer. The latest intruder picks up the envelope that Gracie had dropped and slips it into the pocket of a heavy coat, and quietly steps next to the killer. Startled, the executioner lost balance and fell forward. A muscular elbow breaks the fall; a loud cracking noise came from beneath the elbow.

"She's dead. I broke her nose, sounds like. What are you doing here? Get out!" the assassin growled.

There was a noise coming from the kitchen. Upon hearing the noise, the two figures left through the bedroom window, making certain to close it behind them before making their retreat. Sandalphon again flies above. Through the raven's eyes, Miriam watched the pair disappear into the woods. Miriam waits in the corner.

A figure appears at Gracie's door. This figure is not hooded or cloaked as the others have been, but the room is too dark to make out the face of this latest intruder. The shadowy figure stares across the room into the corner where Miriam stands. She slinks into the dark corner; her view is obstructed by the shadows. The shadowy figure lingers beside Gracie's bed and then focused on Gracie's gold watch.

The intruder picks up the watch from the nightstand, then turns and leaves Gracie's house through the front door. Sandalphon follows the shadowy figure; Miriam, once again, watches through Sandalphon's eyes, Sandalphon circles high above. As the figure slowly walks to the edge of town, Sandalphon swoops down to touch the murky form. Before the figure disappears into obscurity, Sandalphon looks closely into its face. Sandalphon returns to Miriam. Moments pass, then as if invited in, Miss Wallace walked in the front door, she made her way to Gracie's bed she pulled the cover off of Gracie's dead body.

"I didn't expect this mess, Gracie, you were only supposed to sleep. Now I got to sweep up a little." She arranges the lifeless body and properly tucks Gracie in as if she is peacefully sleeping. She didn't find the deed in Gracie's hand, nor did she find it on the floor.

"Good. It's gone." Miss Wallace set a bottle of sleep aid on the nightstand next to Gracie's death bed.

"Night, Gracie. Sleep tight." Miss Wallace left the house.

∽

"How was your day? You don't often take a day off in the week. Are you feeling all right?" Mike worries about Vicky, he knows she pretends to be stronger than she really is. "I feel fine. I just had some things that I had to take care of before we leave. You shouldn't worry about me, Michael. I'm fine."

"Where's Miriam?"

"She's in her room, changing. She's primping for Paul. I ordered pizza."

"Is she all packed? Primping? It's Skype, no one looks any good on Skype. Anyway, I don't think Paul will notice how she looks, he's in loooove." Mike laughs.

"I think she's finished packing. I'll check on her packing later on tonight. What's going on with the sheriff over in Kumquat?"

"I talked to him, he's watching Roberts, but he hasn't seen anything unusual."

"So, any other leads, Michael?"

"No, the case is getting cold again unless something unexpected happens it'll be dead in the water, I'm afraid. What did you get on the pizza?"

"Everything combo, and wings."

"Good, wings. Miriam, there you are, you look ravishing!" Mike hugs Miriam and tussles her strawberry blond curls.

"Stop! Mike, I want to look sexy for Paul."

"Does she know what sexy is?" Mike whispers to Vicky. This is something new he thought he might need to know. Although, he doesn't really want to know. Mike is just glad that this young woman is Vicky's charge or challenge, not his.

"We had the talk." Vicky smiles; Mike winces. A knock sounds at the front door.

"Pizza's here," Vicky calls out. Rocky runs to the door. Mike ushers in the cheesy delight that always suddenly appears at the door whenever Vicky calls out Pizzashere!"

"I got the anchovies separate just for you, Miriam. Here, yuck." Vicky passes Miriam a small ramekin full of oily wonderful. Everyone drops a piece of cheese on the floor for Rocky. Rocky doesn't mind the mess and she certainly doesn't mind the added smelly little bits that are only on the cheese that Miriam drops. Rocky has learned that these smelly bits are called yuck. Rocky likes yuck a lot. Then they heard the familiar Skype tone.

"It's Paul. Answer it, quick, no Vicky wait, do I look all right?" Miriam fluffs her hair and gives Mike a don't you dare mess it up again look. Mike chuckles, stretches his hands out, and makes exaggerated hair messing movements with his fingers as Miriam passes.

"You look great, sugar. Relax," Vicky answers the skype call and puts her laptop on the table. Now, Paul can see everyone. It will be a long distance double date. Actually, the plan is to firm up the arrangements for the group to spend the Fourth of July holidays in the mountains at Paul's cabin.

"Hi, Miriam, I miss you. You look wonderful."

"Oh, thank you, Paul. I hardly had time to comb my hair. I've been out all day." Miriam twisted a curl around her finger. Vicky winks at Mike.

"Who is she learning that from?" Mike whispers although he knows that Vicky is teaching her all kinds of lady tricks.

"Mike, buddy you ready to go?"

"Yeah, bro. We have our reservations and we'll be taking off in the morning."

"You're staying for the week, aren't you?"

"Yeah, five days and nights," Mike reassured Paul.

"Vicky, you're looking good as usual."

"Thank you, Paul, but remember my boyfriend is sitting right here."

"Oh, I get 'ya, Vic. Miriam, you are really going to like it at the cabin, it's beautiful!"

"I am very anxious to see you again, Paul." Miriam blushes. The group finalizes their plans and Mike excuses himself.

"Listen guys, I'm going to have to say good night now, we've got an early morning ahead of us. See you tomorrow, Paul."

"Sure, Mike, I have to get going now too. It was good talking to you, Vicky and Miriam. I'll see you soon, but even tomorrow isn't soon enough."

"Good night, Paul, sweet dreams," Miriam said.

"Sweet dreams, Miriam. See you tomorrow."

"Are you all packed, Miriam? Did you pack your bathing suit?" Vicky follows Miriam to her room.

"No. I think it shows too much of my skin." Miriam whispers as she holds the chic sailor styled bathing suit up to her adorable little self and scowls.

"It's not too revealing, Miriam. I won't let you look like a floozy. Pack it!" Vicky demands.

"All right, Vicky." Miriam tries to close her suitcase. "Help me," Vicky sat on top of the piece of luggage, just as Miriam did for her. Miriam closes her bag and now is ready to go. "This will be a nice holiday. We could all use a break. We haven't had much time to talk about what happened when you went to Kumquat this morning."

"I know. I thought it would be simple. I expected that I would see what happened to Gracie and then we would know exactly what to do. But now I'm more confused than I was before. I have told you everything that I saw. I just do not understand it at all."

"It's all confusing, sugar. But it'll keep until we come back. Let's try not to think about anything except having a good time for the next five days. Okay?"

"Yes, I like how that sounds. We will have a good time only."

"Yes, only a good time, no worries, pinky swear." Vicky crooked her little finger and held it up to Miriam.

"What is wrong with your finger, Vicky?"

"Oh my goodness, sugar, I can't believe I haven't taught you pinky swear."

"No, you have *not* taught me. I think you cheated me from pinky swear." Miriam smiles.

"Look here, whenever you make a promise or an oath you crook your pinkie with the other person's pinky and then you each say, 'pinky swear'. Then you are bound to the promise. See, like this." Vicky crooked her pinky around Miriam's.

"I see. Let's pinky swear now.

"What do you want to pinky swear?"

"I want to pinky swear that we will always look after one another and each other's children, and their children also."

"But I have no children, Miriam."

"You will Vicky. Let's swear."

"All right." Vicky and Miriam crooked their fingers, intertwined their pinkies, and swore a pinky swear.

❧

"Miriam, wake up! Michael is going to be here at six-thirty. We have to be ready as soon as he gets here. Our plane leaves at nine and we have to check in two hours ahead. Come on, get up now." This was Vicky's second attempt to rouse Miriam from her sleep. Vicky pulls her luggage to the door and starts coffee.

"Rise and shine, hon."

v"What time is it?" Miriam sits straight up in bed. Gracie has succeeded where Vicky had failed.

"Your time, or my, time?" Gracie laughs.

"All right, Gracie, I am awake. I have to get dressed now. I am going on holiday, you know."

"Yes, hon, I know. I just stopped in to tell you I hope you have a hi-oh spell with your fella." Miriam thanked Gracie for her wish. Whatever it is, she knows Gracie means well.

"Oh, good, you're up. Get going. Michael will be here soon." Vicky is glad she doesn't have to pull Miriam out of the bed this morning.

"Ja, Gracie got me up." Miriam yawns.

"Oh, Gracie's here?"

"No, she left. She just wanted to wish me a hi-oh something." Miriam dresses as she talks. Vicky leaves the room. She doesn't have the time to try to decipher Gracie and Miriam's foolishness.

"Drag your bags to the front door. Michael will put them in the taxi," Vicky calls out.

"What about Rocky?" Miriam follows Vicky.

"Don't worry, Ted is going to look after her," Vicky reassures Miriam as she pushes her bags up to the door. Finally, all the bags are at the door. Vicky and Miriam have just finished their last sip of coffee when the doorbell rings. Before long, everyone and their luggage had piled into the taxi. Then off they went, like a herd of turtles, as Vicky's grandmother often said.

❧

Hours later, Paul met them at the airport. Paul spots Miriam and hurries to help her pull her bag from the luggage conveyer.

"Ugh, what have you got in here? It weighs a ton." Miriam wonders if Paul really wants to know what she has in her luggage, and if he does, why?

"Paul, good to see you, brother." Mike pats Paul's back and struggles to pull another bag off the conveyer.

"Good to see you. Have you got enough to carry? Let me take one of those." Paul took a piece of luggage from Mike.

Paul drove through the city, into the farmlands, and then up into God's country 'almost heaven' West Virginia.

"Paul, this is beautiful." Miriam looks out the car window, down into bottomless ravines and up into magnificence. She, of course, has seen mountains before in Germany, but this is different though. This is not just looking, this is seeing, this is experiencing. Something has changed. It seems to Miriam that colors are more vibrant, smells headier, the world tastes glorious. Her senses are coming to life. This *must* be almost heaven, as Paul has claimed.

"Here, we are. This is *my* piece of paradise." Paul parks under a canopy of hickory nut trees. Paul and Mike start unloading luggage.

"Yeah, this is a great place. Have you had it long?" Mike put significance in the pride of workmanship that has obviously gone into the creation of Paul's cabin. Paul's 'cabin' stands in the forest as if it has grown there. It is not pretentious by any means; it is *exquisite* by any standard.

"My father and grandfather built it years ago, not long after World War II. I inherited it from my grandfather." An image of Paul's grandfather flashed through Miriam's mind.

"My grandmother lived here until she got older then she moved into a senior village in town. I come up a few times a year and visit her, on holidays and birthdays."

Paul and Mike set the bags down in the entry. There are three bedrooms upstairs. The master bedroom is on the other side of the main floor. A balcony which also serves as a hall to the second floor rooms, stretches above the entirety of the main floor. The great room holds a massive fireplace; the dining area and kitchen is tucked behind the great room; the kitchen opens to a deck that stretches out to a magnificent view of paradise. It is not a large place, but it certainly is comfortable, and there is plenty of room for Paul's guests.

"You all can choose whatever room up there that suits you. Come on, Mike. We'll get these bags up there for these ladies."

"Okay, I'm ready." Mike made a muscle pose and picks up Vicky's bags.

"Come on, Michael. It's not that bad." Vicky and Miriam follow Mike and Paul up the stairwell. The group settles into their rooms and then meet back downstairs. They sink down into the deep and generous armchairs in Paul's living room.

"How about something to eat? Anybody?" Paul offers.

"I'm not hungry just yet, but I'd love a cold drink," Vicky says.

"That's why I have a pitcher of sweet tea in the fridge. How about you, Miriam? I've got lots of lemons."

"Ja, I would like some tea, but nothing to eat, thank you."

"Mike, how about you? I know you're hungry I'm starved."

"Yeah, I'll come help you." Mike pulls himself out of the chair and follows Paul.

"And we'll make ourselves a sandwich," Paul insists.

"Yeah, I think I would like a sandwich," Mike agrees.

"Later, we'll start some coals and grill something. It'll be the welcome party," Paul calls out from the kitchen.

"Woo hoo! A party!" Vicky is already losing the city cares.

Mike smiles, he welcomes that "woo hoo."

~

The friends sat in Adirondack chairs watching the shadows that are racing across the mountains. The sunset is making a complete spectacle of itself.

"That was great barbecue, Paul."

"Thanks, Mike" The guys sit back in their chairs; both, in a red meat stupor having put away a very large chunk of rare cow.

"Paul, you and Mike relax. Miriam and I will clean up the kitchen." Vicky stands and motions to Miriam.

"I have a better idea. You and Mike relax, and Miriam and I will clean up the kitchen." Paul takes Miriam's hand and pulls her out of the chair.

"Aww." Miriam feigns unwillingness but actually is happy to leave the group to steal a bit of time alone with Paul.

"Come on, girl, it's time to earn your keep." Paul didn't waste any time. Once they reach the kitchen, he gathers her into his arms and gently kisses her. Miriam gave herself over to newly awakened senses.

"Wow!" is the only word that Paul's mind is able to fashion into an acceptable declaration. Paul starts gathering dishes. Miriam doesn't appreciate this sudden change in Paul's actions but decides it will be a good thing if she helps with the cleanup.

"What are we going to do tomorrow, Paul? That is the Fourth of July, the Independence Day." Miriam stacks dishes on the counter.

"There's always a Fourth of July celebration in the little town in the valley. It's lots of fun, food, and games. Everyone shows up. My grandmother will even be there. I want her to meet you. My father and her are all the family I have left."

"Oh, I understand. Vicky is the only family I have."

"Vicky?" Paul knows all the particulars of Miriam's coming and goings, here, there, and elsewhere, but this is new information.

"Yes, we did a pinky swear." Miriam holds her crooked pinky up. "Oh, a pinky swear, huh?" Paul knotted his pinky with Miriam's.

"So, you know, pinky swear, ja?"

"Ja, ja. I know, pinky swear," Paul teased.

"I love you, Miriam."

"Pinky swear, Paul?"

"Yes, pinky swear, Miriam. I do love you." Paul took Miriam into his arms and nuzzled the top of her head.

∾

The band paraded down Main Street, they marched into the town square playing a John Phillip Sousa patriotic medley, heavy on the sousa.

The band looks as much like toy soldiers marching as any genuine toy soldier could have. Sporting white pants, red, epaulette adorned jackets, and tall royal blue band hats, the band put on what was nothing less than a spirited performance. A presentation which causes a body to want to break out in a sappy old song like Gary Indiana or My Hometown. So, went the grand opening of the towns fourth of July celebration. It was colossal!

"Miriam, do you like cotton candy? We can get some over there." Paul points across the park. Miriam looks at Vicky for enlightenment. Vicky nods an emphatic yes, and mouths 'you like it'. Paul took Miriam's hand, and they were off.

"She's adjusting." It is more of a question than a statement from Mike.

"Yes, she is." Vicky hopes this will satisfy Mike.

"Does she ever remember anything?" Mike pressed.

"No, she never talks about her past. If she remembers anything, it must be just too painful."

"Poor kid. She's lucky she has you." Mike slips his arm around Vicky's waist and gives her an affectionate squeeze.

"Look, Mike, a football toss! Go on, try to dunk the clown. Go on, win me a bear."

"I know what this is. You think I can't do it. Well, step right up, little lady, be mystified and marveled."

"Three throws for a dollar, sir. Win the lady a bear," the hawker called out.

"The sign says the money goes to charity. Which charity?"

"Make a wish foundation."

"Okay, here's a ten, you can keep the change. I'll get him on the first throw," Mike bragged. Mike won Vicky a bear on the first toss. Just as he had predicted.

"There you go, Vicky. Never doubt me." Mike looked deep into Vicky's eyes. Mike and Vicky poke through the craft and art exhibits. Then they're off to the petting zoo where Miriam is showing Paul up in the chicken rodeo. Miriam has three angry hens in her pen, to Paul's big fat *none*. Mike heckles from the stand. The crowd is in an uproar. Finally, the time buzzer sounds, and Miriam is crowned the chicken rodeo queen. She wears her feather crown with pride and grace. She promises to be a kind and benevolent monarch.

"Let's go to the picnic area. There's someone that I want you all to meet over there, especially you, Miriam." Paul leads his friends to the wooden tables that sit in a shaded field. He introduces his grandmother, he calls her Oma, the first word he spoke as a child, the German word for grandma.

"Oma, these are my friends from Florida. The ones that I have been telling you about."

"Don't shout, child, I can still hear. It is nice to meet you. Friends from Florida… that would-be Tampa. He thinks I don't remember, but I remember what I please. Let me think, you would be Mike, of course, that would be you." Oma touches Mike's arm "and you are Vicky." The old woman smiles.

"And you must be Miriam." Oma takes Miriam's hands in hers. Her fingers dash across the opal ring; a spark of approval dances in her eyes.

"You are a beautiful girl."

"Dankeschön."

"And German, too. Very good, Paul." Oma smiles at her grandson.

"Oma brought us lunch." Paul opens the basket, and the friends feast on the delicious lunch that Paul's Oma has prepared.

After lunch, Mike and Vicky lounge under a shade tree, listening to the music streaming from the band shell. Paul cheers on the young boxcar racers, while Miriam enjoys another stick of cotton candy; this amazing treat confirms Miriam's thought that Vicky is an extremely wise woman.

When the sun finally sets on the day's exuberance, the town gathers at the baseball field, they fill the wooden stands, others ready their blankets on the ground. Now the grand finale will begin, the fire works! The town's people stand as the band plays The Star-Spangled Banner, then the fireworks began. The sky is ablaze. The entire town fell silent, only the sound of the fireworks bursting, and the strains of America, the Beautiful could be heard. The show ends with countless red, white, and blue exploding stars falling toward the spellbound crowd.

It is late the next morning before anyone begins to stir in the cabin. The night before had not ended for the friends at the grand finale. Instead, they stayed up late into the night talking and laughing and, most importantly, nurturing their friendship.

"How about if we go down to the creek today?" Paul suggests at breakfast.

"Creek… how far is that?" Vicky asks.

"It's just back in the woods a little way. There's a nice path to it. I keep it clear, there's no brambles or anything."

"No spiders?"

"No spiders." Paul assures Vicky, Miriam snickered.

"Don't worry, sweet pea, I'll protect you. Paul, can I get another sausage?" Mike passed his plate over to Paul.

"Sure Mike."

"Thanks, Paul, these sausages are great.

"Yeah, Vicky, she'll run down a bad guy by herself but don't put her up against anything with more than two legs," Mike whispers to Paul as he passes Mike his plate back. Vicky pretended she didn't hear Mike's tease.

"Thanks, bro, good breakfast."

"The creek sounds great! Miriam and I have been wanting to try out our new swimsuits." Miriam furrowed her brow at Vicky. Vicky pursed her lips and squinched her eyes. Pursed lips and squinched eyes always trumped furrowed brow.

Miriam and Vicky changed into their swimsuits while Mike and Paul pump up the inner tubes.

"We've had a lot of rain lately, the creek is deep enough to tube in, and the current is good, not too strong," Paul speaks as he works.

"I've been thinking about something, Mike. I want to run it by you." Paul stopped inflating the big pink tube he is working on.

"This one's for Miriam. Nice, huh?"

"Yeah, it's a beauty Paul. What do you want to ask me?"

"It's about my work. I've been thinking about moving it to Tampa."

"Really Paul?" Mike keenly studied Paul.

"Miriam?" he asked.

"Yeah, mostly, but Tampa is a busy city, and my work can easily be moved. It's mainly just computers. What do you think, Mike? Tell me the truth, I trust you."

"Well, Tampa just keeps growing, and I can see where you're coming from. If it were me, I'd do it. That's all I can say, bottom line is you have to decide."

"That's why I haven't said anything to Miriam. Thanks, Mike." Paul appreciates the input.

Vicky sticks her head over the second story veranda and calls down. "Are y'all about ready?"

"We're waiting on you. Come on down, bring towels." Paul answers.

There is a bend in the creek just past the end of the path. At the bend, the creek pools out to a pond then flows back into the creek. The pond is the destination. The giant hickories shade much of the pond; one of the giants even sports a heavy rope which it wears with a manner of self-importance.

Mike swings from the rope and drops into the crisp water then Paul follows, one time after another, they swing and drop. Miriam and Vicky float along the shady edge of the pond.

They are entertained by the guys' clowning around, a show that is being put on, entirely for the ladies' enjoyment and delight. The swimming hole turned out to be a most enjoyable experience.

By the time, the aqua fest was over and done, lunch had been pressed into a new time slot. They each tried to come up with a name for a meal between lunch, and dinner. Mike offered linner, Vicky thought a combination of lunch and supper would work best. She presented sucher with rave reviews. Paul and Miriam conferred and brought the winner to the table, dilusup; a combination of dinner lunch and supper, something for everyone depending on what one's preferences are. After 'dilusup', they gather on the veranda to lend a hand to the setting sun, after which the swim team is exhausted, and turn in early. They have made plans to ramble around in Shepherdson Town the next day.

⁓

Shepherdson Town is amazing. German Street looks as if it has been picked out of a book of fairy tales and then magically placed in the picturesque town. They spend the entire day sightseeing. They poke through galleries and antique shops in the story book town. With souvenirs of their day, in hand, the group motor back to Paul's cabin. *

On the final day of their stay, the friends rest in the tranquility of a tender mist that caresses and delights the eager mountain.

"To life!" Paul made a toast. "There's something that I would like to say." Everyone focuses on their host. "I have been thinking about something, and I have made an important decision that will affect my entire life. I have weighed my options and sought council before coming to this decision. I have decided to move my work to Tampa."

"Wow, that's wonderful!" Vicky applauds, she's thrilled.

"Great!" Mike shakes Paul's hand. He is certain that Paul has made the right decision. Miriam is silent, Paul is concerned.

"What do you think, Miriam?" He asks.

"If you move your work to Tampa then what will you do in Indiana?" Paul explains his intentions to not only move his work to Tampa but to also move himself. Miriam hugs his neck, she is ecstatic. They made plans together and enjoyed their dinner and looked forward to many more.

∽

"Here we go ladies, remember, I'll need a ride home, Vicky." Mike's phone rings as he is bringing the luggage into Vicky's house. Mike let it ring, if it was important, they would call back. He carries the bags to the laundry room as per Vicky's request. Mike checks the caller ID; the station had called. He hit the callback option.

"Yeah, this is De Augustino, I just got a call. I'll hold." Mike waited. A few seconds passed.

"Yes, sir, we just got back." Mike became silent.

"When? Alright, I'll' be in. Yes, sir, about an hour." Mike hung up.

"What is it, Michael?" Vicky stood frozen. She knew that Mike had received bad news.

"There was an explosion; it was Victor's houseboat." Mike sat on the couch; he was numb. Vicky sat beside him and without a sound comforted him.

"He thought he and his family would be safe there. Less than a month ago, he was in my office, now he's gone. He was in my office." Mike shook his head, as if to sharpen his mind's eye of a vague memory. He took his wallet out of his pocket and pulled a small scrap of paper from one of the folds. It was the number that Victor had given him in case of an emergency. Mike dialed the number, the voice mail answered. Victor spoke,

"Hi, Mike. If you're just dinkin' around, hang up. If something has happened, call extension 336." Mike dialed the extension.

In the message, Victor went into antidotes about the summer that Mike and Rolando had helped him rebuild a car. They had worked together that entire summer between their junior and senior year. The stories continued. Each story concerned nothing other than Mike, Rolando, Victor, and the GTO, that they had spent a summer restoring. Then Victor ended his stories with a simple 'see you again, Mike'. Mike knows that there has to be more to these stories than merely fond memories. Mike is sure that Victor would not send a message from the grave to ramble on about an old car. Mike returned the paper to his wallet. He will go home and shower, then he will start looking into his friend's death.

THE HARVEST

"Mike's been working on Victor's case nonstop. I'd be surprised if he's had eight hours of sleep in the last two nights." Vicky put a bag of groceries on the kitchen counter.

"Is there anything that we can do? Do you think we should get the twenty-four box of root beer the next time?" Miriam put the twelve pack of root beer in the fridge.

"I don't think so, sugar. He's got to just work through it. He'll be okay."

"You don't think we should get twenty-four root beers next time?" Miriam is not being flip; she is suffering for her friend.

"No, sugar, there's nothing we can do to help Michael. Get as many root beers as you like."

"I'm sorry for Mike. Has he been working on Gracie's case?" Miriam changed the subject. It is the best she can do.

"No he hasn't as much lately, there haven't been any new leads. Unless someone wanders in with a written confession in their pocket, it's a cold case."

"Do you think anyone is going to do that?" Miriam looks innocently hopeful at Vicky.

"Sorry, sugar. It's not very likely."

"Oh." Miriam is disappointed. She flops onto the couch and surfs through the movies. "What are you doing today, Vicky?"

"I'm finishing my wash up from the trip. Do you have anything to add?"

"No, I finished already."

"Well, what's your plan today? Are you just going to watch movies all day?" Vicky finishes putting the groceries in the pantry.

"I have no plans."

"Well, I sure do, hon." Gracie joined Miriam on the couch.

"Hello, Gracie." Miriam yawns.

"Sheese baaaack!" Vicky attempts an eerie greeting then trudges into the laundry room to work on the mound of dirty clothes that awaited her.

"Tell Vicky hi from me."

"Gracie says hi from me." Miriam called to Vicky.

"I was listening, and I had an idea." Gracie was off and running.

"Oh, but first, hon. How was your trip?"

"It was fun, we did not worry about a thing. Until we got back." Miriam hung her head.

Good, I'm glad you had fun. I'm sorry you're sad, but now we have to get back to work. I think that we should step over to Sondra Kinsman's house."

"To Sondra's house. Why?"

"Well, since the day that you and Vicky came to my house, I've noticed Miss Wallace and Sondra with their heads together a lot. I'm just thinkin' that we should go snoop around her house, maybe we'll find out what they're up to. I bet it's no good."

Vicky emerged from the laundry room long enough to fix herself a glass of ice water then returned to the drudgery of wash.

"All right, I'll change." Minutes later, the nun appeared.

"Hon, why do you always walk in the realm in your nun outfit?"

"Because of what you said about some people seeing or getting a glimpse of me. But I am almost unrecognizable in the habit. It's my disguise, you see." Miriam proudly curtsied.

"Oh, okay. Good, let's go." Gracie stood next to Miriam.

"I have to let Vicky know that I'm going away. I am going away," Miriam called to Vicky. She lifted her hand and whispered, "Sandalphon." The bird flew to her shoulder.

"Where are you going, sugar?" Vicky called from the laundry room.

"To Sondra's."

"What? I couldn't hear over that washing machine." Vicky looks around her living room. "Where in the world did she go now?" Vicky returns to sorting her wash.

Miriam and Gracie stand in Sondra's living room. The curtains are drawn, Sondra sat in a dim corner of the room. She places a compress over her eyes and lays her head onto the back of the winged chair. A noise from the back startles her. She jumps to her fee and begins using the compress as a dust rag. Miss Wallace had come in through the back door.

"I was hoping that it was you, but I thought it might be Wield." Sondra laid the compress on the chair.

"What did you want to see me about, Sondra?"

"I just don't feel right."

"Did he beat you?" Miss Wallace is aware of the abuse Sondra suffers from her husband.

"No. Not too bad." Sondra never speaks of the punishments.

"You did everything that I told you to do, didn't you?"

"Yes, I told you I did."

"Then you should go to the police." Miss Wallace gently places her hand on Sondra's shoulder. Sondra pulls away.

"I'm afraid he will kill me if he finds out." The sound of Wield cleaning the mud from his muckers at the front door caused Miss Wallace to hurry out the back door before Wield discovered her.

"For God's sake, open the curtains! Get some light in here. It looks like a damn dungeon." Wield stomps back to his room to shower. When he emerges, Sondra is still sitting in the darkened room.

"I'm going into town. You better be happy when I get back or we'll see about it." Wield slams the door on his way out. Sondra locks the door and returns to the dim corner. She stared at the ceiling.

"I have an idea," Miriam said. With Sandalphon on her shoulder, she quickly stepped out and back into the realm that obscured her.

Sondra looks toward the shadowy blur but dismisses it as imagination. Miriam moves across the room and repeats the exercise, again Sondra takes notice. Each time Miriam repeats her action, Sondra's reaction becomes more intense.

Our work is done here for a while. We will leave Sondra alone for now." They return home.

"You are really somethin' hon. How'd you come up with that trick?"

"I thought of it from what you said about if anyone happens to get a glimpse of the other realm, no one believes that they really saw anything."

"Glad I could help." Gracie grins.

"I really think that the habit is a good disguise. Don't you?" Miriam spun around.

"I guess it is. So, go change now, it creeps me out."

"Alright Gracie, I will, but the next few nights are going to be yours," Miriam explains her plan to Gracie. Miriam changes from her dark disguise. Gracie went home to anxiously await the witching hour.

In the dead of night as Sondra restlessly turns in her lonely bed, Gracie appears at her bed side, she leans close and begins to whisper in Sondra's ear.

"Wake up, Sondra. It's Gracie," She whispers. Sondra turns, Gracie again whispers in the restless woman's ear. Sondra turns in her bed again.

Through the night, Sondra thrashed as Gracie whispers in her ears. That night is followed by another uncomfortable night for Sondra, then another and another. Gracie stands ready to repeat her nightly game. She will never tire of this match until it produces the desired outcome. Sondra sleeps quietly in her bed. Gracie glides to the bedside as she has each night before and whispers Sondra's name. Sondra whimpers, and it grows to a low moan, the moan turns to piercing scream as she opens her eyes and glimpses Gracie leaning over her. In a sudden burst of light, Gracie vanishes. Wield entered Sondra's room.

"What the hell is going on in here?" Wield stands at the bed of a very frightened Sondra.

"It was Gracie. She was here! She was standing by my bed. Oh my god! She was right here. Oh my god!" Sondra calls to a deity that she has little if any belief in. Wield punched Sondra's face, bloodying her lip.

"It's true, Wield. She was here," Sondra cried. Wield pulls her up from her bed by her meaty arm.

"Shut up, bitch. I've heard just about enough out of you." He punched her face once again before tossing her back on to her bed.

"Go back to sleep." Wield closes the light as he left Sondra's room.

After Wield left the next morning, Sondra calls Miss Wallace.

"I'm going to the police today."

"Does Wield suspect? Remember our agreement."

"No, he has no idea."

"Did he hit you again?"

"Yes."

"Why?"

"I screamed."

"Because he hit you?"

"No, when Gracie appeared in my room."

"You poor thing, you *better* go to the police."

~

Sondra could have gone into the Kumquat Sheriff's office, but she didn't want to take the chance of being seen. Truth be known, she is more than a little frightened of Adrian and Jessamine Thomas. That considered, Sondra drove into the Tampa police department in the middle of the busy town where she can walk in, namelessly. Sondra checks in at the desk. Soon, she is ushered to an officer who begins taking her complaint.

"My name is Detective Duncan. How can I help you. Mrs. Kinsman?" The young detective scanned the paper he had been given. It is obvious that the woman had been beaten.

"My husband hit me last night."

"Do you want to press charges against your husband?"

"No, I mean I don't know."

"Were you fighting?"

"No, he was angry because I screamed at night."

"What did you scream?" The detective expects the woman to out with a string of obscenities.

"I screamed because I saw a ghost."

"A ghost, huh?" Duncan continues taking notes but has decided that this woman might need psychiatric care.

"What did the ghost say to you?"

"Nothing."

"Why do you think that the ghost was there?"

"Maybe I should leave, I'm afraid."

"Are you afraid of the ghost? Do you want to press charges against the ghost?"

"No! Don't be ridiculous."

"Do you want to press charges against your husband then?"

"Not unless I have some kind of assurance that he can't hurt me."

"Okay, Mrs. Kinsman, let me get another detective in here to help." The young man realizes he is in over his head with whatever is going on with this woman; he excuses himself and walks across the hall to Mike's office.

"Mike, do you have a minute to come over? I think I might need help over there."

"Sure, Duncan." Mike follows the young detective to his cubicle. The officer introduces Mrs. Kinsman.

"Hello, I'm detective De Augustino." Mike quickly assesses the battered woman.

"What's going on with you, Mrs. Kinsman? I hope I can help." Mike knows that this woman will respond to a kind word. The woman drew a deep breath and began her story of years of abuse and the appearance last night of the dead woman, Grace Standard.

"So, you saw the ghost of Grace Standard in your bedroom?" Mike knew that she knows more than she has said. Mike is determined to find out exactly what it is that she knows.

"Yes. Do you think we could speak in private, Detective?" Sondra glances over toward Duncan.

"Certainly. Please come into my office," said the spider to the fly.

"Can I get you anything, Ms. Kinsman? A cup of coffee? Or water?"

"Thank you. I would like water, please." Mike got Sondra a bottle of water and stopped at the front desk.

"Vicky, I'll be busy for a while, don't send any one back." Mike hurries back to his office.

"Now, what do you want to talk about?" Mike plans to gently extract every possible bit of information from Sondra that he can.

"Detective, I'm going to need your assurance that I will have protection from my husband."

"We can send you to a safe house, that's no problem. Tell me what's on your mind. I think I can help you."

"There's one last thing you have to promise me."

"What's that, Ms. Kinsman?"

"I want impunity from prosecution for what I'm going to tell you."

"I can't promise impunity from prosecution, but I can make recommendations to the D.A."

"Good." That is exactly what Sondra wants to hear. She had been down this road before.

"I'm going to record what you have to say, Mrs. Kinsman."

"I understand." The recorder ran as Sondra told her tale.

"Please state your name."

"Sondra Lynn Kinsman." She took a deep breath.

"It all started when that woman moved into the old house; that would be Grace Standard. There were a lot of people who had their eye on that property including the church and the city council. Everyone thought that the woman, Gracie would stay in the old house for a short time and then move on, but as time passed and she didn't leave, some people got impatient. Some made a lot of trouble for her, especially the church and the city council."

"How do you know this, Mrs. Kinsman?"

"I'm on the council so is my husband, Wield Kinsman, and his brother, Mark Kinsman are also on the council."

"Thank you. Go on."

"Oh, and Mark's wife, Rietta Kinsman, she's on the council too. There is a woman, Barbara Ann Wallace who is also on the council; one day just in conversation she mentioned that the owner of the property had willed it to Grace Standard."

"How did Barbara Wallace come by this information?"

"She was friends with the old man who owned the property."

"What is the owner's name, Mrs. Kinsman?"

"He's dead now but his name was Henry, Henry Givens. Barbara Wallace said that he told her that he had already made his will. After Miss Wallace spread the news about the will, a few people were worried, most didn't believe it. But some did, and they weren't taking any chances."

"Did Barbara Wallace say that she saw this will?"

"She didn't say that she actually saw it, but she believed Henry. He was known in Kumquat as a man of his word."

"Okay, go on."

"Well, Rietta, Mark's wife, was especially concerned."

"Why was Rietta so concerned?"

"She was concerned because she had paid the council two hundred thousand dollars to condemn the property and then sell it to her for taxes owed."

"Are you asserting that Mark and Rietta Kinsman bribed the city council members?"

"Yes, they worked it all out. Rietta even wrote an anonymous letter to the council complaining about the property. That's when the council voted to condemn the house."

"Was the head of the council involved with this scheme?"

"Certainly, yes. Mark Kinsman is the head of the council," Sondra answers. Mike is stunned, but he remains focused.

"Why did Mark and Rietta Kinsman want the property?"

"They wanted it for their son who is in business with Mark."

"So, Mark Kinsman is in business with his son. What is his son's name?"

"Junior, his son's name is Mark too, but everyone calls him Junior."

"What business are they in, Mrs. Kinsman?"

"Transportation."

"Like truck drivers or limos?" Mike needs specifics.

"No, like drugs."

"Medical drug transportation?"

"No illegal drug transportation."

"Out of Kumquat?" Mike is increasingly amazed as Sondra's story unfolds.

"Yes, out of Kumquat, but beside drugs, Mark also makes trips to Mexico to pick up illegal aliens."

"Where do these drugs go?"

"Mark has a horse barn that he stores the drugs in until they can ship them out."

"Is there anyone else involved in this operation?"

"Yes, a man, his name is Jeffrey Roberts."

"Jeffery Roberts," Mike repeated. This is getting better all the time. Better, better, better, the musical strains played in Mike's head.

"Then what do they do with the drugs and the illegals?"

"They ship the drugs to Tampa; the illegals are mostly young women. They go for prostitution or are sold and sent out of the country."

"Tampa?" Mike's heart skipped a beat.

"Yes. Tampa. Junior is a special envoy between the drugs and humans that travel from Kumquat to Tampa."

"Is there a name that you remember associated with the Tampa connection?" Mike held his breath. Could this be the connection that he has been searching for? The connection to link Vicente to Red Deutzman.

"Joseph Vicente." Mike listens as words leisurely fall from Sondra's mouth. He feels as if time is playing a cruel prank as he anticipates every syllable.

"Joseph Vicente, are you certain that is the name?"

"Yes, that's the name I hear Wield and Mark mention whenever they talk about Tampa." Mike is beside himself. This woman is a gold mine of information. He calmed himself and continued.

"Mrs. Kinsman, after all that you've told me, you haven't explained exactly what happened between you and your husband last night and how or if it has anything to do with what you have just told me."

"That's the worst part," Sondra begins again. Mike thought he had already heard the worst but, much like 'the best', the worst is yet to come!

"It was right after the council voted to condemn the house, like I said before. Miss Wallace had mentioned that the property was going to be willed to Grace Standard."

"After that, Rietta and Mark started to get worried that they would lose the house and the money that they had used to bribe the council. So, Mark and Wield put their heads together and decided that they should get rid of Grace before a will showed up, if it was going to."

"What do you mean get rid of?"

"Murder."

"Alright, go on."

"On the evening of November 9, 2015, Wield crept into Gracie's house to strangle her. He slipped while he was choking her. He landed a pretty hard blow on her face, I'm pretty sure he broke her nose. Poor girl didn't deserve all that."

"Wield Kinsman broke Grace Standard's nose while attempting to strangle her."

"Is that what you are saying?" Mike wants that crystal clear, the broken nose is not information that has been put out, it was purposely held back. Anyone who knew that Grace Standard's nose had been broken had to have personal knowledge of what had happened that night.

"Yes, Wield knew he broke her nose, but, he didn't know that I found the will on the floor and stuck it in my coat pocket."

"Where's the will now?"

"Still in my coat pocket, hanging in my closet, Wield will never find it there. He really searched for that will. Funny, as soon as Wield and Mark saw that the police were not coming around Gracie's house as much, they turned that house upside down, but they never found that little insurance policy of mine because it was right there in the closet in Wields own house." Sondra smiled smugly.

"Can you describe that coat for me, Mrs. Kinsman?"

"Long grey cashmere. It's my favorite."

"Mrs. Kinsman, we're going to put you in a safe house for battered women for now. You will have to stay here for a while. There is a conference room, I will have a policewoman stay with you."

"Are you going to protect me?"

"Believe me when I tell you that when the D.A. hears your story, you will be the most protected person in the southeast." Mike called for an officer to escort Sondra.

"Thank you, Detective." Sondra was led from Mike's office to a conference room. The officer locked the door as she left, Sondra made herself as comfortable as possible. She dialed her cell phone.

"Hello, Miss Wallace," she whispered. "Yes, I'm still at the station, uh huh, I told them everything you told me to."

"No, not about the sleeping pills. That was the deal, you help me, and I protect you. Just like we agreed. Don't worry." The doorknob rattled.

"Bye, got to go." Sondra slipped her phone back into her purse.

❧

Red and blue lights flashed as the Tampa police and the Kumquat sheriff cars raced up Sweet Blossom Road, speeding into the Kinsman's compound, brandishing shooting irons and ordering that they be allowed to enter. The officers thoroughly searched the homes of Wield and Mark Kinsman, as well as their property; their belongings and their barn. The horse barn held bales of marijuana and stashes of methamphetamine and cocaine. The sheriff handcuffed Mark, Mark's son, Junior, and Wield. Adrian Thomas proved to be as good as his word, and a force to be reckoned with. A truck sped from behind Mark Kinsman's barn, a sheriff's deputy pursued. The police officers confiscated papers and documents from both houses and a cashmere coat from Sondra's closet. Mike discovered a gold watch pendant on Rietta's dressing table, the same pendant that he had seen Grace Standard wearing in a picture.

"Does this belong to you, Mrs. Kinsman?" Mike asked Rietta.

"Yes," she answered. She didn't seem flustered. Mike is surprised since now she has been caught in possession of stolen property.

"It looks like an antique. How long have you had it?"

"I haven't had it very long." Rietta was nonchalant.

"Where did you get it?" Mike is curious what her story is going to be.

"I was in my yard when a raven dropped it at my feet."

"Sheese! Rietta Kinsman, you're under arrest for possession of stolen property and for thinking I would believe a cockamamie story like that!" Mike informed Rietta of her rights.

"A raven gave it to me! I swear!" Rietta chose not to remain silent; she screamed hysterically as she was put in the back of the police car in handcuffs.

The truck that sped away from Mark Kinsman's barn is being raced along country roads at breakneck speeds by a drunken Jeffrey Roberts. The officer in chase slows down to keep from flying off the road at dead man's curve, Jeffrey did not. He is dead before the officer reaches the wreckage.

❧

It was early on that July evening when all hell broke loose in Kumquat. July is usually a quiet month in the south. It's much too hot to cut loose and really kick up your heels, so mostly folks loll about on their porch and drink sweet tea. But that evening was an evening that the town folk will whisper about for a long time to come. When it was all done and over a lot of people were ashamed of themselves. The rest were surprised, maybe even shocked by the events that came to conclusion on that hot July evening.

THE ABBEY

Mike studied his phone. He called the number that Victor had left him. The voice mail picked up the call, as it had done every other time that Mike had called. He had been calling the number for weeks now, the calls amounted to a number that Mike did not keep track of. He had continually dialed and then redialed the number, hoping that he would discover what Victor was trying to make him understand. He desperately wanted to know the secret that lies hidden in his friends puzzling message.

"Mike, are you busy?" Miriam stands at Mike's office door.

"No, I'm just looking at this phone number that Victor gave me.

"That is a lot of extra numbers. What do they mean, Mike?" Miriam peers over Mikes shoulder and studies the numbers.

"I don't know, Miriam!" Mike didn't mean to snap at Miriam, but this quandary is consuming him.

"I have some mail for you. I hope you figure out what it means." Miriam lays the mail on Mike's desk.

"Thanks, Miriam." Mike smiles.

"Figure out what it means? She says the strangest things," Mike mumbles. He puts the paper in his desk drawer. He promises himself that he will not look at it again until tomorrow.

"Figure out what it means! That's it, that's it. Figure it out!" Mike opens his desk drawer and hurriedly pulls the papers out. What *do* the numbers mean? He studies the numbers. 762-6957 extension 336. Mike went to the phone keypad, 7=p 6=o 2=b 6=o 9=x 57. P.O. Box 57! Extension 336, the zip code for Tampa. This is what Victor is telling him! Mike hurries to the front desk.

"Look, Vicky, Miriam helped me figured it out! She didn't know it, but she did. Look, it's a P.O. Box number. P.O. Box 57 in Tampa. Amazing!"

"What are you going to do?"

"I'm going over to the post office."

"Now?"

"Yes, now!" It is only a few city blocks to the post office from the police department. It won't take Mike long to get there. Especially at the hurry up pace he is traveling. Mike finds box fifty-seven. There is no mail in it. There is nothing. Nothing except a single key lying inside the box, the key to the GTO! Mike decides not to use his authority to have the box opened. He knows that any wrong move could undo the progress he has just made. There is something about the GTO that Victor wants him to know; some secret that is precious enough to Victor to make sure it is shared. Mike examines a few more boxes then asks about the cost to rent one. Satisfied that he hasn't aroused the curiosity of anyone who might be watching, Mike returns to the station. He listens to Victor's message again. There must be one more piece to the puzzle inside Victor's riddle. Then he realized GTO is the key. The key is in the PO Box, and the key, of course, would get him into the GTO so GTO must get him into the PO Box, logical. Mike put the corresponding numbers from the phone pad to the letters GTO on a piece of paper and put the paper in his pocket. He would return to the post office and open the box. He is certain that he will open the box!

Mike stops at the post office three days later. He has plenty of time before he has to clock in at the station. He has memorized the numbers that he is certain will open the box. He turns the tumblers of the lock. The numbers 486 stand in a row daring Mike to turn the knob. Mike accepts the challenge and opens the box; he retrieves his prize.

Now all Mike has to do is find the car. His thoughts return again and again to the days of restoring the classic car. Where would Victor park the car that it will be safe? Mike rules out any of his father's many warehouses. Victor would not have parked it there; he cut ties with them long ago.

Mike calls every private storage lot that he can find, not one is storing a GTO. Mike is feeling nostalgic, he thought of his old friend Rolando. Victor couldn't have restored the car without Rolando's help; he is a genius with motors. Mike regrets that he never made the time to keep in touch with Rolando. He will call Rolando soon just to say hi. Mike's phone rings.

"De Augustino," Mike answers.

"Mike, what's up?"

"Paul, good to hear from you, didn't recognize your number. It's been almost a month."

"Yeah, I've been busy."

"Me too. What's up, brother?" Mike talks as he walks to the station.

"I got an apartment in Tampa. Haven't seen it yet, only pictures. Hope it's as nice as it looks."

"Wow, Paul. That's as bad as being set up on a blind date by your mother." Mike chuckles.

"I know man. Anyway, I'm going to be moving in after the first of the month."

"Wow, great. Let me know when you're going to get here. I'll help you."

"Thanks, I knew I could count on you."

"Sure thing. Bet Miriam is happy."

"I think she is. Mike, I have a call coming in, I got to go. See you in a few weeks."

"Later Paul." Mike puts the phone in his pocket. Then he remembered his promise to reconnect with his old friend Rolando. There's no time like the present. Mike found two numbers for Rolando Rodriguez; one is a home phone the other is the business number. Mike dials the business.

"Rolando's Classic Restorations."

"Rolo?"

"Yeah, who is this? No one has called me Rolo since high school."

"Mike De Augustino. I've been thinking about you."

"Mike, good to hear from you, man!"

"Yeah, Rolo, you've been on my mind lately especially since what happened to Victor."

"What happened?"

"You didn't hear? Sorry to tell you this, his houseboat exploded."

"Oh, no! Are there any survivors?"

"No, there's not."

"Wow. I was wondering why he hasn't been around lately."

"Victor kept in touch with you?"

"Yeah, I did a lot of motor work for him."

"Oh."

"Come over to my place soon, Mike. We can catch up. I live in the house I grew up in. We can throw back a few beers and talk about old times." Rolando is shaken by the news.

"Sure Rolo, tell you what, I get off around five. How about if I come over tonight, I'll even bring the beer."

"That sounds good. See you after five then."

"See you then."

~

Mike drives down the familiar street to Rolando's house, his second home growing up. Mike and Rolando were the kid kings of that Ybor City neighborhood. They were always together, where one was the other was not far away. If one lied the other swore by it, as a best friend just instinctively does.

Now, after some pretty hefty urban renewal and a lot of midnight relocations of the Ybor City street people to Hernando County, the spit shined and rearing to go Ybor City, is Tampa's fun place to be. From the beautiful Columbia Restaurant to the con brio Seventh Avenue clubs and into the Santeria gift and voodoo store. Ybor never disappoints.

"Mike! Come on in, it's good to see you man." Rolando welcomes his old friend.

"Yeah, shouldn't have waited so long. Here, have a beer." Mike hands a cold one to his old pal.

"This one is for Victor." Rolo raised his bottle.

"To Victor." The friends tossed back the first tribute to their friend and moved to the living room of the small row house.

"When did it happen, Mike?"

"A couple of weeks ago now. I thought you must have read about it. I'm sorry, I should have called."

"Was there a service?"

"Cooper's family had a small private service, that's all."

"Any beers left?" Rolando asked. He and Mike had reminisced for hours.

"Yeah, last two." Mike pulls a warm bottle out of the six pack.

"Throw me one."

"Here ya go."

They raised their bottles, "To friends here and friends forever."

"Hey, Mike, I got my own shop now."

"I figured that when you answered with Rolando's Classic Restorations. "Pretty sweet, man."

"It's in the garage in the back. Want to see?"

"Yeah, really I would."

Mike followed Rolo back to the old garage behind his house. He and Rolo had fixed many a bicycle chain, and pounded their sisters' roller skates onto pieces of scrap wood to make skateboards, in that old garage. Then they sold skateboards to the neighbor kids for three dollars. What Rolando has transformed that run-down garage into astounds Mike.

"Rolo, this is amazing. Did you do all of this?"

"I had help."

"Help? You must have had an army."

"No, just Victor."

"Victor?"

"Yeah, I was really struggling fixing cars, and boat motors, and doing other odd jobs. Victor came by one day and asked if I could work on a car for him, it was a sweet antique Peugeot. It was perfect when I got finished with it."

"Victor made me a loan to get this started. He said he believed I could make it good. He was right; with his help, I did. That was Victor, always ready to help."

"There's one more thing that you're going to like." Rolando and Mike walk back behind the garage and pull a tarp off a classic 1965 GTO. Yellow with a black top.

"It's here! Rolo! It's here!"

"I knew you'd like this." Rolando smiled.

"How long have you had this?"

"Not long a few months, maybe. It still runs like a dream."

"You have the key?"

"Sure, Victor gave me a key. He said to keep it running for him till he came to get it. He said if he never came back, that I should give it to you. I thought that was a strange thing for him to say then, but not so much now. Guess he knew something." Rolando takes a single key out of his pocket and hands it to Mike.

"He said to give it to me?" Mike is choked up.

"Yeah, he even signed the pink. This is the only key I have. It opens the doors and starts it up, but it doesn't open the glove box or trunk."

"Can you tow it for me?"

"Sure, Mike, where do you want it to go?"

"My place. I'm over in Ballast Point, 2911 Ballast Point Drive."

"You want to take it now?"

"If you got time, sure."

"I got more time tonight than I will tomorrow." Rolando smiles.

❧

The yellow GTO sits in Mike's drive, calling attention to itself like a huge metal caution flag. Mike opens his garage and drives the car in. Once inside the private space of the garage, he reclines the driver's seat. Memories of the afternoon that Victor rushed him to his father's side, in this very car, flood his mind. The car will remain out of sight in Mike's garage until he has some satisfaction regarding what happened to Victor and his family. Mike takes his key ring from his pocket and adds the key to the GTO ring, and then separates the single key that he had retrieved from Victor's post office box. He tried the key in the glove box, it opened, he found an envelope with his name on it, the letter inside reads:

Mike,

If you're reading this... no wait, man, that's way too sappy, not my style. Sweet ride, eh? I hope you enjoy it. Rolo knows it inside and out; he'll keep it in good shape for you. It's been... well, anyway, it's been!

Victor

P.S. I left some things in the trunk. Will you take care of it for me? If the big plan emerges, it's your inheritance. She's all yours now. Thanks Mike.

In the trunk, Mike finds Victor's smelly old running shoes, a moldy drink bottle, assorted pieces of children's clothing, and a file box brimming with papers. Mike is stunned as he sifts through the box. All of the papers are copies of receipts and business transactions. The receipts are dated as far back as the 1950s. Mike takes Victor's secret into his house. When Mike has finally gone through each paper, he sees that they paint a very real picture of the sordid dealings of Joe Vicente and Red Duetzman.

The weeks pass, Mike gathers every piece of evidence that he has on the Vicente family, and the new evidence that he has from Victor, of Red Duetzman's involvement with Vicente. He pores over his findings. He has to determine if he has enough to present to the district attorney. The boy in witness protection is a strong witness, but he is young, his testimony can go either way with a jury. Sondra is his best bet and now with Victor's papers, he is pretty certain he has a good case, but he is cautious. He won't hurry the case to court though. If he lost, he might not get another chance at the people that he believes murdered his father!

~

Vicky wanders back to Mike's office on her first break. Mike is still pouring over Victor's papers.

"Hi, how is it coming with the case?" Vicky has not seen as much of Mike in the last few weeks as she would like, but understands, it is the nature of the beast.

"It's coming along. I have a good case."

"Paul's coming in this weekend. Miriam and I are going over to his place to help."

"Yeah, I told him I'd be there too."

"Good." Vicky would have chatted Mike up for a few more minutes but his phone rang.

"A body at the abbey? It'll take me about thirty minutes to get there."

St. John, Florida is a township in Hillsborough County. It's considered Kumquat's little sister. Saint John is a real peep and plum town. If you peep around the corner, you're plum out of town. The St. John Abbey, the post office and a feed store are the sum and total of the town framework. The St. John Abbey is cloistered, the monks rarely leave, and few people visit, save for the Sunday morning mass.

There are a few lay people who live in secluded quarters on the grounds of the abbey; these are employees of the monks. A gardener prunes a large stand of camellias planted around an effigy of St. John.

"Excuse me," Mike interrupts the gardener.

"Yeah?"

"I'm looking for the abbot. Can you tell me where his office is?"

"I can, but you'd never find it. I'll take you." The gardener put his loppers down and walked with Mike.

"You here about the murder?" the gardener asked.

"I can't really discuss it," is Mike's official answer. Have you heard anything?"

"There's a lot that goes on around here. I hear a lot, but I mostly keep my mouth shut. I like my job; no pressure and a place to live, three squares and a cot."

"Did you know the deceased monk?"

"Yeah, me and him were buddies, he was a maintenance worker, too, before he came here to the abbey."

"How long had you known him?"

"Since he came here, about eight years ago. Nice guy, just regular, ya know

"What kind of maintenance did he do before he came here? Did he ever mention that?"

"He did repairs; plumbing, electric, and painting, stuff like that. He worked for the Duetzman family.."

"Duetzman?"

"Yeah, you know the head Catholics around here."

"Why did he leave that maintenance job?"

"He said that all he did was take care of a couple dozen empty warehouses for the Duetzman's; he started snooping around thinking something fishy was going on. Then just didn't show up for work one morning, instead he showed up here and has never left until now. He had his reasons for coming, I guess.

"This is the abbot's office; the secretary will take care of you."

"Thanks, you've been very helpful." The gardener has unwittingly been very helpful. The gardener walks directly across the sidewalk, picks up his loppers and continues his work. Mike is perplexed. The gardener had taken him on a meandering path that led them to a destination that is no more than a moment's walk across a sidewalk, from the point where they began. The gardener smiles as he worked. Maybe it wasn't as unwitting as Mike had supposed.

The abbot took Mike to the monk's living quarters. Mike inspects the stark room, there are no personal items or comforts.

"Is this everything that belonged to the brother?" Mike asks.

"Yes, we live a simple life." Mike thanks the abbot and is led out of the abbey. Mike approaches the gardener, he takes a card from his shirt pocket, scribbles his cell number on the back, and hands him the card.

"Thanks for showing me around." Mike smiles.

"No problem. I needed a break." The gardener put the card in his pocket and continues his work.

"Come and talk to me if you think of anything else. I put my cell number on the back in case you can't make it in. Call me at that number anytime."

"Will do."

❧

THE LONG ARM OF THE LAW

Mike is at his desk, going over his notes when his phone rings.

"I just got back from there! Yeah, I'll be right there."

"Where are you off to in such a hurry, Michael?" Vicky asked as Mike rushed past. Mike leans close and whispers.

"There's been another murder at the abbey."

"They're busy over there today."

"I'll say!"

Mike stands over the body of the gardener, the crime scene pictures have been taken and evidence is bagged and noted. The gardener had been executed; one bullet in the back of the head, no one heard a shot. The shooter obviously used a silencer. Mike studies the contents of the gardener's pockets. A pen knife and one dollar and sixty-five cents in change is everything that the gardener had in his pockets. In his wallet, he had two crisp one hundred-dollar bills. It didn't appear that robbery was the motive, but Mike has already guessed that. The card that Mike gave the gardener was not in his pocket; he could have thrown it away. There is always a chance that Mike will come upon the card in his investigation.

The local television stations swarm the grounds of the abbey. Two murders at the abbey in one day! This is huge news for St. John, Florida. Actually, this is the only news, for St. John, Florida. The monks scatter trying to escape the imposition of questions and cameras. They dash away each in a different direction like naughty children running from their angry mother, knowing that she will only be able to catch one of them. Finally, the WSUN reporter caught a brother who had inadvertently walked directly into his path.

"Excuse me, brother. May I speak to you for a moment?" The reporter and the cameraman follows the Monk as he quickens his pace, ignoring the reporters request for an interview. The camera man hurries in front of the monk to get a clear shot. The Brother bowed his head, his hooded robe covers much of his face.

"May I ask you some questions, brother?" the reporter insists.

"No!" The brother hurries to the monk's quarters.

Mike returns to the station to make his report. This has been a busy day; however, it isn't over yet. As much as Mike longs for the weekend to arrive so he can carry heavy pieces of furniture and boxes of books up a staircase in the sweltering heat, that dream would have to be on hold for a few more hours.

"Mike, you have a call on line five," Vicky alerted Mike.

"Did the person give a name? I'm pretty busy."

"Yes, it's Mr. Richard Duetzman."

"Are you sure?"

"Yes, Richard Duetzman would like to speak with you."

"Okay, put him through."

"Mike?" Duetzman sounds tired and old.

"Red, what do you want?"

"They tell me you're working on my son's case. I'd like to talk to you."

"I can't really talk about an ongoing case. You know that Red."

"I know you and Victor were friends. I know that you know how it was between you and me, and there's no love lost between us, but I'm old now, and I've lost my son and my grandchildren. I would like to come into the station to talk." There was a certain desperation in Red's voice.

"Well, your ankle bracelet will go off. I'll let the IT guys know, we can meet first thing Monday morning." Mike hung the receiver in its cradle, clears his desk, closes the light, and shuts his office door. Tomorrow, he will be *happily* carrying furniture and boxes of books up a narrow staircase.

～

"Is this all you got?" Mike and Paul are drenched with sweat. Paul's apartment is a maze of boxes and furniture.

"Yeah, except what's in the other truck."

"Other truck!"

"Kidding, man have a beer." Paul hands Mike a cold one.

The law men turned moving men, sat down, and turned to their final beer before Vicky got there and started making suggestions as to what should go where, or maybe over there.

Mike has endured the grueling business of furniture arrangement under the instruction of his mother and four sisters. He has been righteously schooled that silence and doing as you're told is the only clear path to survival. By midnight, a few more beers and pizza delivery, Paul's apartment is pretty well set up. Vicky is not quite satisfied but feels that Paul will probably hang his clothes and arrange his dresser drawers later.

Miriam is a furniture moving savant, her pointer finger is her best and only tool. Everyone relaxes on Paul's couch.

"This looks good guys, nice job," Vicky complemented.

"Ja, what do you think about that bookcase, Vicky?" Miriam points toward the bookcase across the room.

"It's fine, Miriam." Paul took her finger and pressed it to his lips. Miriam smiles.

"Smooth Paul, good save." A fist bump is called for.

"Hush, Michael, act right," Vicky admonishes.

The friends talked only for a short time and then said their good nights. They leave Paul in his new apartment and return to their homes. Mike has promised his mother he will come for Sunday dinner and Paul is planning a day of setting up his computer and putting away his clothes. Vicky will be pleased.

～

Monday morning, Mike is just getting settled in his office when Vicky came to his door.

"Mike, Red Duetzman is here to see you."

"Let him come back. Thanks, Vicky." Red stops at Mike's door.

"Come in, Red, sit down."

"Thanks for seeing me, Mike. How are you doin'?" Red took a seat. There is an intense sadness in the old man's eyes.

"I'm fine. What do you want to talk to me about, Red?"

"Everything. I know that you guys have been investigating Vicente and probably me now."

"Yeah, I have, right now I have enough to put you both away for a long time." Mike didn't blink.

"I'm sure that you do. You see, I've known for a long time about those papers that Victor had, so has Joe." Red looked deep into Mike's eyes.

"You're going to want to get this on tape, Mike. I know my rights and I don't want a lawyer." Duetzman stops talking.

Mike turns on the tape recorder and reminded Red of his rights. Then recorded Richard 'Red' Duetzman's confession.

"Please state your name," Mike began.

"Richard William Duetzman."

"Thank you. Continue, Mr. Duetzman."

"I have been in business with Joseph Vicente for many years. The nature of our business is money laundering; he rents buildings mostly warehouses from me with the money he gets from his illegal drug trade. He pays me many times over what the normal rent fee would be. I keep a percentage and return the bulk of the money through couriers. He then uses the money to again buy drugs from the Mexican cartel. The drugs are delivered and distributed through the warehouses. Each time a part of the profit is used to buy property and eventually build another warehouse. There are more than three hundred of these warehouses throughout the South east.

"All of my sons knew about the family business and participated except Victor, my oldest son. He never would have a part in it."

"Right before he married that woman, Cooper, I found out that he had taken some papers that I had. He said that the papers were insurance. I saw very little of him after that and did not see him at all after his mother passed. God rest her soul." Duetzman crossed himself.

"Vicente asked me about the papers, he said that he heard a rumor long ago that Victor had an insurance policy. He said he hoped that was not the case, but he was going to look into it, and hoped that I understood. I understood good enough alright. I have known Vicente for many years, and I understand exactly what he is capable of doing. That is when I called Victor and told him he should hide out for a while."

"Then when this happened to Victor and his family, one of my cousin's kids told me that Vicente caused the explosion. He found out about the houseboat from one of my sons. One of my own sons, I don't know which one it was, but one of Victor's brothers sold him out to Vicente, it could have been any one of them." Duetzman hung his head.

"Do you need a minute, Mr. Duetzman?"

"No, I will finish this."

"Then, last Friday, Vicente told me that he had the monk killed. He didn't want the monk talking about what he had discovered when he worked maintenance at the warehouses. Then Vicente had the gardener killed after he was seen talking to you."

"Are you saying that someone saw the gardener talking to me and reported it to Vicente and he had the gardener murdered that fast?"

"Yes, Vicente has a big network. I'll probably be next."

"I don't think so, Mr. Duetzman. You are under arrest on charges of money laundering and racketeering."

Richard Duetzman gave up quietly. After living a life of lawlessness; Red Duetzman would now safely lean on the long arm of the law.

∾

Miriam and Gracie stood silently in the old roadhouse. From the window, they can see the shadows are lengthening and the waning afternoon light. The Kinsman's property stands vacant.

"They are all gone now, Gracie," Miriam whispers.

"Come with me, Miriam." Gracie glides into her kitchen; Miriam follows. Gracie stops at the padlocked door.

"Come on, let's go upstairs," Gracie says. She touches the pad lock on the door, and it falls open.

"When did you learn to do that?"

"Oh, I could always do that, hon." Gracie glides up the stairs. They stand in an entry hall at the top of the stairs. A small fireplace stands on one wall. There are three doors. One door is on the wall next to the fireplace and a door on each of the other two walls.

"Why do you keep the upstairs locked, Gracie?" Gracie moves to the door next to the fireplace.

"It is part of the arrangement," she answered.

"What arrangement?"

"The arrangement that I made with the spirits when I moved in. I promised that I would leave them be, take care of their place, and they would leave me be. We got along just fine after that." Gracie cracks the door open. The faint sound of a waltz being played from a music box drifts from the room.

"Come here, peek in," Gracie whispers. She opens the door a little wider so Miriam could see in. Miriam watches what appears to be an old cowboy dancing with a barefoot Victorian lady.

"Can they see us?" Miriam asked.

"If they care to, generally, they just dance. They've been dancin' for a hundred years I reckon."

"Will they go away if we go in?" Miriam wants to go into the parlor.

"Don't know." Gracie opens the door and floats into the room. The Victorian lady fades from sight. The cowboy turns toward Gracie, smiles, and tips his hat before he fades from sight. Miriam gazed into the old cowboy's face before he faded, she recognizes him. He is the shadowy figure that she saw through Sandalphon's eyes. He stood next to Gracie's bed, the night of her death. He picked up the gold watch!

"They'll be back," Gracie assured.

Miriam stands in the parlor; a tiny fireplace shares the chimney with the fireplace that stands in the hall. All the fixtures in the room are Victorian.

"This is beautiful, Gracie. Is this how it looked when you moved in?"

"Yeah, Henry left it like this, so I did too. It *is* pretty though. I'm guessin' this is rather how it always looked." Miriam examines the contents of the room. She ran her hand along the tops of the dusty tables and antiquated pictures of long forgotten residents. A deep sadness overwhelms her; she looks at Gracie, the source of the sadness.

"What's going to happen to this place now that you have passed?" Miriam asked.

"I've made arrangements. There's a letter for you on the mantle." There *was* a letter on the mantle, just as Gracie had said. Miriam opens the letter.

"This is from the sheriff's mother, it's a notarized copy of your will, and a copy of the deed that Henry sent you. I don't understand, Gracie. You *willed* your house to me, and the deed to the house has been signed to me! How can that be? This letter is dated November sixth more than a year ago, two days before you were murdered, you did not know me then. I was not even here."

"I told you Jessamine is a special lady." Gracie winks at Miriam.

"But what am I going to do?"

"You're going to live here and take care of the place, that's the arrangement." Gracie smiles. The air conditioner that hangs in the window rattled.

"I had to put that thing in up here to keep the mildew down, but the sill is loose. The water dripping rotted it. I reckon you'll have to fix that." The unit rattled again.

"There's no electricity on now. Why is it rattling?" Miriam asks.

"Must be the wind kickin' up." Gracie moves over to the window just as the air conditioner falls to the ground. Gracie stuck her head out the window.

"*Boy, howdy*! My, my, my, imagine that Old Miss Wallace under the air conditioner. That's what she gets for snoopin' around."

"What? What happened?" Miriam gasped.

"I don't know, but she looks squished to me." Gracie pulls her head back in.

"Grace Love Standard!"

"Mama!" Gracie turned to face her mother.

"Did you do that?"

"No, Mama, you taught me better."

"You're a good girl."

"Did you come to lead me over, Mama?"

"No, Grace Love Standard, I didn't. You aren't finished here, not quite yet." Mama cast her eyes over to Miriam.

"Mama, you never called me Gracie. You always called me Grace Love Standard. Why is that, Mama? Didn't you love me much? I always wondered?" Gracie began to cry.

"Grace Love Standard, of course I loved you. You are my gift from God. Grace and love are His greatest standard."

THE BIZ

Randall Bizmarq is, was, and will always be a genius. I will say that he has probably lost a few sparks over the last thirty years, but he started out with a few hundred billion sparks more than the average Joe. I think that's a lot of sparks. Anyway, we'll call it a lot. Point is, Randal could afford to lose a spark or two. Randal wandered into the shop where I cut hair during my time as a barber in the eighties. My clients were fiercely loyal; having followed me from one shop to the next, they were glad when I finally settled into the little shop on the sixth floor of a downtown Tampa office building

Jonathan Earthwilder, the owner of the shop, only darkened the door to pick up the bank deposits. Jonathan was known as joni justjoni at The Carousel, a local drinking establishment and drag show; where he wows 'em every Friday night with his Marlena Dietrich cabaret. joni spelled his name with lowercase letters only; not because he was channeling ee cummings or any other esoteric reason. He used the lowercase letters, so he could dot his name with tiny black hearts. I am certain that if joni were artistically inclined, he would have added a tiny dagger through each of the tiny black hearts. That in itself would have been an oxymoron or a paradox, or an oxydox, if there is such. The reason I say this is because Jonathan Earthwilder is actually a well-loved, gentle, and big hearted singing, dancing, delight.

The salon was rightly called Cut Up's because that's exactly what we did. My coworker and I cut up and cut hair all day long; the charge for our service was twenty dollars. Furthermore, I would like to add, that we usually got at least a ten-dollar tip. For the twenty-dollar charge, our clientele could expect a haircut and forty minutes of our undivided attention. If truth be told, the forty-minute, twenty-dollar haircut was in actuality, a fifteen-minute eight-dollar haircut included into forty minutes of sweet talk. Most of our clients were men, happy men.

I was up for the next walk-in client. I escorted a handsome bohemian to my chair and began to work on him, talk, talk, talk, that was me, silence, silence, silence, that was the bohemian. After his forty minutes in my chair, I was exhausted, he was gorgeous. He paid for his haircut, and then he dug into the pocket of his jeans and pressed a wrinkled wad of cash into my hand, then he left the shop. The wad of cash amounted to a thirty-dollar tip and a broken fortune cookie. The fortune read, 'Never offer an explanation, your enemies won't believe it, and your friends don't need it.' I decided then to live by those words.

The next morning when I arrived at work, the handsome bohemian was waiting at our door. He sat in our waiting room the entire day and spoke of extraordinary things of dreams, and wondrous thought. He beguiled us with amazing facts and outrageous imaginations. That was, Randal Bizmarq, the Biz. Of all our clients, he grew to be our favorite. Soon, we were spending our free weeknights and almost every weekend hanging with him. He never failed to entertain us with his stories or quiet us with his classical guitar. Yes, he was everyone's favorite, but I was Randal's darling. None of what I have told you up until now is important. It's just a celebration of fond memories, the shadows in my mind, or creases on my brain, you can decide for yourself; I have. It's what I will tell you next that took me from innocence to world wary.

One afternoon, I found Randal sitting at his cluttered table, a letter in his hand; I watch as he reads and rereads the letter as if he were trying to extract a hidden truth from between the lines. He gave the paper over to me and asked me to read it to him out loud. I read: Hi, Biz. Haven't heard from you in a while, I guess you're up to your old tricks. I'm thinking you're back to chasing girls. I'd like to hear about her, she must be very special to you. I think about our M.I.T. days often. Speaking of the old days, I hope you're feeling okay and taking care of yourself, of everything that's the most important. I hope to hear from you soon.

Thomas.

It seemed to simply be a letter from an old college friend; but Randal wasn't seeing it that way. The words; I'd like to hear about her, she must be very special to you, seemed especially bothersome to him. I told Randal that I thought his friend was just having an attack of nostalgia and not to worry about it. He put the letter back in the envelope and handed it to me. He told me to keep it. Then he went into his bedroom and came back out with his college ring. He dropped the ring in the envelope and asked me to hold on to that, too.

Randal was particularly amorous that evening. He asked me to marry him, I accepted his proposal, and I was thrilled. His college ring would be his pledge until we could pick out a proper engagement ring. It was late that Wednesday when I kissed him goodnight and left his apartment with the promise that I would be back on Friday evening after work. Friday couldn't come soon enough for me but finally the dawn broke on that morning. I had not heard from Randal since I had left him on Wednesday night, but that wasn't unusual. I hurried to his apartment after work. I unlocked the door and walked in. I had made up my mind that I would tackle the mound of dirty dishes that he had probably left sitting in the kitchen sink. However, instead of dirty dishes, I found a thoroughly cleaned and freshly painted, empty apartment. Every trace that any human being had ever lived there had been removed, and Randal was nowhere to be found.

Although, it's been more than thirty years since I've laid eyes on my handsome bohemian. I know he's still here… somewhere. Even though, each night I sleep alone, I can feel him; I dream his dreams, I picture each of his outrageous imaginations and I am quieted by the remembrance of his guitar. In my mind's eye, even to this day, I can still see myself, standing in his stark white, freshly washed, and painted apartment. I can still feel the vast sense of loss that I felt that day. Randal is gone, but I still have his memories, his ring, and the letter.

SPLIT APARTS

"Ms. Thorlakson, are you claiming that a monk you saw on the news last week is not a monk?" Tampa detective Mike De Augustino reads over the statement that the excited woman has given.

"Yes, that's exactly what I'm claiming."

"Why do you think that he's not a monk?"

"Because he's my fiancé." The woman seems convinced,

Mike is not. Mike deliberates on the woman's claim. She continues to maintain that one of the monks at the abbey of St. John is her fiancé and not a monk at all! The woman seems earnest enough, although a bit overwrought.

Mike decides that as unlikely as her story sounds, he should probably hear her out. His decision to listen to this woman's tale is based on one factor and one factor only. A monk and a gardener have been murdered at the abbey. There were news casters at the abbey that day covering the story.

Maybe the woman's fiancé had been at the abbey; it is possible the man she saw on the television is her fiancé, the monk, and the killer. Mike is looking for any lead as to who the St. John killer might be, but this has come to him way too easy.

"Why don't you just relax and tell me about it, Ms. Thorlakson?"

"Call me Trudy."

"Okay, Trudy, tell me what's going on." Mike leans his elbows on his desk and studies Trudy.

"I had just gotten home from work and turned on the news. I fixed myself a little something to eat and sat down in front of the TV," Trudy begins.

"So, I'm sitting there, eating some scrambled eggs and watching the news, and who do I see trying to get away from the newscaster, but my fiancé dressed like a monk. I could hardly believe it, so I rewound and paused it. His head was down, and his face was partially covered by the hood on his robe, but it was him!"

"How can you be sure it was him if his face was obscured?" Mike makes notes on his pad.

"I know it was him because he has a small half-moon shaped scar on the side of his face just right above his jaw, and the monk had the exact crescent shape scar."

"If I were to ask you, how certain you are that the monk and your fiancé are the same man, what would you say?" Mike is beginning to be interested in Trudy's story.

"I would say I am one hundred percent certain that monk and my fiancé are the same man."

"Trudy, why did you come to the police about this? Why don't you just ask your fiancé? Are you afraid that he might harm you?"

"He would never hurt me! I came to the police because he's been missing for thirty years, and I want to file a missing person report."

"Really?" Mike is flabbergasted. Now, he realizes that he has been completely taken in by this woman, this woman who appears so genuine, so honest, so… sane. Mike decides to ask her a few more questions, take her report then dismiss her and her story.

"Did you or anyone file a missing person's report thirty years ago?"

"No."

"Why not?"

"I thought the government took him, so I kept quiet." Trudy hangs her head.

"Really, why did you think that?" Mike is once again surprised, which in itself surprises him, since he didn't think he was going to be surprised again.

"I was the only one," the woman sadly whispers.

"The only one what?" Mike cautiously asks; not knowing at all what to expect.

"The only one that he had to talk to, I mean, really talk to."

"Really?" Now, Mike can't even imagine where this story is going.

"Yes, really. Can I file that missing person's report now?"

Mike guesses that this is as far as she is going and opens his note pad.

"Alright, let's do it. What's your full name?"

"Thruda Thorlakson."

"No middle name?"

"No, I'm Icelandic." Trudy smiles proudly.

"Icelandic, huh? I never met an Icelander before. How do you spell Thruda?" Mike mumbles.

"T-h-r-u-d-a."

"What is the name of the missing person?"

"Randall James Bizmarq."

"When did you last see Randall James Bizmarq?"

"July 30, 1987."

Mike asks Trudy a few more insignificant questions. Then he closes his note pad.

"I think I've got about everything. I'll get back to you if I find out anything." Mike thanks her, and Thruda, no middle name, Thorlakson leaves Mike bewildered and shaking his head.

Detective Davies sticks his head into Mike's office. Rob Davies was Mike's rookie eight years ago. He came to Mike right out of the police academy. He was young, fresh-faced and ready to single handedly take on the world of crime. He had plenty of book learning, but he didn't have the good sense God gave a goose. Nevertheless, under Mike's guidance, he was honed and polished, and then when Mike finished with Robby boy, he really was ready to take on the world of crime.

"How did it go with the Thorlakson woman, Mike?" Davies peeks into Mike's office. "Not mad are you? Should I throw my hat in first?"

"Yeah, get in here, kid, thanks for that. Not mad, but you owe me one, Robby boy. She was a real nut case." Mike shakes his head.

"Yeah, I had her pegged as a nut. Sorry, I couldn't take it. My computer crashed again." Rob chuckles, unwraps a stick of gum and folds it into his mouth. He sat on the edge of Mike's desk.

"You get Ted in there?" Mike doesn't look up.

"Yeah, he's in there now, working on it. He's a genius with that computer stuff, I'm glad he is, 'cause I'm sure not." Rob cracks his gum between his teeth.

"Yeah, sure Robby, a genius. You know that gum cracking drives me crazy, get outta here, kid." "Mike isn't listening to Rob instead he is going over Thruda Thorlakson's statement; all he really hears is gum cracking.

Rob ignores Mike's 'get outta here kid,' and continues. "You know Ted's an interesting guy, Mike. I'm amazed at all the stuff he knows about; of course, he could be pulling it out of his ass for all I know." Rob laughs.

"Yeah, he's pretty smart alright but I don't think he has to be a genius to trip you up Rob." Mike smiles at the young detective.

"What's up with Thorlakson?"

"She wanted to file a missing person's report on her fiancé. Get this, he went missing almost thirty years ago, she thinks the government took him." Mike laughs.

"No really? Did you file it?"

"I wrote it all down, but I don't think it's anything. It's just a guy who got cold feet, and got out of Dodge, I'm not even going to log it in, I'll just hold it for a while, just in case."

"Naw, I wouldn't either, but you never know, ya know." Rob grins and cracks his gum one last time before leaving. "Well, Ted must be done by now. I got to get back to work. Later Mike."

"Sure, later, Rob. Hey, hold up a sec. Ask Ted if he managed to grab one of those Ray's tickets they sent over. We can all go together; but you can drive this time. I hate driving in St. Petersburg."

"Why doesn't Ted ever drive?" Rob asks.

"I don't think the genius drives." Mike chuckles.

Okay, I'll ask him if he wants to come along. That does sound good. You, me, and Ted watching the ballgame and drinkin' beer. So, drivin' St. Petersburg's too much for you, eh, old timer?"

"Go on, get out of here, go catch some criminals, kid." Mike balls up a piece of paper and tosses it at Rob's head, Rob dodges.

"Yeah, I'm gone. Someone has to take up you old guys slack. Oh, and don't forget to take your Geritol before we leave for the game. I don't want you falling asleep before it's over. I guess I better, drive you two old farts." Rob mumbles as he leaves Mike's office. "Later, Mike."

"Sure later, whippersnapper." Mike certainly doesn't consider himself an old fart, although he must admit he has slowed down just a bit since he hit thirty. A few minutes pass. Mike picks up his phone and dials Rob.

"Hey kid, I was thinkin' that I don't have any plans for this Friday and there's a game over at Tropicana Field on Friday night, see if Ted can make it this weekend."

"Yeah, okay. That sounds great. I'm not doing anything this weekend either. Okay, we'll plan it even if Ted doesn't want to go along."

"Sounds good to me kid. Friday it is then."

∿

"Hon, are you busy?" Gracie interrupts Miriam.

"Yes, Gracie, I'm working, no time to talk now. Come back when I am done with this filing."

"Oh, good, I'm glad you can talk." Gracie ignores Miriam and continues.

"Did you see that woman who just came out of Mike's office?" Gracie moves closer to Miriam as if she is going to share some juicy bit of gossip.

"No, I did not, I'm quite busy Gracie, come back later. Maybe tomorrow would be good."

"Oh. . . well what are you doing?"

"I'm filing evidence, Gracie. I told you that. I am busy, very busy." Miriam turns to Gracie; she knows it is useless to resist.

"What do you want Gracie?"

"I was listenin' when that woman was talking to Mike."

"Gracie, you should not listen to private police conversations."

"No one saw me, hon, that's the good part about being a ghost. There aren't too many folks that are gonna' have their nose all up in your business."

"Ja, I think you are the one, with your nose in folk's business, Gracie." Miriam continues filing evidence.

"Well, it 'peers she's lost her true soulmate. That worries me; I was just thinkin' we might take a look at her."

"Oh, Gracie, I almost forgot. Paul and Mike are coming to your house to do some work. I thought you should know that." Miriam changes the subject and continues filing. She hopes that Gracie will give up trying to railroad her into whatever scheme she is brewing up and become interested in whatever might be going on at her house. However, Miriam knows that it's a futile attempt since Gracie's train of thought is actually a train wreck, of thought. Try as she may, Miriam is never able to derail Gracie's wayward notions.

"Is Eliakim coming too?"

"No, Gracie, he's not!"

"Too bad, he's really pretty. Why not?"

"Well, Gracie," Miriam begins. "Pretty or not, Vicky hasn't told Mike anything about Eliakim or how I got here. So, Eliakim is not coming. By the way, Gracie, have you figured out why you are still here? Do you think you should be moving on by now? That is what most dead people do." Miriam again tries to change the subject.

"Oh, I sure do think that I should have already moved on, hon. Yep, I think so, but you know I got stuff to do before I go over. So, here I am, tryin' to do as much stuff as I can possibly do. Well, I think maybe then I'll hit it lucky, and go on, but so far it seems like I always turn up a day late and a dollar short. But I'm not quittin', no siree, not me, I'm no quitter. That's what my daddy always said. He always said to Mama, that Gracie, she's no quitter. No quitter, that is for sure, but good Lord is she a talker! Yep, that's what he said, all right." Gracie smiles, Miriam rolls her eyes and continues her task.

"What is soulmate, Gracie? I have never heard that." Miriam didn't look up from her filing.

"Good, I'm glad we're back on the soul mate subject. This woman that was just in Mike's office. Well, she lost her soulmate; anyway, she thinks he's a monk she saw on TV. He probably is, 'cause you always know your soulmate; 'cause your soulmate is the one that's made just for you."

"Oh, split apart. I know all about split aparts. The ancient lore says that people were originally created as two people who were perfectly matched and blissfully happy together. Except the spirits became jealous of the human's happiness, and split the people into separate halves. Since that time, people have always sought their one true love as their split apart." Miriam is pleased that she can bring some of her own tradition into this conversation.

"Yeah, yeah, that's a pretty story hon, but what are we going to do about this woman? I know what it's like to be split apart from your one true love." Gracie sighs wistfully.

"Adrian?" Miriam whispers and turns to Gracie.

"Yes, hon, Adrian. I did love him deeply and that big ole' man still loves me. I can feel it, so strong. I looked in on him a few days ago; he was just sittin at his desk, lookin at the ceiling. I know he was thinkin' about me, that's what brought me there to him, the force of his true love. I do miss that beautiful man."

"What is your plan for this woman, Gracie?" Miriam asks not to get involved with Gracie's foolishness, but just for curiosity's sake, of course.

"Lord knows, I don't have a plan, hon, that's your job. I'm just the idea person." Gracie vanishes.

"Alright, Gracie I will think about it. Now, can I get back to work?" Miriam speaks to the air. Miriam's friendship with Vicky and Mike has opened the employment door at the Tampa Police Department and provided her with a steady job, filing hard evidence. Some of the officers have noticed that on occasion Miriam talks to herself as she works. However they cut her considerable slack because of her tragic circumstance.

"I hear she took a terrible beating." "Poor thing, she can't remember a thing. It's a wonder she can function at all given, the extent of her injuries."

They whisper. Unbeknownst to them, Miriam must feign amnesia to protect her secret life.

◦

"Good game." Ted rubs the ketchup stain on his shirt as he walks toward the car.

"Yeah, how many hot dogs did you eat anyway, Ted?" Rob stumbles at the curb. Wow, those Ray's, huh, Mike? It was awesome the way they came from behind."

"How many beers did you have?" Mike asks. Rob belches.

"Am I the designated driver?"

"I don't think so, kid. Better hand the keys over." Mike extends his hand.

"We've got a way to walk yet. I might be sober by the time we get to the car. I don't even know if you can get us out of here old man." Rob giggles.

"You're a silly drunk. Give me the keys, kid. I'd hate to ticket you." Rob dangles the keys in front of Mike's face. Mike snatches the keys and unlocks the car doors. Ted continues smearing the ketchup stain into his shirt.

"Ted, I think you made it worse." Rob laughs. Ted frowns and continues working on the stain.

"Did you enjoy the game, Ted? I'm glad you could come along." Mike put the car in gear and pulls out of the parking lot.

"I did, Mike, thanks for inviting me. I don't get out much. These games with you fellows are about it."

"Why's that?" Rob leans forward from the back seat.

"Well, you know I raise and show prize winning roses. Quite time consuming, you know. Most of the rest of my time is spent at my work." "Roses take your time, huh?" Rob asks.

"Well, I do spend some time tinkering with my vintage auto." Ted has quit smearing the stain in, and now sits with his hand covering it.

"So, Mike, how come you aren't hanging with Vicky tonight?" Rob keeps up the conversation.

"She's at the mall with Miriam."

"Ah, I see, shopping, that can be grueling." Rob smiles.

"Yeah, I like to stay clear of it." Mike grins and keeps his eyes on the road.

"I do enjoy a jaunt to the mall occasionally." Ted lifts his hand and checks on the stain.

"I'll probably have to buy a new shirt,"
Rob belches again then giggles.

"Jaunt? Where are you from, Ted?"

"I'm from England."

"Cool, England swings," Rob hums the tune.

"Like a pendulum do," Ted finishes the verse.

"You on duty tomorrow, Mike?" Rob asks.

"No, I have the weekend off. As soon as I drop you two drunks off, I'm going over to Kumquat to help Miriam's friend work on her house. "

"Miriam's beautiful." Ted leans back in the seat, his hand still covering the stain. "Soda water will probably get this stain out," he mumbles.

"She sure is, Ted," Rob agrees, as did most of the red-blooded officers.

"Calm down boys she has a big ole' boyfriend that's crazy about her." Mike laughs. He drove on toward South Tampa. Mike will deposit his friends safely at their respective homes and then head to Miriam's house.

"Okay, last man out." Mike pulls into Rob's driveway He hands Rob back his car keys and watches as he makes his way to his front door. When Rob had successfully unlocked his door. Mike makes his way to Kumquat. He will happily spend the weekend helping Paul work on Miriam's old roadhouse.

&

"Rise and shine, hon."

"No, Gracie, you know it's Saturday, I can sleep late." Miriam pulls the covers over her head.

"Well, I'm here now. Come on, get up. You're burnin' daylight."

"Alright, but I need coffee first." Miriam peeks out from beneath the covers.

"I already made coffee for you," Gracie smiles.

"Ja, really? How nice of you. I didn't know that you can do that." Miriam is out of bed and heading to the kitchen.

"I can't, I was just jokin' you. What do you have planned today, hon?" Gracie follows to the kitchen.

"A cup of coffee," Miriam grumbles, as she starts the coffee maker.

"After coffee, what do we do then hon?" Gracie insists.

"I want to see if Eliakim can go with us." Miriam is still in a snit about the coffee; however, to Gracie it seems to be time to put bygones behind and get to work.

"Where are we going?" Gracie will not stop with the questions until she gets an answer to her liking.

"We aren't going anywhere, Gracie. I only want to see if Eliakim can go into another realm by himself and then come back to me." Miriam watches the coffee drip into the pot, still quite displeased with Gracie's fib.

"That sounds risky; we don't want to dink up that handsome golem of yours." Gracie leans into Miriam's space and grins.

"It could be." Miriam pours her coffee and ignores the handsome golem remark. She knows that Gracie is always just trying to get a rise out of her.

"Sounds like fun. When are we stepping out?"

"Quit nagging me, Gracie. I have to finish my coffee first!" Miriam's coffee frustration has left her a little bit testy.

"Looks like somebody's got their jammies in a wad this morning." Gracie laughs.

~

It is merely a small scrap of paper with one name written on it. That paper with that name written on it, along with Miriam's belief in every aspect of the name, is what causes Eliakim to live. In the corner of her closet, Miriam presses the paper into the clay figure's open mouth. Eliakim awakes and steps beside Miriam. She raises her hand and calls Sandalphon. The raven flies from seemingly nowhere onto Miriam's shoulder. Miriam, Gracie, Eliakim, and Sandalphon step into another realm. Miriam steps back into her natural realm. Eliakim remains in the realm that Miriam had just stepped from, she steps back in.

"Ja, this is good. Eliakim is still here and awake. Did you see that, Gracie?"

"Yes, I saw it but I'm not sure what all that means. What's it about, hon?"

"I wanted to find out if Eliakim could go with us when we go realm stepping. As well as I want to know if he will turn back to clay if I step out of a realm without him. I thought he might, since technically when I step out, I don't exist in the realm that he is in. But he did not turn to clay, so I think that existence transcends the realms. Like you do, but death not life. Understand, Gracie?"

"Sure, I get it, if you're alive or dead on one side, that's what you are on the other side. Well, hon, didn't you say you passed before you were brought here?"

"Yes, Gracie, I did."

"So, I guess if you wanted to go back and say visit your father you would be dead when you go back."

"Only if I went back to after the point where I crossed over."

"So, why are you alive here now if you died before?" Gracie needs an explanation of Miriam's life as it seems an obvious contradiction of dead on one side, dead on the other side notion.

"I am not certain what exactly happened the moment I passed over and how I am alive now. I feel that it is Sandalphon, the spirit, with all of the faces who in some way helped me. I do not have complete remembrance of what happened."

"Well, why don't you go back to before you passed?"

"If I did that, there would be two of me at once in that realm and that might change something, and I cannot change the past."

"Is that the rules?"

"Yes, Gracie, I suppose it is." Miriam smiles sadly.

"But hon, if you went back to after you died, wouldn't you be able to visit your father as a ghost like me?" Gracie is desperately trying to make sense of this puzzle.

"If I did go back, I would not find my father at our home since he went away with the others to work against the German war agenda. I am not even sure if he is living or dead himself, so you see, Gracie, I cannot even search for him. I'm afraid if I did search for him and he is dead, I might be transported to a realm that I did not mean to go to. I really am not familiar enough with this realm walking yet." Miriam is quiet for a moment then sighs heavily and continues.

"Now, there is one more test. I want to find out if Eliakim can go out and come back to me if I do not go with him."

"Oh, hon, what if he gets lost or something?"

"I think that will not happen because his life energy is an extension of mine, and he should be drawn back to me by that very energy." Miriam glances around her room from the cocoon of the other realm; she sees her journal is open on her desk.

"Eliakim, bring me my journal." Miriam orders her golem. Eliakim steps through the wall of energy. He makes his way to Miriam's desk. Then the powerful figure of a man returns to his creator and places the journal in her hand.

"I was right, Gracie, he can do it! We can take him with us when we step. Also, I can let him stand in another realm if I don't want him to be seen. Ja, this is wonderful! I won't have to hide him in my closet any longer. I finally have room for my shoes." Miriam is excited at the thought of extra room for new shoes, which is only slightly more exciting to her than new lipstick. Miriam has a low excitement threshold.

"Pardon me?" Gracie is surprised by Miriam's exaggerated excitement. Truth is, Gracie thinks that she holds exclusive rights to strange remarks.

"Do you want to go to the abbey and find that monk you were telling me about?"

"I thought that was what I heard you say. I sure do, hon." The realm travelers are immediately standing at the abbey of St. John. The Angelus is ringing, it is mid-day at the abbey and the monks stand in silence as the bell rings.

"Let's go, hon, we got a lot of brothers to look at." Gracie is anxious to begin the search for the woman's soul mate. Hidden by the blind of another realm, Gracie, Miriam, Sandalphon, and Eliakim wander the grounds of the abbey; but they did not encounter a monk with a crescent shape scar on his cheek.

"Gracie, can we go to him like you went to Adrian?"

"I think there has to be a connection to just go to someone." Gracie supposed.

"Ja, like the way Eliakim was drawn back to me. There's a connection because I created him. But I don't have a connection to this monk."

Miriam thought for a moment. Her eyes widen as she turns to Gracie, who is studying Eliakim for the umpteenth time.

"But you have a connection, Gracie."

"Pardon me, hon?" Gracie turns her attention to Miriam.

"Don't you see? You were listening when the woman was talking to Mike, and you felt sad about the loss of her true love; you had *simpatico* because you lost your one true love. You had the same feelings as she had, and I think he might share the same feelings as you both have. That's the connection! Those feelings will lead us to him. Think how you felt when you heard her talking to Mike."

"Okay, hon. I'll try." Gracie closes her eyes and sighs. In a moment, they are standing in the monk's room looking at the man that the woman described.

"Look, we're here, that's him!" Gracie is excited.

"Ja, we found him, now it will be easy to find him again. Tonight, I will devise a plan." The monk looks around his small room. His eyes stop where Gracie, Miriam, and Eliakim stand.

"Do you think he can see us, Gracie?"

"No, I don't think he can, hon. He would have reacted if he could see us, but I think he feels us."

"We should go home now." The realm walkers immediately returned home. Miriam and Eliakim suddenly appear standing in Vicky's living room. Startled by their sudden appearance, Vicky gasped as she choked on her last bite of a fried baloney sandwich.

"Good lord, Miriam." Vicky coughs.

"Are you all right, Vicky? If you are choking, you should make the sign for choking. See, you put your hands up to your throat and make choking movements." Miriam demonstrated while Vicky coughed.

"I saw this on P.B.S."

"Thanks for the demonstration, sugar, but I'm okay. Where did you come from? You scared the beejesus out of me. I thought you must have gone off with Paul."

"No, he's at the hard store buying things to fix my house."

"The what store, sugar? Why is Eliakim awake?"

"We went for a walk. The hard store for house stuff, I think Mike went with him." Miriam opens the fridge and pours herself a glass of sweet tea and began slicing lemons. She drops six lemon wedges into her tea.

"Wait! What? You went out for a walk with Eliakim? What if the neighbors had seen you? Or Mike, heaven forbid, I'd never be able to explain that one away. The big lie that I told him about me helping you get Gracie's house with your fund money was bad enough." Vicky shakes her head. "It's hardware store, sugar." Vicky smiles.

"Not that kind of a walk. We went with Gracie. I don't even need Gracie anymore, I just take her along because she likes to go, you know." Miriam sips her tea.

Vicky did know, as a matter of fact she knows things now that only a year ago she had never even thought of. Hell, she knows things now, that no one she has ever known, has never, ever thought of.

"Geez, Miriam, I hope you know what you're doing." Vicky had to give a responsible adult warning in the capacity of Miriam's legal guardian. Vicky also feels obliged to occasionally give Miriam the what-on-earth-were-you-thinking speech, which in fact is something that Vicky does often wonder. Although Vicky knows Miriam's circumstances, even at that, she realizes that she will probably never truly know what on earth Miriam is thinking or understand the twist of fate that brought this exceptional young woman into her life.

"Okay, as long as you're being careful, sugar. We're going over to your house in the morning, Miriam, be ready early."

"Ja, I warned Gracie that Paul and Mike were going to be there. I hope they don't get frightened by any late-night visions." Miriam snickered. Vicky rolls her eyes and just shakes her head.

"Sugar, will you pour me a glass of that tea?" Vicky hands her glass to Miriam

"Ja. Lemon?"

"Sure, but take it easy."

"Only three?"

"I think one will do it. I love you, you big nut."

⌒

Miriam's old house is a Kumquat landmark. Everyone in the small town knows the history of the old house, every sordid detail. In the tedious little town of Kumquat, around the turn of the century, the roadhouse was the favored establishment of which the town's gentlemen called upon. While most of the gentlemen only called on occasion. some of the more vigorous cowboys were more frequent guests.

Lately, the house has suffered neglect, but Paul has determined that since the house is structurally sound, he will put every ounce of his might into relieving the suffering of the old brothel. He plans to replace a few windowpanes, rotted wood, and such. Then, he'll give the whole house, a fresh coat of paint, inside and out, after which the house will be as good as new, or better. He'll enjoy restoring the old roadhouse for Miriam.

"Wow, y'all have really done a lot!" Vicky stands next to Mike in the front yard of the old house.

"Paul, I am so proud of you. You are doing a wonderful job." Miriam stands on her tiptoes and gives Paul a peck on the cheek.

"Yeah, we replaced some rotten siding yesterday, then last night we painted the living room. The color turned out nice." Paul grins as Miriam evaluates the work that he and Mike have done.

"We brought y'all breakfast. Are you hungry, Michael?" Vicky holds up a bag of bacon, egg, and cheese biscuits.

"Good job, sweet pea, we started the coffee already." Mike gives Vicky a hug and takes the bag of biscuits. "I'm starving how about you Paul?" Mike and Paul proceed into the house, with their bag of breakfast.

"I could eat." Paul can always eat. However, even the most dedicated fitness guru will be hard pressed to find even an ounce of extra fat gooing around on Paul's chiseled body.

"After breakfast, let's check the windowsills outside to make sure none of 'em are rotted."

"Good call, Paul. He's really good at this," Mike brags on Paul's architectural abilities. "Yep, he's the brains of this outfit, I'm the brawn." Mike flexes and grunts for effect.

"Yeah, I should be pretty good at it. My grandfather wanted me to be an architect. I studied architecture to please him, and then I followed my dream and went into criminal justice." Paul takes another breakfast sandwich from the bag.

"You're an architect? That explains a lot." Mike has never thought of Paul in any aspect other than law enforcement.

"Nope, I'm a bad guy getter." Paul laughs.

After breakfast, Paul and Mike return to the task at hand.

"Look here, Mike." Paul points to the air conditioning unit that is lying on the ground below the second story window.

"That unit must have been dripping on this sill." Paul gives the sill a slight tug.

"The wood is pretty rotten. That's what happens in these old houses, when people put in those window shakers, the water does a lot of damage, but nothing that we can't fix, eh, Mike?"

"Yeah, we'll have to get some lumber though," Mike agrees. He's enjoying this project. It's is a pleasant reprieve from the stress of police work.

"It won't take much, but most of the wood has to be special cut, the size is off." Paul uses his considerable brawn to yank the piece of the rotting wood from the sill.

"See this old lumber, it's true, a two by four is really two inches by four inches, but now the new boards aren't true, so if you want the new wood and the old wood to match, it has to be cut special," Paul explains.

"Wow, you do know your stuff. I'm impressed."

"Hey, Mike, what ever happened with the kid you were telling me about in witness protection?"

"Ah, Carlos," Mike groans. "He got in touch with me about a week ago. He said he called an old friend just to talk, said that the kid told him that one of the deputies in St John is on someone's pay, he told Carlos that he doesn't want to deal drugs anymore. He says he wants to come into the protection program." Mike struggles with his task as he speaks. "Man, really, I can't get this big glob of paint off."

"What do you make of that kid, Mike? Don't work too hard with that scraper. We'll pressure wash later then we'll paint over whatever doesn't come off."

"Good call. I don't know what to think about Carlos' friend. It could be all bull. I was pretty hard on him, the poor kid. He's lucky, hope he didn't blow his cover."

"Must be tough on a kid in witness protection." Paul continues checking for rot.

"I know he must be going nuts. His whole life has been upended. I hated to be so hard on him. But I think he understands now that he needs to stay out of Vicente's radar."

"You going to be able to take what you got to court soon?" Paul asks.

"I think I'm almost ready, with the kid's testimony, and the testimony of the woman from here in Kumquat. Besides, the papers that I got from Red Duetzman's son; I think I have it."

"What about Red Duetzman? Is he goin' down?"

"I'd love to wrap him up and serve him to the district attorney, but he'll probably only get a slap on the wrist since he's testifying against Vicente. Unless I come up with something that isn't related, that is. Then it will be a new ball game. Not very likely though." Mike is frustrated with the turn of events but will gladly forfeit the little fish to catch the big one.

"Red ratted out his old buddy, huh?"

"Sure did, he came in and confessed to money laundering for Vicente. Then Red told us all about how Vicente runs his operation. Duetzman only came to us because he believes Vicente had his son, Victor, killed."

"Those people are ruthless." Paul and Mike continue scraping, checking for rot, and pulling the decayed pieces off the old house.

"Yeah, well, it does seem that there is something going on between the Mexican cartel in Kumquat and the Vicente family in Tampa."

"Maybe Red knows more than what he's saying," Paul says.

"I'm sure Duetzman is mixed up in it all, but he's done talking. He made his deal; he's a small fish, anyway, compared to Joe Vicente."

❧

As the guys are deep in discussion of sordid mob dealings, Vicky and Miriam stand in Miriam's living room admiring the paint job.

"I love the color you picked, sugar. White with just a hint of pink and it looks so good with the bright white trim. The guys did a good job. I'll have to remember this. I'm going to need my living room painted too, pretty soon." Vicky smiles.

"Thank you, Vicky. Paul did not agree about the color, but he says he likes it now." Miriam and Vicky stand back and are deep in discussion about the effort the guys are putting in, when Gracie pops in.

"I like it too, hon, you know that Paul says he doesn't like pink because it scares the daylights out of guys. Seems like they think their privates will fall off if they really do like pink." Gracie heartily laughs at her joke.

"Good morning, Gracie, I didn't' know that." Miriam turns to Vicky. "Gracie likes the color too."

"What didn't you know, Miriam? Vicky asks.

311

"That Paul thinks his privates will fall off. Do you think that's true, Vicky?"

"WHAT? PRIVATES! Geeze, Gracie, good morning and watch what you say. Don't listen to her, sugar, she's full of beans."

"Where have you been, Gracie?" Miriam asks. She will remember to question Vicky later about privates falling off and full of beans.

"Oh, I've been here and there, mostly here, keeping an eye on your handsome fellas. Good morning, Vicky"

"Gracie says good morning, Vicky." Miriam relays the conversation.

"How do you like what the guys are doing, Gracie?" Vicky greets Gracie, although she doesn't see or hear her. Even though Vicky and Gracie started out on unsteady footing, they have seen the error of their ways. They now have a blossoming friendship. Miriam is glad and relieved.

"I think the house is coming right along, Vicky." Gracie chirped. She also is pleased with the progress of her friendship with Vicky. She's actually glad that Miriam has Vicky to help her along; after all, she figures she will hit it lucky one day and cross over.

"Gracie says it's coming along, Vicky."

"Are you going to paint up the rest of the rooms, hon?"

"Yes, I hope you don't mind that I'm painting, Gracie."

"This is your house now, do whatever your heart desires to it." Gracie winks at Miriam.

"She says she doesn't mind if I paint, she says whatever my heart desires." Miriam smiles. She always keeps Vicky up on the conversations with Gracie. Miriam feels that it's the only proper thing to do, which of course it is. Nobody wants to be the odd man out, not knowing what the ghost is saying. However, Miriam does practice a ten second delay when relaying Gracie's conversations, just in case she has to rephrase. Vicky and Gracie follow Miriam through the house, listening to her plans for each room. Then, suddenly, Miriam becomes silent, she turns to Gracie.

"Gracie, thank you for this house. It is an amazing gift that you have given to me. I promise to you, just as you promised to the others. I will always care for it."

Absolute Power

Poor, pitiful Saul grew up in the lap of luxury in the Duetzman household. That's not to say that being one of six children couldn't have consequences that can carry over into adulthood, especially if the children are left to fend for themselves. It is well known that the child who is not properly nurtured faces the possibility of future troubles, although that is not the case with Saul. His mother was well versed in all of the psychobabble and made every effort to help Saul and his siblings work through the terrible injustice of their privileged birthright. Saul's father on the other hand, took particular enjoyment in pitting the children against each other.

Saul was a sullen child who never played well with others, and discovered early on that some bad behavior here or a scuffle there, was enough to get the attention that he so desperately wanted, and if bad behavior or a scuffle didn't produce the sought-after effect, Saul would ratchet it up a notch. A screaming fit of temper could usually bring forth the desired result, which was everyone's complete and exclusive attention. After all, it wasn't his fault that he had been born after Victor, the golden boy. Much to Saul's distress, Victor the eldest son was everyone's favorite. Even the other siblings preferred Victor's company to Saul's. Moreover, Victor didn't even have to cause a stir to get attention. Quite the opposite, Victor went through life contentedly marching to the beat of his own drum.

Saul, however, has recently taken a well-thought-out path, to the impasse that has always been his older brother. Saul and the Vicente crime family thugs have made certain that Victor and his family are gone forever.

Then there is Brenda, Red's only daughter, the darling baby girl. Saul has regretted not having strangled his baby sister as she slept in her bassinet. However, he resisted his murderous notion then and allowed her to live. A benevolence of which, he now has misgivings. Brenda Duetzman is not a gracious survivor at all, not one bit. Saul may one day, bring her attention around, from her daddy's credit cards, and indulgences, to the reality of his own earlier gesture of goodwill towards her. The rest of the sibling brothers are much the same as Saul, each jockeying for position in the family business.

Saul has married three times, each wife thinking that she would be the one to bridge the gap between Saul's inability to love, to a life of her devoted love. They were wrong.

Saul and Saul Junior are now happily residing in the South Tampa mansion where Saul was raised. Saul has taken charge of the everyday workings of the Duetzman empire such as it is. Red Duetzman is under house arrest in that same mansion. With the ankle monitor securely attached, he awaits the day that he goes to court on charges of money laundering for Joseph Vicente. He will turn state's evidence against his old friend, Vicente. To sweeten his impunity pot, Red will also tell whatever he knows and make up what he doesn't know about.Jorge Hernandez Gonzalez El diMarco, the head of the Mexican drug cartel that operates out of Kumquat. Until then, Red will be safe and comfortable in his home. He could have gone to a safe house for protection but opted instead to stay in his own home, a veritable fortress. Besides, a safe house has nothing on Duetzman's own security system. His protection measures consist of a small army of guards that Red employs twenty-four hours a day, every day, to ensure his safety. These thugs will kill with no compunction, and then without hesitation will skillfully dispose of the body.

Red Duetzman is sitting in his darkened room, nursing a bottle of cheap scotch, when a knock sounds at the door to his suite.

"Who is it?" He growls.

"Mr. Duetzman, Saul's on the phone for you," the thug answers.

"Why doesn't he just come up and talk to me? What a dumbass." Red is a nasty drunk.

"He's not here, Mr. Duetzman."

"Tell him to call my cell. I'll turn it on." A moment later, Duetzman's cell rings.

"What, Saul?"

"There are fires in two of our warehouses. I'm driving by there now. Looks bad, probably a total loss."

"Anything in 'em?"

"Nope, both empty."

"Does Joe know?"

"Yeah, dad, he's the one who called me."

"Did he do it?"

"No, he says it was the Mexicans, revenge for not getting their money."

"Don't they know that there was trouble in Kumquat? Hell, we lost everything and all our go-betweens. What the hell do those crazy bastards think burning the warehouse is going to solve? Crazy bastards."

"Relax, Dad. I'm on my way to talk to Vicente now. Don't talk to the police if they come around tonight. I want to talk to Vicente first. Just go to bed, Dad, I'll be home later."

"Okay, Saul, you're da boss, tonight." Red isn't ready just yet to give complete control of the business over to Saul, but it is good lip service. Red is fairly certain that Joe had nothing to do with the burning warehouses. Plus, he is absolutely certain that Joe Vicente doesn't know that he is under house arrest. That is a secret that the district attorney and the Tampa police will be keeping to themselves.

⌐

Red is having an early breakfast with his grandson, Sauley, Saul's only child. Saul took a seat at the breakfast table.

"What did Joe say last night, Saul?" Red asks.

"He's sure that it was the Mexicans. They are all hell bent out of shape because of what happened in Kumquat. They're making a statement. But I say there's going to bloodshed in Kumquat tonight."

"What's your plan? Pass me a piece of toast, will ya?"

"I'm going to make a statement of my own tonight. I'm going to take out El diMarco's wife." Saul passes the toast.

"Saul, you gonna' hit a woman? Pass the butter, Sauley."

"No, of course not. I'm going to have Billy Fat Legs do it." "Oh, Fat Legs, I see. Thanks, Sauley." Red butters a piece of toast.

"Why aren't you at your clinic working, Sauley?" Saul questions his son.

"I don't have any patients until after ten."

"Alright just don't slack off, idle hands are the devil's workshop, you know." Saul laughs.

"Yeah, right." Sauley finishes his breakfast and leaves the table. Sauley isn't brilliant; and it was obvious early on that the probability of Sauley being any sort of use to society is nil or none. If the truth were known, Doctor Saul Duetzman Junior is not the physician that most would choose, even though he has the best medical degree that money can buy.

"So, this is going to happen tonight with Fat Legs? Did you speak to him about it yet?" Red asks.

"Nope, not yet, but Billy'll do it. I'm going to tell him to do it in front of diMarco's bodega. Angelina goes in every night to pick up the deposit, that's when he'll hit her."

"Sounds pretty dicey," Red cautions.

"Maybe, Pop, maybe not." Saul takes a sip of his coffee. "But it will be, POW, POW, and then it's done and then El diMarco's wife is officially a statement from the Duetzman family, Simple, don't worry." Saul smirks.

"Don't do it, it's not a good idea, Saul." Red gives his final warning to his hotheaded son.

❦

"Michael?" Vicky peeks into Mike's office.

"Good morning, sweet pea."

"It's a nice day, Michael. Do you want to have lunch out in the courtyard with Miriam and me?"

"What time is it?" Mike doesn't look up from his files.

"About eleven."

"I guess I can, in an hour."

"Good, Michael, we'll meet you out there. I don't get to see enough of you since you've been working so hard on getting your case together."

"I know, Vicky, but it'll be done real soon and then I'll have a breather, I hope." Mike smiles at his sweet Georgia peach. He returns to his work and continues leafing through the mound of papers on his desk. "Is that all of the papers that you got from Victor?"

"Yeah, this is all of it, strange how it turned out. Victor thought that the information in these papers would save him, but these papers are what destroyed him."

"He was a good friend, Michael; and you're doing the right thing. He must have known that it could go either way, why else would he make sure that you got the papers?"

"Just in case he didn't make it," Mike whispers. "You're right. I'll see you two ladies in the courtyard in an hour. Now, take your charming selves back to your station." Vicky rolls her eyes, turns, and leaves. Mike's cell rings.

"De Augustino here."

"Stay away from the abbey or there will be problems," the caller whispers and hangs up. Mike makes a quick call from his office line.

"Ted, it's Mike, are you busy? I need you to come to my office."

"Sure, Mike, I'll be right there." Ted hurries to Mike's office. He studies Mike's cell phone.

"Sorry, Mike. I can't trace it. He probably wasn't on long enough. I'd wager the call came from one of those burner phones. You can always change your number."

"I think I'll let this play out. Whoever made that call has to be someone involved in the murders at the Abbey. I might get a lead if I just play it cool. Thanks, anyway, Ted."

"Okay, Mike, sorry I couldn't help with this one, but if they had emailed you, I'd be the one to call. I'm quite proficient at the computer. I'm taking my lunch now, catch you later, Mike."

"Wow, thanks for reminding me. I'm supposed to meet Vicky and Miriam in the food court. Thanks, Ted, see ya later."

"You're having lunch with Miriam? Lucky stiff. Can I come?" Ted smiles.

"Well, you'd have to pay then."

"Forget it, Mike." Ted returns to his desk and his bag lunch. Mike hurries out to the food court.

"Hi, ladies." Mike sits between Vicky and Miriam. A break with his two most favorite ladies is just what he needs.

"How's the case coming, Mike?" Miriam scooches over a bit to give Mike a little more room.

"Oh, you know tying up all the loose ends. I want all my i's dotted and p's crossed." Mike smiles at Miriam.

"I know that you are trying to confuse me, Mike. I know that t's cross and p's..."Miriam furrows her brow; she looks to Vicky. Vicky just smiles.

"Well, p's do other important things, like make you be good." Miriam has not forgotten her idiom lesson on minding your p's and q's. She is glad, it has come in quite handy.

"Mike, are you coming over tonight? Miriam is cooking." Vicky grins.

"Uh, gee, thanks for the invitation, but I really have a lot of paperwork left to do." A gracious thanks, but no thanks is the first response that came to his mind. Mike is afraid it might be her notorious scoodle and isn't taking any chances.

"Sorry, you'll miss it, Mike. Paul's coming over, this will be the first time Paul gets to have Miriam's scoodle." Vicky laughs. Mike feels vindicated.

"Well, I might be able to break free early." Mike will definitely be able break free. He will not miss this.

"Miriam, that smells wonderful." Paul hugs Miriam and hands a bottle of wine over her shoulder to Vicky.

"It's white. I didn't know what goes with scoodle." Paul winks at Vicky. Seems that Paul has been tipped off about Miriam's signature dish.

"I'm not sure either, Paul." Vicky opens the fridge.

"Hey, don't put that wine up; I'll have a glass now." Mike calls out from the couch.

"Me too." Paul sits next to Mike on the couch. Rocky watches as Miriam scoodles in a large skillet.

Scoodle is an interesting dish. It's somewhat like an endless buffet only the entire buffet is all in one frying pan. Scoodle is Rocky's favorite, which is a plus because there are always plenty of leftovers. A phenomenon that hasn't gone unnoticed by Miriam and that significantly pleases Rocky.

"How about another dish of scoodle, Mike?" Miriam offers.

"Oh no, thanks Miriam, I'm driving. But I will have another glass of that wine, Vicky." Mike lifts his glass toward Vicky.

Vicky takes his glass, smiles, turns and extra heavy duty rolls her eyes. Miriam furrows her brow and begins a protest. Mike's cell rings.

"Hold that thought Miriam. I need to get this. Excuse me ladies. It's the sheriff in Kumquat." Mike answers his phone.

"Yeah, Adrian, what's up? Really, shot dead? Yeah, sure, Adrian, send me whatever you have. I'll take a look at it for you tomorrow. Probably spill over from the fires."

"Yeah, I'll talk to you soon. Okay, Adrian, I will." Mike ends the call.

"Adrian says hi Vicky. I didn't know that you two are buddies."

"I get his calls sometimes at the front desk,"

Vicky explains, then in her mind adds… sometimes I call him, since Adrian is much more forthcoming with information than you. Certainly, a thought she will keep to herself. Mike looks suspiciously at Vicky.

"Who was shot dead?" Vicky changes the subject she really doesn't want to talk to Mike about her conversations with Adrian. In point of fact, Vicky has been having a difficult time lately deciding, what she really can, talk to Mike about. What she shouldn't ever, talk to Mike about and what she should always, talk, to Mike about. Usually when there is a question in Vicky's mind concerning the relevance that a conversation has to her relationship with Michael, she just changes the subject. Because after all has been said, it doesn't really matter because, they are split aparts.

"What happened in Kumquat, Mike?" Paul asks.

"Angelina El diMarco, the wife of Jorge El diMarco was shot dead coming out of their family's bodega tonight."

"Wow, El diMarco's wife, the drug lord in Kumquat! Does the sheriff have any idea who did it?" Paul asks.

"Nothing for sure. I figure it must be either Vicente or a Duetzman. I bet it has something to do with those fires last night," Mike says.

"El diMarco's wife, wow, that's huge. What fires, how did I miss that?" Vicky asks again.

"It was late last night, Vicky, two of the Duetzman's warehouses burned to the ground. Now, the wife is gunned down. It's ratcheting up, sounds like war is, coming, to me."

"Yep, I'd say so." Paul agrees.

⸺

"Okay, Fat Legs, calm down, it's not that bad." Sauley helps the nurse bring the bloodied man into a treatment room. Billy Fat Legs is bleeding, just as countless others that Billy has dealt with have bled.

"Angelina, she's dead." Billy fat legs mumbles, as he floats in and out of consciousness.

"Let's get him on the table where I can take a better look. Then you can go on home Lynn." Lynn knows the drill; this is not the first time that she has been sent home early. Neither is this the first time that Doctor Duetzman has patched up one of the not so wise guys. Sauley will dutifully perform the service that is expected of him. Short of having a brain to make it on his own merit, it's the price Sauley pays for having a medical education, license, and practice that is bought and paid for with contributions from the underworld. He will not question fat legs about the wounds; therefore, remaining innocent of any knowledge of wrongdoing. After service is rendered, he will send his patient away.

Fat Legs moans.

"It's nothing, Fat Legs, just a flesh wound. Quit whining, I could take it in my eye." Sauley stops the bleeding and starts an I.V. Hours later; he discharges Billy Fat Legs into the dark of night. Sauley closes up his clinic and steps into the cool fall darkness.

A car speeds by, shots ring out. When the street is quiet, Sauley Duetzman is dead. What a shame, such a waste of an education. Clearly, the Mexican cartel didn't contribute to the Saul Duetzman Jr. scholarship program.

⁓

The body is discovered in the wee hours of the morning by a jogger.

"I saw him lying in a heap right next to the door right there." The jogger points to the spot where the earthly remains of Doctor Saul Duetzman lie.

"Thanks. We have your statement. If there's anything else, we'll contact you."

"What do you think?" Mike approaches the medical examiner. "He's been dead a few hours. I'd say he was killed around two o'clock this morning, give or take. Bag him up and take him to the lab," Eslen instructs his assistant then turns back to Mike.

"That's all I know now, but give me a few hours and I can tell you what he ate for his last meal, if that's what you want to know. Must have been a big meal." Eslen points to the huge dark stain on Sauly's very expensive trousers. "Nice pants, too bad." The medical examiner and his assistant have a hardy laugh.

"Thanks, Eslen." Mike ignores the medical examiner's ghastly sense of humor. Mike supposes he'd probably be a little nutty too if all he did was hang with dead people all day.

Mike drives toward the Duetzman estate; he will have to get a statement from Saul Duetzman on his son's death. Mike plans to ask Red if he knows anything about a deputy sheriff in Kumquat working with Vicente. It is a long shot that Red will admit it if he does know something. Although, possibly Red is feeling particularly generous today, no... that really is a long shot. Given the probability that if Red does know something, the odds that he won't give up any information greatly outweigh the odds that he will. Furthermore, if he doesn't know something now, he will certainly know something if Mike mentions it. Mike decides not to speak to Red at all today, about the deputy in Kumquat. He will keep that to himself for now.

"Mr. Duetzman, Mike De Augustino from the police department is here to see you."

"Let him in." Saul allows his housekeeper to escort Mike into the inner sanctum.

"Saul, I hate to have to come here today like this. I'm sorry for your loss." Mike shakes Saul's hand as he offers his condolences. "I'll be brief. Do you know anyone who wanted to harm your son?"

"No, no one, he was a good, and respected man."

"Have you noticed anything odd in his behavior lately, or any new acquaintances?"

"No, nothing, please Mike, no more questions." Saul is devastated over the loss of his son.

"Thank you, Saul, again, sorry for your loss."

"Thanks, Mike, our man will show you out." One of Red's guards shows Mike to the door.

Back in his office, Mike gathers his thoughts, he considers everything that has happened up until now, and then he calls the sheriff in Kumquat.

"Hey, Adrian, got the papers you sent. I guess you heard about Saul Duetzman's son."

"Yes, I did. Don't you think that the timing of that hit is mighty telling?" Adrian asks.

"Exactly what I think. I'm glad we're on the same page. First, Duetzman's warehouses burn, then El diMarco's wife is killed in the street, and then immediately Saul Duetzman's son is shot coming out of his clinic. Sounds like war. Information seems to be changing hands pretty damn quick. Hold on a second, Adrian, I got a call coming through." Mike put the sheriff on hold and took the other call. A short time later, Mike returns to the call.

"Yeah, Adrian, that was the chief; he says that a body was found floating in the bay, it's William Cox, a.k.a. Billy Fat Legs. Wow this war is really getting hot."

"Yeah, you know, Mike, I've been thinkin' lately there's been some interesting coincidences, and I don't believe in coincidence."

"Neither do I, Adrian. It seems like the cartels are getting a lot more efficient lately."

"Yeah, it's like they each know what the other is thinking. What do you think?" The sheriff is fishing.

"I think they are getting information. I think we've got a mole working both sides."

"Well, that is a coincidence, Mike. That's exactly what I think. I'm just curious who the mole is ultimately working for."

"Yep, Adrian, we find that mole and we got a real foot up."

"Sounds like a plan. Talk to you soon, Mike."

"Catch you later, Adrian."

❧

"Saul, how could this be? First, I lose Victor and his children, now Sauley. Someone in our family sold-out their own flesh and blood.

"Who do you think would do that?" Saul worries that his father suspects him.

"I don't know who, but I believe that someone close is selling us over to Vicente." Red is grief-stricken. He pours another glass of scotch.

"I will take care of it, Dad. Vicente will pay, there will be vendetta."

"Take care of it, Saul. You're in charge."

"I promise you, Pop, that Vicente will feel the pain of losing a loved one. And I will discover who the traitor to our family is." With this vow, Saul voices his loyalty to his father and alleviates any suspicions that his father might have about his involvement in Victor's death. Saul will be certain that his father never discovers his connection with Vicente and the death of Victor and his family.

❧

"Mike, have you got a minute? I want you to look at something I got in the mail today."

"Sure, Rob, what is it?"

"It's a nursery rhyme look at it, it's really creepy." Rob lays the letter in front of Mike. The words of the verse have been carefully cut from various papers and magazines to form a nursery rhyme.

"Wow, some nut really took a lot of time with that." Mike reads the rhyme.

There was a little girl who had a little curl.

Right in the middle of her forehead.

And when she was good,

She was very, very good.

But when she was bad,

She was horrid.

"My mother used to recite that rhyme to my little sister when she was bad." Mike laughs. "And when she was bad, she really was horrid."

"What do you think this means, Mike?" Rob asks.

"I don't know, but I'd probably make a file on it. You never know what the loonies are thinking."

"That's what the chief said. He also said he wants to put me over in the Kumquat Sheriff's Department for a while. He thinks there's a person on the inside over there givin' info to the mobs."

"Wow, undercover. Just be careful, don't try to be a cowboy."

"I don't know how long I'll be there. As long as it takes, I guess."

"Don't worry. Adrian Thomas is a good man; he'll be watching your back."

"I'm not worried, that's why I got into this; to thwart evil doers wherever they may be, and fight for truth justice and the American way." Rob strikes a Superman pose and imagines his hair and cape blowing in the wind as an American flag waves in the background.

"Okay, I've got to get back to work now, Clark." Mike laughs

Mike is glad when his phone rings, he's hoping it's Carlos. He has left a message for him to call. Mike feels bad for being so hard on the kid, even though he knows it is for his own good. Carlos has been in witness protection for almost a year. And now Mike can assure him that this ordeal is almost over. Everything Mike has on Joe Vicente has been sent to the district attorney's office. They will get their case together shortly; Carlos and his mother will be safely relocated.

"Hi Carlos, what's up, man?"

"You tell me Mike, you called."

"Yeah, kid, I got good news; we're going to court soon."

"That's great, Mike, but what about my buddy? He wants to get away from that deputy sheriff in Kumquat. How about him?"

"I'll tell you what, Carlos, give me your friend's number and I'll try to set something up."

"Thanks, Mike." Carlos gives Mike his friend's number.

"It's okay, kid."

THE PLANS

Sylvia Cooper-Fields unlocks the door to her daughter's house. This is the first time that Sylvia has been to her child's home in more than three months. She trips on a dinosaur that has escaped from the children's playroom.

"You're probably searching for your playmates." Sylvia picks up the unruly toy.

"I didn't want to be the one to have to tell you," Sylvia speaks in whispers to her grandchild's toy.

"The children aren't coming home tonight. No, not tomorrow either. I'm sorry, there's been a terrible accident. They won't be coming home." Sylvia holds the dinosaur to her broken heart. She returns the dinosaur to the toy box and begins the sad undertaking of closing her daughter's home.

Lydia Cooper Duetzman has died along with her two small children and Victor Duetzman, her husband. Sylvia doesn't recall what exactly she was doing on the day she heard about the deaths of her only daughter and her family. She only recalls the words, 'terrible accident'. It was those words, which were spoken on that day, that have left Sylvia in an empty world of dark disbelief. She packs the pictures first.

Sylvia holds Lydia and Victor's wedding photograph. There had been some problems in their marriage but not between Lydia and Victor; it had been in-law problems. But they were in love, they worked through it, everyone always said they were meant for each other. It seemed that they were going to make it. She gently touches the faces then packs the photographs away. Lydia had all but given up hope that she and Victor would ever have children, then Kyle came along; his permanent teeth were coming in so straight. Sylvia studied the picture of the smiling young boy, then there was Julia. Julia Cooper Duetzman, what a joy and she looks just like Lydia. Julia carried the Cooper family name well, as has each female child in the lineage for generations, now there will be no more Coopers.

The clothes will go to the Goodwill Store; save for keepsakes of the children's baby clothes. Sylvia breathed the scent that lingered on the tiny pieces of sleepwear. Sylvia would find a special place for Victor's and Lydia's high school letter jackets. She sits on Lydia's bed, holding the letter jacket that her daughter had earned for cheerleading. Cooper was emblazoned across the back in the gold and burgundy of her school's colors. Cooper… Sylvia smiled. That's what Victor called her; she was always his Cooper.

The last room to pack was the laundry room. Neither Lydia nor Victor collected junk, so there would be little if anything in the laundry room to be concerned about. Sylvia will take a quick look before she leaves the house.

On the very top shelf of the laundry room closet, Sylvia found a large cardboard tube covered by a stack of quilts. Inside the tube was a set of plans, plans of The Holy Trinity Monastery. The plans are a work of art; they are the original plans that had been hand drawn by the builder and architect Klaus Duetzman. Sylvia returns the plans to the tube and locks the house. On her way home, Sylvia will stop and show the plans to her architect friend. He will love to see them. Sylvia dials her friend.

"Hello, Corwin. I'm on my way home from Lydia's house. I have something I'd like to show you. Are you busy? Good, I'll be there in a few minutes." Corwin Riggs and Sylvia have been friends for years. They grew up together in Tampa, married their college sweethearts, and through all the years stayed in touch. Now, they are alone together.

"Sylvia, I'm glad you came by. Come in, sit down for a while." Corwin hugs his old friend.

"I've been at Lydia's all day. I want to show this to you. I think you will like this piece of Tampa memorabilia." Sylvia unrolls the plans onto Corwin's dining room table.

"My goodness, Sylvia, this is a beautiful piece of history." Corwin and Sylvia talked over the plans. They relived old times and tender memories. It is comforting chatter and a glass of wine with an old friend.

"Corwin, dear, I must excuse myself, I am completely overdone."

"Certainly, you've had a hard day. Go home and rest now. Can I look at those plans for a day or two Sylvia?"

"Of course, Corwin, I thought you might like to look at them for a bit."

"Thank you, Sylvia." Corwin walks Sylvia to the drive and opens the car door for her. Sylvia graciously accepts his gallant gesture.

～

"Good morning, Mr. Riggs," Corwin's receptionist greets him.

"Good morning, Aggie." Corwin hurries to his office.

Corwin Riggs did not inherit his architectural firm; he built it with honest hard work and long hours. Now, he is the president and C.E.O. of one of the most prestigious firms in Tampa. It's an impressive resume for a self-made Tampa man. Corwin hangs his jacket and buzzes his receptionist.

"Aggie, will you ask Raymond to come to my office please?"

"Certainly, Mr. Riggs."

Raymond Dwyer is Corwin's best friend and business partner. During their sixty-year friendship, they have witnessed many a change in the Tampa skyline; they have even effected many of those changes.

"Morning, Cory, what's the plan today?" Raymond chuckles, he never tires of his play on the words.

"You have to see this, Ray. Silly showed it to me last night!" Corwin is excited as he rolls out the old plans for his buddy to see.

"This is awesome. Where did she get these?"

"She closed up Lydia's house yesterday." Corwin is somber.

"Oh," Ray sighs. Cory looks away, their friend's grief resonates between them.

"I want you to look at these plans Ray. I looked at them for quite a while last night. There are some markings over on one page that I can't make out. Take them to your desk and study them. Maybe you can figure what the old Duetzman was doodling about."

"Sure, I'd love to go over these!"

Raymond rolls the plans back into their tube and returns to his office, plans in hand. Raymond pours over the plans all morning and into the afternoon. He is fascinated with the workmanship that went into the drawing. Every detail of the massive building was hand drawn by the architect.

"Mr. Dwyer, would you like me to pick up something from the deli for your lunch, sir?" Raymond is still studying the plans when the intern draftsman interrupts him.

"Oh, my goodness, I have been so engrossed in these plans, I forgot all about lunch."

Melissa Turnble approaches her supervisor, the draftsman may be an intern, but she certainly is not a man, as the young architects in the office have seen and noticed.

"I've been watching you in here all morning, well, not all morning only when I pass by." Melissa doesn't want Mr. Dwyer to think that she has been goofing off, which she has, or that she is some kind of old guy stalker, which she isn't.

"I understand, Melissa." Raymond chuckles.

"Come look at this, it's drafting history."

"What is this?"

"It's the plans of The Holy Trinity Monastery."

"Really? My great grandfather built that."

"Then he's the one who drew these plans. See, there's his name on the bottom of the page, Klaus Duetzman." Raymond is enjoying sharing this bit of drafting skill with the young woman.

"Cool. So, do you want a sandwich or something? I'm going down to the deli now, Mr. Dwyer."

"Sure, bring me a corned beef on rye. Mustard, please." Raymond is once again captivated by the plans.

"Okay." Melissa bounces off to the deli. She is somewhat impressed by the plans, but only because her supervisor is impressed. She can't really be expected to be totally impressed by some prehistoric member of her family who has scribbled something on a big piece of paper, like almost a million years ago. That is all well and good, great accomplishment, yah-da, yah-da, yah-da... But if she gets some recognition from it, all the better.

~

Richard Duetzman is the youngest child of his parents. Brenda Duetzman Turnble is Richard's youngest child, and sweet baby Melissa is Brenda's youngest. Being the youngest child, of the youngest child, of the youngest child, is much akin to the phenomena of being the seventh son of the seventh son. Save that Melissa's gift is not the clairvoyance of the all-seeing third eye. Melissa's gift is mind-numbing immaturity.

"I love you, grandpa," Melissa whispers. To Melissa's good, she did have enough sense to know that this is a sad visit to her uncle Saul and grandfather.

"Missy, how are you doin' at your internship? You will be the first architect since your great grandfather. I'm proud of you. Here's something." Red took a crisp one-hundred-dollar bill from his shirt pocket and pressed it into Melissa's hand.

"Thank you, grandpa. Know what?"

"What?" Red doesn't mind playing the-know-what game with his young granddaughter.

"My supervisor, Mr. Dwyer, was looking at the plans of The Holy Trinity yesterday."

"He was?" Red plays along.

"Yeah, he was all excited. He says it's drafting history or something."

"Were these a copy of the plans from the city archives?"

"I don't think so, grandpa. He said that the architect hand-drew every detail. He was really impressed, I think."

"Oh, okay, Missy. I have to go talk to your Uncle Saul. Go visit with your cousins for a while." Red finds Saul in an isolated corner talking quietly with friends.

"Saul, we need to talk. Missy saw the plans," Red whispers.

Saul turns his attention from the circle of friends who had come to memorialize Sauley.

"Can it wait, dad?"

"I guess it can." Red turns and walks toward Joseph Vicente and his wife, Christina. Richard Duetzman and Joseph Vicente, without a doubt could have been politicians. Instead, they are the imperial monarchs of Bizarre Shitland. The difference is negligible; much like D.C., Bizarre Shitland is a place where whatever bullshit spews out of the mouths of the sovereigns is immediately transitioned into undisputable truth.

"Ricardo, I am so sorry that we are seeing each other under such sad circumstances. Sauley was a well-respected member of this community," Vicente offers his sympathy.

"Yeah, Joe, Sauley was a good man, he didn't deserve this." Red swallows the contemptuous feelings he is harboring toward Vicente.

"It's the Mexicans, they are out of control. We have to work together now more than ever. Am I right, my friend?" Vicente redirected.

"Yeah, Joe, you're always right, my friend," Red spews exaggeration.

"Don't tell him that, Red, he's hard enough to live with." Cristina gives Red a hug.

"Christina, you look good. Thanks for coming."

"I liked Sauley, he was a good kid." Cristina lies she really didn't give a damn about Sauley. Christina Vicente has been well cared for. She is a striking woman, Cristina is a woman who is always seen everywhere she goes, because everywhere she goes, she always makes a scene. Cristina is not afraid to stomp her perfectly pedicured foot or shake her polished finger and her well-coiffed head of curly black hair at anyone who dare to irritate or disappoint her. Nevertheless, at the end of the day, Christina and Joe Vicente are perfectly matched and blissfully happy. Proving the old adage that there's never a pot so crooked you can't find a lid for it! Red and Joe step away for a private conversation.

"We lost fat legs, too."

"Yeah, Red, that's too bad, but I have other shooters. Don't worry. Do you mind if I smoke? Would you like one?" Vicente pulls two cigars out of his coat and offers one to Red.

"Thanks, Joe." Red lit his Hav-a-Tampa. "We need to teach those crazy Mexicans a lesson." Red's grief has turned to rage.

"I think you're right, Red.

"Yeah, Joe, I am. We'll talk about it later on." Red turns and walks across the room to where three of his sons quietly talked.

"Saul, come with me." Saul follows. Red takes a seat in his favorite chair. Saul sits with his three brothers.

"Boys, we have had some harsh things come down on us lately." Red reaches into his coat pocket and withdraws four quite hefty straight sticks. He hands a stick to each of his sons.

"Sticks, Pop?" Wendell, the youngest brother is puzzled. Lawrence and Fredrick the twins just look quizzically at their father and begin stick sword play.

"Yes, Wendell, sticks, how 'bout you Freddy, got any smartass remarks? How 'bout you Larry, any shit you got to say?"

"No, Pops, we're good, go on," Lawrence speaks for the group.

"Good, then quit horsing around and shut the hell up, dumbasses." Red continues, "The sticks in your hands, try to break them."

The boys look at each other wondering what the trick could be to snap a rather insignificant twig between their fingers, but otherwise did as their father requests. Each son easily snaps the stick in two.

"What's up, Pop, did you think we couldn't do it?" Saul askes.

"Shut up, dumbass." Red reaches down beside his chair and picks up five bundles of five straight sticks. Red hands each son a bundle of sticks and keeps one for himself. "Now, try to break the bundle." The boys smile and nod, certain of the outcome. Try as they may they are not able to easily snap the bundle.

"You see boys, one by one, we can be easily be broken but as a whole, it will be much more difficult to take us down. Remember this lesson." Red left his sons and returned to the guests.

~

After all the friends and family members had left the Duetzman's home, Red and Saul retire to the privacy of Red's den.

"Saul, Missy told me she saw Raymond Dwyer looking over the plans for the Holy Trinity Monastery."

"So?"

"So, Saul, they've been missing for years."

"So?" Saul leans back in his chair.

"Saul, she saw the original hand-drawn plans."

"And why do you think I'm interested in that?" Saul closes his eyes.

"I can't believe you don't know about those plans."

"Nope. What about them?" Saul puts his feet up on the ottoman and tries to get comfortable. Red explains to Saul how valuable those plans actually are. Saul sits up straight in his chair. Saul is quite interested now.

"So, those plans are part of our heritage, huh, dad?"

"I would say so."

"Well, why don't you just ask this Dwyer guy for them? You know him, he'd probably give them to you."

"He might but he doesn't have to, and anyway, I don't want to draw too much attention to it. I think that I have something better figured out."

"What are you thinking, dad?"

"I'm thinkin' that I get a couple of those security guys out there to watch Dwyer and then they can take the plans from his office," Red explains.

"That sounds like a good plan, Pop. I'll talk to them."

"Be clear, Saul. They're not that smart, you know."

"I know how to talk to those idiots, don't worry."

∽

"Ray, hi, glad you stopped by," Corwin greets Ray at his front door.

"I wanted to bring these plans by."

"Come on in, Ray. You could have kept them a few more days." Raymond hands the plans to Corwin.

"I've been looking at them for more than a week now, I wanted to bring them over. I don't feel right keeping them any longer. Anyway, these plans are pretty valuable and a nice keepsake."

"How about a glass of wine, Raymond? Sit down, stay awhile. What do you think about those notes Duetzman scribbled in the margin?"

"You know I ran those numbers and letters through my mind so many times, I can't even count. I got nothing, the first part of the scribbles are numbers and then the word auzz; I tried to find a translation but couldn't find one. I don't know, what do you think Corwin?"

"It must be something that only meant something to him, some kind of shorthand or hieroglyphics maybe. I'd love to know what the old guy was thinking." Corwin shakes his head and stares at the doodles.

"Yeah, it could be his shorthand, but I noticed that there is not even one other doodle or mark on those plans. I think that he was reminding himself of something."

"Yeah, probably his honey-do list." Corwin laughs.

"Yeah, don't forget to pick up some milk on your way home, Klaussie, my little Schnitzel," Ray jokes.

"Schnitzel? Maybe, Ray." Corwin chuckles.

"So, how is Sylvia doing Corwin? I'm worried about her."

"As well as can be expected. She's a strong lady. She'll get through it."

"Yeah, I guess she will. Do you ever think that at our age we have more friends and family on the other side than we have here?" Ray poses the spiritual question to his friend.

"Yeah, Ray, I have thought of that. I think that's the plan so then when it's our time, there isn't that much holding us here."

"I think your right Cory."

"Raymond, Silly is coming over for dinner. I'm just going to grill some chicken and open a couple beers, how about you join us?"

"Oh, I don't know, Cory, I don't want to intrude." The doorbell rings.

"Too late, now you have to stay; she's here." Corwin smiles at his friend and then they both greet their friend at the door.

"Hi Ray, where have you been keeping yourself? I hope you're staying." Sylvia hugs Raymond.

"Cory's got me chained to my desk. How are you, Silly?" Ray asks.

"I'll be fine, Ray," Sylvia answers.

"He was trying to run off," Corwin tattles.

"Oh, I don't believe that. Ray knows how good your grilled chicken is."

"Let's go out on the deck and throw back a few beers, huh, what do you say Ray?" Cory led the way.

"I say great. Come on, Silly." Ray dubbed Sylvia, Silly early into their friendship, and the name has stuck.

"I totally agree," Sylvia follows.

"Your plans are on the dining room table, Silly, don't forget them when you leave," Ray informs Sylvia as they make their way to the deck.

"Thanks. Now, let's get to that grilling, I'm famished," Sylvia declares.

The old friends talk and laugh well into the night. Once again, they are the carefree teenagers who stole away from the prom to drink beer under the bleachers. Sylvia breaks up the party with her announcement that at any moment she will be turning into a pumpkin and hopes she will make it home beforehand. The guys sweet-talk Silly into staying for one more beer, after which she did not turn into a pumpkin, but went home anyway.

Cory and Ray finish the rest of the beers. Raymond leaves his good friend with the promise that the late hour will have no bearing on his punctual arrival to his desk the next morning.

❧

Ray opens the door to his dark house. He didn't intend to be out so late. Prissy is probably mad. Ray figures he can expect a juicy hair ball in his shoe first thing in the morning. He decides that a little bit of tuna might allay her temper. Raymond turns on a dim light and heads into the kitchen.

"Come on, kitty. Here, Prissy, how about some tuna?" Prissy rubs against Raymond's leg. Raymond flips on the kitchen light. The light illuminates enough of the living room for Raymond to see that his home has been completely turned upside down.

"What went on here tonight, kitty girl?" Raymond bends down to pick up Prissy; a bullet flew through the air just above his head. Someone had shot at him but missed. Raymond hides himself behind the kitchen island. Maybe the intruders will leave. Raymond remains still for what seems an eternity, and then he hears the sound of his back door shutting. Now he can get to the phone and call the police. The house is quiet. Ray picks up his kitchen phone, then three shots end the call.

～

"What do you mean he's dead?" Red bellows. He has been awakened by one of his security guards.

"Dwyer came home while we were still in his house, we had just finished looking," One of Duetzman's brutes offers an explanation.

"You were supposed to go to his office, not his house, you imbeciles." Red is beside himself with rage.

"We did watch him at the office, Mr. Duetzman. But when he left his office, he took the plans home. Then when Dwyer left his house, we went in, but they weren't there."

"Just shut the hell up. Where did Dwyer go?

"Don't know where Dwyer went, we didn't see. We just thought we should let you know that we finished looking, and what we were looking for isn't there."

"Bet he parked in his garage, huh?"

"Yeah, boss, the garage."

"The plans must have been in his car, idiot. Where the hell is Saul?"

"We thought…"

"Shut your face. You just thought? You should have just thought before you decided to kill Dwyer. You just thought. Where did you morons get the idea that you could think?"

"Saul said to think about what we're doing."

"Jesus H. Christ! Forget what Saul said, I'll take care of Saul. Are you sure it isn't there?"

"Yeah, Mr. Duetzman, we tore the place up."

"Just get back to your post."

Red returns to his bed. He will speak to Saul about this screw up tomorrow.

~

"I thought you knew how to talk to those idiots. Don't worry, I know how to talk to those idiots, that's what you said. And then you tell them to think. Where the hell is your head? Who's the idiot now, Saul?" Reds anger toward Saul has not subsided.

"But Dad, I didn't tell them to go to Dwyer's house. I said he was looking at the plans in his office and to watch him. I don't know how they got go to Dwyer's house and kill him out of that."

"I don't know either, Saul, I got to think. Maybe the police will decide that Dwyer was killed in a burglary gone bad. You're just lucky the night wasn't a total loss; at least we know where the plans aren't. Now, we will have to take a look at Riggs."

"Do you want me to take care of those two dumbasses?"

"No, Saul! You're the dumbass. I don't want you to take care of anything. Just go on, do something that you can't screw up. We'll just sit tight. It'll be okay." Reds anger was somewhat abating.

~

"Victorian Garnet, that's the color, that matches." Paul and Miriam stand in front of her house. They are making the final decision on the color she will choose for the exterior. Paul holds the chip next to the piece of wood that he has pulled off the side of Miriam's house. They look from the house to the paint chip, to the house, and back to the paint chip and then they looked once or twice again.

The color chip matched exactly the paint that had been preserved under a hundred years of fresh coats of paint. The house has been painted and repainted numerous times but never Garnet, the original color of the old brothel. Miriam steps back and imagines her roadhouse in its glory days. At last, she decides.

"Ja, I like this color, and my house likes it. This is what we choose."

"Good. Mike and I will go get the paint and start painting this afternoon."

"Alright, Paul. I am going to pick up Vicky. Then we are going to Publix to get a few groceries. What do you and Mike want for lunch?"

"I don't know, surprise us. Get ice though, we'll probably be getting pretty thirsty."

"Ice, I won't forget. See you soon, Paul."

"See you soon."

"Mike, where did you go? Are you ready to get paint?" Paul walks to the porch where he had left Mike

"Paul, I need to talk to you." Mike steps from inside the house onto the porch and sits down on the step.

"Oh, no, Mike are you breaking up with me?" Paul laughs as he takes a seat on the step next to Mike.

"I've been getting some threatening calls lately."

"Wow, Mike, you can't keep that kind of stuff to yourself. "What's going on, man?"

"Someone has been calling, warning me not to pursue the case at the abbey."

"Are the threats specific?"

"No, I guess there more like warnings, no specific threats."

"Mike, have you told anyone else?"

"Just the computer guy. I thought maybe he could track the call, but he couldn't."

"You got a partner or someone you trust?"

"Yeah, I do, my rookie Rob. He's a detective now."

"Tell Rob, and then you know you got someone who's got your back. And remember Mike, I got your back too."

"Thanks, Paul, I feel so safe now." Mike puts his head on Paul's shoulder and offers a goofy, dreamy eyed grin.

"Geez, Mike, get a hold of yourself." Paul laughs, as he pushes Mike off the step.

Mike brushes himself off and heads to the car. "Let's go get that paint. You don't want Miriam to come home and find you goofing off, do you?"

"No, I'm kind of scared of her," Paul admits.

"I feel 'ya bro, I feel 'ya," Mike commiserates.

~

"Thomas, I didn't expect to see you," Christina Vicente greets her new friend.

"I was just driving by, and I saw you coming out of the spa. I thought you might like to get a drink."

"Well, yes, I'd like that, but I do have to get back early. Monday night is Joe's and my date night."

"I just got a wonderful new bottle; it's an import and it's divine. Would you like to try it with me?" Thomas got out of his classic Bentley and opens the passenger door for Christina. Christina takes Thomas' hand as he helps her in.

"Yes, that would be superb, Tom, and anyway, I would love to see your place." Christina has been curious about this eccentric Englishman that she met at the day spa.

"Perfect, little girl, let's go to my place then." Tom smiles and speeds away with his prize.

~

"How long has your wife been missing, Mr. Vicente?" Rob took Joe Vicente's report.

"She went to the spa this afternoon, and then she was going to the Plaza. Then she was going to come home."

"Has your wife disappeared before?"

"No, of course not, oh she's been late sometimes, but she would never miss date night."

"Date night?"

"Yeah, date night. I take her shopping, buy her a nice trinket and then we have a romantic dinner. We do it every Monday night, every week without fail. But she didn't come home. She would never blow off date night. I'm worried."

"Okay, I'll put a bulletin out, Mr. Vicente." Rob logs the report into his computer, then he crosses the hall to Mike's office.

"Mike, did you see who just came in?"

"Yeah, I did, Rob, what's up?"

"He claims his wife is missing."

"Wow, I bet he's beside himself, especially with all that's been happening lately with this war."

"He is. Well, I got a description of her car out there and her license plate number. We'll hear right away if any of the guys spot it."

"Yeah, we will. Mike leans back in his chair and clasped his hands behind his head."

"You look pleased with yourself."

"I am. All the files are ready to go over to the DA's office, and I feel like a hundred-pound weight has been lifted off my shoulders."

"That's good, Mike. You worked hard on that case." Rob starts to the door.

"Hey, Rob, there's one thing that I want to tell you."

"Okay. What is it?" Rob turns back and sits on the corner of Mike's desk.

"I've been getting some calls lately. They're from someone warning me to stay away from the abbey."

"Calls here at the station?"

"The calls are to my cell phone."

"Wow, Mike, how did someone get your cell number?"

"The only thing that I can figure is that whoever killed the gardener at the abbey found my card. I gave the card to the gardener and put my cell number on the back so he could get in touch with me."

"I'm glad you told me about this, Mike. I'll be keeping an eye on you now, old timer." Rob laughs.

"Get out of here, kid."

❧

"Mike, come on, they found Christina Vicente's car," Rob calls to Mike as he hurries by.

"Where is it?" Mike is out from behind his desk and only a step behind Rob.

"Parked in the parking lot at the spa on Neptune. Get this, she's in the car naked and dead."

"Let's roll." Mike and Rob rush to the scene.

"What you got, Eslen?" Mike didn't think he would be seeing the medical examiner again quite so soon.

"Female dead from exsanguinations."

"What's that?" Rob asked.

"All of her blood has been drained from her body, and get this, there isn't a drop of blood anywhere on her, somebody was really tidy. And there's this." Eslen directs the detectives to a ghoulish point.

'when she was bad, she was horrid'. The words had been carved into Christina's abdomen.

"Mike, it's the nursery rhyme!" Rob is staggered.

WASTED

"Plant Park? Yeah, I know where that is. Martin, did you talk to my guy yet?"

"Yeah, but he needs you to meet us at the park. So you can tell him that I'm your friend. He won't make a deal with me if he doesn't see you."

"Okay, dude, when is the meeting?"

"Tonight, at ten o'clock, down by the river walk, under the bridge."

"Yeah, I know where that is. Good deal, Martin, I'll be there."

Hidden deep in shadows under the Platt Street Bridge, the boy waits for his friend. Martin has been running in street gangs since he was in middle school, but lately he's been hanging with the big boys.

"It's almost ten. I can't wait much longer, kid."

"He'll be here, and then we can finish up our business."

"Hey, Martin, where are you, bro?"

Martin's buddy calls into the shadows.

"Dude, over here." Martin calls out to his friend, but he still cannot be seen. Martin steps out from the dark and bear-hugs his friend.

"Hey, dude, long time no see."

"Good to see you, bro. Where is he?"

"Right here." A tall figure holding a revolver steps out from behind a bridge piling.

"Martin? What's going on?"

The man fires one shot into the boy's skull, and the young boy falls.

"Okay, Sheriff, I get paid five more big ones now, like you promised."

"Sure, kid, like I promised." One more shot and another young life is wasted on the river walk. The deputy sheriff tosses his gun into the deep water of the Hillsborough River.

～

St Johns Abbey is hushed. The monks have retired to their private quarters for the night. Gracie hovers beside the bed of a sleeping monk.

"Thruda has been looking for you," she whispers.

The monk sits up in his bed and stares into the darkness of his room. Gracie draws closer to the monk. He shivers and pulls his covers close.

"I know that you are here, spirit. This is not the first time that I have felt your presence." The monk's eyes dart as he searches his room for a glimpse of the specter. Gracie moves to the end of the bed and sits at the monk's feet.

"Your presence is not something that I fear, but I do wonder what has drawn you to me. Possibly it is my belief in the definite existence of one's soul and a life after this one. However, perhaps it is something much less pious." The monk smiles. Gracie moves across the room to the monks writing table. She had watched him as he sat at the table and studied a tattered old photo of himself and Thruda Thorlakson. Gracie disturbs the photo; it flew to the floor. The monk switches on his bed light. He sees the photo of his one love has fallen to the floor. The monk returns the photo to its place on his table and sits down in the chair.

"I see that you are interested in the photograph. I will tell you about it, but first, I would ask that, if it is in your means, curious spirit, show yourself to me."

The bed light dims and then the room went black for a moment. Gracie has used the energy from the small lamp to illuminate herself. For a brief moment, the monk sees the tiny lady who is his midnight phantom. Then the room is once again illuminated by the bed lamp. Gracie can no longer be seen.

"The picture is of my love, Thruda. I have not seen her face for more than thirty years; we would have married, but for her own safety, I left her. Spirit, I will not say anymore as it is a painful remembrance. Now, I hope that what I have told you will quell your interest and I can return to my sleep. Thank you, spirit, for whatever concern you have and goodnight." The monk returns to his bed.

◦

Mike has been in his office since daybreak. He has come in early to go over his case against Vicente one more time. He knows the case is solid and that he has thoughtfully and thoroughly put it together.

However, he has to look at his notes once more, not even so much for the case but for his friend, Victor.

"Michael, Carlos' mother is here to see you, she seems upset." Vicky is concerned.

"Geez, what is she doing out? She has to quit that," Mike scowls and shakes his head. "Send her right back."

"Mike!" Joniqua staggers to a seat.

"Joniqua, what's wrong?"

"Carlos is missing."

"Missing how, when?" Mike is shocked by this news.

"He was gone this morning when I woke up."

"Has he ever snuck out before?"

"No, I don't think so."

"When did you see him last?"

"Right before I went to bed last night, he was watching TV."

"Okay, I'll put a bulletin out. Don't worry, Joniqua, I'll make it a priority."

"Thank you, Mike."

"Go home and sit tight. I'll have one of the officers drive you home, wait here." Mike leaves his office to arrange a ride.

"I need an officer to drive Joniqua home." Mike stands at Vicky's station and makes his request.

"What's up with Joniqua?" Vicky asks.

"Carlos is missing."

"Oh no!"

"Yeah, I need to get an officer to drive her home."

"Mike, before you do that there's one thing."

"What's that?"

"There's a report that just came in. Two young John Does were found dead in Plant Park." Vicky is gripped by dread.

"Oh my God, give me strength," Mike whispers.

Mike hurries to the medical examiner, he finds Carlos there. He supposes that the boy found with him is his friend Martin. Mike had bonded with the boy that he has been protecting; now the boy lies dead in the medical examiner's lab. Mike returns to his office, he now has the most dreaded duty. He must tell Joniqua that her child is dead.

"Joniqua, I'm sorry. The report just came in. It's Carlos, he's been shot."

"Where is he? Where is my boy?"

"He's being taken care of, he's with the medical examiner now."

"I want to see him. I want to see my son," Joniqua cries.

"Vicky will take you home, you will be able to see him soon. I'm sorry, Joniqua."

"I knew he was gone when I woke up this morning. I just knew. He is all I have." Joniqua cradles her head on Mike's desk and sobs.

"I'll help you, Joniqua." Vicky gently laid her hand on the woman's shoulder.

"Thank you, Vicky." Joniqua and Vicky left the station.

"Tough break, Mike. I'm really sorry." Rob comforts Mike.

"Thanks, Rob. I should have looked into what the kid was telling me."

"What was that, Mike?"

"He had a friend who wanted protection. I was going to contact him, but I've been so busy that I put it off. That's probably the other kid he was found with."

"What are you going to do?"

"I'm going over to Kumquat and talk to the street kids."

Mike spends the rest of the morning putting the final grim details in Carlos' file, then he heads over to Kumquat. There aren't many school age kids on the street in Tonya Town, the moniker given to the ghetto neighborhood of Kumquat. Mike picked the hour before school let out to come to call in the Tobacco Road type town. The good kids are all in school and the ones that are out on the streets at this hour are looking for trouble, and today they might just find it. With a picture of the two dead boys in his shirt pocket, Mike heads toward a group of high school age teens smoking reefer in an alley, behind a popular bodega. As Mike approaches, the teens glare.

"Did I miss something? Is it a school holiday today?" Mike hopes the teens will assume that he's a truant officer.

"No, it's not a school holiday. Who the hell are you, dude? We know you aren't the truant officer."

The talkative teen is obviously the man with the questions and probably the answers. Mike is right where he wants to be. He takes the picture of the boy that was found dead with Carlos from his pocket.

"No, I'm not, the truant officer dude." Mike flashes his badge.

"So, you gonna arrest us for smokin' weed?" The teen is insolent.

"I didn't see any weed, if I get some answers, capiche?" Mike is doing his best sopranos impression.

"Who is this kid? Or, I should say who was, this kid?" Mike hands the picture to Mr. Talkative.

"He's dead?" Talkative goes pale.

"Yeah, he was found dead this morning, executed." Mike put his index finger to his head and pulls an imaginary trigger. One of the other teens take the picture from Talkative. The teen sinks to the graveled path of the alley.

"His name is Martin, he's my cousin." The teen holds his head in his hands.

"What's your name, kid? Mike asks.

"Anthony."

"Who has your cousin been hanging with lately, Tony?"

"I don't know, he quit us months ago."

"That answer is going to get the whole bunch of youse arrested. I can arrange a ride to the station for all of you." Mike put his hand on his radio.

"Wait! No, really, he just comes around sometimes. When he does, he's always flashing lots of green. We all figured that he was dealing for El di Marco or Vicente, all the same no matter."

"When was the last time that you saw him?"

"A few days ago when he came around and he was flush."

"Lots of cash, huh?" Mike is starting to form a theory.

"Yeah, lots."

"Did you ever see him talking to anyone, a stranger maybe? Or did he ever get picked up by the police?"

"There was a sheriff that stopped him a lot. Seemed like this dude really had it out for him. But Martin always walked away; he was pretty slick."

"Who was the sheriff? Did Martin ever say a name?"

"No, never."

"Where did Martin live?"

Tony gave Mike his cousin's address. Now, again Mike would have to give another painful report.

⁓

Mike sits at his desk and closes his eyes. In an hour, this day will finally be over. He recalls every heart wrenching moment. He goes over his notes. Tony has unknowingly confirmed Carlos' story about his friend and the sheriff. Now, all Mike needs is a name.

"How did it go in Kumquat?" Rob stands at Mike's door.

"I think Martin convinced Carlos to meet in the park, he was connected to the deputy somehow. I think the deputy must have followed Martin there, I don't really know how it went down." Mike leans back in his chair and studies the ceiling. "I guess Carlos was right. There is a dirty deputy."

"Yeah, I think so too, Mike. I'm going over to the Kumquat sheriff's department starting tomorrow." Rob perched himself on the corner of Mike's desk.

"Good, Rob, we need you on the inside."

"I asked the chief if I can leave the mother goose murder with you."

"Is that what you're calling Christina's murder?"

"Yeah, I guess." Rob shrugs, he isn't concerned with the Vicente murder now; thoughts of undercover in Kumquat are heavy on his mind.

"Sure, Rob, I'll take it. Have you got anything on it yet?"

"Naw, not a thing. I even went to the spa to look at their surveillance footage." Rob takes two sticks of gum from his shirt pocket an offers a stick to Mike.

"No, thanks, kid. Nothing on the film, huh?"

"Ha, it's what wasn't on the film." Rob stuffed the two sticks of double mint into his mouth.

"What wasn't on the film, Rob?"

"I thought you'd never ask, old man. The CCTV footage of the street outside the spa shows Christina Vicente talking with somebody but the person was blanked out. She obviously left the spa with that someone who took her somewhere, did the deed, then brought her back, put her dead body in her car and somehow blanked that all out."

"This one is pretty smart." Mike sighs. "Don't worry, I'll handle it."

"Good, Joe Vicente's coming in next week." Rob picks at his thumbnail and cracks his gum.

"I guess Eslen will be done with her, and the Vicente's will have all paid their last respects by then." Mike squeezes the bridge of his nose with his thumb and forefinger. "Really a lot of shit going on," he mumbles.

"I guess so. You didn't happen to catch the name of the sheriff from those kids, did you, old man?"

"No, I didn't, Rob. I talked to the sister of the other kid, she is understandably upset, and she blames the sheriff department too. But she didn't have a name either."

"So, the sister knew about the sheriff." Rob is taking in all the information he can.

"Maybe. She must have at least had suspicions all along. But she liked the extra cash that the kid was bringing home. I don't know. Why else would she not make some kind of complaint to the sheriff's department? All I know is her brother is dead, and now she's alone."

"It's a tough place, Mike, down there in Tonya Town."

"She could have at the least made an anonymous tip that might have saved two boys lives." Mike is going through the what ifs, and the should'a, woulda, could'of's.

"The streets of Tonya Town scream strife. It's a shame, not much we can do about it though, a lot of it is self-inflicted. You believe that the kids you talked to don't know the deputy sheriff?" Rob asks.

"Yeah, I do. None of them has ever even seen him, but the cousin said one thing that was very telling."

"What did he say, Mike?" Rob wants all the information he can get before he starts at Kumquat.

"He said Martin was dealing for El di Marco or Vicente. Then the kid said it didn't matter it's all the same, like it was one organization which we know it's not. Rob, there is still something that we don't know."

"I think you're right, Mike. When I'm undercover, we'll find out what piece of this puzzle we're missing."

"That's the plan kid."

Rob has the exuberance of youth on his side. Mike on the other hand is just tired of the bullshit. Mike sits back in his chair. In an hour, he will go home and have a beer. Maybe, he will ask Paul to come by, and they will polish off a six-pack or two. Then they will watch a mindless survivor reality show and laugh. It will be a distraction from the reality of survival in Tonya Town.

～

"I went to Saint John's last night, hon."

"Why did you go there?" Miriam isn't surprised by Gracie's announcement.

346

"I just wanted to poke around a bit. I figured that I might find out if the monk truly is Thruda's lost love."

"What did you decide, Gracie?" Miriam acts nonchalant, but she knows that soon enough, she will be wrapped around Gracie's axle and dragged into whatever scheme she has dreamed up.

"I decided you should get those two back together."

"Ja? He's a monk, Gracie. Do you think I'm a matchmaker or something like that?"

"Yes, exactly like that, hon." Gracie has no idea why Miriam seems so contrary to being a matchmaker. Gracie continues, "Hon, you are the only one with the where-with-all, to do it. Anyway, he hasn't always been a monk, and plus, I think he really is her split apart. It's a shame that they are torn apart." Gracie uses Miriam's own words to convince her.

"You are probably right, Gracie. I will make my plan today, and then tonight, I will see about it. Now, will you leave me alone so I can do my work? You know it costs money to care for your house." Miriam smiles.

"I'm gone, hon, I got irons in the fire." Gracie vanishes. After all, Miriam now seems agreeable to her proposal and that is what is important.

⌇

Sister Mary Katherine with Sandalphon, perched on her shoulder, stands in the monk's room. Vespers will soon be over, and the monk will return to his room for the night. The monk enters his room.

"Scholastica?" Upon seeing the vision of an ancient nun, he calls out the name of Saint Benedict's' sister, Scholastica. The saint, who by traditional accounts, was accompanied in her travels by a raven.

"No, I am not. I have a message from Thruda."

"Is Thruda in the spirit?"

"No, she is alive. She mourns for you."

"Who are you?" The monk approaches.

"I am a friend. Do not come near me, it may be to your detriment," Miriam warns. The monk takes no further steps.

"Tell me, spirit, what message do you have of my one love?"

"Thruda will come here to the St. John chapel to pray. Then it is only for you to decide what path you follow. But she will come, you must watch for her. Now, I bid you goodnight my brother, and I ask only one thing of you; that you never speak of me."

"I will never."

"Peace be with you." Sister Mary Katherine steps back into the realm that brought her there and disappears.

"And with you," the monk answers.

~

Sister Mary Katherine and Sandalphon appear at the bed of Thruda Thorlakson.

"Trudy, wake up."

"I'm not sleeping." Trudy sits up and looks at her visitor.

"Don't be frightened."

"I am not frightened; I have seen a ghost before."

"I am not a ghost. I am a visitor. I have news of your love, Randal. You will find him at the abbey chapel when you go there to pray."

"I knew that monk was Randal. But how do you know this?" "You will find him there. I have no reason to say this if it is not true."

"Who are you?"

"I am a friend, but you must never speak of me."

"I won't."

"Peace be with you." Sister Mary Katherine vanishes.

"And with you, my friend."

~

Miriam flops on to her bed. She feels that the weight of the habit's heavy black material was the only thing holding her to this earth. She is exhausted.

"What's wrong, hon? You did a good thing tonight." Gracie sits on the bed next to Miriam.

"I don't know where I belong. I am tired, Gracie," Miriam cries.

"Hush now, go get your jammies on and try to get some sleep now."

"Will you stay with me, Gracie?"

"Yes, I'll stay, hon."

"Will you sing, Gracie?

"Yes, child, I will."

The abbey is quiet. The morning mass is over, and the brothers have all filed out of the chapel. Trudy has studied the face of each monk as they pass; none wore the face of her love, Randal. Trudy closes her eyes, maybe she didn't pray hard enough. Maybe she prayed too hard, she didn't know, she couldn't know. All she knows is what the strange visitor told her. Now she is certain that Randal is here at the abbey.

Trudy will return to the abbey for the next mass. Trudy passes the confessional, a priest steps from behind.

"Would you like to give your confession?"

"Yes, father, I would"

"Someone will speak with you, daughter." The priest smiles as he holds the door to the confessional.

"Forgive me father for I have sinned." Trudy sits in the cramped confessional.

"Stop, Trudy, it's me, Randal."

"Randal!" Trudy puts her face to the screen. She strains to see the man on the other side.

"Trudy, listen to what I am going to tell you and know that a day has not gone by that I have not loved you."

"I love you, Randal. Why did you leave me?" Trudy whispers.

"Trudy, I did not leave you, I was taken away. I would have never left you and even though I was taken away, I never really left you."

"Did the people from the organization take you?"

"Yes, do you remember when we first started seeing each other and I was taking the medicine that the doctors from the organization prescribed? Do you remember when you encouraged me to start cutting down on the pills?"

"Yes, I remember."

"Well, I did some research on the medicine. I learned that the medicine they gave me was strong psychotropic drugs. They were using the medicine to control me, so I totally quit taking the drugs, and I got better. The fog started lifting from my mind, I felt like my old self, but I made one mistake."

"What mistake did you make, Randal?"

"I quit going to the hospital to pick up the prescriptions. That's how it got back to the organization that I was off the drugs. That's when they came to my apartment and took me back to the hospital. I was locked in the psych ward for years; they locked me up because they didn't want me telling anyone that they had forced me to work in their laboratory creating biological weapons. We were creating chemicals and viruses that they were testing on our population. I pretended to take the medicine, and after a while, they thought it was safe to let me return back to society. They set me up in an apartment, then after a year of still pretending to swallow their mind-altering poison I walked out of the apartment and hitched a ride. That's how I got here to the abbey. This is where I've been for the last twenty-four years."

"What about your roommate Thomas, couldn't he help you?"

"On the contrary, Trudy, Thomas was as interested in me taking those drugs as the organization was. Thomas was also drafted by the organization. It was while we were comparing notes of what we were doing in the lab that we discovered that we were splicing D.N.A. to create new organisms. We were making deadly, new and unknown diseases. I was very upset about what we had uncovered but Thomas did not seem to be bothered at all. Even though we didn't see eye to eye on our lab work, we got along alright. He was quiet and mostly kept to himself; and I was busy with other things. Then one Christmas holiday, that all changed. I was always gone for the entire holiday break. Thomas was usually gone for only a few days. But that year he said that he was staying in the dorm, and that he was not going to England to visit his parents for the holiday. His parents, he said were coming to their home in the states for Christmas. The day that I returned to the dorm I saw his plane tickets to England, lying on a table. By the date on the ticket, I knew he had lied to me about staying in the dorm. I did not question him, or even acknowledge the tickets. The tickets promptly disappeared from the table. Thomas then began acting very strangely; he was odd anyway, so I didn't give it much credence."

"A few days later, the police came to the dorm and told him that his parents had been murdered. After that day, he continually asked me about my holiday. I told him that the holiday was no different than any other holiday that I had spent at home, and I enjoyed the time away. But I know that Thomas suspected that I had seen the tickets, although I never admitted it. I'm certain that Thomas is the one who turned me in to the organization. I think he figured that if I had indeed seen his tickets, then I probably suspected that he had murdered his parents. The organization would be his best chance to get rid of me. I told him that I was going to refuse to work in the organization's lab; Thomas knew that the organization would not allow me to walk away free and clear. That's when they took me the first time. The second time they took me, from my apartment, it was right after I received Thomas's letter inquiring about you. Thomas knew my address and somehow knew of you. It was clear that the organization had been monitoring me; I knew that I had to disappear for good. To save you I could never return to you. I had to disappear from your life completely. Trudy, I hope you understand it was not to save myself, but to save you. I have missed you; I have longed for you. Thruda, I love you; I will always love you." Randal touches Trudy's hand at the screen.

"I will always love you." Trudy whispers

WRONGFUL DEATH

The Mother Goose murder, the name of the case as Rob labeled it. Mike spends the morning reviewing the file; he wants to make sure he is up to speed before Joseph Vicente comes in for an interview. Christina's body has been released and the family has said their final goodbyes. Now, Christina Vicente sleeps with her ancestors. Mike's mind wanders as he studies the details of the murder. The specifics don't fit the profile of a mob execution, unless of course the mob has recruited a psychopath to do their bidding. Mike junks that thought. It was a doubtful notion, in view of the fact that everyone knows that the psychopaths have very strict union regulations; they are only authorized to work alone. However, if it is a sociopath, their union allows them to do whatever the hell they please. Mike doesn't make the rules, he just enforces the law. Mike closes the file; he has reviewed enough. Now, Joe Vicente is on his way back to his office.

"Mr. Vicente please have a seat." Mike stands to greet Vicente.

"Thank you, Mike." Vicente is familiar with Mike De Augustino, but even more so with Mike's father, the detective who had dogged him for years before his untimely demise.

"I'm sorry for your loss, Mr. Vicente. I know how difficult it is to lose a loved one. I'll be brief. Were there any threats against your wife's life before her death?"

"No, none."

"How often did she go out to the day spa?"

"Maybe once or twice a week."

"Did she ever mention anyone that she had problems with at the spa? Did she befriend anyone there or mention someone who she considered weird?"

"No, she just went for massage or nails or other lady stuff, we never discussed it much."

"So, did she have any disagreements with anyone lately?"

"Well, my Christina was not an easy woman. She could speak her mind, but it was usually about something like someone didn't have the right color or size of something she wanted. She could make a fuss over nothing, but she was all blow. When people got to know her, they really liked her. She was a very kind person."

"There's one last thing, and I'm sorry that I have to bring it up, Mr. Vicente. Do the words when she was bad, she was horrid, mean anything to you?"

"Yeah, those words mean there's some sick bastard out there who's going to pay and pay dearly for hurting my Christina." Vicente stands, now towering over Mike's desk. He slams his fist into the wall. Joe Vicente walks out, the interview ended.

~

Corwin looks out across the Tampa Bay, the lights of downtown Tampa and Davis Islands shimmer in the calm dark water. Corwin reaches across the table and pats Sylvia's hand but says nothing. Sylvia cups her other hand over her friend's hand in answer. The waiter greets them, and places the menus at their table

"Good evening, Mr. Riggs, Miss Sylvia. Can I bring you a drink?"

"We would like three bottles of beer, please."

"Yes, sir, that will be right out."

"This place sure has changed a lot since we were in high school," Corwin says.

"How many times do you think we drove through this place on Friday nights?"

"I hate to think, and here we are once again." As he speaks, Corwin watches the moon light dance on the still waters of the bay.

"We had some good times, you, me, and Ray." Sylvia touches Corwin's clenched hand to comfort him and also herself.

"Remember the night when Ray came to your parent's house in his father's old beat-up work truck?" Corwin asks.

"Yes, we were all just going to watch TV, but then we convinced him to take us for a ride in the back of the old truck." Sylvia is sixteen all over again.

"Then we insisted that he take us through the drive-in here, knowing that the rich kids would all be hanging out showing off their fancy cars. I don't know which one of us came up with that bit of foolishness. I think it was you Silly."

"But the funny part was when we laid down in the back of the truck bed, so it looked like Ray was just crusin' through the Colonnade in his dads' old beat-up truck. That was so funny." Silvia laughs.

"He was so embarrassed. We did have a good laugh over that one."

"Like the time we TP'd your father's car, it looked like a huge pastel marshmallow when Ray and I got done with it." Sylvia wipes a tear of laughter from the corner of her eye.

"You two must have used dozens of rolls of toilet paper to cover that car."

"Well it took a lot to cover that big caddie your dad drove."

"Yeah Remember everyone called it the bat-mobile? We had some good times in the bat-mobile, didn't we?"

"We did, Cory. Good times." Sylvia smiles.

Sylvia and Corwin are lost in the memories of the good times when their waiter brought their drinks. Corwin and Sylvia tap their beers on the neck of the bottle that sat at the empty place setting. Corwin raises his bottle to friends under the bleachers on prom night. Sylvia and Corwin spend the rest of the evening honoring and properly remembering Raymond Dwyer. As it should be, they pay tribute to their friend, at their spirited high school hang out; The Colonnade, an establishment that matured as gracefully as the friends.

"Sylvia, I was cleaning up Ray's office today and I came across some old photos you might be interested in seeing.

"Yes, I would, I'd love to see them."

"What do you say we go to my house, have a night cap, and go through the pictures?"

"Sounds like a good plan, Cory. I'll follow you to your place."

Corwin unlocks his front door and gives a justification for the clutter. "I apologize for the mess. I haven't gone through all of Ray's papers yet, so it's a little untidy." Corwin opens the door and switches the lights on.

"My lord, Cory! I would say it's quite untidy."

"Oh my, I think I've been robbed, Sylvia." Corwin's home has been thoroughly ransacked.

"Don't touch anything, Cory. Call the police."

⌒

"What time did you get home and find this, Mr. Riggs?" The officer stands in Corwin's living room and studies the mess.

"Around eleven or eleven-thirty."

"So, you say that you and Ms. Cooper had spent the evening at the Colonnade?"

"Yes, that's correct, officer."

"And Ms. Cooper accompanied you home and was present when you discovered the break in?"

"Yes, she was."

"Mr. Riggs, was anything taken that you can tell?"

"It doesn't appear that anything was taken but I guess I'll know better when I go over everything."

"One more question, Mr. Riggs, have you made any big purchases lately or bought any high-end items online that someone might be interested in?"

"No, nothing, nothing at all."

"Mr. Riggs, this is your case number." The officer hands Corwin a card. "You will be assigned a detective. You can come in anytime tomorrow and talk with the detective. Just give the number to the front desk they'll get you to the right person."

"Thank you, officer." Corwin closes his front door and faces the chaos.

"Corwin, come and stay in my guest room tonight. Tomorrow, I will help you with this mess. We'll get it all back together in no time."

"Okay, Sylvia, thanks. I don't think I would sleep very well here tonight anyway."

⌒

"Hello, I'm here about this case." Corwin Riggs gave the officer the card with his case number on it. The officer typed the number into the computer.

"Sure, Mr. Riggs, I'll have an officer come up."

Corwin and Sylvia are escorted back to the detective's office. Corwin and Sylvia settle into the rickety folding chairs that are provided in the young detective's small cubicle. Sylvia pats Corwin's hand and encourages Corwin with a smile.

"I apologize for the makeshift quarters, but I'm just getting set up in my new cube. My computer isn't even ready to go yet, but I am detective Duncan." Christopher Duncan smiles.

"Just pretend that I'm not here. I'm just the I.T. guy." Ted stuck his head out from behind the detective's computer and tries to put Corwin and Sylvia at ease in case his presence might cause them some reservations. However, Corwin seems unruffled by Ted's activity. Sylvia simply smiles, Ted returns to his work.

"I've looked at the report that the officer filed. I just have a few questions for you today. Mr. Riggs, have you noticed any strange persons canvassing your neighborhood lately?"

"No, not that I can think of."

"Has anyone come to your door and solicited work like tree trimming gutter cleaning or anything like that?"

"No, no one."

"Have you answered or bought anything from a personal ad?"

"No, I haven't."

"I'm going to go over everything and run prints before I have anything to tell you Mr. Riggs. Thank you for coming in and if you think of anything or find that anything is missing let me know right away."

"Thanks, Detective, I appreciate your time." Corwin shakes the young detective's hand, and he and Sylvia leave the office. Sylvia takes Corwin's arm as they walk.

"Sylvia, I should go over to my office. I need to finish up with Ray's things."

"Cory, darling, have you forgotten? You rode with me. Don't you need help with that?"

"No, Silly, I need to do this alone and since it's Sunday I'll have some quiet time over there. I'll get a cab. See you back at my place in about an hour, huh?"

"Okay, if you're sure. I have a few errands I can run. I'll see you back at your house in about an hour then." Sylvia gave Corwin a quick hug and hurries along.

Corwin turns the key in the door to his building, the lock jams, Corwin jiggles the key, the lock clicks open.

"Better have maintenance take a look at that in the morning," Corwin mumbles as he walks to his office. His office door is ajar. He pushes the door open. His office is in shambles.

"Oh my God, what has happened? What is going on? How can this be?" Corwin steadies himself against the wall as he sinks to the floor of his office. He cradles his head in his hands carefully examining his fragile basket of thoughts. Thoughts painted up like Easter eggs, each egg its own unique design, a swirl of colors seeming without rationale. Each unreasonable thought dipped into a color, each color spun into a pattern, a guide, an outline, a blueprint, a plan. Time has no lucid order. Corwin's cell phone rings.

"Hello," Corwin whispers.

"Corwin, where are you? I've been waiting for you. Are you all right?"

"Sylvia, I'm at my office, everything is ruined."

"What! What's ruined? What are you saying Corwin?"

"My office has been trashed, someone was searching for something, and I think I've figured it out."

"Corwin, I'll be right there. Stay there, I'll come and get you. We'll go back to the police."

"No, Sylvia, stop. Don't come here yet. I want you to go home, get the monastery plans and put them in your safety deposit box. No, no, it's Sunday, the bank is closed. Take them out of the tube, fold them, and put them in a big handbag or briefcase. Put the empty tube in your fireplace and burn it. Then come here to my office. Call me when you leave your house. Bring the plans."

"Corwin, why? I don't understand."

"Sylvia, it's got to be the plans, it's the only thing that's different. Nothing else has changed, hell, nothing ever changes in my life, and Ray's life was equally as boring. It's those plans, it has to be the plans that someone is searching for. Do just as I said, bring the plans and we'll figure it out."

"Okay, Corwin, I'll call you."

Corwin leaned back on the wall and assessed the damage. Someone had pounded through every piece of dry wall, obviously searching the walls for a safe or a secret closet. The bookcases had been overturned; pictures had been ripped from their frames nothing had been left unsearched. The damage done in the hunt for this cursed set of plans was vast, but everything could be replaced, everything except his old friend and partner, Raymond. Corwin's cell rings again.

"I just left my house."

"Good, do you have the plans?"

"Yes, they're in my handbag like you said."

"Come into my office when you get here. Don't mention the plans."

"Okay, Corwin."

"See you soon." Corwin hangs up.

~

"I'm sorry, Miss, this is a crime scene; you will have to wait outside."

"It's all right officer, she's a friend of mine I asked her to come," Corwin calls out.

"Corwin, why is this happening? Who do you think is behind this?" Sylvia whispers while the officers are dusting for prints.

"Sylvia, there has always been whispers about the Duetzman's and the mob, but I don't know why either Duetzman or the mob would want the monastery plans so badly."

"But Cory, if it's the plans and someone knows that Ray had the plans, and you had the plans, why didn't they come to search my house? They must know that I had the plans too. I'm worried, Corwin."

"I thought of that. If say it's Duetzman and he for some reason is looking for the plans, why wouldn't he come to you first? He would have if he knew. Sylvia, it would have been very simple, but you didn't have the plans long enough. Ray and I on the other hand had the plans in the office for some time. Everyone in the office knew about them, they were quite the conversation for days. Hell, a professor from the drafting school even heard of them and asked if someone would bring them to his class. Show and tell, I guess. Anyway, I think that you were never in the equation."

The officer interrupts, "Mr. Riggs, you mentioned earlier that your house was broken into last night. We're done here, but you should come down to the station and give a report now."

"Yes, certainly, officer, we'll go right away. Thank you."

~

"Mike, can I talk to you? I think I need some help, man." Christopher Duncan stood at Mike's door.

"What is it, Duncan?"

"That guy that came in earlier this afternoon, about his home that was broken into Saturday night."

"Did they get the perp?" Mike interrupts.

"No, but he went over to his office today and it was completely ransacked too, nothing left standing, it was a mess."

"Wow! Who is this guy?"

"Riggs is his name, Corwin Riggs."

"The architect?"

"Yeah, and a friend came in with him a Ms. Cooper."

"Moral support?"

"No, they were out together when both break-ins happened."

"What do you think, Duncan?" Mike knows what the detective's next move should be but what Mike wants to know is if the detective knows what his next move should be.

"I think I should talk to them separately. What do you think Mike?"

"Yeah kid, I think that you should start with Ms. Cooper, hope you got a good address."

"Yeah, condo on Bayshore Boulevard."

"Fancy. Need company?"

"Yeah, really. Thanks Mike." Chris Duncan is relieved.

"Okay, let's roll."

"This is my first case, Mike."

"It's okay, kid. Don't worry, you'll do fine. Just remember the game face. That's the most important, game face." Mike keeps his eyes on the traffic. It is a five-minute trip from the station to the Bayshore high rise, where Sylvia Cooper lives.

"What do you mean, Mike?"

"Be professional, ask the questions, but stay aloof, play it cool, got it, kid?"

"Yeah, sure, game face. Play it cool, got it." Duncan is frantically scribbling Mike's wisdom into his note pad.

Mike parks and the detectives take the elevator to the twelfth floor of the posh high rise.

"This is some place, eh, Mike?"

"Yeah, and she's probably some stuck up old broad with a dog named Muffin. Don't let her intimidate you, kid." Mike laughs and Duncan scribbles. Christopher Duncan rings the bell and studies his notes.

"Hello, detective Duncan. Can I help you?"

"Ms. Cooper, I'd like to ask you a few questions if you don't mind. It will just take a moment. May we come in? Oh, this is my partner detective De Augustino." Christopher turns to Mike.

"Mike?" Sylvia peers around the young detective to get a better look at the partner.

"Miss Sylvia!" Mike squeezes Duncan aside, throws his arms around the stuck up old broad, and spins her around in the hall. "It's you, you are Ms. Cooper now. I didn't know it was you!"

Duncan keeps an eye on the goings on as he is desperately searching his notes.

"Mike, it's been so long, come in, please come in." Sylvia invites the men into her living room. "Sit, there's so much to talk about." A tear clouds Sylvia's eyes.

"So, Ms. Fields, you took your family name?" Mike only knew Sylvia by her married name, Fields.

"Yes, after the divorce, I guess I just wanted to start over and since Lydia was out of the house, I decided to drop my married name and use my mother's family name."

"I'm sorry about Lydia."

"Thank you, Mike. That means a lot to me. You and Victor and Lydia, and that other boy that worked on the cars. What was his name?"

"Rolando."

"Yes, you all were such good friends. Y'all were always into something." Sylvia smiles and turns to Christopher. "Detective Duncan, you said you have a few more questions. What is it that you need to ask me, young man?"

"Yes, Ms. Cooper. Ahem." Duncan clears his throat. "Is there anything that you remember that you would like to add to the statements that you and Mr. Riggs made?"

"No, nothing. Would you like some sweet tea? Mike? Detective?"

"That would be nice. Thank you, Miss Sylvia." Mike graciously accepts. Christopher also accepts although he would have graciously declined if Mike had not beaten him to the reply. Christopher Duncan leans toward Mike and whispers, "What happened to game face?" Mike ignores him and continues chatting with Miss Sylvia.

Christopher Duncan now is not really certain if game face still pertains, but he will at least still play it cool as Mike has suggested. He guesses that he has a lot to learn, and that twirling the stuck up old broad around in the hall was about as cool as it gets. He did wonder though where Muffin is hiding.

~

"So, Ms. Cooper is the mother of the woman who was killed in that big boat explosion? The mob hit?" Duncan asks as they rode back to the station.

"Yes, Victor Duetzman was her daughters' husband. He was a good friend of mine."

"Really?"

"Don't go all ape shit, kid, he wasn't mob."

"But he was a Duetzman."

"What can I say, kid? I knew him well and he wasn't involved."

"Okay, Mike. What's next?"

"Nothing, just wait."

"What about Riggs?"

"If he knows something more, he'll come out with it, maybe he's scared. If Miss Sylvia knows something, I think she would have said it. It's almost quitting time, just write it up as a follow up and log it in, then go home and have a beer."

"Thanks, Mike."

"It's okay, kid."

~

"Hi sweet pea, what's up, how was your day off?" Mike called Vicky from his office. He leans back in his chair and relaxes he has a few minutes before he clocks out.

"Hi, sweetie, we had a good day. Miriam and I spent some time in Kumquat. Her house is really coming along. She says she would like to have thanksgiving there if everyone agrees."

"That sounds like a plan."

"Are you coming over, sweetie?"

"I can stop in for a minute on my way home."

"Good. I'll see you soon then."

"Yeah, about twenty minutes. Hey, I got a call coming in. See you soon. Bye, sweet pea."

"De Augustino here."

"Mike, this is Sylvia Cooper, I would like to talk to you, in private. Can you come to my home? It's important."

"Yes of course I can come right over."

"Thank you, Mike, see you soon then."

"Yes, Miss Sylvia, see you soon."

Mike dialed Vicky. "Sorry, something has come up. I'll try to come by later. If not, I'll see you in the morning at the station."

"Okay, Mike, I'm tired anyway. I'm going to turn in early, be careful. Bye now, sweetie"

"Bye, sweet pea."

"So, you found these plans when you closed Lydia and Victor's house?" Mike sits in Sylvia Cooper's dining room and studies the papers that Sylvia has laid out in front of him.

"Yes, then I showed them to Corwin Riggs who let his partner Raymond Dwyer study them. Raymond had them for about a week when his house was broken in to and he was killed, but he didn't have the plans then, he had already given them back to Corwin and Corwin had immediately returned the plans to me."

"And now, Riggs' house and his office have been broken into, and these are in the middle of it all," Mike says.

"That's what Corwin thinks too. I hid them in my bag like Corwin said and I intended to put them in my safe deposit box tomorrow morning." Sylvia shoves the plans into Mike's hands.

"Can I keep these, Miss Sylvia?"

"Yes, please. I don't want anything to do with them. I'm scared, Mike. I think they will come to me next, looking for these plans."

"It's okay. I'll take care of it, don't worry."

~

It is midnight and Mike insistently rings Vicky's doorbell. He can hear Rocky pawing at the door, it is pretty late but at least Rocky doesn't mind.

"Michael, it's late. I was in bed."

"There's no time for that." Mike grins. "We have to go over to the station. Put some clothes on. Hurry up, sweet pea. Time's a wasting."

Vicky threw on a pair of jeans and a tee, and they hurry out the door. As they rush to Mike's car, he explains what has transpired since they last spoke.

"I want to make copies of these original plans and blank out some doodles that I haven't figured out yet, but I have a hunch that they mean something. It's a gut thing. I want to do that before anyone sees them. Then I'll turn the copies into evidence. Later after I figure this out, I'll replace the copies for the original. Get it, sweet pea?"

"Yeah, your gut wants to tamper with evidence, and you want me to be complicit." Vicky raises her eyebrows.

"It's just temporary. I'll have the originals swapped back before anyone even knows. It'll be okay."

"Geeze, Mike, you're as bad as Miriam." Those birds flew out of Vicky's mouth before she even thought, and now they are in the air.

"I know there's something going on with you two. I don't know what it is, but we'll talk about it later, sweet pea." Mike drives to the station at breakneck speeds. They screech into the parking garage and slip into the station.

"Okay, Michael sweetie, I know how to work this old cranky copy machine. Good thing they haven't hooked that new one up yet or you'd be out of luck. Just a good thing I'm here, sweetie. You'd have to put your ID into that new baby before you can get any copies out. But don't worry, Michael, I can master this old machine." Vicky smiles and lays the Michaels and the sweeties on pretty thick. She's hoping that will numb the part of his brain that is concerned about what's going on between her and Miriam. She is relieved that he doesn't want to pursue his suspicions right then. She will have time to make up a good story and a backup lie just in case it's needed. Anyway, Mike could forget… or probably not.

～

"Good morning, Michael, did you sleep well?" Vicky lays a stack of mail on Mike's desk.

"Naw, you snored all night." Mike grins.

"Hush, Michael. Did you turn those copies over?"

"Yep, they should get filed into evidence today. Don't forget to call the Trib and tell them about the historic Tampa memorabilia that the

TPD has in evidence. That'll be a great human-interest story." Mike winks at Vicky before she turns to leave.

"The story will be out by lunch, sweetie." Vicky winks back.

"You have two people waiting for you up front; the sister of the boy killed with Carlos and her lawyer."

"Okay, send them back."

Mike stands as the lawyer and his client enter his office. "Mike De Augustino," he introduces himself.

"Good morning, I'm Don Evans from Evans, Higginbotham, and Clay, and you know my client, Miss Sanchez."

"Yes, good morning, Ms. Sanchez. How can I help you?"

"You are the detective on the case of the murder of the two boys Carlos Ramones and Martin Sanchez, aren't you?" Don Evans answers for his client.

"Yes, I am." Mike looks askew at the attorney.

"Miss Sanchez has some information that she received about a certain deputy sheriff in Kumquat. The information is hearsay, but she wishes to pass this information on," Don Evans comes to the point.

"Where did this information come from, Ms. Sanchez?"

"My client is not prepared to give that information at this time."

"What information is your client prepared to give?" Mike snaps, he doesn't have time for the bull.

"The name of the Deputy Sheriff who her brother was working with."

"When will your client be ready to give this information, Mr. Evans, and what's in it for her?"

"If this sheriff is involved in her brother's death, my client will pursue a wrongful death suit along with the murder charge that he will face. I have advised her to hold off any proceedings. When we are satisfied that the case is thoroughly investigated and there is evidence enough for a formal accusation, then we will proceed with a wrongful death suit against this sheriff."

"So, Ms. Sanchez will give us the name of this deputy, but if you or your client feel that we aren't pursuing this case properly, you will go full ahead immediately with a wrongful death suit? Do I understand you, Mr. Evans?"

"Yes, detective, that's the deal."

"Since any proceedings that Ms. Sanchez might initiate prematurely might damage our case. I'll agree to her terms and keep you abreast of our investigation, so it's a deal. What's the name of this sheriff?"

"Garnett Cox," Ms. Sanchez whispers.

"Cox, huh? That name has come up before." Mike shakes his head. "Okay, got it. Thanks, Mr. Evans." Evans and his client left with the information. As Mike's office door closes, Mike calls Rob's cell phone.

"Hey, Robby, can you talk?"

"Yeah, what's up, old guy?"

"Garnett Cox. Know him?"

"Yeah, he's a mealy- mouthed little rooster."

"Well, the kid's sister just dropped his name."

"Okay, got to go, I'll check him out."

Rob stays behind for lunch, feigning an oncoming migraine. When the station is quiet, Rob searches Garnett's desk, he finds nothing. Rob's curiosity leads him to the row of parked cruisers. It is Garnett's day off and there sits his car. Rob goes back to the desk and grabs the keys for the cruiser. He searches the trunk, nothing there. He opens the passenger door and sits in the seat. He checks the console and the glove box, still nothing. Then he looks down at the floorboard; a tiny corner of a white calling card shows out from beneath the floor mat. Rob bends over and retrieves the card, a Tampa Police Department Detectives card, Mike De Augustino's card; with his cell number scribbled on the back. Then Rob's world turns black.

THE BIG MEET

Joe Vicente and Saul Duetzman stand in a dark corner of the old warehouse. Their conversation is hushed. However, the acoustics of the old structure mimic those of an ancient amphitheater, their quiet conversation resounds through the deserted warehouse.

"Well, now were stuck with this guy. Why did you snatch him anyway?" Saul continues questioning Vicente.

"I didn't have him snatched," Joe protests, as he took a long drag off his cigar. Saul doubts the accuracy of Joe's plea of innocents.

"Whatever, Joe. He's already poked around the station in Kumquat and no telling how much he's overheard here. I'm sure one of the boys would get rid of him. I'm tellin' you, Joe, the guy knows too much. We got to get rid of him. Just let your guys do it," Saul argues the point but is making little headway.

"No good, Saul. If I let my guys do it then I will have to get rid of the boys that did him. No, I just can't spare the men." Vicente flicks the heavy ash that hung on the end of his Hav-a-Tampa.

"Well, how 'bout if we get the Mexicans to do it?"

"We'll see, Saul, maybe we can make that work. We'll see about it."

"We better move on this pretty damn quick. I say he knows too much. He knows about Garnett, and he has probably figured out about the merger by now. We can't afford a slip up. The longer we keep him, the better the chance is for a cluster fuck." Saul glances across the dank dusty room. Two of Vicente's men, guard, semi-conscious, bound and gagged Rob Davies.

"Calm down, kid, I've been doing this for a long time. I'll give you a little sage advice." Vicente leans into Saul's space and blows a cigar smoke ring into the air. "Don't panic 'til the last minute." Saul laughs.

～

Vicky stands at the door of Mike's office, "I wasn't sure if you were back from lunch yet. I have this for you, Michael, you probably need to see it." Vicky puts an envelope on Mike's desk. Mike looks at it; it looks troublingly familiar.

"Oh, damn, not another one."

"Looks like it, that's why I brought it right to you."

Mike opens the letter and stares at the note that is painstakingly spelled out in letters cut from magazines and newspapers. The note reads:

I sing, I sing.

From morn till night.

From cares I'm free,

And my heart is light.

Mike's phone rings. "De Augustino here. Okay, captain, I understand. I'll get on it right now." Mike hangs up the phone. He looks at Vicky with the weight of the world reflecting on his face.

"What is it, Michael?"

"It's Rob, he disappeared from the station in Kumquat yesterday around lunch time. He didn't come in this morning. Also, Garnett Cox is missing."

"Oh no, Michael." Vicky sits in the chair in front of Mike's desk. "What are you going to do?"

"I'm going over to Duetzman's. I'll start with Red; he might have wind of what's going on. He will most likely talk to me if he knows anything. Especially given his certain set of circumstances. He won't want to be complicit in a cop kidnapping. Not right yet, anyway."

"Be careful, Michael."

"Yeah, don't worry. I was born careful, see you later." Mike hurries to the door then turns back. "See you tonight, sweet pea."

Vicky knew that she worries more since she came back to work. She sees that she is a bit timid, a little more skittish and a lot less likely to take a chance. Maybe it's just the wisdom of age. Maybe the responsibility of looking after Miriam has grounded her a bit. But it's most likely that the thought of getting shot again just plain scares the stew out of her.

Mike doesn't break any speed limits getting to the Duetzman's place, but he wants to. He wants to break the speed limit. He wants to break every rule in the book, he wants to break every bone in Red's body. More than that, he wants to race over to Red Duetzman's place, storm into his home, grab his sorry self by the collar and shake the truth out of him, if in fact there is or ever was any truth in him. Mike pulls into the Duetzman's driveway; a security guard meets him at the car door. Mike is escorted to the front door and screened by the security guards in the video booth. Saul opens the door and invites him in.

"What's going on, Mike? Is this about Sauley?"

"No, Saul, I'd like to speak with your father."

"Sure." Saul leads Mike to Red's suite.

"Mike, how can I help you today?" Red sits his glass of scotch on the table and stands to shake Mike's hand. "Please, sit."

"Red, have you heard anything about one of the deputies who disappeared from the Kumquat Sheriff's station?" Mike takes a seat on the couch.

"I haven't heard nothin. When did this happen, Mike?" Red sits at the end of the couch and picks up his Scotch. He takes a long hard slug.

"If you know anything, it will look bad for your case if you don't out with it now, Red."

"Just a minute, Mike, are you accusing me of something?" Red pulls his pants leg up and pointed to the GPS tracker strapped to his ankle. "It would be pretty hard for me to get around with this thing- a- ma-jig on my leg."

"Don't try to BS me, Red, I know if you want something… anything, done. All you have to do is make a call and it's taken care of."

"Yeah, Mike, that's true, but this time I don't know . Let me get Saul in here, maybe he heard something." Red picks up the phone on the end table "Send Saul up to my suite. Yeah, now, dumbass." Red hangs up. "These guys are morons."

"Yeah, Dad, what is it?" Saul pours a glass of Scotch and sits in the armchair across from Mike.

"One of the deputies has disappeared from Kumquat. Our friend, Mike, here has come asking if I heard about this. I don't know nothin about it. Have you heard anything, Saul? You better say if you did. Understand?"

"Sure, Pop, I understand, but I haven't heard anything." Saul sits his glass on the side table.

"There you have it, Mike. My son knows nothin either."

"Well, Pop, I might be able to figure something out. I know Vicente's operation."

"What do you mean, Saul?" Mike asks.

"Well, if Joe or maybe even the Mexicans let's say, snatched someone, say like a cop, he would probably hide him out for a while. I think he wouldn't just go and kill him, it's not his style. Anyway, he might want to find out what the guy was doing before he makes up his mind how to handle the situation."

"So, that's what you think, Saul?" Red has a suspicious eye on his son. "Tell us what else you think, son."

"I think he'd hide him in one of his warehouses, maybe even one out of state." Saul tosses that last bit in to throw Mike off the trail.

"Is that it, Saul?" Red asks.

"I think we can help our friend out here, Dad." Saul turns to Mike. "Tell you what, Mike, let me nose around a little and I'll get back to you. I have your number; I'll give you a call."

"Okay, Saul, I expect to hear from you soon."

"Hey, man, it's the least I can do since you've helped the old man out so much. I'll get back with you soon." Saul shakes Mike's hand. "Come on, Mike, I'll walk you out." Saul escorts him to the door. Mike heads back to the station. He's certain that Red is clueless, and that Saul is up to his eyeballs in Rob's disappearance.

"SAUL, GET YOUR DUMBASS IN HERE." Red calls out. "Yeah, Pop what is it?" Saul appears at Red's door.

"You tell me what it is, Saul."

"I don't get it, Pop, what do you mean?"

"Cut the crap, Saul. Maybe you think you fooled Mike, which I doubt. Maybe you think I'm too old and don't know my ass from my elbows anymore and can't figure out what's going on. I know you are in cahoots about something with Joe and you better let me in on it right now."

"Hey, Pop, it's not cahoots, not what you think at all. Joe's been talking to me and El diMarco about a merger."

"What about the cop, Saul?"

"El diMarco got the cop. He's at one of the warehouses."

"What the hell, Saul? Whose warehouse is the cop at? Better not be one of ours. Dumbass," Red sputters.

"Don't worry, Pop, I got this under control. I swear." Saul doesn't have it under control just yet, but hopes that the tide will soon turn in his favor.

"Why do you say El diMarco grabbed him, Saul?" Red is trying to get to the bottom of this totally fishy story.

"It came up in conversation. Anyway, if there's a merger then instead of fighting all the time, we make a bigger operation and split even three ways, that's it, I swear." Saul put his hand over his heart for emphasis.

"Came up in conversation? That's it, huh? And you trust what Vicente says. Yeah, real smart dumbass. Vicente lies, and you swear by it. Damn, Saul, use your brain for once." Red finishes off his scotch

"We only just started talking about merging with the Mexicans. I was going to come to you today with it, I swear."

"Merge with those crazy bastards?" Red shakes his head. "But yeah, it might just work. We'll get them to kill the cop, the crazy bastards. Okay, that's it. Go tell Joe I said okay." Red pours himself another glass of scotch, and sinks back into the couch.

Mike sits in his office staring at the clock until it hit five. At five after five, Mike stares at the clock again for another forty minutes. Mike wants to be lost in his own thoughts. He tries to be, but somehow his own self relentlessly fights his way clear of any ease or comfort that might be afforded in some bottomless space of his head. He himself hurls him back into the real time of Mother Goose murders, Mexican drug lords, dead teenagers, and injured and missing partners. Mike will drive to Vicky's house now and show her that he has yet again emerged victorious. He will show her that he has been cautious and then he will be sheltered in her company for an evening. He will teach her that there is nothing to fear except fear itself. Fear, a deep abyss, and dangerous fun.

The lights are on in Vicky's house when Mike pulls into her drive. They are beckoning him to the door. Mike rings the bell.

"Michael." Vicky throws her arms around Mike. "I was wondering where you were. Come on in, sweetie."

"Just getting things together in my office. You were already gone when I got back to the station." Mike sits on the couch.

"Are you hungry? We had Chinese food, there's leftovers."

"No, sweet pea, not hungry, but I'll take a glass of wine."

Vicky brings them both a glass of wine and snuggles down next to Mike.

"What did you find out this afternoon?"

"Saul Duetzman had a lot of interesting speculation. I suspect he knows a lot more than he's admitting. He says he might be able to find out where Rob is." Mike rested his head on the back of the couch. He stared at the ceiling and sipped his wine.

"Well, that's good, huh?" Vicky gently runs her hand across Mike's chest.

"It could be. I don't trust him, but he's all I got right now." Mike moves Vicky's hand to his lips; he gently kisses her fingertips.

"What about Mother Goose?" Vicky whispers.

"I don't want to talk anymore." Mike kisses Vicky. Soon the lights are out in Vicky's house and Mike allows himself comfort in Vicky's arms.

❧

The back streets of Drew Park are dark and quiet. Save for the sound of the jets arriving and departing Tampa International and the roar of the crowd at the baseball park. Vicente, Saul Duetzman, and El diMarco meet in a dim corner of Duetzman's warehouse.

"You know what they call me in Tonya Town? They call me El Diablo; the devil, and I will take you to hell if I find out that you killed my Angelina." El diMarco cleans beneath his fingernails with a Bowie knife as he speaks to Vicente.

"George, rest assured my organization had nothing to do with your wife's murder. As a matter of fact, I light a candle for her every time I go to mass." Vicente always addresses Jorge El diMarco as George; he thinks that it's about time the devil assimilated.

"Yes, I believe you, Joe." El diMarco smirks. "I don't think you would do this terrible thing to a woman. Oh, maybe one of your whores, but not my Angelina. What was so important to talk about so late in the evening?" El diMarco sheaths his knife.

Saul wishes he could disappear into the shadows of the old, abandoned factory. He has heard that this El diMarco guy is a bad dude, but he figured that it is all Mexican urban legend. Now, Saul is beginning to believe this guy really is the devil. Saul steps back a bit.

"Well, George, there's been too much fighting going on between us. Too much war. We need to make amends and work things out. We both want the same thing, to have enough to take care of our loved ones. If we go together, you can make more than you ever dreamed, we will be unstoppable. What do you say, George?"

"Are you talking a merger?" El diMarco laughs. "In Mexico, that would include a wedding, but my daughter is only eight and I'm not ready to give her away just yet."

"No, no George. No wedding, just a gentleman's agreement."

"First, I want to know who is the little weasel of a gentleman standing in your shadow?" El diMarco pulls his knife out of its sheath and steps toward Saul. "What's your name, weasel?" El diMarco held the tip of his knife to Saul's gullet.

"Saul Duetzman." The words squeak from Saul's throat.

"Duetzman. What do you know about my wife?" El diMarco presses the point of the knife a little harder into Saul's neck. A tiny drop of blood trickles to Saul's collar.

"It was my dad. I told him not to do it, but he was in a rage. I could not convince him not to. Please don't kill me, I'll give you my father."

"Why did you come here with Joe, weasel?"

"I brought him, George, and believe me when I tell you, this is the first I heard of Red Duetzman's involvement in Angelina's death. Weasel, I mean, Saul is here because the Duetzman family has been very helpful in the business, and I have asked him to merge with us. Now, of course, it's up to you."

"Weasel, bring me your father then we talk." El diMarco knows that Saul is lying but this is a perfect opportunity to get rid of Red and possibly Saul. "Joe, there's one more thing as an act of good faith. We have an undercover cop tied up in the hall, he needs to go. I say the weasel takes care of the cop or no deal." El diMarco keeps his eyes on Vicente.

"Deal, George."

"One more thing, Joe I want to see the weasel with the cop

"The cop dead or alive?" Vicente clenches a soggy cigar between his teeth as he speaks.

"Both, show him to me now then show me when he's dead."

"Okay, sure, George.

"He's here in the hall all tied up in a nice package, okay, weasel, show me what you got." El diMarco pulls his knife and hands it to Saul.

"Wait a minute, George, I got some interviewing that's need to be done before we finish." Vicente tries to regain control.

"Okay, let's see how well you work with your hands, weasel."

Saul walks to the chair where Rob is tied. Scarcely conscious Rob is still suffering from the beatings he has taken from Garnett Cox. Saul kicks the leg of the chair. Rob opens one eye, the other is swollen shut and encrusted with dried fluid. El diMarco laughs.

"I said work with your hands, weasel. My little daughter can do better than that."

Saul leans into Rob; puts his hand on the back of the chair to steady it. Rob's head bobbles. With his other hand, Saul lands a heavy blow to Rob's jaw. Rob falls forward, the chair falls sideways. Saul falls back. El diMarco roars with laughter. Saul scrambles to his knees and begins to thrash Rob. Saul whispers to Rob as the blows fall, "I'm working with Mike to get you out." Rob goes limp.

"Let me know when it's over. Joe, good to see you. Weasel, take care of business." El diMarco walks away. Joe turns to leave.

"Joe, dad says okay to the merger," Saul calls out.

"Okay, Saul, tell your dad I'll call tomorrow to talk." Joe stomps his spent Hav-a-Tampa into the warehouse floor as he makes his hasty exit.

"Sure thing, Joe, talk to you tomorrow." Saul heads to his car, but he won't go home just yet. He needs to unwind. He heads toward The Carousel, where he would have a few drinks and take in the drag show, and then if he's lucky, he will be home first thing in the morning.

~

"Where have you been, Saul? You don't come home at night now? What the hell's wrong with you? Dumbass."

"Relax, Pop." Saul flops into an easy chair and cradles his aching head in his hands.

"You should at least take one of the boys out with you when you go out. Those crazy Mexicans are gunning for us, you know."

"Relax, Dad, I've got it covered. I need a drink."

"Yeah, hair of the dog, that'll do it. I just bet you got it covered just like you had Dwyer covered. Damn, dumbass." Red crosses the room to the dry bar and pours a generous glass of Scotch takes a big slug and hands the glass to Saul.

"Thanks, Pop." Saul downs the remainder in one big gulp.

"Where were you? You left to talk to Joe and El diMarco and then I don't see you till the next morning? What's going on, Saul?"

"Joe wants to meet us at the warehouse with the Mexicans, where he's got the cop."

"Geeze, Saul, did you forget about this?" Red lifted his pants leg as a reminder to Saul, the ankle bracelet blinked. "I can't go anywhere."

"I've got it, Dad, that's what I was doing last night."

"Don't get ya, Saul. What's up?"

"I know a guy who knows a guy who can help with the bracelet."

"Who's this guy who knows a guy?" Red is wary of Saul's plan, whatever it may be.

"A guy I met at the bar last night. He knows a guy, real smart with tech stuff, he called him Widget."

"Did you get this other guy's name too?"

"Tom, his name is Tom. He took my number and said Widget will call me. So, now we wait."

"Great, now I'm waiting for another dumbass, damn Saul." Red pours another glass of Scotch, seems the Duetzman's are having a liquid breakfast. "So, when's this guy supposed to call?"

"Tom said he will talk to him this morning; I told him to put a rush on it." Saul's phone rings.

"Is that him?"

"No, it's Joe." Saul took the call. "Hey, Joe. Yeah, I talked to dad he says he can break free maybe later today, tomorrow at the latest. Sure, the warehouse, we'll see you there. I'll give you a call to firm up. Okay, Joe, later. Yeah, we're on plan."

"What's the plan, Saul?" Red really doesn't trust Saul's administrative ability.

"We're going to have the first meeting, then we'll all decide together what to do with the cop."

"Somebody needs to get rid of him." Red will make that decree at the big meeting, not knowing that the rest of Saul's plan might involve getting rid of him soon after they get rid of the cop. Saul is weaving a dangerously unpredictable tangled web.

～

"Dad this is Widget. Widget this is my father Mr. Duetzman." Saul makes the introductions.

"Top of the Mornin' to ye Mr. Duetzman." Widget leans on his cane and touches the brim of his cap, losing his balance he stumbles a bit forward. Saul takes Widget's arm to steady him.

"Good Morning Mr. Widget." Red studies the odd little man.

"My father would be Mr. Widget, I'm just Widget." Widget cocks his head from side to side as he speaks.

"Are you alright Widget?" Saul asks.

"Aye Laddie, I walked a long-crooked mile for this crooked sixpence." Widget smiles.

"You're Irish." Red's proclamation is as much a question as a statement.

"Ah and it would seem so, now wouldn't it, Mister?"

Red sits in his easy chair and raises his pant leg. "Can you get this thing off or not?" Red is finished with the niceties besides; he is quite put off by this strange fellow.

Widget cocks his head, first to the left and then to the right then back to the left. He looks Red in the eyes and smiles.

"We'll see now won't we Mister?" Widget opens his satchel and digs deep into the moldy old bag. "This will cost you a pretty penny, a pretty penny indeed Mister of mine." Widget looks again into Reds eyes, but he does not smile. "I saw a pretty little kitten when I came in, I will require her."

"Callie the cat? What the hell do you need her for? This is crazy Saul." Red bellows as he pushes his pant leg down and stands up. Widget begins putting the pieces he has retrieved from his bag back into its deep recesses.

"Sit down dad. Hold on Widget." Saul intervenes. "My Dad's just upset. He's been through a lot lately. Please cut him a little slack, just this one time. Tom told me that you are probably one of the best at this sort of thing, give him another chance. I promise it will be worth your while."

Widget violently jerks his head around to face Saul, and then he smiles into Saul's eyes. "Tom? Well, since you put it that way, laddie. Be more than happy to help." Widget sits on the floor in front of Red and again unpacks his bag.

"What is all this?" Red asks.

"Tools of the trade my good man, tools of the trade." The smile never leaves Widget's face as he works. "I'm still going to need that kitten, Laddie."

"Sure Widget, I'll get her, but I don't get it. Why do you need a cat?"

Widget let out a shrill cackle. "I don't. A dog would do just as well, laddie. But the cat is here so here it is." Widget continues chuckling as he arranges his paraphernalia. He picks up a tiny chip from the pile and studies it. Widget studies Red's ankle bracelet picks up a different chip, and studies it, then he begins feverishly entering information into his laptop.

Saul collects Callie and brings her to Widget. "Good kitty." Widget strokes Callie's thick fur as he speaks. "Timing. Now it's all in the timing. So, you will have to lie very still little pretty." Widget continues stroking Callie; until she is sleeping soundly next to him. Widget cocks his head toward Red who has fallen asleep in the easy chair. Widget smiles. "Good. Good girl kitty." Widget picks a collar from the pile; he inserts the chip that he has chosen into the collar. Callie purrs as Widget securely fastens the collar around her neck. "I'd suggest not letting her outside for a bit, Laddie." Widget returns to his laptop, and with another few strokes of the keys Red's ankle bracelet quits blinking, at that precise moment, Callie's collar begins to blink. "That Laddie is how it's done." Widget closes his laptop and packs his bag.

"What exactly did you do Widget?"

"Simple, laddie. I programmed the cat's collar the same as your father's ankle bracelet. Then I turned her wee collar on and his off. That of course is a simple answer for such a simple person as yourself." Widget smiles.

"How much do I owe you?"

Widget looks around at the opulence that is Duetzman's home. "That will be twenty thousand, cash, that will cover turning it off. It will be another twenty thousand cash, when I come to turn it back on."

"Alright Widget. I'll be right back."

"I'm certain you will Laddie." Widget looks down at Red sleeping in the chair. "Appears, he, won't be back for a bit though." Widget cackles.

"Yeah, I'll let him sleep. Like I said he's had a tough time lately." Saul excuses himself for a few minutes, returns with twenty thousand cash, and then shows Widget to the door.

"Don't try to cut that bracelet off his leg Laddie just tape it down. It shouldn't be noticeable under his slacks." With that last bit of advice, Widget is on his way.

Saul left Red sleeping in his chair. He made himself a sandwich for lunch and enjoyed the peace and quiet. He especially enjoyed the reprieve from his father's continual berate. Saul's phone rang. The caller was Mike De Augustino.

"Hello, Mike."

"Hey Saul, do you know anything about the missing cop yet?"

"Yeah, well, I do. I was just going to call you." In Saul's haste to do business with Vicente and El diMarco, Saul had forgotten about his agreement to call Mike. Now he would have to change plans, but a change of plans might suit Saul, and actually work to his advantage.

"What do you know, Saul?"

"I heard that the cop is being held in a warehouse in Drew Park. I think the Mexicans got him."

"There's a lot of warehouses over there. Can you be more specific than that?"

"Yeah, it's two blocks off of Air cargo behind the Ball Park. There are only a few guards one or two at the most, shouldn't be too hard to get him out."

"Thanks, Saul, I know the area."

"Sure, Mike glad to help, especially with all you've done for Pops." Saul hung up and dials Vicente.

"Hey Joe, it's Saul."

"Yeah, Saul, when does Red want to meet?" Vicente was surprised to hear from Saul so soon.

"Something's come up, Joe."

"What is it?"

"De Augustino just called. I think he's trying to rattle my cage or something. He said he heard something was going on in Drew Park and asked if I know anything about it. I just want you to know I'm pulling our guys out of there today."

"Why would he ask you, Saul? That sounds strange to me." Vicente has been suspicious of Saul ever since he sold his brother Victor out, anyone who would do that certainly couldn't be trusted. Furthermore, lately he has been even more wary of Saul since he was not up front about Angelina's murder. Vicente's not the man who likes surprises. Vicente likes to manage; he needs to be in control. To Joe Vicente, the nature of surprise is reality unmanageably out of control.

"Yeah, Joe, Mike was weaving a tale about Sauley's murder and the Mexicans. Like I said, he was probably just trying to rattle me, you know, get me to say something. Whatever it was, I'm getting our boys out. You should get your guys out too just in case there's a raid. Leave the Mexicans to take the heat. He probably got information from them anyway. The crazy bastards."

"Yeah, you're right. I'll get my guy out soon. Thanks for the heads up, Saul."

"Yeah, Joe, it's okay. I'll be calling my guys back this afternoon. Call El diMarco and tell him we'll set the big meeting next week sometime."

"Good plan, that gives us time to see if the cops got some good information, I'll call him this evening."

"Okay, we'll talk later."

"Sure, Saul."

∽

Mike calls his captain immediately upon hanging up from his call with Saul Duetzman.

"Captain, it's De Augustino here. I just got a tip that Rob Davies is being held in a warehouse in Drew Park. Yeah, I know there's a lot of them, but I got a pretty clear picture of where it is."

"I'll get some guys over to Drew Park to help nose around. We'll have to be sure before we break in over there. As soon as we have an address, I'll get a warrant. I'm putting a priority on it, Mike."

"Got it, captain. I'm ready to roll." With any luck, he will have his warrant before this day is over. Then Mike and as many officers as are available will comb the back streets of drew park for the warehouse where one of their own is being held.

∽

As Mike waits to begin his search of Drew Park, Saul dials Nebo. Nebo is a very large thug who is equally as stupid as he is big.

"Hello, Mr. Duetzman, it's Nebo."

"I know it's you, Nebo, I called you."

"Oh yeah. Whatcha want?"

"I want you and Trey to walk down to the corner and have pizza for lunch."

"Can't we drive, Mr. Duetzman? It's kinda hot out."

"No, I think you need the exercise."

"I like pizza. But I worked out and jogged today already, Mr. Duetzman." Nebo scratches his head as if that will clear the fog.

"I said walk, you need the exercise."

"Okay, we'll walk. What should we get on the pizza, Mr. Duetzman?"

"I don't care what you get on the damn pizza. I just want you and Trey to walk down to the pizza place on the corner and have a pizza."

"Okay, Mr. Duetzman. When do you want us to walk down there?"

"RIGHT NOW, NEBO, I WANT YOU TO DO IT RIGHT NOW. RIGHT NOW, DO YOU UNDERSTAND ME, NEBO?" Saul raises his voice in pure frustration.

"Yes, Sir Mr. Duetzman, we're going right now." Nebo hangs up.

"What's all the yelling in here about?" Red wanders into the kitchen and digs around in the fridge for a snack. He sits at the kitchen bar next to Saul and bites the end off of a cold kielbasa."

"I was talking to Nebo."

"I understand. Nebo's a dumb ass." Red shakes his head.

"Yeah, he sure is."

"What did he want?"

"I called him, Pops."

"Why?" Red chews as he talks.

"I told him to take Trey and walk to the pizza place down the road."

"Not drive, Saul?" Red, took a big bite of his kielbasa.

"No, walk."

"Well, the only reason I would tell my guys to walk away and not drive is so that it doesn't look like they aren't coming back."

"Yeah, Pops, I'll go over later and get their car. I guess I learned from the best. I'm pulling our guys out today. Joe's pulling his guy later."

"Why you pulling them?" Red took another big bite of his kielbasa.

"Mike called I told him the cop is there."

"Risky Saul. What does Joe think?"

"I made him think maybe the Mexicans are talking. We decided to let El diMarco's guys burn."

"Okay, good, we'll get Mike his cop back. Joe and El diMarco won't be any the wiser and we'll make some points with the Tampa cops. Sounds good to me." Red burps. "I need a drink."

"I'm going to the pizza place to pick up the guys. Oh, and one more thing, we're going to have to get Widget to come turn your bracelet back on."

"Damn it, Saul, dumb ass, and you were doing so good." Red walks out of the room.

Saul smiles.

❧

Deputy Sheriff Garnett Cox sits in a dirty wooden chair in a corner of the dank old warehouse and watches El diMarco's men play cards. His phone rings.

"Hey Joe, what is it?"

"Are Duetzman's guys there?"

"No, they went for pizza a couple of hours ago, they never came back. Can't figure it out, their car is still here."

"Are El diMarco's guys there?"

"Yeah, they're still here, playin' cards."

"Good. Duetzman pulled his guys out."

"Why'd he do that? Somethin' up?" Cox catches on quick.

"Duetzman got word something is going down there with the police."

"So, I better get outta here too, Joe."

"Yeah, Garnett, you better, do it right now but tell diMarco's guys that Nebo and Trey got arrested and you have to go bail them out. Don't say anything else. Understand? Better be sure to get out now Garnett, we don't know how soon this thing is going to happen."

"Sure thing, Joe, get with you later." Garnett makes a quick call before he leaves.

❧

"What do you think, Emilio?" Rico lays his cards against his chest.
"What do you mean what do you think?"

"Well… I see it is almost midnight, we've been playing cards all day and I have seen no one since lunch. There are no cars in the parking lot, no Garnett in the back and there is no Nebo and no Trey anywhere, something funny is going on."

"Oh, yes, that Trey fellow, he is very much funny; he always make me laugh. Always joking, funny guy." Emilio grins a toothy grin.

"That's not what I mean, Emilio. We have been abandoned here."

"Gin, Rummy." Emilio lays his cards down.

"Emilio, you don't get it."

"Yes, I did get it. Just like you taught me. Four of one and three other of another, or all the same. I did get it, Rico."

"Santa Maria Madre de Dios, Emilio. This is not good." Rico swears to the holy mother of God.

The next sound that Emilio hears is the front, back, and side doors of the warehouse being battered down. Smoke bombs roll into the warehouse through the beaten-down doors. The building is thick with heavy smoke. Rico and Emilio hit the floor face down and began screaming hysterically. They shouted don't shoot in English and Spanish.

"Don't worry, we're not going to shoot you. You can't talk if you're *muerto*." Mike handcuffs Emilio and Rico. The night air hangs heavy with the smoke that wafts from the warehouse. Mike puts Emilio and Rico in the back of the cars and taps the roof. "Take 'em' in."

Rob Davies, bruised and battered, is being wheeled out of the warehouse to the waiting ambulance. Mike catches up before Rob is loaded into the vehicle.

"Hey, kid, you look like hell."

"I feel great," Rob struggles to whisper. "Good thing it's me not you, old timer. You wouldn't have made it." Rob closes his eyes; the drugs that the EMTs administered take effect.

"Yeah, kid, you're right. I couldn't have taken it. You did a good job, cowboy." Mike watches as the emergency team pushes the stretcher and Rob into the van. Mike turns as the vehicle races away; he closes his eyes and takes a long deep breath. The rancor of smoke fills his lungs and burns his eyes; no one will suspect that he shed a tear. Mike turns back to the warehouse. The smoke has cleared but the rancor that hangs in the air burns his throat with each breath. Mike knows that the men they picked up are disposables. He looks over the warehouse, hoping to find something that will lead to the kidnappers but there is nothing to be found. Mike heads toward the exit. On his way out he notices something on the floor. Mike kneels for a closer look; he pokes the soft object with his pen and drops it into an evidence bag.

The station is quiet when Mike gets back there. Emilio and Rico wait in the interrogation room. Mike and the chief watch through a two-way mirror. The chief pulls a chair over and sits in front of the mirror, he moans ever so quietly and rubs his knee.

"You good chief?"

"Yeah, that shot I took a few years back to the kneecap is acting up. I'm not getting any younger you know."

"Yeah, I guess we're all getting older chief. Have they said anything between themselves?" Mike hands the chief the evidence bag. "I got this out of the warehouse."

"I'll send it to the lab maybe it's something." The chief turns back to the window. "They haven't said much. The skinny one, Emilio, keeps asking the other one, Rico, if they will be executed. I think Emilio's fresh over the fence."

"Good I'll talk to him first. Put him in another room. I'm going to clean up then I'll talk to him." An hour and a long hot shower passed before Mike stormed into the room where Emilio sits. Mike slams a folder brimming with papers that he pulled from his trash-can onto the table. Emilio's eyes widen as he looks at the folder.

"Yeah, take a good look buddy." Mike leans back in his chair. He opens the trash file and pretends to read.

"We got some pretty interesting stuff back about you Emilio."

"I don't know what you mean." Emilio is shaken.

"We took your fingerprints. That's all we need to find out everything we need to put you in prison for a long, long time. Who knows maybe the rest of your life?" Mike continues to leaf through the papers. He smirks as if he is reading something, especially corrupt, he looks up.

"This bit of information here could easily get you put away for life, or longer." Mike grins toward the mirror knowing that the chief got a chuckle out of that statement.

"What is it? What does it say that I have done? I promise you I have not done something that wicked."

Mike lays the folder down and leans forward. "You know, I believe you."

"You are right to believe me. I did not even know we were holding the policia."

"I think if you tell me what you know, I can talk to someone on your behalf. Understand?"

"Yes, I understand." Emilio hangs his head.

"Good. Tell me who you work for."

"I work for El diMarco, but I have worked only a short, while, since I came here."

"Chasing the American dream, huh, kid?" Mike mumbles.

"Pardon me, sir?"

"How long have you worked for El diMarco?"

"Only a short, while, like I said. Maybe only two or three months."

"Tell me about Martin Sanchez. Who did he work for?"

"He worked for a policia named Cox, Garnett Cox."

"Did Cox kill Martin and his friend Carlos?"

"Si, he did kill them. Cox killed them both so they would not talk."

"What about the boy on channel side that was murdered? Tell me about that, Emilio."

"I know nothing about that, sir. I swear to you, I have been truthful, but I know nothing of this. As the Holy Mother is my witness, I know nothing." Emilio crosses himself.

"Okay, man." Mike stands, takes a deep breath, and stares at Emilio for a moment then turns and walks out.

"But sir, can I go now?" Emilio calls out as the heavy door to the interrogation room slams shut.

Mike enters the adjoining room and stands next to the chief. They silently watch Emilio through the two-way mirror.

"What do you think, chief?" Mike asks.

"Life or longer? Really?" The chief shakes his head. "Honestly, I think El diMarco's lawyer will have them both out by the end of the day, and nobody will ever see them again after that."

"Well, I guess I better talk to Rico while I have a chance then."

Mike takes a seat in the interrogation room across from where Rico sits.

"Rico, te gustaria tomar una Copa?" Mike offers Rico a drink.

"Yeah man, a glass of water would be good."

Mike leaves the room and returns a moment later with a cold bottle of water. He tosses the water to Rico. Rico raises his cuffed hands and catches the bottle at the precise instant before it hits his face.

"Good reflexes, kid," Mike laughs. "You should have been a ball player." Mike takes his seat. Rico smiles but never takes his eyes off Mike as he twists the cap off the bottle.

"Yeah, I was good when I was a kid."

"And now you're an old man of what?" Mike looks at Rico's arrest report. "Nineteen. Wow, you're ancient." Mike laughs.

"Go ahead laugh cracker, you don't live where I live. When I was ten, my brother was shot and killed right in front of me, he was eight, it was his birthday. Last week, my neighbors were on their front porch just sittin' there when they were all killed in a drive-by shooting. The baby was shot sitting on her grandfather's lap; she was only a year old; so yeah, I guess I am ancient by those standards."

"I guess you are, kid, I guess you are. How long have you been in diMarco's organization?"

"A little more than eight years."

"That's a long time."

"Yeah, I went looking for him after my brother was killed. I figured it was better to make peace with the devil than be caught in his rage."

"Guess you've seen a lot. Ever want to get out?"

"Yeah, I've seen a lot all right, and sure I think of walking away, but I got no place to go if I do."

"What do you know about the kid that was killed and dumped on channel side a while back?"

"I don't think I know anything about that."

"Eight and a half years and you don't know about that. I think you do, Rico."

"What if I do? If I tell you I'll end up in the same place that kid did."

"What if I could keep you safe?"

"Forget it. Then my mother and sisters would be at diMarco's mercy."

"You mean if you thought it was safe for your mother and sisters, you would talk about what you know about diMarco?"

"Forget it, I said. He's El Diablo, no one is safe from him."

"Excuse me, kid." Mike hurries into the adjoining room

"What do you want to do, chief?"

"Make the offer. I'll smooth out the details."

"What about the other kid?"

"Yeah, we'll look after him too."

"Great, chief." Mike hurries back into the interrogation room.

"My chief says we can send you and your mom and sisters away if you agree to tell us what you know."

"So, I would be safe like Carlos? You know what, cop? There was a bunch of us guys who were pulling for Carlos. We were glad that he had the cojones to do what he was doing. But it didn't turn out well for him. Why should I think it would be different for me?"

"I don't know, Rico. I can't promise anything, I can only offer you hope. That's all, hope for a better life for you and your mother and sisters. I guess an ancient guy like you knows that there are no promises in this life but there is hope." Mike stands to leave.

"Wait, sit down. Before I talk, I want you to have my mother and sisters picked up and taken somewhere far away. Deal?"

Mike turns to the mirror. A quiet voice comes over the intercom.

"Yes, Rico, it's a deal."

"Okay, Rico, that's the word. All I want to know right now is about the kid that was killed on Channel Side and what was going on at the warehouse."

"Yeah, the kid was killed by diMarco because he skimmed five hundred bucks off the top of a drug sale. El diMarco won't stand for any theft so he had him taken care of; it was a warning to the others. He brought someone in to do it, don't know who. As far as the warehouse goes, Garnett Cox kidnapped the cop and stashed him in the warehouse, don't know why, and I heard Vicente and Saul Duetzman talking and they didn't know why either. Joe didn't want to kill the cop; Saul was okay with it but didn't want his guys to do it. I don't know who Cox is working for, some say Duetzman, some say Vicente, but they both act like they don't know nothin' about him. I think Cox killed the gardener at St. John. That's what I heard anyway."

"What about the monk that was murdered at the abbey?"

"Lots of ideas about that but no one knows for sure though. It had to be either Duetzman or Vicente, but no one knows why."

"Okay, kid, you're doing good. I'm going to put you in a holding cell for now, but we'll have you out of here before dawn."

Mike can hear the sounds of distant thunder. There is a tropical storm in the gulf. The torrential rains will soon begin. Mike speaks quietly to the captain, "Yes, it's agreed. The kids will be out before dawn."

DUST UP

Mike hurries down the hospital corridor to Rob's room. He knows he is okay, but he needs to see his buddy for himself. Mike slows his pace as he nears the room.

"Mike! Here." Rob waives Mike into his room with the arm that isn't rendered unmovable by tubes.

"Hey, kid, when are you going to quit gold bricking and get back to work?" Mike takes a seat in the chair next to Rob's bed.

"Right, man, I told them last night that I was okay, and I could just go on home, but the EMTS wouldn't hear of it. Go figure, huh?" Rob squirms in the bed trying in vain to ease his suffering.

"Yeah, you're a real cowboy, you did good. I'm proud of you, kid." That is as sappy as Mike is comfortable with. Rob smiles.

"Thanks, Mike, that means a lot to me... old timer." Rob closes his eyes and sighs.

"I won't stay long; the nurses said you need your rest." Mike stands to leave.

"No, Mike, I need to talk about it." Rob motions Mike back to the chair.

"Okay, Rob, go ahead. I'm all ears." Mike takes his seat and leans in closer.

"First off, I found your card in Garnett Cox's patrol car."

"So, there's a good chance that Cox did kill the gardener. What happened then?"

"Then I was knocked out and woke up bound and gagged in that warehouse. I heard Saul and Joe talking about making a merger with El diMarco. Later, Cox got a call from Vicente telling him to get out. After the call with Vicente, Cox made a call and said that he is going to need a place to hide out. Then, he told El diMarco's guys he was going to bail out the other two guys because they got arrested. Sometime after that, all hell broke loose, and someone was throwing a gasmask over my face and pushing me to the floor. Now, here I am." Rob raises his arm to further display the medical paraphernalia hanging from it.

"Okay, Rob, that's a lot of good information, but now you're milking it, put your arm down. The nurse said I could only stay a few minutes." Mike stands again to leave.

"Wait, Mike, I saw a news bulletin on the TV that two prisoners were killed early this morning while, in the holding cell. How could that happen?

Mike leaned over and whispered, "The official story is that the generator failed for a short time during the storm; that's supposedly when someone killed the Mexican kids that we picked up. But the truth is that we moved them and their family's out to a safe place."

"Good, Mike. I was hoping it was something like that." Rob closes his eyes. Mike walks to the door. "Oh, wait, I got you a get-well gift." Mike takes a pack of double mint gum from his shirt pocket. He tosses it on to Rob's bed tray. "Enjoy. Get some rest now, cowboy. I've got to hit the bricks."

～

"How's Rob, Michael?" Vicky lays a stack of notes and mail on Mike's desk.

"He's doing good. You should go see him when you get off."

"I think that's what Miriam and I are going to do after the mall. I was afraid we wouldn't get him back." Vicky leans against the wall.

"Yeah. It was touch and go there for a while, but I wasn't afraid. He had a good teacher, you know, sweet pea." Mike knows that Vicky worries a little more than she did before she was shot, so he smiles and shows the game face, but he was afraid. He was afraid now, just as he was when he thought that he wouldn't get her back.

Vicky smiles. "Come over tonight, we can watch some TV. Miriam is trying a new recipe."

"Oh, now, I am afraid."

"Stop, Michael, she's getting better, but we need to encourage her."

"No, we need Pepto Bismol."

"I'll see you tonight." Vicky starts out the door.

"I didn't say yes I was coming over."

"I didn't ask if you are coming, I said come over. You need to pay attention, Michael." Vicky laughs as she makes the short trek back to her station.

"No, Pepto, that's what I need," Mike mumbles.

A minute later, Mike's phone rings.

"Mike, Saul Duetzman is here. Can I send him back?"

"Yeah, Vic, send him back."

Saul strolls into Mike's office and takes a seat in front of Mike's desk. Mike is silent. He waits for Saul to spill whatever is on his mind. "Mike, buddy, I'm glad it turned out so good for the cop. That was close though. If Pop and I hadn't stepped in, it could have been all over for the cop, you know."

"Yeah, thanks, Saul." The words stuck in Mike's craw. But he guessed he should play the game a little longer.

"Seems like you owe us now." Saul smiles.

Mike suddenly feels as if the life has been drained from his body. He is all at once scorching hot and freezing cold. He bites his lip and grits his teeth. Finally, he speaks, slowly and deliberately, through his clenched teeth.

"Get out of my office now, Saul, while you can still get out on your own steam."

Saul, the weasel, scrambles to his feet and hastily leaves Mike's office. Mike dials the front desk.

"Vicky, can you come to my office for a minute?" Mike has to talk about this before he explodes.

"Sure, Michael, Miriam just came up, I'll have her hold the fort down. I'll be right there."

"What fort, Vicky?" The desk phone rings.

"No fort, sugar. Stay here, I have to hurry. Get that phone, I'll be right back."

"Okay, then." Miriam picks up the receiver. "Hello, Tampa police department. How may I help you?" Miriam answers just as Vicky has taught her.

"I would like to speak to Thomas Dylan who is in the departments employ." The person speaks in a heavy British accent.

"Can you hold?

"Yes, but this is a long-distance call, please just a brief hold."

Miriam checks the employee's directory. No Thomas Dylan. She decides to call the chief, he knows everyone.

"Chief, do you know Thomas Dylan?" she asks.

"Sure, that's Ted."

"Ted?" Miriam was befuddled.

"Yes, Thomas Elijah Dylan, initials T.E.D."

"Oh, yes, I see. Thank you sorry for the bother, chief." Miriam gave Ted's number to the caller and hangs up.

"I think Vicky could have taken a minute to explain. Maybe when she comes back." Miriam grumbles as she sifted through the notes piled on the desk. She is disappointed that Vicky didn't have time to explain about the fort to her. She is still deep into the fort mystery and Vicky's notes when Gracie pops in.

"What's up, girly girl?"

"What's holding down the fort, Gracie?"

"Holding down a fort? Humm forts are pretty hefty. I don't reckon one would need to be held down unless, of course, it was in outer space, no gravity you know." Gracie smiles, her up-to-something as usual smile and continues, "Let's figure this intrigue out. So, holding down the fort is what you are asking, is that correct, hon? Of course, it is, and here you are at Vicky's station, looking through her notes." Miriam quickly put a handful of notes back down on the desk. "And where is Vicky?" Gracie gazes into the ceiling and then bends over to check behind the counter. Then she taps her temple as she supposedly contemplates the fort question.

"Vicky left and she said to hold down the fort. So, do you know or not, Gracie? Miriam gripes.

"Oh, sure, hon, I get it. It's a good thing, important job." Gracie smiles.

"But what is that, Gracie? I certainly don't want to fail at such an important responsibility." Even though Miriam is still not satisfied she felt slightly better, now that she knows whatever holding down the fort is, it's important.

"What? What's what, hon?" Gracie grins.

"The fort. That's what Vicky said, 'hold down the fort' so I want to but, what is it?"

"It's just an expression. I don't have time to go into it right now, hon. Did you see the guy that just skedaddled out of Mike's office?"

"Expression, geeze, Gracie." Geeze is also an expression she has learned from Vicky, of which she hasn't an inkling of the literal meaning. She just knows it doesn't mean good.

"Yes, I was up here talking to Vicky when he hurried by."

"Well, Mike got pretty hot under the collar at him."

"Were you eavesdropping again, Gracie?"

"Sure, I was. Anyway, Mike told him to get out before he put a world of, hurt, on him."

"Mike said that? That sounds like a lot of hurting to me," Miriam says.

"Well, that's not exactly what he said but that's what he meant. Hey, that's real good, hon, you figured it out. Do you want to follow the guy and see what he's up to?"

"Ja, it's real good I did figure that out. No, Gracie, I have to stay here for Vicky. The fort, you know, it's very important."

"Okay, I'm going to catch up with that rascal since you're holding down the fort so good." Gracie laughs and vanishes.

"Not funny, Gracie." Miriam speaks to the air. Vicky returns to her station.

"Is Mike okay, Vicky?"

"Yeah, why do you ask?" Vicky starts looking through the stacks of notes cluttering the desk, tossing the out-of-date and just plain ridiculous ones in the trash.

"Gracie said he had a fight with someone in his office."

"Was she eavesdropping again?" Vicky shakes her head and continues tossing notes.

"Yes, she was."

"No wonder she's always on top of the station gossip. Glad she doesn't read these notes I get. Listen to this one." Vicky cleared her throat and began to read.

"Vicky, you must get really tired of answering the phone all day. I wonder if you'd like to come to my office for a little break. I've been watching you. I think you're kind of cute. M." Vicky rolls her eyes and shakes her head. "Mike, what a goof." She sticks the note in her pocket.

"I tell Gracie to mind her own business, but she doesn't listen you know."

"I sure do know, sugar. Anyway, it was nothing really; Saul Duetzman just said something inappropriate. Mike lost his cool for a minute, that's all. Is Gracie here?"

"No, she's gone now, I have to get back to my files. See you later, Vicky." The desk phone rings as Miriam turns.

"Okay, sugar, later." Vicky answers the phone. "Tampa Police Department, front desk. Hey Ted, yes, Mike is in today. Isn't this your day off? Sure, come on in, he's doing paperwork today. I'll tell him to expect you." Vicky rings Mike.

"Mike, Ted just called he's coming in, says he needs to talk to you."

"Thanks, Vic."

⁓

Gracie sails along the busy downtown Tampa sidewalks searching for the 'rascal' that has hurried from Mike's office. Finally, she catches sight of him. Saul steps to the windshield of his car and pulls the parking ticket from under the wiper.

"Shit, another one." Saul crumples the ticket and discards it into the street. Saul heads toward home with his unseen passenger riding shotgun.

"Where we goin', rascal? This is some nice fancy car you got here. What is it one of them Mercedes Bends or somethin'? So, looks like we're goin' over to the other side of the tracks. Well, to each his own I say." Gracie chatters all the way to the Duetzman estate. Saul pulls into the drive. "Wow, this is way on the other side of the tracks." Gracie follows Saul into the Duetzman estate and did what she does best; she listens.

"Don't you greet your sister?" Red scolds Saul for his disrespect.

"Yeah. Hey, Brenda." Saul nods to Brenda who's sitting next to her father.

"I'm going upstairs, I've got some calls to make. Saul, talk to your sister, be nice." Red disappears up the stairs.

"So, you, Vicente and El di Marco are meeting, what are you up to, Saul?"

"Go to hell, Brenda." Saul walks across the room to the dry bar. Gracie follows Saul.

"Tsk-tsk, no way to talk to a lady. Anyway, you'll be the one going to hell, Saul, because that's exactly where Pops will send you whenever I decide to tell him that you're the one who sold out Victor to Joe Vicente."

"Bullshit, that's a damn lie, you little bitch." Saul pours himself a drink and sits in his armchair.

"Really? Well, I guess Christina Vicente was mistaken then." Brenda smiles as she pours herself a straight scotch, neat and walks over to where Victor sits. Brenda stands over Saul still smiling as she sips her scotch.

"Christina?" Saul turns pale.

"I guess she was whispering sweet nothings in Joes' ear." Brenda flicks Saul on the temple with her forefinger. Saul swats her hand.

"Well, Brenda, Christina's dead now so what matter does it make?"

"Yeah, what matter? You and I and Vicente are the only ones who know your dirty secret. I'll tell you something, Saul, my friendship with Christina really served me well. Joe, Christina, and I became quite close. Did you know that we all used to go to mass together at the abbey? It is there that I recognized the monk that was Pops' old maintenance guy. I identified him to Joe and had him taken care of." Brenda laughs.

"And in case you still have doubts about the scope of my influence, Cox reported to me that the gardener at the Abbey had been talking to Mike. He killed the gardener because I told him to."

"So, did you have the kid in witness protection killed too?"

Brenda laughs. She leans in close to Saul's face. "No, Cox did that for El di Marco, even though he was working for me, but now he belongs only to me. This little dust up that I have caused between the families is really working out for me, and when the dust settles, who do you think is going to be the top dog Saul?" She steadies herself on the arm of the chair and leans a bit closer; Saul can feel her hot breath on his face. "It'll be me, Saul. Me, this little bitch right here, me! So that's the answer to your question, that's the matter that it makes. Now, believe me when I say if you give me even a hint of trouble, I will be of one mind only and I will tell Pops that you had Victor and his family killed." Brenda turns and leaves. As the front door slams shut, Red descends the stairs.

"What were you fighting about this time? You shouldn't fight with a lady, Saul. Pour me a drink." Red sinks into his armchair.

"That's no lady, that's my sister." Saul mumbles as he turns to fix Red's drink.

"Where's Brenda going? Why'd she take off so quick?"

"Business, I guess." Saul pours himself a double

"Hey, Ted. What's up?" Mike looks up from the file he is studying.

"Hi, Mike. I came by because I was going over some things on my computer at home and when I got to Duetzman's GPS I noticed that there was a short blip. Wanted to let you know. Not really worried, just thought I should come straight away with it."

"A blip? What does that mean, Ted?"

"It was like an interference."

"How long did it last?"

"Maybe two or three seconds, that's all. I can't explain it and it's working fine now."

"Okay. Ted, watch it close. Let me know if it happens again and I'll go over and take a look."

"Sure, Mike. I'll let you know."

"Thanks, Ted, appreciate it." Mike walks to the front with Ted so he can stop at Vicky's station.

"Hi, sweet pea," Mike whispers. "What's going on tonight?"

"Miriam and I are going to the mall this afternoon after work. Why don't you come over later? We'll order out."

"That sounds like a good plan." Mike leans closer and whispers.

"Do you promise we're ordering out?" Mike doesn't want any scoodle surprises.

"What sounds like a good plan? I couldn't hear what you two were whispering about. Hi, Vicky, you're looking good as usual." Paul squeezes Mike out and stands in front of Vicky at the desk.

"Paul, bro. What brings you around?" Mike stands up straight, clears his throat and nudges Paul back.

"Okay, boys, act right. Quit horsing' around," Vicky scolds.

"I got some stuff I need to talk out. You got time, Mike?"

"Yeah, sure, come on back."

"Good to see you, Vicky." Paul was on his way down the hall.

"Hey, Paul, hold up."

"Sure, Vicky, what is it?" Paul turns.

"I'm just getting off duty. Miriam and I are going over to the mall but come on over later, we're ordering out."

"Sounds great, Vicky." Paul accepts the invitation and heads back to Mike's office.

"What is Paul doing here? He didn't come and say hi to me." Miriam furrows her brow as Paul disappears down the hall.

"I don't know, Miriam. It's just guy talk, nothing you want to know about anyway. They're just going to hang in Mike's office. Come on now, we've got to hurry. I want to get to the mall then to the hospital before visiting hours are over."

"Okay, but he could have said hi, anyway."

"Let it go, sugar, you can't fault a man for being a man. Anyway, I invited him for order out tonight." Vicky took Miriam's hand, in case she had to pull her along.

"Wait, Miriam, I got something to tell you." Gracie pops in.

"I'm going to the mall, Gracie. See you later." Miriam calls out on the fly.

"Okay, see you later." Gracie kept pace.

"Not too early. Paul's coming over."

"Humph, Paul..." Gracie grumbles, "I guess I can't blame her for that. He is right pleasant to look at." She mumbles. "Oh, well." Gracie vanishes.

Vicky and Miriam rush home, throw on a change of clothes and are back on the road in no time; unaware of the dark SUV that follows.

～

"Wow, Paul the FBI. Wow, what did they say?" Mike grins.

"They said there's an opening in the field office here."

"How did this happen? Does Miriam know yet?"

"Well, in my work, we cross paths pretty often, we even worked together a few times. Anyway, they contacted me and asked if I would be interested, so I sent in my resume. It all happened kind of fast. I haven't said anything to Miriam."

"So, Paul, did you hear anything back yet?"

"Yeah, I did. They want me." Paul looks at Mike and half smiles.

"Good, but you won't have to leave Tampa, eh, bro?"

"I'll have to go to DC for a while for training but that's all."

"Well, that's good, we're kind of getting used to you hanging around. Really, that's great, Paul. What do you think?"

"I think I'm going to go for it."

'Good, I'd do the same if I were you." Mike gives Paul a congratulatory slap on the back.

"Glad to hear that, Mike, I value your input. So, tell me, what's going on with you these days?"

"Got two kids and their families in protection. One's been with El di Marco for eight years. He's giving some pretty good information so far."

"Good, then you might get Vicente and El diMarco all wrapped up soon."

"Yeah, I might." You know, those kids don't have a clue what they're getting into. They're just kids, all passion, full of vim and vinegar."

"And Hollywood," Paul adds.

"By the time they figure it out, it's too late. They're dead in an alley somewhere." Sad memories give Mike pause. "I'm sure hoping to get Vicente and El diMarco soon, it looks good so far. But they're like roaches you get rid of one or two, and a dozen more come out of the woodwork." Mike's phone rings. "Don't leave just yet Paul. We'll go get a beer. Let me take this call real quick."

"Go on, get it. I got nothin' but time." Paul clasps his hands behind his head, leans back, and grins.

"De Augustino here."

"You got my boys. I'm not buying the, murdered in the cell' story. You'll get Ms. Knight back when I get the boys." The phone went dead. Mike went pale.

"Who was it, Mike?"

"The caller I told you about, he said that I get Vicky when he gets the boys. They got Vicky!"

"Quick, Mike, call Vicky. Maybe they're not at the mall yet."

"Already dialing."

Vicky's cell rang. "Hello, sweetie. Miss me already?

"Where are you, Vicky?"

"Just pulling into the mall parking garage. Great rock star parking." Vicky parks her car.

"Vicky, I just got a call it was…" static interrupts the call.

"Sorry, Michael, you're breaking up. Can you hear me?" Vicky and Miriam walk toward the entrance of the mall. "Can you hear me now? What did you say? I'm almost out of the garage, lots of interference."

"Yes, Vicky, I hear you. Just listen to me, get back in your car and drive as fast as you can back to the station. Don't stop for anything."

"What is it, Michael?"

"There has been a threat called in on you. Get back here now."

"Okay, Michael. Come on, Miriam, we got to get out of here." Through the phone, Mike hears the sound of tires squealing, "Someone has blocked us. It's a dark SUV, looks like a Lexus. Four men in masks in the car." Vicky describes the scene to Mike as she and Miriam turn and run back into the garage toward the safety of their car. Static again interferes with the call.

Another car turns the corner in the garage and fishtails to a stop in front of Vicky and Miriam. Two men in ski masks get out; one man grabs Vicky. He presses a handkerchief over her mouth and nose; Vicky goes limp, her cell falls to the ground. The man throws her into the back of the car, and they speed off. The second man pushes Miriam to the concrete floor of the garage. The SUV following the speeding car stops and the second man jumps in. The SUV races out of the garage.

"What's going on, Mike, where are they?" Paul is at Mike's side.

Mike holds a dead receiver. He drops the phone into its cradle and turns to Paul. Paul can see the fear in Mike's eyes.

"Mike, what's going on? Tell me!"

"They were already there at the mall. They took them, the line went dead." Mike dials his captain.

"Captain, Vicky and Miriam were taken by the cartel at the International Mall. They want to trade for the boys."

"I'll get some cars out there. You get over there now!"

"Paul Linder is here with me, we're on our way out. We're looking for a black Lexus SUV, that's the only thing I got before the phone went dead." Mike slams the receiver down.

"Come on, Paul, we're out of here"

Mike and Paul speed to the parking garage of the International Mall. The security cop is already at the scene as they pull up. EMTs are attending to Miriam. Paul bounds out of the car toward the stretcher where Miriam is lying.

"Miriam!" He calls out as the EMTs are loading her into the ambulance. Paul tries in vain to get into the back of the ambulance.

"Hold on, sir, are you related to this woman?" The EMT holds Paul back.

"Yes, I'm her husband. Now, let me go." The EMT allows him into the ambulance. Paul knows that the lie will get him to Miriam. He also knows that nobody will be asking for a marriage certificate as proof. Paul makes his way to the head of the stretcher. Miriam is semiconscious, her eyes are unresponsive and fixed on the ceiling.

"Miriam, I'm here, it's me. I'm here, Miriam." Paul turned to the EMT. "What happened? Why isn't she responding?"

"She hit the pavement pretty hard. Looks like a concussion. We have her on a board and in a collar just in case there's any neck or back injury. She's had quite an ordeal, she's in shock."

Paul takes Miriam's hand and presses it to his lips. "Miriam, I'm here. I won't leave you; I will never leave you. Remember, I love you, pinky swear." Paul twists his pinky finger around hers; wipes a tear from his eye and gathers his strength.

The ambulance races to Tampa General Hospital. The EMTs rush the stretcher through the doors. David Knowles meets them as they wheel Miriam into a room. He examines Miriam, and the x-rays, then he finds Paul in the waiting room.

"Husband, huh? Congratulations. I hadn't heard." David raises his eyebrows.

"Yeah, I lied."

"It's okay, man. I would probably have done the same thing."

"How is she, David?"

"Let's walk back to the ER while we talk."

"Is she okay?" Paul is worried. Doctor Knowles and Paul stand next to the bed where Miriam sleeps. Knowles studies his notes once more then closes the chart.

"Well, no broken bones. She's in shock from the trauma. Too much too soon, but she's strong. I think she'll snap out of it quickly. Other than some bruising, that's it. We'll put her in a room overnight for observation then maybe you can take her home tomorrow. You can sleep in the lounge chair next to the bed. I'll tell the nurses it's okay. She's been sedated but she'll need to see a friendly face when she wakes up. Glad you're here, Paul. Take care of her, she's a special lady."

"I know she is. Thanks, David."

"I'm sure you do. She'll be all right, don't worry." Doctor Knowles shakes Paul's hand and leaves him with Miriam.

"Mr. Linder?" The nurse enters the room followed by an orderly. "We are going to move the patient to a room now. The doctor says you are going to be our guest tonight." The nurse smiles. She unlocks the wheels of the bed. Paul follows the nurse to the room where they are quickly slipped away in a private room overlooking the channel.

"Thank you, nurse." Paul pushes the lounger as close to Miriam's bed as possible.

"You're welcome. It's usually quiet up here. If you need me, just buzz."

"Thank you, I will." Paul sits in the lounger and fiddles with the controls.

The parking garage has been cordoned off. A crowd of shoppers have gathered, unable to breach the cordon to get to their cars. Mike and the officers comb the garage for evidence and take pictures of the tire skid marks that are found close to where Miriam was found. Mike interviews the eyewitness who had been leaving the mall at the time of Vicky's abduction.

"Thanks for coming forward, it's very brave of you. What exactly did you see?"

"I saw the two women walking toward the mall, one woman was on her cell when a black SUV cut them off. A man in ski mask started to get out. The women ran the other way, but they didn't get very far when another car cut them off. There were three men in the other car. Two men in masks got out. One of those men caught up with the woman on the cell phone. He put his hand over her mouth and nose, it looked like he had a handkerchief or a tissue in his hand. Then she went limp, and the man tossed her into his car; that's when she dropped her phone. Then the car tore out of the garage. The other woman was running toward the woman on the phone. The second man ran toward the other woman. He pushed her to the pavement; he really sent her flying. Then he ran back to the black SUV, and they took off."

"Did you get a good look at the other car?"

"Yes, but it wasn't really as close, and I'm not good at identifying cars. I know it was a nice car. It was black; you know nice like a Mercedes. Sorry, I can't tell you anymore."

"Thanks, you've been a big help." Mike hands the girl a card. "If you happen to remember anything, give me a call."

"I will." The girl drops the card into her bag and hurries into the garage. Mike's cell rings just as he finishes questioning the witness.

"De Augustino here. Another Mother Goose victim! Behind the Carousel, yeah, captain, I know where that is. Sure thing, captain, I'll get Duncan to finish this. I'll be over at the carousel in a few." Mike fills detective Duncan in on what he got from the first witness and then rushes to the Carousel and into the world of Mother Goose and murder.

The proprietor of the Carousel is waiting for Mike in the alley behind the bar. He is a big boned man. probably five-eight or nine if he stretches. For this man's bone structure, he should have hit at the least the six-foot mark. From the looks of the heavy stage makeup that he is sporting, he dazzles 'em with his brilliance. He obviously takes to heart the kitschy makeup trend of 'when in doubt, add glitter'. He wears it well. Mike parks his car and approaches. The medical examiner and his assistant are just finishing.

"Oh, oh, oh, officer." The man shrills to Mike, his sequined stilettos hit the asphalt hard as he runs. "I'm so glad you're here. Officer, this is dreadful, just dreadful. My lord, I think I've sprained my ankle now. Dreadful, just dreadful." The man leans against Mike and bends over to gently rub his ankle.

Mike helps the man to the backdoor of the establishment. The man leans over once again to examine his ankle, then stands up and proudly announces, "Nope, not sprained. I never buy a pair of stilettos that I can't run in. You never know, you know." Mike just shakes his head, not certain how to respond. He takes out his notebook and flips to a new page.

"I'm Detective De Augustino, you found the body?"

"Yes, Detective. Dear, baby Jesus, yes, I certainly did. Right over there by the dumpster. The man pulls a feathered fan from the sleeve of his kimono and uses it to point toward the dumpster. Then he leans against the back door and dramatically fans himself.

"What is your name?" Mike walks ahead to the dumpster. "Bruce, Bruce Haywood." The man follows from afar. He hurries to catch up.

"Bruce?" Mike looks sideways. "Is that your given name? Do you know the victim?"

"Not personally, only from the show. He called himself joni justjoni all lower case. j, lower case. j, lower case. j, lower case. Yep, it is."

"Yeah, I got that lower case. Yep, what is?" Mike looks up from his notes.

"Bruce. My given name. I guess my mom knew I was going to be a tranny. Bruce…humph," the man sighs a huff. "Really trite, pedestrian you know. Anyway, ironic, huh?" Bruce shrugs then studies his perfectly glittered inch-long nails. "Anyway, I was opening the bar, getting ready for the show tonight. It's my club." Bruce waives the fan towards his club.

"You own it, huh?"

"Sure do, every inch."

Mike pulls a card from his pocket and hands it to Bruce. "Will you come into the station tomorrow? I'd like to ask you some questions. Nothing to worry about, just routine."

"Sure, I can come in." Bruce stuck Mike's card down his bustier and heads back into the bar.

"Hey, Mr. Haywood, do you have CCTV in your place?"

"Sure do, Detective. I know right where you're going, I'll bring in the films and any photos I can get my hands on. Tootles now, see you soon." Bruce waives Mike a feathered fan goodbye.

"Thank you, Mr. Haywood." Mike walks toward the medical examiner.

Mike studies the body. A thin man with shoulder length platinum hair lie dead and naked beside the dumpster. The words, 'from cares I'm free' are carved deeply into his abdomen. Mike turns to Eslen.

"Another one, eh, Eslen. Got time of death?"

"Between two and four am. Like the other, this isn't the murder site. Death by exsanguinations, again we didn't find a drop of blood. And there's the message carved into the abdomen postmortem. Yeah, Mike everything points to another one. I hear you're calling 'em the Mother Goose murders."

"Yeah, Mother Goose." Mike is tired. He closes his notebook. "I got everything I need for now. I got to get to the hospital."

～

The nurse checks and notes Miriam's vitals then quietly returns to her station. Paul sits in the lounge chair next to the bed fiddling with the chair's settings. Mindlessly moving up and down, forward and back. Mike watches from the door.

"Where 'ya goin' on that thing, big guy?"

"Mike, glad you're here, bro." Paul gets out of the chair and bear hugs Mike.

"How's she doing, Paul?"

"Knowles says she'll be okay. They got her knocked out. She'll probably sleep through till morning. What about Vicky? Do you know anything yet?"

"No, not much yet." Mike sits in a chair next to the bed. Paul takes his place in the lounger. "All I know is that there were two vehicles, one SUV and the other was a late model sedan. That's all I know. Had to give it over to Chris Duncan. I got another Mother Goose victim."

"Geeze, no, Mike. Are you working the Mother Goose and Vicky's case?"

"As soon as I talk to Duncan I'll know more. I'll be on Vicky's case anyway. The Mother Goose doesn't take a lot of my time. No clues, no nothing. I'll be in the station in the morning. The guy who found the body is coming in."

"You suspect him?"

"I don't know, just going to ask some more questions. No suspects yet." Mike squeezed in between his eyes at the bridge of his nose. "I've got a real head banger coming on. I think I'll go to the drink machine. Want anything?"

"Yeah, bring me a Coke and chips, just plain chips."

"I could probably find you something downstairs, if the deli is still open."

"No thanks, there's nothing worse than hospital food. Miriam's Scoodle is even better." Paul chuckles.

"I heard that." Miriam whispers.

Paul leans close and gently strokes her hair. "Hi, I'm glad you're awake. I love you."

"I'm glad you are here, Paul." Miriam takes Paul's hand.

"Where else would I be?"

"Hey, Miriam, good to see you awake. Paul, I'll be right back with your chips." Mike left the room. He would take his time. Paul and Miriam needed some private time, and he needed a Coke and a handful of aspirin.

"Don't forget the Coke, bro."

"Yeah, Coke."

Paul turns his attention back to Miriam. "Doctor Knowles says you can go home tomorrow."

"Is Vicky home?"

"No, she's not home yet."

"Where is she?" Miriam begins to wrestle with the bed covers.

"Hold on, girl, where are you going?"

"Does anyone know where Vicky is?" Miriam continues trying to break free of her bed.

"Calm down, Miriam, the department and Mike are all searching for her."

Paul's answer does not satisfy Miriam. She continues her struggle. She tries to pull herself up by grabbing the I.V. stand next to her bed. The stand falls and hits the monitor, the monitor sounds an alarm. The nurse quickly appears at Miriam's bedside. She administers a sedative, and Miriam slumps to her pillow.

"Paul." Miriam whimpers.

"Yes, Miriam?"

"Tell Mike I will find Vicky tomorrow. Sandalphon and I will find her..." Miriam mumbles before she gives in to the drug.

"Hey, got your Coke and chips. What happened in here?" Mike watches as the nurse straightens the bed covers and checks the I.V. and the monitor.

"Miriam is a little emotional. She's disoriented too. She tried to get out of bed."

"Did I hear her right? Did she say that she and the bird are going to find Vicky?"

"Yeah, like I said, she's confused." Paul didn't volunteer any further explanation. He is lost in concern for Miriam and conflicted over the deep secret he is keeping from his friend. He knows Vicky and Miriam have not included Mike into the facts of Miriam's mysterious past. Furthermore, he is certain that Mike hasn't been brought into privy of Eliakim, or Miriam's golem raven or her ghost cohort. He hopes for resolution to the conundrum that is wrapped around his friendship with Mike and Miriam's existence. Paul took the Coke and chips.

"Thanks, Mike."

"Miriam's a good girl. She says some odd things sometimes that's for sure." Mike chuckles and sits back in the side chair.

"That she does." Paul smiles.

"Vicky seems to understand her pretty good though."

"Yeah, Miriam is lucky." Paul knows it isn't luck that brought them together but he's not really sure what it actually is. "Don't worry Mike, you'll find her."

"Yeah, I will." Mike rubs his forehead and closes his eyes. Three hours later, Mike opens his eyes. Paul is asleep in the lounger. Mike quietly leaves the room.

BUMPER CHICKEN

"How long have you been here, De Augustino?" The captain stands at Mike's door.

"Since about three this morning."

"I know you're worried, Mike, but we've got everybody available in the department on this and the FBI. We'll find her Mike." The captain steadies himself on the door then walks in to Mike's cubicle.

"I feel so helpless, Chief. I don't know where she is. I need to know that she's okay. I have to know. Chief, can anyone in the department tell me she's okay? Can the FBI assure me that she'll be okay? That she'll come home?" Mike hangs his head. The captain sits in the chair in front of Mike's desk.

"Mike, whoever took her needs her alive, she's a bargaining chip. Because of that, you can be assured that she's alive. That in itself gives us the upper hand. We have the time and resources to find her, and we will."

"You're right, Chief. We'll find her."

"Keep the faith, De Augustino, keep the faith. Tell me about this new Mother Goose now."

"Just got the basics. The owner of the Carousel found the body, he's coming in this morning so I can ask a few questions."

"Suspects? Anything to go on?"

"No, clean just like the Vicente case."

"Darndest thing I've seen in a long time, De Augustino, but they always screw up, always." The chief leans toward Mike as he speaks.

"Yeah, chief, I know, but how many victims will there be before he gets sloppy?" Mike's desk phone rings.

"Don't know, I just don't know." The chief quietly moans. Pushes himself up from his chair by steadying himself on Mike's desk. He slowly walks back to his office.

"De Augustino here." Mike answers. "Yes, thank you, please send him back." A robust man knocks on the side of Mike's door.

"May I come in, Detective?"

"Yes, but I only have a moment, I'm waiting for someone to come down."

"Bruce Haywood?"

"Well, yes. Who are you?" Mike is surprised that this man knows who he was waiting for."

"I'm Bruce Haywood."

"Oh, excuse me; I didn't recognize you without the… uh."

"Kimono?" Bruce laughs.

"Please, come in, sit down. I have a few questions."

"Anything I can do to help, detective. Joni was one of the favorites over at the show, and a very nice guy. It's such a shame, such a shame." Bruce hangs his head and gathers himself.

"This has been a difficult case. I'll be honest with you; this is the second victim and we got nothing."

"I was reading in the Trib that ya'll are calling it the Mother Goose murders."

"Yeah, that's right. So, Bruce, do you remember anything that seemed out of place or suspicious the night of the show? Was there anything unusual?"

"No, nothing more than the usual unusual." Bruce smiles.

"Did you notice if joni seemed worried or distracted?"

"No, not at all. As a matter of fact, he put on a brilliant show. He performed his best Marlina Dietrich ever. He was dazzling, actually he won the show. It was really a great show, joni was at his best."

"So, nothing suspicious?" Mike asks.

"Now, I wouldn't say this is suspicious, just different. Someone sent him a huge bouquet of roses backstage. As many times that joni had performed, that never happened before. So, I figured he had a new friend, I didn't notice anyone new, but the place was slammed."

"Roses, huh? Was there a card?"

"There sure was, it's here with the pictures. This is all the photos that I could get." Bruce laid a stack of photos on Mike's desk.

"That's a lot of pictures."

"I have the CCTV tapes too." Bruce shuffles through the pictures.

"Here, look at this." Bruce pointed out one patron in particular dressed to the nines.

"This guy here I had never seen before. Which isn't all that odd, but this guy really didn't fit. And I think he sent the roses."

"Why do you think that?" Mike makes a note on the picture.

"One of my servers heard him on the phone talking about roses."

"Thanks, Bruce, we'll run him through facial identification." Bruce stands to leave.

"Oh, one more thing, he had a slight accent. British, I think."

"Thanks, good information. I hope it gets me somewhere. I need a break on this one."

"No problem, glad I could help."

Mike stands and extends his hand. "I think that's about all, Bruce. If you remember anything else, just let me know."

Bruce took Mike's hand and vigorously shook it. "You are most welcome. Oh, and feel free to come check out our show."

"Thanks, but..." Mike stumbles.

"I know you're not gay. So what? Nobody's perfect." Bruce smiles. "Come anyway, everyone's welcome."

"I just might, thanks for the invite."

"No problem, hope to see you, detective." Bruce turns to leave, takes a few steps toward door and turns back.

"Detective, there is one thing that I remember from my childhood. I have always considered it an urban legend. I'm not sure it's even important."

"Well, tell me. It might be." Bruce returns to his seat and begins.

"I grew up on the outlands of the Ozarks, in southern Alabama. As a kid, I did a lot of camping in the woods with my friends. Good fun, ya know, which always included a lot of s'mores and terrifying ghost stories. The tried and true scary story was of the four princes who lived under a big stone in the woods. The princes would come out and kidnap someone that they had been watching, take them to their stone in the woods, drain their blood, carve their initials in their dead bodies, and then take the bloodless bodies back where they got them. It was pretty scary stuff as I remember, but of course, it was just a legend. But seeing joni like that brought it all back."

"Ozarks, huh?" Mike is quiet for a moment. "What else did you do when you were a kid?"

"I helped an old guy at the car graveyard build a bumper chicken once. It ended up being around fifteen feet or taller when we got finished."

"A bumper chicken?" Mike laughs.

"Yeah, I swear, a fifteen-foot chicken built out of old chrome bumpers. Took us a powerful long time but it was great. That's where I learned to weld. If you're ever traveling up state road 221, check it out. I bet it's still there, it's awesome." Bruce is grinning with pride. The sadness and horror of the past days had succumbed to a pleasant remembrance.

"You know, I think that would be worth seeing. I might try to get my girl to take a road trip up there." Mike is keeping the faith. "I'm going to think about that legend too. You never know it could be something." Mike shakes Bruce's hand.

"Thanks again."

"You're welcome, and good luck." Mike starts sifting through the pictures.

"This is a lot to go through," Mike mumbles, he dials Ted.

"Hey, Ted, can you bring a video player to my office? No, I'm not watching porn, you old perv." Mike chuckles. "I have the CCTV from the carousel drag show. I want to go over it. Okay then, I'll see you in a bit. Bring popcorn, the owner said it was a great show." Mike and Ted watched the show, without popcorn.

"Mike, old man, what do you know of this fellow, besides that he puts on a good show?"

"He told me that he built a fifteen-foot chicken out of old chrome car bumpers when he was a kid." Mike laughs.

"That's a good start." Ted smiles. "Car bumpers, hmm. Amazing, fifteen feet tall, did he say?"

"Yep, that's what he said. He says it's still standing out on state road 221. Then he told me an urban legend from his childhood about four princes that lived under a stone in the back woods of the Ozarks. Legend says they drain the blood from the bodies of their victims and carve their initials into them. Sounds close, but no cigar."

"I have heard the stories of the four princes long ago in Brittan. But how could one ever track them down? They live under a rock for pity's sake." Ted laughs at the absurdity.

"Yeah, it's just a fable, but an eerie similarity just the same."

Ted stands and stretches.

"I have to be off to my cubby. Will you want to keep the video machine?"

"Yes please, leave it for a while, Ted."

"Sure, Mike, catch you later. Good show, quite campy."

"Right, Ted, catch you later."

Mike studies the pictures carefully. At one point, he brings out his magnifying glass to clear up the picture that Bruce pointed out. The man in the photo looks vaguely familiar, but it's grainy, a tough call. He will give the pic to Paul, maybe he can run it through his facial recognition.

"This is a lot. I'm going to call it a day." Mike grumbles he picks up the card that had accompanied the bouquet of roses. The sentiment of the card is the words of the Mother Goose killer. 'From cares be free. Love forever. Thomas.' Mike's legs buckle.

"They always make a mistake," he whispers. He picks up his phone and dials the carousel.

"Hello, Mr. Haywood, this is detective De Augustino. When you get this message, will you please send me the CCTV that you have for the week before the show? Please send it as soon as possible. I hate to rush you, but I think I might be on to something. Thank you." Mike couldn't wait until morning to leave the urgent message, he had to do it immediately, it's urgent. Now, he will urgently hurry home, urgently take a hot shower and urgently relax. Then he will go to bed and urgently worry about Vicky all through the damn urgent night.

~

The first thing Mike does the next morning is dial Paul's cell. Mike has tossed and turned most of the night. What little sleep he was afforded was nightmarish.

"Hey, Paul, are you at Vicky's with Miriam yet?"

"We'll be there soon. I just got her out. We're on our way there now. What's up, bro?"

"I'd like to come by if it's okay. I've got some things to go over. Would really like your input. How's Miriam?"

"Sure, Mike." Paul chuckled. "Miriam's pretty loopy, they've got her all doped up for pain and anxiety. Knowles says she'll be pretty much out of it today. She nodding off, now."

"Is she okay?"

"Oh, sure, she's kinda' like a bobblehead right now though. Knowles just wants her to stay quiet for a day or two then he'll take her off the anxiety stuff."

"Glad she's okay Paul, you can trust David, he knows what he's doing. He did okay for Vicky. I'll get cleaned up and catch you at Vicky's."

"Sure thing, see you later." Paul looks over at Miriam sleeping next to him.

"Hey, hold up, Paul. I know you have to catch a plane this afternoon. How about if I drive you to the airport?"

"Yeah, great, Mike, sounds like a plan. Later, bro. I have to catch Miriam now before she slides away."

∾

Paul pulls his car into Vicky's drive. He sprints to the front door, unlocks it with Miriam's key, then sprints back.

"Miriam, wake up bobble head, you're home."

"You know what, Paul?" Miriam opens her eyes and smiles at Paul.

"Probably." Paul answers as picks Miriam up and carries her to the door.

"I think you have my key."

"I do have it. I told you I probably know what." Paul chuckles.

Miriam had spent only a day and a half in Tampa General, but it seems like an eternity to Paul. It is a half day longer than Miriam anticipated, and what's more she isn't all that happy about it.

Paul readily carries Miriam to the couch. He set everything up the night before in the eagerness of bringing her home. He gently positions her on the pillow and lays the blanket over her legs. Rocky cautiously approaches, jumps onto the couch, and curls up at Miriam's feet.

"Rocky, you are a good girl." Miriam reaches out to pet Rocky but falls back on to the pillow and whispers, "Don't worry about Vicky, I will bring her home."

"Are you all right? Are you comfortable?" Paul tucks the blanket under Miriam's feet. He is being a helicopter boyfriend.

"Yes, Paul, I am fine. I could have come home yesterday, but Doctor Knowles said no." Miriam pouts, her eyelids hang heavy as she speaks.

"Yes, I know, Miriam." Paul agrees so as not to upset Miriam any further. Rocky sits up and cocks her head.

"It's okay, Rocky, she's going to sleep for a while." Rocky rearranges herself back on the couch and settles in.

Paul leans over and whispers, "Sleep now, Miriam. Mike is coming over for lunch. We have some things we have to go over before I leave."

Miriam's eyes flew open. "Tell me Mike that I am going to find Vicky. Sandalphon and I will find her. I promise. Where are you going Paul?" Tears cloud her eyes.

"Miriam, don't you remember? I have to go to DC to start school. Remember FBI?"

"Ja, I do remember. I do see about FBI on the television. They are very important police for America. It is an important job. Am I right?"

"Yes, you are right, Miriam."

"But Paul, I see on the television the FBI is in New York City. Are you going to leave me?" Miriam is fighting back the tears.

"No! Miriam, I'm not going to leave you. I'm only going for training. Remember?"

"Ja, I remember, you will be home soon. I'm so proud of you." Miriam closes her eyes.

As Miriam sleeps, Paul decides to check out the fridge and pantry for something to fix for lunch. He chooses crusty bread and chicken soup. He takes a frozen block of soup from the freezer and sets it in a pot to defrost. As Paul turns, he knocks a pot off the kitchen counter. The clatter wakes Miriam from her sleep.

"Paul?"

"Yes, I'm here." Paul goes to Miriam. He pulls the armchair closer to the couch.

"I am going to find Vicky. Eliakim and Sandalphon will help me. We will bring her home."

"I know, but maybe you should rest up a little first. That's a lot to do with only a crow and a statue." Paul tucks the blanket and smiles; he figures he can get a little rise from Miriam. It will be good for her. "He's a raven," Miriam grumbles. "I'll ask Gracie to come." Miriam gives as good as she gets.

Paul sits in the armchair and leafs through the glamor magazines. "Maybe I'll ask Gracie to come." He chuckles. Miriam begins to stir, she gently moans. He leans over and Miriam opens her eyes.

"It's you, Paul."

"Of course, it is. It will always be." Paul gently kisses Miriam.

"You were moaning in your sleep. Are you hurting?"

"No, I have been having the same bad dream over and over. Each time, I dream this certain dream there is something new about it."

"Do you mean like a continuing story?"

"Ja, good, Paul, that is exactly what I mean." Miriam is pleased that Paul gave her the words to clear up a bit of her bad dream. "A continuing dream. Very good, thank you. Now I know."

"What is this bad continuing dream about?" Paul asks.

"I dream that I am in a forest with Sandalphon. Four men bring a woman into the forest. The men are in black robes the woman is in a purple robe. They stand around a large flat stone alter on the ground. Sandalphon is perched in a tree above them. Then the woman is forced to lie on the stone alter. Sandalphon flies down from the tree to the woman. When he touches the ground, he becomes an enormous raven towering over the robed men. Then Saldalphon lifts the woman from the alter with his talons and flies away with her. When I wake from the dream, there is always a black feather on the floor."

"Miriam, Doctor Knowles gave you medicine for pain. That's probably why you had a bad dream." Paul calmed her. He will hold the dream and feather conversation another time, with a lucid Miriam.

"No, not only dreams of now, but also from before, but now the dream is the same but different."

Paul took Miriam's hand and kissed her fingertips. "Don't worry, Miriam. It was only a dream."

"I know, Paul. I love you."

"I love you too. Now, tell me your same but different part of the dream." He supposes this is as lucid a Miriam that he's going to get today and now he must do his best to comfort her.

"You think I'm cuckoo, don't you?" Miriam exaggerates a pout.

"No, I think you're feeling better, but loopy. Tell me the dream." Paul whispers, he catches a stray lock of Miriam's hair and gently twists it between his fingers.

"Now, I only dreamed about the woman who was lying on the stone. She came to me in my dream. She said her name is Lizzie and asked me to help her. Then I awoke."

"Were you frightened?

"No, I was sad because I did not know how to help her." Miriam closes her eyes, as tears escape.

Deep in thought, Paul, lowers his head. There on the floor he sees a black feather just as Miriam had foretold. Paul picked up the feather and put it in his pocket. Miriam stirs.

"Miriam?"

"Yes, Paul?"

"Will you write all of these dreams down? If you do, when I come home for Thanksgiving, we can talk about them."

Miriam sits up and relaxes against the back of the couch. "Thank you, Paul."

"For what?"

"For listening." Miriam struggles to stay awake.

"Yeah, and I didn't even roll my eyes." Paul gathers Miriam close.

"Did you want to?"

"Certainly not! Well, maybe a little bit." Paul teases.

"Ja? Maybe I need another boyfriend." Miriam closes her eyes.

"Oh, ja?" "Well, sorry girl, you're stuck with me."

"Pinky swear." Miriam lifted her pinky as sleep again took Miriam into the never-ending saga of a deep green forest, a woman and a raven. Paul gently twists his pinky around Miriam's and whispers.

"Pinky swear."

The doorbell sounds. Rocky jumps from the couch, runs to the door, and begins turning circles, clearly signaling for one of her people to open the door and allow her friend to enter the den.

"Okay, Rocky, I get it, that must be Mike." Paul opens the door. Rocky turns a few more circles then flops on the floor and rolls over for a belly rub.

"Good girl, Rocky." Mike gives her a quick belly rub. With which she is totally satisfied and returns to her spot on the couch.

"Hey bro, how's your girl?" Mike greets Paul.

"She's all right a little loopy, like Knowles said, but she'll come out of it."

"That's good. Is lunch ready? I'm starved."

"Almost ready." Paul and Mike tiptoe to the kitchen and finish preparing lunch.

~

"This is a great lunch Paul." Mike keeps his eyes on Miriam.

"Thanks, bro," Paul is also closely watching her.

Miriam spreads a large gob of jelly over her toast. Most of it falls on to her blouse, but she is unconcerned. She spoons another gob onto her toast. As Miriam lifts the gooey bread to her mouth, the jelly falls from the toast on to her hand. Miriam studies her hand; the sticky jelly poses a difficult challenge. She gingerly turns her hand and licks the confusing mess away. A few bites and a bit more jelly later, with a self-satisfied grin, she announces that she is finished with lunch. She leans back in her chair and her eyes close.

Mike whispers, "Is she sleeping?" Paul, whispers a reply. "Not sure." And shrugs.

"Not sleeping. Quit whispering." Miriam mumbles. "I made the soup. He just toasted the bread."

"She's tellin' the truth." Paul chuckles, "You should see all the soup she has squirreled away in that freezer. Shameful, little soup hoarder." Paul slurps a spoonful of soup for drama. "Too bad there's no dumplings." Paul is quite aware of Miriam's love of dumplings and that a perceived dumpling error pushes the envelope a bit. He expects a dispute.

"If you wanted dumplings, you should have chosen the pack marked with D." Miriam can ignore most of Paul's foolishness, but an accusation of a dumpling misstep is above the pale. "D for dumplin…cup!" Miriam hiccups.

"I'll clear the table. I have your next dose of meds ready, Miriam." Paul clears the table; Miriam swallows the pills. The guys get down to business. Miriam hiccups.

Mike lays the pictures out in piles and explains to Paul and Miriam that these pictures were taken at the carousel the night of the Mother Goose murder. Miriam hiccups and holds her breath.

"I know this is a lot of pictures, but I feel like I don't have a lot of time. I am chasing a serial killer and I need help, your help. I'm asking you because I know I can trust you."

"What are we looking for Mike?" Paul is anxious to get started.

"I don't know Paul. All I know is that the victim got a large bouquet of roses." Mike picks up the card. Miriam hiccups, she holds her breath again. Mike and Paul stop to watch.

"This is the card that came with the bouquet."

Mike shows Paul the card. "See, the words 'from cares be free'. "These words that are written on the card, are similar to the words that the mother goose murderer sent in a letter, and the words carved into the latest victim. If we can get information on who sent the roses, we might finally be on to something." Miriam frantically gasps for breath. Paul and Mike turn, their attention is now fixed on Miriam. She looks to Paul and then to Mike. She takes a larger-than-life breath and exhales.

"See. No more hiccups." Miriam smiles triumphantly.

"So maybe we might see the flowers being delivered." Mike continues his thought.

"Yeah no hiccups, good, Miriam." Paul smiles. "Even if we just see the florist's delivery van; we can get a name."

"Got it. Give me my stack of pictures. Do you want to help me look through my stack, Miriam, or do you want to lie back down?" Paul catches Mike's eye and discreetly motions toward Miriam whose eyes have a doll-like glass to them.

"How many pain pills did you give her?" Mike whispers.

"Just her dose, I think she should lay down." Paul whispers.

"No, I said quit whispering. I want to help you Paul, h-e-l-p." Miriam smiles. Paul grimaces and pulls Miriam's chair closer to him. Paul and Mike begin to study the photos. Paul shuffles through the photos while Miriam voices her excitement with ooohs and awwws and repeated comments on what a fun party it appears to have been. It seems that she is totally not understanding the task at hand when unexpectedly she takes the pictures from Paul.

"Wait! I need to see this." She pulls a photo out of the pile and shows it to Paul.

"Look at that, that man has a beautiful silver tattoo on his hand." She gives the photo back to Paul.

"Well, Miriam, I don't see a tattoo." Miriam grabs the photo again and insists that man at the bar has a silver tattoo on his hand, then gives it back to Paul. Paul studies it for another few moments.

"I just don't see it." He hands it to Mike. Mike shakes his head and leans toward Paul and whispers,

I don't see it either. Are you sure she's okay?" Mike whispers and returns to studying the picture.

"Alright, guys go-ahead whisper, geeze. It's an expression." "Miriam, you've met Ted the computer guy, haven't you?" Mike asks.

"Yes, a few times." Miriam is checking out her fingernails.

"How do you like this color, Paul?" She puts her hand up to Paul's face, palm first. Paul gently turns her hand and looks at her nails.

"It's beautiful." Paul kisses Miriam's fingertips and returns to looking at the pictures.

"Come on, guys, pay attention." Mike hands the picture back to Miriam.

"Do you think this is Ted?"

"Ja, it looks like him, but Ted doesn't have a tattoo."

"No, he doesn't." Mike's befuddled.

"So, it can't be Ted. Ted, that's funny, ja?" Miriam giggles until she snorts.

"Dude, really, how many pain pills did you give her?" Mike worries, but also wonders why all the amusement about Ted.

"Just one dose, I swear, but she is really loopy, right?

"Yeah dude, more than usual."

"Paul, do you know someone named Lizzy?" Miriam asks between giggles and snorts.

"No, I don't," he answers.

"Neither do I. I will ask Vicky when she comes home." Miriam gives Paul an exaggerated wink.

"Yes, I know. When Vicky comes home, you can ask her." Paul pacifies Miriam, "Come on, girl. I think it's time for you to lie back down." Paul helps Miriam to the couch. She is asleep before her head hit the pillow.

"Is she okay?" Mike asks again.

"Yeah, I guess Knowles was right. She is pretty of out of it today. Anyway, the home nurse will know what's up. She's supposed to be here this afternoon." Mike and Paul sort through the rest of the photos while Miriam sleeps.

"Paul?" Mike begins.

"Yeah, bro?"

"I'm a mess about Vicky. I feel so helpless." Mike admits. "I'm frozen with fear; I can't do anything because I don't want to do the wrong thing."

"I know how hard this is, Mike, just with the mother goose alone, you've got plenty on your plate and now with Vicky's kidnapping. It's more than anyone can handle. Just remember, they took Vicky for a reason. They want something. She is alive because she is of no value to them otherwise. Soon they will contact you and once they reach out, we will deal with them. As sure as I am sitting here with you, I know that we will get Vicky back. "Trust me on this one, bro. I got the word."

"Thanks Paul, it's good to have someone to sound off to, you know." Just then, the doorbell rings. Mike checks his watch. "Looks like it's about time to get you to the airport."

"I guess it is. That's probably the home nurse now. She'll be staying with Miriam for a few days." Paul invites her in.

"Hello, my name is Scarlet Indigo." The nurse introduces herself to Mike and Paul and a very curious Rocky.

"Hi, Scarlet. I sure am glad you're here, thanks for coming. That's Miriam asleep on the couch." Paul motions toward the couch.

"She's been out of it most of the day." Paul's nervous concern was on display.

"That sounds pretty normal." Scarlet smiles, her calm manner sets Paul at ease. "Don't worry about a thing. Doctor Knowles has acquainted me with Ms. Davidson's condition. We will get along very well. Also, I understand that you have a flight to catch." Scarlet seems to be a pleasant young woman.

"Yes, Scarlet, I'm sure you and Miriam will get along just fine. Now, I have to go catch that plane. Thank you again for coming. We better hit the road Mike."

"Gotcha. Let's roll." Paul and Mike say their goodbyes and hurry out the door. They throw Paul's luggage into the trunk of Mike's car and are off to Tampa International.

❧

The dawn broke. Gracie, with Sandalphon on her shoulder, has stood watch over Miriam the entire night. Scarlet slept soundly on the couch. Gracie had been pulled from her realm into Miriam's and Vicky's reality in the parking garage. She had witnessed the entire kidnapping. She had followed Miriam to the hospital. Satisfied that Miriam was safe in Paul's watch, she searched for Vicky and had finally found her, drugged and unconscious, bound in the corner of an abandoned building. Gracie gently tried to wake Miriam.

"Miriam, hon, can you wake up now?" Gracie sits on the edge of Miriam's bed. Miriam opens her eyes.

"Gracie, I am glad to see you." Miriam realizes she is no longer on the couch.

"I'm glad to see you too, hon."

"How did I get in my bed?"

"Scarlet, the home nurse, helped you to bed. Paul left you a note on the dresser."

"Gracie, Vicky is gone." Miriam begins to cloud up. She struggles not to cry.

"Don't cry, hon, I know where she is. I saw her."

"Gracie! You know where she is?"

"Well, not exactly, but I can go back to her. I know she is in a building somewhere. I came to you as soon as I found her last night. I was so excited I didn't have the where with all just then to figure out where the building is."

"It will be all right. We can go to her now." Miriam quickly sat up. The room spun; she fell back to her pillow.

"Hon, I heard Doctor Knowles tell you that you have to take it easy for a few days. Just lie back, I will keep an eye on Vicky."

"I didn't tell Doctor Knowles how dizzy I am. I knew if I did, he would have kept me even longer in the hospital. I want you to go to Vicky and take Eliakim. He can stand in the other realm and guard her until I can get there. Gracie, go now to Vicky, I will get Eliakim ready. Come back later and he will go with you." Miriam closes her eyes, Gracie vanishes.

❧

The doorbell rings. "Come in." Scarlet welcomes Mike.

"Good morning, Scarlet. How's the patient?"

"She's doing well. I just got off the phone with Doctor Knowles. I gave him her update. He says everything sounds good." She returns to putting out Miriam's morning meds.

"Thanks, Scarlet." Mike heads to the kitchen. Rocky leaps from Miriam's bed and bounds to the kitchen. Rocky stands poised in anticipation. Mike greets Rocky.

"I bet you're hungry. Eh, girl? Want some cheese?" Rocky edged up next to Mike in front of the fridge. "Here you go girl, cheese. Catch." Rocky caught the cheese midair and then settled in on the couch.

"She likes coffee with cream." Miriam shuffles to the kitchen table. Paul's note is in her hand. Mike notices that she is pale and drawn.

"How are you feeling this morning?"

"The nurse checked on me, so did Gracie. Can you make me coffee? I have a terrible headache." Miriam studies the paper she holds in her hand.

"Sure, Miriam, coffee. I got ya covered." Mike wonders about Gracie, who checked on her, but figures that Miriam is still in some sort of altered state. Kind of half-awake due to the drugs Knowles has her on; not to mention the nasty bump on the head. Mike starts the coffee.

"What ya got in your hand, Miriam?" Mike takes two cups from the cabinet.

"A note that Paul left. He's gone to be an important FBI policeman. Do you know that? Rocky likes the kitty cup." Mike brings two cups of coffee to the table, one for Miriam and one Kitty cup coffee for Rocky. Mike sits at the table.

"Yes, I do know that." Mike smiles. "It's a good thing." Mike isn't sure if Miriam needs convincing, so he just casually threw that out for good measure.

"I know, it's very important." Miriam looks at the note. "He says he will be back for Thanksgiving. He says I can visit him in Washington DC sometime."

"That's great, Miriam. So, do you need anything? If not, I'm going to head to the station. Call me if you need me. You have Scarlet here and my cell number if you want anything."

"I will call if I need anything. Don't worry, I will be fine. I will watch TV with Rocky and then I will sleep. I am very tired. Thank you for coming over, Mike. You can come after work if you like."

"Okay, Miriam If I don't get caught late at the station I will come by. Bye now, rest." Mike locks the door as he leaves. Scarlet pours herself a cup of coffee and sits down at the table next to Miriam.

"Good morning, Miriam. We didn't get to talk much earlier this morning. I talked to Doctor Knowles and he's happy with your vitals. Everything looks good, but he says you still need another day of complete bed rest. I will take care of you until you recover, probably only a few days, we'll see. Now, it's been a busy morning for you." Scarlet sips her coffee.

"Ja, busy. Mike is worried about his friend Vicky." Miriam answers, seemingly still in a dream state.

"Yes, I gathered that." Scarlet smiles. "Are you done with your cup?' Scarlet reaches for Miriam's empty cup.

"Yes, I am. Thank you." Scarlet takes Miriam's cup to the sink and returns with her meds.

"Time for your morning meds, then you should rest." She puts the pill cup and a glass of water in front of Miriam. Miriam falls silent. Bewildered, she can only stare at the silver tattoo on Scarlet's hand.

DOUBLE CROSS, DOBLE CRUZ, DOPPIO GIOCO

Mike is at his desk in his office. He has brought his lunch today, a salami sandwich, the very exact sandwich that he brought yesterday. He didn't eat it yesterday because he didn't want to be chewing when 'they' called. It has been four days since Vicky was taken. Four days, and nothing, not a word, nada, zip, zilch, zero. A big fat nothing. Mike slams his sandwich down onto his desk. Mike is impatiently waiting. He knows he has to keep the faith; he knows Paul's advice is right. He knows Vicky is alive and 'they' will contact him. Who the hell are 'they' anyway? Mike put the sandwich back in the desk drawer. It'll still be good tomorrow.

Mike's cell rings. Finally, hope springs eternal.

"De Augustino here."

"Hi, it's Bruce Haywood. Got your message. I can send that CCTV you asked for, of the full week before the show. But if you can hold on for a couple days? We're having a memorial show for joni. I thought you might want to look at that."

"Yes, I would be very interested in seeing that. Thanks, Bruce."

"Sure, I'll send it over soon."

"Thanks, again."

"No problem, have a good day, detective."

"You too." As soon as Mike finishes his call with Bruce his cell phone rings again

"De Augustino here."

"Bring us the boys and drop your investigation of Garnett Cox. If you don't agree, there will be no further contact, and you'll never see the girl again. If you agree, then we give her to you unharmed."

"We need proof of life, or we won't deal." Mike asserts. The caller hangs up. Mike dials the captain,

"Chief, they contacted me."

"I'll be right there. I'll let Ted know."

It took Ted all of six seconds to get to Mike's office. Mike is pacing his small cubicle when the captain arrives.

"Who was it?" Chief asks.

"Pretty sure it's diMarco's guys, heavy accent."

"Did they call your desk or cell?" Ted asks.

"Sorry, Ted, it was my cell. I know you can't trace it."

"But I can try to triangulate it. I might get an approximate area."

"What did they say, Mike?" the captain asks.

"They want the boys we just put in protection, and they want me to drop the investigation into Garnett Cox. So, that tells me Cox is definitely mixed up with diMarco. I told them that we need proof of life, or we won't deal. That's when they hung up."

"Good, they'll get back to you when they figure out how they will give proof of life," the captain says. Then Mike's cell rings.

Mike answers his phone, it's a video text. The video is of Vicky blindfolded. She is tied to a chair in a small room. The brick walls are decorated with graffiti. The only light shines from a line of small windows just below the ceiling. Her hands are bound to a chair and her mouth is taped shut. Someone calls out, "Move your fingers, cracker, so your boyfriend can see." Vicky wiggles her fingers.

"Mike, how do you know it's not a video from four days ago?"

"Look at the time stamp, it's today. She's alive." Mike was overcome, he whispers. "She's alive, alive."

"When they call back, tell them that you need some time to set things up. Ted, if Mike sends you a copy of the video, do you think you can glean anything from it?"

"I'll give it my best, captain. Send it over to me, Mike."

"Doing it right now, Ted."

Ted hurries back to his cubicle.

"Chief, I have some paperwork to do, then I'm going over to the Duetzman's. They might help given Red's situation."

"Good. Keep me posted." The captain shuffles back to his office.

❧

Gracie stands in front of Vicky, she is lifeless. Gracie whispers in her ear, she kisses Vicky's forehead. Vicky moans but does not wake.

Three men are guarding Vicky. They pay little or no attention to her, save for occasionally pushing a damp rag over her nose.

"Aren't you afraid you will overdose her with that stuff you're using on her?" one of the men asks.

"Nah, that stuff is safe enough for a baby."

"Who the hell would chloroform a baby?" the man mumbles. He truly doubts that it really is a harmless exercise. He pulls a rickety old wooden chair up to the old wooden chair he sits in, props his feet upon it and rests his head on the cold graffiti festooned brick wall behind him. The third man walks past his resting cohort and kicks the rickety old chair from beneath the resting guy's feet.

"There's only two chairs in this whole damn place. You think you get both?" He sat in the chair and scrolls through his cell phone.

"Ass." Resting guy leans his head back on to the brick wall.

The other man sits in the corner opposite of where Vicky is tied, he scowls. He stretches his legs and positions himself so he can keep a wary eye on the jokers he has been paired with.

"You two should just shut the hell up." Wary eye snarls.

"Make me." Cell phone dude grumbles.

"What are you, twelve? You're an idiot." Wary eye mocks phone dude. "HEY!" Wary eye calls over to the resting guy. "Bet you a twenty, the next sentence out his mouth is, I'm rubber, you're glue." Wary eye and resting guy have a good laugh at cell phone dude's expense. "Dude, you got any of that MD20 left?" Wary eye asks phone guy.

"No, drink your own." Phone dude isn't sharing even though he still has three bottles of MD left from when diMarco pulled him and the other two off the street.

"I already drank it. This is shit." Wary eye moans. He really needs a drink.

"It's better than the street." Resting guy closes his eyes.

Gracie has heard enough from these rascals. She begins her search for some indication of where this building is exactly. She wanders through the building. It is a big empty nothing except for empty crates and stacks of long forgotten paper labels. She studies a label. Golden Girl Oranges.

"These are the packing labels for the crates…orange crates. This is an old packing house." Packing oranges, that is a most important industry in Kumquat. Gracie has a hunch that she discovered the location of the building. One last look around and she will be certain. All at once,

Gracie stands on the highest peak of the roof of a massive tin building. Old smokestacks and rickety old fire escapes honeycomb the outside of the building. Gracie looks down at the street. She is standing on the roof of the old Kumquat packing house.

"I have to tell Miriam." Gracie instantly stands in Vicky's living room. Miriam is flipping through the channels.

"Miriam!" Gracie raises her voice to get Miriam's attention.

"AHH!" Miriam shrieks. "Oh, Gracie, sorry, you startled me."

"Hon, I know where Vicky is. I figured it out."

"Where is she? How do you know?"

"It was the labels. Golden Girl Oranges. She's in Kumquat." Gracie grins.

"Kumquat? How can you be sure?"

"I stood on the roof. It's an abandoned packing house, right at the edge of town."

"You stood on the roof?"

"Yes, hon, don't worry I couldn't have fallen to my death?"

"Ja, I guess not."

"That's how I made sure where I was. I'm sure now. We can get Vicky."

"I feel like I need a day more to rest. I must be certain that I am ready. Eliakim is ready to go with you. He will stay there in the other realm. No one will see him, but he will be guarding Vicky until I get there."

"So, you don't think we can go get her right away." Gracie is disappointed.

"I am afraid not yet. I think the medicine that I am taking causes me not to think right sometimes. The fog must clear from my mind, then I will be ready. Until then, it will be you and Eliakim. Have you ever seen a silver tattoo, Gracie?" Miriam's mind again wanders.

"I can't say that I've seen a silver tattoo. You get some rest. I will take care of Vicky."

"Good, Gracie. I know you can do it. Eliakim is in the other realm. He will obey, just call him to follow you and give him instruction when you get back to Vicky."

"I'm standin' on go. But wait, I'm not goin' yet. I have to tell you what was so important that I was going to tell you the day y'all were going to the mall."

"What is it, Gracie?"

"Well, hon, if you remember I was tracking Saul down. I caught up with him and hitched a ride along to the Duetzman's place. His sister Brenda was there. They had a terrible fight. I thought, there was gonna be bloodshed, for sure. She said she knows that he and Vicente had Victor killed. Then Saul said he knows she had Sauly killed. Then she said she is going to take over everything."

"I think we should watch Saul and Vicente."

'I think so too, hon."

"You should probably keep watch on Brenda too." Miriam added.

"Will do, boss."

"I'm going to sleep now. Take Eliakim with you."

"Sure will. Come on, Eliakim, let's go." Gracie and Eliakim disappear. Miriam covers her head and sleeps.

∾

"Hey, Tom, this is Saul Duetzman. Sorry to call this early but I need Widget to come and turn Red's bracelet back on asap. Tell him there will be an extra G in it for him if he gets here early today. Thanks, Tom." Saul leaves the message on Tom's machine. Now, he hopes for the best. The best being Widget will get there and turn the bracelet back on before Mike comes snooping around and everything goes south. Saul is truly hoping for the best. Realistically, though Saul knows that with Widget things can go either way. Saul wanders into the kitchen. Red sits at the bar eating a bowl of fruit loops.

"That crap is going to kill you." Saul grumbles.

"Yeah, if your dumb assness doesn't kill me first." Red picks up the bowl and drinks the sweet milk.

"You're disgusting." Saul digs through the fridge for something to eat.

"Whatcha looking for?" Red wipes his mouth with the back of his hand.

"Geeze, Pops, where's the cook?"

"I fired her."

"Why the hell did you do that?"

"I didn't like her. She hid my fruit loops."

"Stupid," Saul whispers. He takes out a half pound of bacon, six eggs, and a package of Velveeta cheese from the fridge.

"What are you making?"

"I'm making an omelet."

"Good, be sure to wash it down with a big glass of whole milk and don't forget the toast and butter." Red laughs and sets his bowl in the sink.

"I'm going up to my room. Don't forget to get that wizard guy to come and take care of this mess." Red lifts his pajama leg and points to his ankle bracelet. "Dumbass." Red starts up the stairs.

"Already taken care of. He'll be here soon. Stupid," Saul whispers. He puts his bread in the toaster, takes the butter out of the fridge to soften, and pours himself a big glass of whole milk, and then enjoys his breakfast.

❧

"Mr. Duetzman, that little man is here again, says he has an appointment."

"It's okay, Nebo, let him in." Saul yells up to his father to come downstairs.

"Are you sure, Mr. Duetzman?" Nebo questions.

"Damn it, Nebo, just let him into the den." Nebo shows Widget in.

"Top of the morning to you, laddie, and to you, mister. Let's get right to this. I got no time to waste." Widget prattles as he is unpacking his bag.

"What's your hurry, Widget?" Red asks.

"I'm working on my costume for the memorial show at The Carousel. I'm on a deadline. Got to hurry, got to hurry."

"You go to the shows at The Carousel?" Saul asks.

"Indeed, I do. I do indeed. Yes, yes, I do. Occasionally." Widget talks as he works. Red takes a seat in the armchair closest to Widget and leans closer.

"What is your costume, Widget?" Red just had to delve into this conversation.

"I'm going to be a wee fairy. I will dance The Ring of the Nibelung." Widget didn't look up from his frantic computer work. Red is more than amused and stifling a giant hee haw.

"Do you want the cat?" Saul asks.

"Can she dance?" Widgets fingers fly across the computer keys. "Does she have her own costume. It's extra if I have to make her costume too." Widget cackles.

"No costume. For the computer chip."

Widget looks at Saul as if he is a total idiot. "Laddie, this is the precise part. It must be done with the utmost of timing. The first time was simple, nothing to it. Smoke and mirrors. Don't bother me with trifles." Widget hit two keys simultaneously and Red's bracelet starts blinking.

"Give me that little pretty now. I will be needing her collar."

"Thank you, laddie, quite the gentleman you are." Widget took the cat from Saul. "And you've been a bonnie lass. Now, I'll be happy to take that twenty-one thousand." Widget packs his tools into his bag. He strokes the cat and unfastens her collar. He slips it into his bag.

"Twenty-one? Is that what we agreed on? Christ on a cracker! Twenty-one G's to turn the damn thing back on?" Red complains.

"Aye, and so it is. If that isn't suitable to you, I will gladly turn that pretty bauble back off, then that will make the grand total of forty-two thousand if you please to have it turned on again sir…" Widget is interrupted.

"Twenty-one thousand is fine. Thank you. I appreciate what you did here. Widget." Saul pays Widget.

"Sure, and aren't you the grandee young, Mr. Duetzman." Widget tips his hat and continues his goodbye. "May the road rise up to meet you, and may you be in heaven for a day before the devil even knows you're dead." Widget stuffs the twenty-one Gs' into his bag. He heaves the bag over his shoulder and dances an Irish jig to the door, cackling the entire way.

"Where the hell do you think he's going?" Red is feeling rather surly and not the least bit appreciative.

"I don't know, Pop. I guess he's probably going to hang out with his friend Tom." Saul really has no idea about Widget's coming or goings, neither is he interested in a discussion with his father of such matters.

"I'll be at my desk until lunch. Don't disturb me." Saul retires to his den and locks the door.

~

Mike stares at the envelope on his desk. He dreads the news it carries. He opens the envelope and reads the verse.

Mistress Mary quite contrary.

How does your garden grow?

Mike is holding the latest Mother Goose message in his hand. Ted taps at his door.

"Mike, have you got a minute?"

"Sure, Ted, what's up?"

"I triangulated that call, but they have it pinging off multiple towers. Somebody's good at what they do. Anyway, I couldn't pin them down. Sorry Mike. Also, I told you I'd let you know if I noticed another blip on Duetzman's bracelet and sure enough there was one this morning."

"I have to go over there anyway and persuade Duetzman to help with Vicky." Mike doesn't look up.

"Are you all right, Mike?"

"Yeah, sure, Ted. I just got another letter from the goose. Come in, please sit."

"You have been through the ringer lately. Sorry, Mike."

"It's been four days, but it seems like forever."

"What about the Mother Goose? Are you getting anywhere with that?"

"The pics that the owner brought from the night of the murder looked pretty wild, but innocent enough. The owner says that there was nothing unusual. Anyway, I'm going over the pictures of the crowd again." Mike shuffles through the pictures as he talks.

"That could turn up something. Are the pictures of good quality?"

"Passable enough to put through facial recognition."

"Really? I'd like to look at them if I may. I might be able to clear them up. I'm pretty good on the computer, you know." Ted perks up.

"Yeah, that would be okay. I'll let you take a look when I get done with them. Bruce, the owner, invited me to come to a memorial show for the victim. He says everyone is welcome. Have you ever been to a drag show, Ted?"

"No, I don't really have the time for clubs. Have you been?"

"Sure, it's great fun. I had a friend in college who is gay. We went a few times. Sorry, you don't have time. I was going to say we should go check the memorial out."

"A professional, check it out? Yes, I see." Ted considers Mike's proposal.

"Yeah, Ted, professional."

"I'll try to make time, I guess." Ted smiles

"Great, we'll plan it." Mike has his reason for asking Ted to go with him to the drag show. He is a little surprised that Ted agreed to accompany him. Maybe his suspicions are unfounded, he reasons.

"I have to get to my cubicle, back to the grind, you know." Ted makes a hasty retreat. Mikes cell rings.

"De Augustino here."

"De Augustino, you have forty-eight hours to get it in gear. You bring us the kids and drop the investigation of Cox, or the deal is off. 48 hours, De Augustino. We'll meet in 48 hours at the old barracks on Lois Avenue in Drew Park. Bring the kids." The line goes dead. Mike grabs his car keys and heads to the Duetzman's place. Oddly enough, Red Duetzman now seems to be his only hope to save Vicky.

❧

Saul sits at the kitchen bar, peacefully eating his lunch. The housekeeper comes in.

"Mr. Duetzman, Mike De Augustino is here," she announces. Saul puts his fork down and quickly gulps a mouthful of water. Saul coughs frantically. The housekeeper slaps his back; he slaps at her hand.

"I'm not choking. I'm f-ing drowning. Leave me, take him in to the den." Saul gets himself together and greets Mike.

"Hey Mike, have a seat. What's on your mind?"

"I need to see your father."

"Sure, Mike."

Saul takes out his cell phone and calls Red. "Pops, Mike's here. Come down he wants to see you."

"He'll be right down. Would you like something to drink?"

"No thanks, Saul. I'm fine."

Saul pours himself a glass of scotch. "Are you sure? It's single malt."

"No, I'm on duty, Thanks anyway." Mike states the obvious. Saul aggravates the crap out of Mike, he always has. Even as a kid Saul was a total ass.

"Mike, what's up? Saul, did you offer Mike a drink?" Red pours a generous drink for himself.

"He's working, Dad."

"Well, how can I help you, Mike?"

"First, I need to look at your ankle bracelet. There's been some slight static on it, so I just need to check. Probably nothing to worry about but I have to check."

"Do you need a search warrant for this?" Red laughs and lifts his pant leg. The bracelet is blinking. Mike examines it for any signs that it has been tampered with, there are none.

"Looks good, Red. Now, we need to talk." Mike returns to his chair. Saul and Red take the two remaining chairs in the conversation area.

"Listen, it's no secret that I've gone over all the papers that Victor left me. Those papers tell me that your family and Vicente's family have a close relationship. You understand that, don't you?"

"Yeah, we know that you know all about the business," Red admits.

"What I don't know, or care about, is what your relationship with Vicente is now. Understand?"

"Yeah, Mike, what's your point?" Red wants the bottom line. "Is that what you came all the way over here for?"

"It's six blocks from the station, Red. What'd you mean all the way?"

"You got somethin' else on your mind?" Red grins.

"Yeah, I want to know what you know about Joe, El diMarco and Garnet Cox's involvement in the kidnapping."

"What are you talking about, Mike? We know nothin' about any kidnapping. You know somethin,' about a kidnapping, Saul?"

"No, Pop, I don't."

"I'm going to give ya'll the benefit of the doubt, just because I'm a nice guy, you know?" Red and Saul certainly did not know that, nor did they in the least believe it. Mike continues, "I know that Vicente is planning a merger with El diMarco, and I know that your man, Garnett Cox, is involved with El diMarco. Now, I'm giving you two a big break because I don't even want to know how you're involved in that cluster fuck. Got me, Red?"

"Come on, Mike, cut the crap. Give it to us straight." Red empties his glass with one big gulp.

"This is it, Red. I got a call from diMarco's guy, he wants a trade." Mike is spoon feeding them the details. Hoping that they trip up with their story.

"What are you talkin' about? Get to it, cut bait or fish, Mike." Red demands.

"They snatched Vicky and want to trade her for two of their boys that we have."

"Someone snatched that cute blond cop you go around with? Saul, you know anything about this cop kidnapping?"

"No, not a thing, I swear." Saul crosses his heart.

"What do you want, Mike?"

"I want Vicky returned unhurt."

"You got a plan?" Red questions.

"Are you prepared to help the department get Vicky away from diMarco, Red?"

"If we can help, we will. Not saying that I know anything but maybe I can help you if it helps me. I'd hate to see that girl hurt, you know that, Mike." And Mike didn't know that in the least, but he will have to deal with the Duetzman's. Mike hates that he has to make a deal with Red; however, he will deal with the devil to get Vicky back safe. He dials the captain.

"Chief, I'm talking with Red. Can we help him if he helps us?" Mike listens for a few moments.

"Yeah, chief, okay. I'll work something out." Mike put his phone back in his pocket.

"Chief says if we get good information about Vicky's whereabouts, number of guards, and weapons. He will put in a good word for you. Do you understand? He can't get you let off, but maybe you'll get leniency. Understand?"

"Yeah, I get it." Red looks at Saul. Saul nods.

"What do you want us to do?"

"Saul," Mike begins, "I know that you have been the kingpin lately dealing with this merger. So, I want you to go to Vicente and tell him that I know everything. If he questions, say we have an informant. Tell him I keep the boys, but I drop the investigation of Cox. In exchange I get Vicky, and everyone walks away. Make an exchange date. Go to Vicente today. Got it?"

"Yeah, Mike, we got it, but why would they agree to this?"

"Because the FBI is coming in on this; and they don't play around with cop kidnapping."

"That's a dirty shame snatching a girl." Red shakes his head and pours himself another strong scotch.

"We have forty-eight hours to turn the boys over and drop our investigation on Cox."

"Garnett Cox." Red snarls.

Saul and Red trade glances. Mike continues.

"The department is all out to find Vicky. We know it's diMarco who took her, we know Cox is involved. We just don't know where she is, but when we find out, El diMarco and Cox will be done for. Remember if you can get anything out of Vicente, the department is willing to work with you. That will be to your benefit all the way around. Don't forget that El diMarco gave us forty-eight hours to turn the boys over. So, you have limited time to get the information to Vicente and back to us."

"I tell you the honest truth when I say we don't know nothin' about the girl, but we do know it's true that Cox and El diMarco are planning a war. We don't want nothin' like that. I think Saul can talk to Joe. Is that so, Saul?"

"Yes, that's so, Pops."

"Before I go, I want you to see this video from El diMarco." Mike opens his phone and shows Saul the video. "Do you recognize this place?"

"Yeah, that's one of our warehouses out in Pasco County, it's abandoned."

"I need the address."

"You gonna raid the place?" Saul scribbles the address on a scrap of paper and gives it to Mike.

"Not until you have El diMarco sidetracked. A raid will be too risky for Vicky. I just need to know where it is for now so we can watch it." Mike folds the paper and sticks it in his pocket.

"You work something out with Joe. Let me know as soon as you talk to him. I have to get back to the station now." Mike leaves Saul and Red to their business.

∾

"Thanks for seeing me, Joe.

"Sure, Saul. It sounded pretty important when you called. How come your father didn't come?"

"It's private between us, you know."

"Yeah, come on in. Saul, we'll talk." Joe escorts Saul into his study. "Would you like a drink Saul?"

"Scotch would be good. thanks."

"There you go, cin-cin." Joe hands Saul a good measure of Scotch and toasts. "What's this about, Saul?"

"Listen, Joe, I have to tell you diMarco is full of shit. He doesn't want a merger he wants war."

"What are you talkin' about? He is all for a merger."

"No, he wants to take over all the businesses. I'm tellin' you, Joe, he hates Pop and wants war with him."

"Are you lying to me, Saul? I've known you from a child, you were always a sneak."

"No, Joe, this is the truth, on my mother's grave it is. God rest her soul." Saul crosses himself. "I did lie though when I said dad killed Angelina."

"Why did you lie about that, Saul?"

"I lied to save myself because I knew diMarco would slit my throat just to start a war with Pop. I had to give him something. It was a lie that my father killed Angelina. El diMarco knew it was a lie because he had his wife killed himself, but he couldn't argue that dad didn't do it. What he doesn't know is that I know he did it. I never intended to give him my father."

"Why the hell did he kill his wife?"

"El diMarco had his wife killed because he found out that she was running around on him, with fat legs, Billy Cox." Saul had to tell the whole story to Joe to protect himself and his dad. Saul needs Joe to be agreeable.

"Fat legs? She was cheating with fat legs?" Vicente shakes his head.

"Go figure, fat legs, huh? How do you know this?" Vicente is very interested in Saul's source. Saul continues.

"I was going to have Angelina taken care of myself because I was so mad about El diMarco burning our warehouses. Dad told me not to, but I was going to anyway. I went to Billy fat legs and proposed the hit to him. He refused, which really surprised me. Then he told me that he was fooling around with her. That was a real shock, I'll tell you.

Anyway, El diMarco's men hit Angelina, and the same night they hit fat legs, but he survived. That's how I know El diMarco killed Angelina. I don't know how he knew about Angelina and Billy, but he sure did. He killed Sauley because he knew that Sauley worked for you and Pop, and I think he killed your Cristina for no reason at all. He just wants war."

"If this is all true, there will be war. But tell me, how do you know El diMarco wants war?"

"One of our guys overheard my sister Brenda and Cox talking out by the pool the other night. Don't you see, Joe? El diMarco thinks that he and Cox are taking over, but Cox is working with Brenda. They're planning to get rid of El diMarco after he gets rid of us and takes our business. Also, Mike's undercover guy knows, and he has been talking to him about us. Mike came to the house to question us because he got a video from the kidnappers that shows Vicky tied up in our warehouse. You know he came to show Pops the video because we own most of the warehouses around here and sure enough it's one of ours. Then Mike says he's supposed to do an exchange, Vicky for the kids, at the old barracks in Drew Park. El diMarco knows you own the barracks Joe, and he knows we own the warehouse. He's trying to throw suspicion on us for this kidnapping. Mike threatens that FBI is going to finish whoever is involved in this kidnapping. Joe, don't you see? It's a double-double-cross."

"Brenda, your sister, is involved with Cox? When did she get with Cox?"

"I don't know when, but I suspect she's been scheming with him for a while."

"What's the plan, Saul?"

"I think you should tell El diMarco that he hasn't thought this kidnapping through. Tell him he will get Red at the merger. Tell him we can take care of the boys in protection, no problem. Then tell El diMarco that the FBI is on him, and they will finish us all because of his actions, and tell him to give up Vicky. If he doesn't, the FBI comes after all of us since he has implicated us all with the warehouse and barracks. Tell him to move Vicky to one of his safe places soon because the police will raid the warehouse. Say that if he acts now, the warehouse will be empty when the cops get there."

"Good plan Saul, then we inform the cops where she is. Then they find the girl at El diMarco's place and it's all on him and Cox." Joe is very satisfied with a triple cross. Joe pulls two Have-a-Tampa's from his cigar box. Joe and Saul light up and take a deep puff.

"Okay, Joe, you talk to El diMarco. I'll spin it to Mike."

"All right, Saul, be smart."

"Always." Saul left Joe quite pleased. He dials Mike.

"Hey, Mike, are you still at the station? Great, can I come by?"

"Good, I'll be there soon."

~

"Joe dials El diMarco."

"You got plans tonight, George?"

"No, Joe, I have nothing planed."

"Good, we have to talk."

"Talk, my friend."

"Well, George, I just got word that you better get your girl out of Duetzman's warehouse. The FBI is on the case, and it looks like there is going to be a big raid there tomorrow."

"How do you know this, Joe?"

"Ha, you doubt me? That's okay. Do you know how long I've had Tampa in my pocket?"

"No, Joe, I don't."

"Well, neither does Tampa." Joe laughs. "This is just a courtesy call, one gentleman to another. Trust me or don't, but I tell you, there will be a raid on that warehouse sometime tomorrow."

"You've never steered me wrong, Joe, I'll get her out tonight."

"You're right, George, I never steer you wrong. Now I'm going to save your life, so you listen, or you pay the price. You have brought the FBI down on yourself, and have implicated me, my family, and my friends. That was a big mistake."

"I don't understand, Joe."

"I will break it down for you. You've made three big mistakes, big mistakes. Snatching that girl cop was your first big mistake. Then you stashed her in my good friend, Red's, warehouse. That was your second big mistake. Then you involve me and my property in Drew Park in your kidnap scheme. That's you're third big mistake. Now, George, I understand that you don't know how we take care of business here in this country. You see, we have a saying here 'it's three strikes and you're out'.

But I'm giving you a chance because I like you. I really do, George. I don't want to strike you out, but I'll have to if you don't right these big mistakes."

"How can I satisfy your anger? I want to make it right. Joe, tell me what I can do."

"Give it all up now. We'll do the merger like we talked, and everything is good."

"Yes, Joe, that's what I want and what I will do."

"One last thing, George, I ask you this kindness. Tell me what you know about my Christina's death?"

"Joe, I swear on my eyes, I do not know. But I have heard of the type of murder they speak of. It was when I was a child in Mexico. Stories of, like you Americans say, the Boogeyman."

"Boogeyman? Okay, George, whatever you say. Get that girl out of the warehouse or you'll hang. FBI don't play." Joe hangs up. "Lying piece of crap." he whispers.

❧

"Rise and shine, hon."

"I'm awake, Gracie."

"Good, it's time you get up and start feeling better. Anyway, I have something to tell you."

"I do feel better today, Gracie." Miriam buries her head in her pillow.

"How did Eliakim do last night?"

"He was fine. I had him run around and scare the daylights out of those rascals."

"Gracie! That is not what you were supposed to do." Miriam sits up and swings her feet to the floor.

"I know. I didn't do that. I just said that because I want to get you outta bed. Since you're up now, I want to tell you something, but first, I want to go on a road trip."

"Where do you want to go?" Miriam is pulling clothes out of her dresser drawers. She settles on jeans, a tank top, and a light sweater.

"Just to Kumquat. That's all." Gracie smiles.

"Alright, I'm ready. We can go to your house."

"That's close enough."

"I'll call a taxi. I'm not ready to drive yet." Miriam takes her cell phone out of her pocket.

"We can just step over. It would be good for you." Gracie put her hand over Miriam's phone.

"I can see through your hand, you know, Gracie."

"Yeah, but not very good."

Miriam sighs, takes a deep breath, and then sighs again. "I don't know what to do, Gracie. Vicky's not here. Paul has gone to the FBI, and Michael is working really hard to find Vicky and I need to help." Miriam hangs her head and looks into her unhappy thoughts.

"Hon, you can do this. You're a strong woman." Gracie chastises.

"You have had more things pass through your life in the short time of your existence than most have in their complete life. Hon, this is not the last and most probably not the worst thing that will come to pass before it all ends. It is what it is, and what it will be is what it will be. Now, pull up your big girl panties and let's step to Kumquat. I got fish to fry."

Miriam raises her hand. "Sandalphon," she whispers. He flies to her. They vanish. In a second, Gracie, Miriam, and Sandalphon stand in the dusty old building. Miriam turns to Gracie.

"How did we get here?" I thought we were going to your house." Miriam looks suspiciously at Gracie.

"Well, this is where I want to go. Vicky is here."

"I want to see her." Miriam and Gracie immediately are standing in a room next to Eliakim. The men guarding Vicky are shooting dice in the corner.

"Is she unconscious?"

"She's sleepin'. They keep her asleep; it's good though because she won't know nothin' when she wakes up. That way there won't be a need to kill her. Anyway, they don't want to do that. They want the kids Mike has."

"How do you know that, Gracie?"

"I listened to their plans last night."

"What is their plan for the kids in protection?

Gracie shakes her head. "Not good. El diMarco will kill them as soon as he gets them back."

"That makes it more difficult. If we take Vicky out now, then El diMarco goes on to eventually find the kids and kill them. I have to figure this out. There must be a solution." Miriam rubs her head, teeters a bit and softly moans.

"Hon, are you okay?"

"Ja, I will be. My head hurts a little."

"We maybe should go back to Vicky's now."

"Not yet, I want to stay with Vicky a little longer."

"Okay, a little longer. But now I have to tell you something, Miriam."

"What is it, Gracie?"

"Last night, I decided to look in on Mike. He was at the station, he seemed really worried, so I stayed with him for a while. Then his phone rang, and he said, yeah come on over, so I stuck around and waited to see who came. Low and behold, it was Saul Duetzman. He told Mike that Joe Vicente was going to talk to El diMarco and then the police would be able to rescue Vicky from the warehouse here. Saul told Mike that there are only three guards, and they aren't armed because Vicky is kept drugged and unconscious. Well, besides, El diMarco doesn't want to give guns to a bunch of drunk street people anyway."

"When are they planning to get Vicky?" Miriam asks.

"They weren't really clear about when. I'm thinking that Mike's going to do it today. So, we need to take Eliakim home now because TPD could break in here like gang busters anytime, then Eliakim is liable to do something crazy."

"You're right, Gracie. We will go back to Vicky's and wait." They are immediately standing in Vicky's living room. Miriam and Gracie step from the blind of the cocoon. Eliakim remains hidden.

"There you are. I was wondering where you were." Scarlet walks through the kitchen from the laundry.

"I went for a walk."

"I washed your jammies and sheets." Scarlet gathers the folded wash. The jammies tumble to the floor. "Oh, fudge." Scarlet holds the folded laundry to her chest and bends to pick up the jammies.

"Well, now would that be the silver tattoo you were talkin' about?" Gracie asks.

"You can see it?"

"Big as life. Right there on her hand."

"Can I see what, Miriam?" Scarlet asks.

"I'm sorry, I have spoken wrong. I mean can you see it, the button that fell?"

"I didn't notice a button fall." Scarlet studies Miriam. "But I'll keep my eyes open." Her eyes fixed on Gracie, for a split second. Gracie turns away.

"I am very tired. I will rest now. Let me take those." Miriam takes her clean sheets and jammies and hurries to her room. She stuffs her sheets in the closet. Miriam flops on to the bed. Gracie steps to Miriam's room with Eliakim in the blind.

"I will leave Eliakim in the corner. He's safe there in the blind. I don't want Scarlet to find him in the closet." Miriam stares at the closet as she speaks.

"Goodness gracious, no, you don't want to scare poor Scarlet half to death." Gracie agrees with Miriam although she reckons that Eliakim wouldn't be the oddest or most fearsome thing Scarlet has ever seen.

"Gracie, do you know about the silver tattoo?"

"Can't say that I do, hon. Anyway, I don't recall. Why do you ask?"

"Because I think Scarlet can see you. I have tried to read her, but I cannot. It is only recently, for the first time, that I saw a silver tattoo in a picture. Paul and Mike did not see it though."

"Miriam, don't fret about what Paul and Mike did or didn't see. You're special, you see a lot of things that others don't."

"But you saw it too, on Scarlet's hand."

Gracie smiles.

"I do see more strange things now that I've passed. Things that I never saw before, but I don't think much of it. Kind of like a fly on an outhouse. Well, maybe Scarlet is special. Who knows maybe I'm special too." Gracie laughs.

"But I'm going to keep my eye on that girl anyway."

"I'm going to rest now, Gracie. I'm tired."

"You go on, you need your rest. I'll go on back to Vicky, but first, I want to visit Mike."

Gracie immediately stands in Mike's office. The captain, several officers, and the SWAT team stand in the room listening to the captain's instruction on how they are going to proceed.

"We will be traveling to Kumquat in unmarked cars. We have reliable information that Vicky is being held in the old packing house off of Main Street. The address is two four seven two Orange Blossom.

"We have been told there are no more than three guards who may or may not be armed. Officers will all be wearing their vests as a precaution. We will batter the doors and use smoke to draw the guards out. Officers will be using rubber bullets. The SWAT sharpshooters will be fully armed and ready. Also, our informant tells us that Ms. Knight has been kept heavily sedated and will not be responsive. De Augustino will partner with a sharpshooter. He will immediately, upon entering the building, ascertain Ms. Knight's whereabouts and bring her out. The sharpshooter will accompany him until Ms. Knight is safely outside and out of danger. Are there any questions or concerns?" The room is silent.

"Okay, men, go get her." The troop files out of the station and travel to Kumquat. Gracie follows. The cars park along the side road and the officers begin their advance.

Mike motions to his partner, he points to a brick wall, it's the front of a small brick building, tucked away under the great tin packing house. They quietly approach the door; it opens to a long dark hall. The hall is decorated in great swirls of neon graffiti. The hall leads to a room that is lit only by a single line of windows just below the ceiling line. The walls are covered in graffiti.

The sharpshooter calls out, "CLEAR"!

It is the room Mike saw in the video, the room where they took Vicky. The room where Vicky isn't anymore. Mike is devastated. The officers return to the station without, Vicky and without answers.

Gracie tries to go to Vicky, but she cannot. Something is blocking her. She follows Mike, he stays at the station long enough to write the report of how he failed to rescue Vicky. Then he dials Saul.

"Saul."

"Yeah Mike." Saul is expecting the call.

"I'm coming over." Mike races to the Duetzman's, he pushes past the guards and pounds on the door.

"Come in, Mike." Saul opens the door.

"Your guards are worthless. I pushed right past them."

"I told them to expect you. What's up?"

"Vicky wasn't at the packing house."

"What?"

"Don't play dumb, you self-serving weasel."

"I swear, Mike, I went to Joe and told him exactly what we agreed on. Joe must have played fast and loose with the plan. Wait, wait, wait, Mike, how do you know she's not there?"

"We went over there this morning."

"What! Are you kidding me? That wasn't the plan. Man, talk about fast and loose. Amateurs I'm dealing with, damn amateurs." Saul mumbles.

"Why did you do that? We only talked about this last night and this morning you guys go in. What were you thinking?"

"Well, after you came by yesterday and told me about the guards and everything. I sent a scout over to check it out, he looked around, came back, and told me it was three homeless guys guarding her, they had no weapons, like you said. They were just playing craps and drinking. They were like sitting ducks. So, we went over just before noon today and she was gone."

"Damn it, damn it, damn it. Joe did this." Saul is putting his spin on this; he didn't expect Mike to jump the gun. Saul needs the FBI to raid the packing house and see that it's empty. He needs to know where Vicky is so she can be found at diMarco's place. This is a kink in the plan, but he can bring it back around. Saul takes a deep breath and continues his rant.

"That bastard always has to be the boss. Listen, Mike, let me try to find out what Joe's up to. Don't let on that you know she's not there. If they know that you know, she's gone they will suspect I'm working with you to set them up. If they call arrange the trade, stall if you need to, but we have time, you won't need to stall. I'll find out where she is, and we will be on track. Don't do anything, just sit tight for a day. Joe's up to something. I got a day to find out what."

"Alright, find out where they took her." Mike turns to leave; Gracie returns to Miriam.

"I'll do what I can." Saul breathes a sigh of relief. They are on track. Joe did good.

www.ingramcontent.com/pod-product-compliance
Lightning Source LLC
Chambersburg PA
CBHW061209190726
48288CB00001B/115